LOST LIVES

LOST LIVES

ALAN HARVEY

Sage & Onion

First published in 2026 by Sage & Onion Books

A CIP catalogue record for this book is available from the British Library.

ISBN 978-1-0676001-0-5 (Paperback)
ISBN 978-1-0676001-1-2 (ePub)

Typeset by Clare Brayshaw

Manufacturer: York Publishing Services Ltd
64 Hallfield Road, Layerthorpe, York YO31 7ZQ
Tel: 01904 431213 | Email: enquiries@yps-publishing.co.uk
Website: www.yps-publishing.co.uk

Represented by: Authorised Rep Compliance Ltd.
Ground Floor, 71 Lower Baggot Street, Dublin D02 P593, Ireland
www.arccompliance.com

Contents

1

Push Comes To Shove

Tuesday, 27th March 2018

The room was small, claustrophobic. No window. Two vacant seats waited before them – ordinary office chairs, but with all the dark appeal of 'Old Sparky' greeting the condemned. On the opposite side of a large desk that ate up most of the room sat Sarah Morton, the supervising social worker from hell. Bitch. To her left, in the middle, Andrew Chilwell, the Deputy Manager of Fostering. To his left sat a third, unknown person, ominously dressed in black, like some kind of Reaper.

'What's all this about?'

Chilwell spoke. 'Sit down, Mr Blundell, please.'

'I wasn't expecting the bloody Spanish Inquisition.'

'No one expects...' Chilwell checked himself. 'Mr Blundell, please... Mrs Blundell...' He indicated the chairs.

Heather Blundell sat. Matthew Blundell followed suit.

'Mr Blundell, Mrs Blundell. There's no easy way of putting this. We've asked you here today because issues have been raised concerning your conduct regarding children placed in your care. A review panel has assessed these issues, and I've outlined our primary concerns in a letter that I'd like you both to read.'

The figure in black eased two copies of a letter silently across the smooth surface of the desk.

Dear Mr & Mrs Blundell,

Following various concerns brought to my attention by your supervising social worker, Sarah Morton, relating to various children placed in your care, a review panel has confirmed that the following issues will be subject to further investigation:

1. *Refusing to take a child to hospital after a violent incident and their having sustained an injury and failing to report this incident immediately to Ms Morton.*
2. *Not seeking medical advice for a trauma sustained in a further violent incident and failing to phone the out-of-hours service to report this incident.*
3. *Having a negative opinion of some of the children in your care.*
4. *Allowing a child access to adult games rated 18+ on their tablet.*
5. *Supplying another foster carer with an insufficient amount of medication for use by a child during a week's respite.*
6. *Inappropriate questioning of a child in your care who had sustained injuries at her mother's hand.*
7. *Demonstrating an inability to cope with a child with a medical condition, leading to that child being relocated.*

Your current placements, James Henderson and Grace Walker, will be removed from your household with immediate effect, and you are to have no further contact with them. You will continue to be paid your allowances, although pay rates will decrease accordingly on a phased basis.

You are entitled to independent representation to provide support and to advise you during all meetings and interviews. Any questions should be raised at the first investigation meeting, the date of which we will set in the next few weeks.

We regret that this action has been deemed necessary; however, we feel it to be in the best interests of all parties concerned.

Yours sincerely,

Andrew Chilwell

Deputy Manager, Fostering.

The silence that had accompanied the reading was shattered.

'It's all bollocks! You know it is! That bitch has had a vendetta against us from the start!' Matthew Blundell's trembling finger pointed at Sarah Morton.

'I don't understand...' Heather Blundell stared at her copy of the letter. 'Matthew, they're taking the children.'

Matthew Blundell was off his seat, his slim, six-foot frame towering over the desk. 'Do you really feel it's in James and Grace's best interest to be removed from a stable home, Mr Chilwell? For Christ's sake, Sarah, James has been with us since he was a few days old! You've registered our interest in adopting him... Or have you?'

'James isn't up for adoption,' said Sarah Morton.

'But at some stage, he will be.' Matthew Blundell was shaking. 'This was our dream of finally having a child of our own. You know how much it means to Heather.'

Sarah Morton looked at him – cold and silent.

'You callous bitch!'

'Mr Blundell, please. Sit down. You're doing yourself no favours.' Chilwell, too, rose from his chair.

'Matthew, please...' Heather Blundell tugged at her husband's sleeve.

'That's better.' Chilwell sat back down. 'Now, if we can all just calm down... My next step is to complete my inquiry and write my report, which I anticipate will take about two weeks, given that I've already spoken with many of the relevant third parties. Then I'll visit you at home to discuss matters with you and hear your side of the story. I suggest we set a provisional date for the meeting as Tuesday, the 10th of April, if that's okay with you. Until that time, I cannot comment further or answer any questions, as difficult as that might be. You will receive a letter from me in due course, confirming the date of my visit. Is all that clear?'

'Clear? Clear, my arse! The only thing that's clear, Mr Chilwell, is that this is a stitch-up!' Matthew Blundell jabbed a finger in Chilwell's direction. 'Where's that medicine bottle and those missing supervision notes, eh? You'd better come prepared to that meeting, I tell you, cos this is our life you're fucking with. One of these days, Mr Chilwell, I...'

‘Matthew, stop it!’ Heather Blundell pulled back on her husband’s outstretched arm. ‘Mr Chilwell, tell me: if this investigation shows that we’ve done nothing wrong, will we get James and Grace back?’

‘I’m ending this conversation now, Mrs Blundell. But in answer to your question: No. No, you won’t.’

2

Upheaval

Two years earlier...

Good Friday, 25th March 2016

Matthew and Heather Blundell planned to make good use of the Easter holiday and spend all four days packing. Their last foster child, three-year-old Seamus, had recently moved on following a successful adoption, and so Heather, as the primary carer, had already begun sorting through their clutter the week before. Matthew had been working as a patient transport driver, travelling daily all over Kent from their home in Maidstone. Having only worked his final shift on the Thursday, he had risen early on Good Friday and, while limbering up in his pyjamas, had announced his availability to handle the more physically demanding aspects of lifting and shifting.

He started after breakfast by bringing everything down from the loft, starting with the suitcases, which Heather immediately commandeered as she deliberated over which wardrobe to empty first. She was a self-confessed 'fashion freak' and deciding what to take and what to give away was a gut-wrenching ordeal; choices and decisions were frequently reversed by instant separation anxiety. Matthew, who was anything but a fashion freak, preferring what he referred to as the "casual James Dean look", in white t-shirt and jeans, finished in the loft and joined her in their bedroom, feeling hot and dirty, and turned his efforts to building flatpack boxes from the multitude delivered the week before.

He looked across at his wife. 'You take that much stuff and you'll sink the bloody Isle of Wight,' he said.

Heather was kneeling on a bulging suitcase full of her clothes, struggling to keep her long blonde hair out of her eyes and mouth as she attempted to zip it up. 'Well, we're moving to a bigger house, so we'll have more space, won't we,' she said.

Matthew nipped at a roll of brown parcel tape. 'So you're planning to fill four bedrooms instead of two?'

'Funny,' said Heather, finally forcing the zip home. Her face was flushed, and she winced as she massaged the zip imprints on her fingers. She looked up at Matthew. 'So, no last-minute regrets about moving, then?' she said.

Matthew cursed as the long strip of tape he'd bitten off twisted and tangled, rendering it unusable. 'Well, it's a bit late to be doubting ourselves now.'

'You don't think we're taking on too much with the new place?' said Heather.

'Here we go again.' Matthew raised his eyebrows and started over with the parcel tape. 'How many times have we discussed this?'

'Yes, Matthew, but you know what I'm like – I worry. The fact that we're here packing our lives into boxes and suitcases has made it real all of a sudden. It's hit me that we're actually doing this.'

Matthew sighed. 'We had no choice, Heather. We want to foster more kids, so we need a bigger house, and we can't afford the finest the Isle of Wight has to offer, so we've taken on a project. Yes, that means there's a lot of work to do, but we can cope.'

'I guess it's no different from all the work we've done here.'

Matthew nipped at the parcel tape and carefully put down the roll with his left hand, while the length he'd removed dangled precariously in his right. 'Exactly,' he said. 'I don't think anyone had touched this place since they built it in the First World War. We've totally transformed it.' He took hold of the bottom end of the tape with his left hand and looked up at his wife. 'Just try to focus on the end goal, Heather. With more placements, we'll earn more, and I won't need to supplement our income with a full-time job. That way, we both get to focus all our attention on caring for foster kids. We'll be living the dream. Now, come and hold this together.'

Heather grasped the cardboard box and lined up the two bottom flaps so they were flush. Matthew carefully laid the length of tape across the join and smoothed it down, allowing for a little excess to run up each side. 'There,' he said and flipped the box the right way up. 'One down, forty-nine to go.'

Heather returned to the wardrobe and removed another armful of clothes. She dumped them on the floor next to Matthew. They landed on the carpet with a dull thud. 'Don't get me wrong,' she said. 'I am excited about the move. It's just...'

'You worry. I know,' said Matthew. 'Come on, think positive. Tell me the one thing you're most looking forward to, and I'll tell you mine.'

Heather smiled. 'That's easy. I'm looking forward to being ten minutes away from Shanklin beach. We've always loved it there, haven't we?'

Matthew closed his eyes and breathed in. 'I can almost smell the sea air and taste the fish and chips.'

'So,' said Heather, 'what's yours?' She reached over and dragged another suitcase towards her.

'The bathroom.'

'Really? I thought we agreed we'd have to rip that out and start again?'

'Ah, yes. But it's upstairs! Not that I'm getting old, but going down those bloody stairs every night just to have a piss is a nightmare – especially in winter.'

'Typical,' said Heather. 'Trust you to think of your bladder over everything else.' She picked up a pink and white floral blouse from the pile of clothes on the floor and held it up to examine it. 'Now, when did I last wear this...?' She buried her face in the silky fabric and breathed in. 'This smells musty,' she said. 'In fact, it stinks. I'll have to wash it before it goes to the charity shop.' She cast it to one side and picked up the next item.

By the time Matthew had put together most of the boxes and distributed them around the house, ready to be filled, the monotony of the task was getting to him. He'd just about had enough for one day. Heather was clearing the bookshelves in the lounge when he wandered in. There were substantial numbers of hardbacks and paperbacks in precarious-looking piles, littering the floor.

He didn't bother to hide his annoyance. 'There's no way we're taking all these, Heather. We'll have to get rid of some.' He picked up a stack of cookbooks, which promptly toppled, and a thick tome landed, corner first, on his foot.

'Fuck!' He hopped around, clutching his toes.

'Hey!' said Heather. 'Watch what you're doing with those!' She bent down to retrieve the book. 'Look, you've damaged the cover!'

'Never mind the cover! What about my fucking foot?'

'Matthew! How many times? Stop that swearing!'

'Don't blame me; blame bloody Delia Smith!'

'Delia Smith's got nothing to do with this. You need to curb that temper.' Heather looked up at the clock. 'It's no wonder you're irritable. Look at the time. It's gone two. I suggest we stop for lunch.'

'Good idea.' Matthew hobbled over to the sofa and collapsed into it. He groaned, massaging his foot.

'Cut the amateur dramatics,' said Heather. 'We don't need to bust a gut. The removal men aren't coming till a week on Monday. We've got plenty of time.'

3

New Life

Monday, 4th April 2016

The removal lorry arrived at 8:00 AM and left just after midday, leaving Matthew and Heather with the final task of dropping off the house keys at the estate agent. Heather welled up as they drove away – the doubts and fears she harboured for this new venture into the unknown mingled with tears for the life she was leaving behind.

They expected the journey from Maidstone in Kent to the Portsmouth ferry port would take around two hours. They drove in Matthew's silver Citroën C3. Heather had sold her Volkswagen Polo, which had seen better days, and the plan was to buy something like a seven-seater Volkswagen Caravelle once they had established themselves and had a family to cater for. The journey included a traditional stop for a mug of tea and a bacon roll at a café set in the woods off the A3.

'We've stopped at this godforsaken place every summer since we first went to the Isle of Wight on our honeymoon,' said Matthew, pushing aside his empty plate and wiping his mouth with a napkin. The rich, greasy smell of fried food emanating from the serving hatch was overpowering. 'Remind me why we do it?' He picked up his mug and idly swilled the contents, staring at it in distaste.

Heather looked around at the faded decor. 'It hasn't changed much since 2009, has it? I guess it could do with a bit of TLC.'

'I doubt it's changed much since the bloody seventies.' Matthew slurped his tea and pulled a face. 'When exactly *did* milky tea become an essential part of our holiday experience? They should let you put your own milk in. I've got a bloody good mind to...'

'Have we really been married seven years?' said Heather, before Matthew had the chance to make his displeasure publicly known. 'You haven't got the itch, have you?'

'Itch? Me? No, I've got a cream for that.'

'You've got a cream for everything, Matthew.'

Matthew placed his mug on the Formica tabletop and reached across to Heather. 'Give me your hands,' he said.

'You what?'

'Just give me your hands.'

Heather brought her hands out from under the table and placed them in Matthew's.

Matthew squeezed gently. 'Heather Blundell, I can honestly say that I haven't looked at another woman since I first laid eyes on you. You're the best thing that ever happened to me. I adore you.' He locked his fingers into hers and squeezed again. 'Today is the beginning of a new chapter for us. It's a big step we're taking. We're moving away from all of our family and friends. I don't think we'd be doing that if either of us were scratching an itch. Am I right?'

Heather smiled. 'You know, sometimes, Matthew Blundell – when you're not talking out of your backside – you know just the right thing to say.' She stared for a moment at her hands in his. 'I just wish I had your confidence that we're not over-stretching...'

'Over-stretching, my arse!' Matthew withdrew his hands and sat back in his chair. 'That chill pill I slipped into your tea isn't working, is it?' he said. 'How many times, Heather? Okay, so we've eaten into the money your mum left you; it was either that or a huge mortgage. We've still got some of it left to do the necessary work on the house and tide us over until we get up and running. As long as we get the placements, we'll make ends meet just fine.' He folded his arms across his chest.

Heather picked up a napkin and began playing with it. 'That's just it,' she said. 'I'm worried there won't be enough fostering opportunities. I know we still have some inheritance money, but what happens if the fostering doesn't work out?'

'Heather, for Christ's sake, it'll be fine. The council has pretty much guaranteed they'll approve us over there – in fact, they almost begged us to come over, they're so short of carers. What's to worry about? Worse comes to worst, I'll find other work. I've always fancied going back into landscaping. If anything's bothering me, it's having to deal with those pernickety social wankers – I mean workers.'

Heather placed the napkin back on the table and smoothed it out. 'They can't win with you, can they, Matthew? You hold a grudge because you say they neglected you when you were a foster kid, and now they're too "pernickety".'

Matthew glared at her. 'My foster parents bullied and belittled me, Heather, and those bastards responsible for my welfare did fuck all about it.' His voice had risen. 'And all these years later they're as inept as ever – just in different ways.'

Heather glanced around. 'Don't you think it's about time you buried your demons, Matthew? Times change. Half the people responsible for your care back then are probably dead by now.'

'Probably – but some wounds never heal, Heather – you of all people should know that. Yes, times change, but the pendulum's swung too far the other way. Now, they suffocate you. I've probably got more relevant life experience than half the bloody social workers out there.' Matthew leant back, glaring across the room. 'If it weren't for Tony and Barbara adopting me, who knows what kind of reprobate I'd be?'

Heather resisted the obvious comeback and raised her hands in a placatory gesture. 'Look, we've got a new start on the Isle of Wight. You never know; you might actually find that you like the system over there.'

Matthew turned to her. 'I've said it before; I'll say it again: the system's gone bloody mad. All this politically correct, risk-assessed, health and safety compliant, arse-covering bureaucracy. Where did common sense go? Oh shit, little Billy's sneezed – where's my manual on how to wipe his nose without infringing his human rights?'

Heather sighed. 'Well, you constantly raging against the machine isn't going to solve anything. I suggest you keep your thoughts to yourself – you've pushed your luck in the past. If the authorities on the Isle of Wight get wind of your attitude, you could jeopardise everything.

Anyway, it's about time we got going, or we'll miss the four o'clock ferry.'

'Always worrying!' Matthew pushed back his plastic chair, which scraped on the linoleum. Both appeared to be relics from the seventies. He stood and waited patiently while his wife pulled her purse from her handbag and left a small tip. She stood and looked up at him. Matthew looked down into the gorgeous blue eyes appraising him, and his mood softened. 'Come on, short-arse,' he said.

'Oi! I'm five foot four and still growing, I'll have you know.'

'If you say so.'

'I do. And while we're getting personal, why don't you comb that rat's nest on top of your head and have a shave?'

'Funny you should say that – one of the first things I'm doing when we get there is having my head shaved. It's all coming off.'

'Hmmm. I quite like the military look.'

Matthew relaxed into a smile. 'Me, Burt Lancaster – you, Deborah Kerr.'

'You what?'

'That famous scene – "From Here To Eternity". Want to get salty with me in the Isle of Wight surf?'

'Yes, I'm familiar with the scene, Matthew. But you, Burt Lancaster? Don't make me laugh. Burt Kwouk, more like.'

'He wasn't six feet.'

'Once you've had that brown mop shaved off, nor will you be. Now, are you ready?'

'Let's go then, my little blonde bombshell – and it's your turn to drive.'

They timed their arrival at the Portsmouth Gunwharf car ferry port to perfection and passed through the barrier half an hour before departure. The attendant ushered them into waiting lane seven. There were no delays, and Heather breathed a sigh of relief. One less thing to stress over. One less thing for Matthew to get upset about.

Boarding the Wightlink ferry, St Clare, proved to be a straightforward affair, and they pulled into an oil-stained parking space on the upper car deck. As they got out, people were hurrying past them to get up the stairs and into the lounge above, hoping to get a much-coveted window seat. Matthew and Heather were in no rush. They had worn winter coats and were planning to join the few hardy souls who would be out on the forward-facing sun deck, in the late-afternoon sunshine, where the views across the Solent would be worth braving the cool, crisp April air and the wind blowing a saltwater mist into their faces. Once out there, they found a bench on the upper level, away from the small crowd that had congregated below, and sat down.

Matthew drew in a lungful of sea air, closed his eyes and tilted his head back, basking in the sunshine. He looked down and checked his watch. 'Ten minutes and we should be off,' he said. 'It's a forty-five-minute crossing, so we should be in Fishbourne by quarter to five. I reckon fifteen minutes to get out of the terminal, so we should get to the estate agent in Shanklin just before they close at half five.' He bent down and rummaged around in the rucksack they had brought on deck with them.

'Great. So, we can relax for a while.' Heather looked out to her left. Five miles distant across the Solent lay the Isle of Wight. The known and the unknown. A new life, with all its uncertainties. She pushed aside her nagging doubts and tried to focus on the positives. Perhaps Matthew would benefit from a fresh start and a slower pace of life, away from Kent, with all its past associations. And of course, they were moving to a bigger house where they could accommodate more children and both become full-time foster carers – that was the dream. The wheels were already turning. They'd spoken with the fostering department on the island to start the process, highlighting their background and experience. Based on that, they'd been invited to a face-to-face meeting in two weeks' time at the council offices in Newport to address the formalities.

'Coffee?'

'Eh?'

'Do you want some coffee?' Matthew held up a flask.

'Sorry, Matthew, I was miles away. No, I'm okay, thank you.'

'Are you still worrying? I told you; it'll be fine.'

'Yes, I know. I'll just be happier when we're settled in, have some new kids to look after and some money coming in.'

Matthew undid the flask and poured himself some coffee. 'Smell that,' he said, breathing in the earthy aroma. 'Kenco's finest! You don't know what you're missing.' He replaced the flask's stopper then sat back and looked out across the water as he took a sip from his cup. He sighed contentedly. 'You were right earlier. I need to try to put the past behind me. I'll make more of an effort to toe the line in future.' He hung his head in mock shame and then smiled. 'We've got some great memories, though, haven't we? I was reminiscing earlier. Remember the time we tried to get Lucas to feed himself and you gave him that bowl of spaghetti?'

Heather smiled. 'He banged the table with his spoon and then stuck his face in the bowl. I can still see him, covered in tomato sauce.'

'And the time we went to the beach at San Tropez and Ethan kept eating the sand every time we put him down.'

'Yes, some good memories,' said Heather. She reached out and patted Matthew's knee. 'Perhaps I will have a little of that coffee.'

The St Clare's four diesel engines had been idling gently in the background. Now, they powered up, and the water churned violently at the rear. The ferry eased away from the dock and navigated its way out of the terminal, turning left into a narrow channel. It passed the Round Tower on the port side and Fort Blockhouse on the starboard before heading into the Solent and arcing off to the southwest, its bow pointing directly at Fishbourne.

After the short crossing and a relatively smooth disembarkation, Matthew and Heather drove south to Shanklin, where the estate agent had hung on for five minutes after closing to hand them the keys. It was about a three-mile drive from there to the house in Alverstone. The removal company wasn't due to arrive until the following morning. Having spent all morning loading up in Kent and all afternoon journeying down to the coast and across the Solent, they had deemed it too late in the day to unpack at the other end. Except for a few things they had brought in the car, all Matthew and Heather's belongings were being held over at the company's storage depot in Lake, ten minutes down the road.

'It's been a while since we were last here,' said Heather, as she walked through the hallway and into the lounge. 'These rooms look huge now they're empty.'

'Make the most of it,' said Matthew, 'tomorrow they'll be full of our clutter.'

Heather walked over to the large bay window and looked out across the street. 'We'll have to put up some net curtains.'

Matthew joined her, resting his hands on her shoulders. He massaged her gently. 'It's another eight o'clock start in the morning,' he said. 'In which case, I'm all for an early night. Let's blow up the inflatable mattress, and then we'll pop out for some fish and chips.'

The fish and chips were from a shop on the seafront that they had discovered on a holiday to Shanklin two years previously. They took them back to the house and ate them on the floor of the lounge.

'Bloody marvellous!' said Matthew, still chewing a mouthful. He screwed up the greasy sheets of paper he'd been eating out of.

Heather rose from her perch on the edge of the mattress and took the scrunched-up ball from him. 'Cup of tea?' she said. 'I brought the kettle.'

'Please,' said Matthew. 'That'll round things off nicely.'

Heather disappeared through the lounge door and towards the kitchen at the far end of the hallway. She returned a few minutes later with the tea and then disappeared again. When she reappeared, she was singing.

'Happy birthday to you. Happy birthday to you. Happy birthday, dear Matthew. Happy birthday to you.' She bent down and placed a thickly iced chocolate cake, still on its silver cardboard base, on the floor. A solitary candle burned in the centre.

'My birthday's not until tomorrow.'

'I know,' said Heather, 'but we'll be rushed off our feet tomorrow, so I thought since we had nothing better to do...'

Matthew blew out the candle. 'Thank you.'

'Here's your present.' Heather reached behind her and produced a parcel wrapped in red metallic paper that had been tucked away in her skirt.

Matthew took it and squeezed. 'A jumper?'

Heather smiled and said nothing.

Matthew ripped off the paper and held up a set of blue overalls. Heather had embroidered "DECORATE" across the chest. 'Decorate?' he said.

‘Turn them over.’

Matthew turned the overalls around. Heather had embroidered “MY ARSE” across the backside.

‘Decorate my arse?’ said Matthew.

‘Yeah. You’re always saying it: this, my arse; that, my arse.’

Matthew rubbed the rough stubble on his chin absent-mindedly. ‘Well, I guess, now you mention it... I am rather fond of “my arse”. Thank you.’

‘My toy boy is thirty-nine,’ said Heather. ‘Make the most of it – it’s the big 4-0 next year. Mid-life crisis and all that.’

‘Crisis is my middle name.’

‘Here,’ said Heather, handing him a card in an envelope.

Matthew opened it and read aloud.

‘To my dear husband...

The future is ours; the future is bright,

Here’s to our new life on the Isle of Wight.

May your dreams be fulfilled in the year ahead,

Don’t fight the system; embrace it instead.

Happy Birthday.

All my love.

Heather.’

‘I mean it,’ said Heather. ‘You need to start off on the right foot.’

‘My fighting days are over,’ said Matthew. ‘But you won’t find me embracing any social workers.’

‘So long as you don’t antagonise them.’ Heather raised her hand. ‘Or you’ll get a slap!’

‘Slap, my arse!’ said Matthew.

‘I thought you’d never suggest it,’ said Heather. ‘Now, let’s have this tea and cake and then try out this new inflatable mattress!’

4

Square One

Thursday, 21st April 2016

'Good morning, Mr and Mrs Blundell. Come in and take a seat. I'm Rachael Ash, and I'm the Foster Care Admission Coordinator.'

Rachael Ash rose from the table where she sat and came over to greet them. She was impeccably turned out. Straight, shoulder-length, fair hair, like a silky waterfall, and an immaculately tailored, royal blue, two-piece suit: jacket and skirt. Matthew approved. 'I hear you've come to us from across the water?' she said, offering her hand.

Matthew leant in and shook it. He smiled. 'Good morning, Rachael. That's right, we've moved here from Kent.' Her perfume was subtle. Matthew was no expert, but he thought he detected delicate notes of sweet pea.

'I expect you'll find it a completely different lifestyle over here – much quieter.'

'That's why we've chosen the Isle of Wight,' said Heather, smiling and reaching out to shake hands with her. 'We're looking for a more relaxed way of life.'

'Please,' Rachael Ash indicated two of the chairs in the room, 'do have a seat. Would you like a tea or coffee?'

'Oh, no, we're fine, thank you,' said Matthew, pulling out a chair and sitting down.

‘Actually, I wouldn’t mind a tea,’ said Heather, taking the chair next to him.

‘Oh, go on then,’ said Matthew. ‘Make that two teas. Thank you.’

Rachael Ash went over to a hot water dispenser on a small table in the corner. She took two plastic cups and placed a tea bag in each. With a flip of the dispenser tap, she filled the cups with hot water. She brought them over to the table, placed them in front of Matthew and Heather and then returned to the drinks station. She came back with a few small pots of UHT milk, some sachets of sugar and a couple of plastic teaspoons.

‘Any chance of a biscuit?’ said Matthew.

Heather punched him on the arm, and Rachael Ash laughed. ‘I’m afraid the council’s budget doesn’t stretch that far,’ she said.

The meeting was being held at the council offices in Newport. The room was a typical council office. Clinical décor with plain white walls and grey carpet tiles on the floor, and just large enough to accommodate a large white table, four white chairs with grey upholstery and the drinks station in the corner. The half-height stud walls topped with glass panels didn’t lend themselves to privacy.

‘Obviously, you’ve fostered before,’ said Rachael, ‘so you don’t need me to give you all the basic background information.’ She had made herself a coffee and now sat opposite the Blundells. ‘This meeting shouldn’t take too long – it’s just a chance to put faces to names and to start the application process formally. My job after today is to collate all your documents and basically manage the whole journey from here to the panel interview.’ Rachael moved some papers to one side and picked up a pad and pen from the table. ‘So, I know a little bit about your fostering background from our telephone conversation, but perhaps you can tell me a little bit about yourselves. Heather, do you want to go first?’

‘Yes, of course.’ Heather poured the last of her milk into her tea and stirred it. ‘I grew up in East London,’ she said. ‘After school, I studied computer science at the University of London and then trained to become a teacher. I taught ICT and computer science at Barking & Dagenham School until 2004...’ She shifted in her seat. ‘After that, I worked for NatWest in its IT department. That’s where I met Matthew in 2006. Three years later, we married and moved to Kent.’ Heather glanced to her left at Matthew. 'Those were the happiest days of our lives, weren't they, my love... What are you doing?'

'They were indeed, sweetheart.' Matthew was mopping up some spilt UHT milk with a tissue, having had a disaster attempting to open his first pot.

Heather smiled awkwardly and looked back at Rachael. 'Sorry,' she said. 'Where was I?'

'You met Matthew at the bank and got married,' said Rachael, looking up from making notes.

'Oh, yes, that's right. Well, we first considered fostering after we were both made redundant by the bank in 2011. Obviously, we spent the first year going through the vetting process and doing all the training, and we've been fostering for the last four years now. We've had thirteen children come and go in that time and have had some very rewarding experiences.'

'Why did you leave teaching, Heather?'

'Oh,' Heather shifted in her chair, wondering if Rachael had been doing some background research and was steering the conversation. 'There was an incident that got out of hand, and after that, I sort of lost my passion for teaching – it knocked my confidence a bit. It was nothing I'd done wrong,' she added hurriedly.

'Well, obviously, any incident where children are involved is relevant to your application. Can you tell me about it?' Rachael sat with her pen poised above her notepad.

'There's not much to tell, really.' Heather's face flushed, and she shifted nervously again. 'A pupil accused me of something I didn't do. The school investigated; he was found to have psychological issues and was moved to a special needs school. I was completely exonerated, but, as you can imagine, the whole thing took its toll on me – and people never look at you the same way after something like that...'

She caught Matthew's warning look out of the corner of her eye. He hadn't known her at the time she'd been a teacher, and he knew virtually nothing about her ordeal. Even so, he was clearly wary of what she might say. She had played it down whenever he'd asked about it until he'd given up asking. She didn't want to talk about it. She didn't want to remember.

'Well,' said Rachael, noticing Heather's discomfort, 'if you were fostering for Medway Council for four years, then they must have looked into that and verified the account with the school. We'll cross-check with them, just to dot the i's and cross the t's at this end. Okay, excellent. Matthew, can you tell me something about yourself?'

'Of course.' Matthew finished brushing a few stray grains of sugar from the tabletop. 'Well, I was born and raised in Kent – which is why Heather and I bought a place in Maidstone when we got married. When I left school, I did landscaping for a few years, which I enjoyed; but then, in 1998, I got a job at NatWest. Heather and I were working in the same department in 2011 when they outsourced the work we were doing. As she said, we were both made redundant, and that's when we started fostering.' Pausing, he looked at Rachael, who was writing notes. He noticed her tanned hands and how immaculately painted her fingernails were. He took a sip of his tea. When Rachael looked up, he continued.

'I was in foster care myself when I was a child, so I thought I could build on my own experience. Knowing what it's like, I thought I could, perhaps... well, how can I put this politely... learn from the mistakes of others and improve on the care I received. On top of that, I've just finished a five-year contract as an ambulance driver doing patient transport. Going forward, I'm looking to join Heather, doing foster caring full-time.'

'That's great, thank you,' said Rachael, finishing some more notes. 'Interesting that you were also in care yourself, Matthew. Personally, I believe your ability to fully appreciate the experience through the child's eyes is a big positive. This is a sensitive question, I know. I note that you've had no children of your own. May I ask why?'

There was a moment's silence and then Heather answered. 'We tried unsuccessfully for a couple of years to have a family...' She cleared her throat. 'Eventually, I saw a specialist, and he told me I couldn't have children. That's one of the reasons we turned to fostering pre-school children after the redundancy.' She reached for her tea, took a sip and clasped the cup as if to warm her hands.

'I'm sorry to hear that, Heather.' Rachael took a sip from her own cup of coffee. 'That must have been tough for you both.'

'It was,' said Heather, 'but to be honest, fostering the little ones is so rewarding that I don't have too many regrets anymore.'

Rachael placed her cup back on the table. 'I'm pleased to hear that,' she said. She made a quick note on her pad. 'I do recall when we spoke,' she continued, 'that you expressed a preference for placements of a pre-school age. Is that still the case?'

'Yes,' said Heather, 'I think so. For the time being. Ideally, we're looking to take on children anywhere up to four years of age. The youngest we had previously was Emily, and she was six months old when she arrived. We'll make sure we're prepared for any eventuality, though.'

Rachael Ash nodded as she wrote. 'And with your move from the mainland, I'm guessing you've left a support network behind. Are you likely to have anyone here able to support you?'

'Well, we did have a lot of help from family and friends, especially at the start,' said Heather. 'Matthew's adoptive parents, Tony and Barbara, have always been good; though, sadly, my mum and dad are no longer with us.'

'Oh, you were adopted, Matthew?' said Rachael. Her soft blue eyes looked his way.

'Yes – just after my ninth birthday.' Matthew smiled. 'I have to say, I couldn't have asked for better parents than Tony and Barbara.' His smile faded. 'Especially after seven years of hell in the care system.'

'Oh, I'm sorry to hear that...' Rachael paused. 'Apologies, Heather, I interrupted you.'

'That's okay. Support? Well, we don't have family here – or friends, come to think of it. Matthew speaks with Tony and Barbara most weeks, and they're always there for us. They recently retired to Bude in Cornwall, so they're not a million miles away. To begin with, we would use our supervising social worker, the out-of-hours service and perhaps even the children's own social workers, if necessary. Saying that, we do have all our years of experience to fall back on, which I would like to think counts for something.' Heather took another sip of her tea and placed the cup back on the table.

'Absolutely! It sounds as if you have a lot of experience between you, working with children and caring for others.' Rachael put down her pad. She reached for the papers she had pushed to one side earlier. 'Okay, so, as you are now residents on the island, I can give you this application pack. Unfortunately, just because you've fostered before, it doesn't mean you can automatically pick up from where you left off in Kent. Obviously, you will be working with a new council here on the Isle of Wight, so you will have to apply from scratch and go through all the usual formalities: the Skills to Foster course, the final panel interview... The good news is that we can write to your old council to request a reference and, presuming there are no problems, fast-track you through the process. Once you get these forms back to me, I can start the ball rolling. And once we've finished, I'll allocate you a supervising social worker. I'm sure you're familiar with the process – they will come out and meet you at your home and do all the normal safety checks. Oh, and I'll notify you of the professional fees you'll be entitled to. I think you'll find our rates are competitive.' Rachael sat back in her chair. 'Do you have any questions?'

'How long do you think it will be before the home visit is arranged?' said Matthew, leaning forward in his chair.

'Well, I'm sure you know that these things can take a considerable amount of time. As I've said, in your case, we can fast-track you to a certain extent, but I imagine it's still going to be around two to three months.'

'That's good to know,' said Matthew. 'We've plenty to do in the new house to get it ready, so we can crack on with that.'

'Perfect,' said Rachael. 'In the meantime, I'm afraid you'll have to complete the three-day Skills to Foster course again. But the good news is you won't have to do the three-day first-aid course or the two-day paediatric one. You only need to repeat those every three years, and I've noted from our previous telephone conversation that you attended both last year. If you can provide me with the certificates confirming that, I'll be grateful. After that, as you know, it'll be down to the panel to decide if your application is approved. Anything else?'

Matthew shook his head. 'But I'm sure we'll think of something the minute we leave.'

'Well, if you do think of any questions later, then just give me a call,' said Rachael, rising to her feet. 'That's it, really. I said it would be short and sweet. We'll get cracking once you've completed those application forms.' She offered her hand across the desk, and Matthew stood, reached out and shook it.

'In that case, we'll get them back to you as soon as possible,' he said.

Monday, 23rd May 2016

The application forms had been completed and returned, and while the council dealt with all the formalities, Matthew and Heather had devoted all their time to unpacking and working their way through a long list of DIY jobs. Some work required professionals, however. The estate agent on the Isle of Wight had warned them that there could be a considerable wait for recommended tradespeople, and they had, therefore, made prior arrangements with a company to carry out the necessary electrical and plumbing work once they'd moved in. However, the company wasn't able to start until four weeks after Matthew and Heather's completion date. Typically, the start date had then been delayed and, of course, the work to rewire the entire house, put in a new bathroom, new pipework and install a new combi boiler had taken longer than expected. To compound matters, Rachael Ash had proposed the earlier-than-expected date of Monday, the 13th of June, for their home visit and allocated their supervising social worker: Ms Sarah Morton. Keen to push on, Matthew and Heather had agreed to the date of the visit. But now that the workers had left, and the dust had settled, time was running out as they turned their attention to the decorating. Sensing Matthew's rising agitation during one of their weekly telephone calls, his parents, Tony and Barbara – who had never been to the Isle of Wight and were keen to see the new house – had offered to come over for a week and lend a hand. Matthew and Heather had gratefully accepted.

'They've arrived,' said Matthew, pulling back the net curtain in the lounge bay window. He watched as his father, Tony, pulled up on the sloping section of concrete drive behind Matthew's Citroën, which was parked in a flat bay in front of the house. 'I'll go and help them with their bags.'

Matthew exited through the front door and entered the porch, with its waist-high brick walls and wood-framed, single-glazed windows. To his left was the house wall and a row of coat pegs. Matthew walked through and down the drive.

Tony emerged from the driver's side of a black Mercedes. He was over six feet tall and very slim, with a healthy head of silver hair. His face was tanned and lined, and he looked good considering he was well into his sixties. Anyone who didn't know that Matthew was adopted would naturally consider that they were father and son, given their physical similarities. Barbara emerged from the passenger side. Unlike Tony, she was short and rotund, with long grey hair pulled back into a ponytail. Both were elegantly dressed: Tony in a white shirt with brown trousers and a sports jacket, and Barbara in a blue jacket, white blouse and a heavy blue woollen skirt.

Matthew shook Tony warmly by the hand, and they embraced. 'Great to see you, Dad,' said Matthew. He rounded the front of the car and hugged Barbara. 'Did you have a pleasant journey, Mum?'

'Long,' said Barbara. 'It took us almost four hours to get to Lymington, and the weather coming over on the ferry was miserable, so we were confined to the lounge. We were last on, so we didn't even get a window seat.' She looked accusingly at Tony.

'What?' said Tony. 'You were the reason we were late setting off – faffing around at home.'

Barbara shook her head. 'He insisted on giving the houseplants a final water, right at the last minute,' she said to Matthew. 'Never mind. We're here now.'

Tony retrieved their luggage from the boot of the car, and Matthew carried their bags into the house. He put them down in the hallway. 'Right,' he said, rubbing his hands together. 'A tour of the house?'

'I think your mum and dad might like to sit down and have a cup of tea first,' said Heather, who had also given Matthew's parents a warm welcome.

'No, no,' said Barbara. 'We've been sitting in the car for the best part of an hour. I've been looking forward to seeing the house. We can have tea afterwards.'

'Great,' said Matthew. 'Let's start upstairs. I'll bring your bags, and we can put them in your room.' He led the way up a staircase to the left, on the opposite side of the hallway to the lounge. A dogleg to the right took them onto the upstairs landing. 'That's our room,' he said, indicating the room directly opposite. He looked to his left. 'That's the new bathroom down there – at the end on the right. The other two rooms will be kids' rooms.' He turned and walked into the bedroom on his right. 'This is your room,' he said. 'Obviously, it's not decorated yet. That's where you come in. We're going for neutral colours.'

'That makes sense,' said Barbara. 'You need to cater for boys and girls.'

Matthew left Tony and Barbara's bags in their room, and they wandered in and out of the other rooms upstairs, all of which had the floorboards exposed, awaiting new carpets. All were in desperate need of a coat of paint.

Downstairs were similar scenes of disorder. They had almost completed work on decorating the lounge. The walls were magnolia, and it was due to be furnished with a cream-coloured carpet and a turquoise four-seater sofa and armchair. Heather was halfway through making matching curtains and cushions. On the far side, a door led through to a narrow room the width of the lounge, which Matthew and Heather planned to use as an office. Further up the hallway, on the right, was a dining room. To the left were the stairs with an under-stairs cupboard, and at the far end was the kitchen. In the kitchen and off to the right was a door leading to a utility room and a shower room and toilet. To the left, in the far corner, a doorway led to a single-storey extension that would serve as a playroom.

'Wow, it's like Aladdin's cave in here,' said Tony, looking into the playroom and marvelling at the assortment of furniture and belongings that were stacked high and crammed into every inch of available space. Matthew and Heather had brought with them their old cots, beds, stair gates, walkers, car seats, buggies and a large playpen. They had also stored all their new furniture and equipment there, waiting until they had finished decorating.

In the kitchen, Matthew approached the sink and looked out of the window overlooking the back garden. 'The garden is going to require a bit of work,' he said, 'but the main thing I need to do is fill in the pond. We won't pass inspection if that's not done.'

'Well, I can give you a hand with that,' said Tony. He peered through the window and surveyed the overgrown lawn, the flowerbeds choked with weeds and a small pond just below the window. 'So, when do we get started? There's plenty to do.'

'Well, let's get our priorities right and have that cup of tea first,' said Heather. 'It's going to be a long week.'

5

The Visit

Monday, 13th June 2016

'I'm Ms Morton. I believe you're expecting me.'

Without so much as proffering a hand, Sarah Morton sidestepped them and invited herself into the lounge. By the time Matthew and Heather had recovered their wits, closed the front door and followed her in, she had already settled herself in the new turquoise armchair in the far right-hand corner by the window. She had a navy leather briefcase on her lap and was pulling out what looked like a clipboard with a checklist attached. 'Right, let's get started,' she said as they entered the room. 'Take a seat.'

Matthew and Heather, slightly stunned, sat down obediently on the new four-seater sofa that took up most of the wall on the opposite side of the room. Matthew stared at Sarah Morton as she sorted through her paperwork. She was short, barely five feet tall, and her BMI was probably slightly more than her doctor was happy with. But Matthew's overriding first impression was mutton dressed as lamb. She was getting on for what? Sixty? And yet she was comically made up in a vain attempt to present herself as a hip twenty-something. She had bleached, shoulder-length, blonde hair and too much make-up – some of it glittering. Piercing eyes peered through pink designer glasses, which matched her pink eyeshadow, and perched on her thin, pointed nose. Her lipstick was a deep fuchsia pink and matched her shoes. Her white blouse was unbuttoned way too low so that Matthew could see the top of her sagging breasts, but at least she had been professional enough to wear a navy skirt suit – though the skirt was a little on the short side and rode up when she sat down.

Sarah Morton placed her briefcase beside the armchair and turned her attention to Matthew and Heather. Brown eyes, so dark they almost appeared black, appraised them through her pink glasses. 'First things first,' she said. 'The purpose of my visit today is to assess the condition of your home – from cleanliness to safety and security.' She paused as if waiting for them to say something. When Matthew and Heather remained silent, she cleared her throat. 'Safety is paramount,' she said. 'For example, do you have up-to-date electric and gas safety certificates? Do you own a fire blanket? Have all the kitchen cupboards got child safety locks on them?' Silence. She sat forward. 'I have to say, I've been doing this job for more years than I care to remember, and in my experience, prospective carers often find the home visit the most stressful part of the application process. I hope you're prepared?'

Patronising bitch thought Matthew. He scowled.

'Well, we do have some previous experience,' said Heather. She forced a smile. 'Would you care for some tea or coffee, Sarah?'

'I think we'll stick with Ms Morton for now, if you don't mind, Mrs Blundell. And I haven't got time for tea or coffee. Actually, if it's alright with you, I'll just get on with the home checks. I'll start upstairs.' With that, she stood up, headed out through the lounge door and disappeared.

Matthew looked at Heather. 'Fuck me,' he said in a low voice. 'What a moody bitch. We've got a right one here.'

Heather listened for a moment. 'I suppose we shouldn't take it personally,' she whispered. 'Perhaps she's just having a bad day, or she's got other appointments to go to. Best we just let her get on with it.'

Ms Morton spent what seemed like an inordinate amount of time upstairs. When she finally made her way back down, she proceeded to scrutinise the downstairs rooms, wandering in and out of each one, without a word, making notes on her clipboard. She let herself out into the garden through the double doors in the playroom. When she came back in, she found Matthew and Heather loitering in the hall and directed them back into the lounge. As they returned to the sofa, she settled herself back into the armchair in the corner and placed the clipboard on her lap, neatly aligned with her legs.

She looked across at them. 'So, I've had a thorough look around. You seem reasonably well prepared – I suppose I should be impressed. Still, as you say, you have some previous experience.'

'We'll take that as a compliment, shall we?' said Matthew under his breath, as Ms Morton paused and looked at the clock, which was above a flueless gas fire to the right of the lounge door.

'I looked through your application form before I arrived,' she said, turning to face them again. 'Interesting. I see you were a teacher at Barking & Dagenham School, Mrs Blundell.'

'Please, call me Heather. Yes, I was – between 1998 and 2004. I wasn't Blundell back then, though. I was Matterface.'

'Yes, I remember that from your application, Mrs Blundell. An unusual name, Matterface. I'm familiar with Barking and Dagenham. I used to live in West Ham with my husband. We're divorced now.'

'Oh, right. West Ham. Just down the road...' Divorced. Why was Heather not surprised. 'I'm sorry to hear about the divorce, Sar... I mean, Ms Morton. That must have been tough.'

'Yes, it was all rather unpleasant. Still, had Douglas and I not gone our separate ways, I wouldn't have met his replacement, Chris – so something good came out of it.'

'Getting back to the matter in hand,' said Matthew, 'is there anything you've noted that we should be aware of?'

'Oh, it goes without saying, Mr Blundell. Nowhere ever gets a clean bill of health the first time around. At least, not from me. I daresay there are other supervising social workers who are not quite so discerning. For instance, I can see two problems right in front of me.' Ms Morton looked pointedly from Matthew to Heather. They stared back at her blankly. She smiled. 'For a start, you have no fireguard in front of that gas fire. And all those wires coming from the back of the TV and those connected boxes are way too accessible for little ones.'

'Well, that's easily fixed,' said Matthew. 'We have a fireguard in the loft. When it's not seventy-odd degrees outside, we'll get it down. And I'll get those wires cable-tied and out of sight.' He watched as Ms Morton pushed a few stray bleached blonde hairs over her shoulder. He noticed her dark grey roots.

'Fine,' she said. 'Well, I'll write up my report and let you have a copy; then it's up to you to address the issues. I'll be back to check that you've carried out all my recommendations before signing you off.' She leant forward, retrieved her briefcase from beside the armchair and placed it on her lap. She opened it and packed away her clipboard. 'Now, just so we're quite clear,' she continued, 'my job is to support you, but the needs of the children remain paramount. I'll be visiting you on the first Monday of every month. We'll discuss the children, and I'll collect your daily logs. Those need to be handwritten in pen – we can't have you changing your notes after the fact, can we? I'll also check that you're adhering to policies and procedures and, where necessary, arrange any training. I'll go away, type up my supervision notes and then, at our next meeting, we'll sign them off and I'll return your daily logs to you. Be warned,' she clicked her briefcase shut, 'sometimes, I'll turn up unannounced, which is something you'll just have to get used to. We need to be sure that you're conducting yourself in a professional manner and maintaining a safe environment all day, every day.'

Ms Morton slapped her thighs, lifted her briefcase and rose from the armchair. 'I think that covers everything. I'll leave you in peace.'

'I'll...' began Heather, preparing to get up.

'Don't worry, Mrs Blundell. I know where the front door is.'

'... show you out,' finished Heather, sitting back down again, as the front door opened and then clicked shut.

'Christ,' said Matthew. 'We're going to have a barrel of laughs with that one. What's her problem?'

Heather's disbelieving stare was fixed on the doorway of the lounge. 'Beats me,' she said. She was silent for a moment. 'But you were very restrained in the circumstances, I have to say. Well done.'

'Maybe a little *too* restrained,' said Matthew. 'I've never known such blatant rudeness. She walked in like she owned the place, and then all she did was patronise us. I've got a good mind to put in a complaint.'

Heather turned sharply. 'Oh, that'd get us off to a great start, wouldn't it? Antagonising the first social worker that crosses our path. No, we've put everything on the line here, Matthew. We can't afford to mess this up. Don't you dare go rocking the boat.'

Matthew slumped back into the cushions on the sofa. 'Well, if that wasn't painful enough, we've got the bloody Skills to Foster course next week. I can't believe we've got to sit through all that again.'

'Well, unfortunately, it's part of the process,' said Heather, recovering her composure. 'They won't approve us if we don't attend.'

Matthew groaned. 'It's just another example of the crazy system nowadays. For fuck's sake, we've got four years' experience on the job and they want us to sit through a three-day induction course just so they can tick a bloody box.'

'Matthew – embrace it, don't fight it, remember?' Heather turned and prodded him playfully. 'Do you remember it all then, smart-arse?'

'Of course I do,' said Matthew. He thought for a moment. '... the need for fostering, the role of a foster carer... attachment, trauma... loss, neglect, abuse...'

Heather sighed. 'I must admit, it's heavy-duty stuff – I'm not looking forward to it. But it's not like learning to fly. We'll get through it.'

Matthew buried his face in his hands. 'I don't know what's worse,' he said, massaging his eyes, 'the course or the panel interview – sitting in the bloody dock, being judged by twelve jurors, deciding if we're fit to be foster carers.'

Heather stood up. 'But it's not going to be like the first time, is it. This time, with our proven track record, it's more of a formality than anything.' She looked down at Matthew. 'They hold them on the last Monday of every month, don't they?' she said.

'I believe so,' said Matthew, removing his hands from his face and sitting up. 'But it's already too late to be invited to the one in June. My understanding is that everything has to be submitted to the panel two weeks before they sit. By the time we've completed the course, Morton's signed off the home visit and Rachael Ash has wrapped it all up, we're looking at the end of July.'

Monday, 25th July 2016

It was the last Monday of the month. Matthew and Heather Blundell had been seated before a panel of twelve referees from various walks of life: social workers, teachers, nurses, senior foster carers... References had been requested, DBS checks carried out, the home visit conducted, the Skills to Foster course attended and, now, a series of final questions had been asked. Matthew and Heather waited patiently in a side room while the jury retired to consider its verdict. In a matter of minutes, the panel chairman entered the room. He reminded Matthew of an ageing Mr Bean in his grey-brown jacket, white shirt and red tie. Matthew and Heather stood as he approached them with a somewhat comical gait.

'Congratulations, Mr and Mrs Blundell,' he said with a broad smile. 'I'm pleased to say that everything's been approved. All quite straightforward, really. We'll recommend to the ADM, that's the Agency Decision Maker, that your names be added to the council's register. She'll consider our recommendation and write to you formally, advising you of her decision. All being well, you'll receive your certificates and, no doubt, your supervising social worker will be in touch.' He shook hands. 'I wish you every success.' With that, he turned and left the room.

And that was it. The gavel had come down with a resounding crack, and in the case of Matthew and Heather Blundell, it was 'application approved'.

Heather breathed out and sat down heavily in a chair. She looked exhausted. 'It's over, Matthew. Everything's going to be okay.'

Matthew grinned. 'Told you so.'

6

James

Tuesday, 9th August 2016

Heather was thinking about lunch. She walked from the kitchen into the playroom and stood looking out through the open double doors leading into the garden. There, she saw Matthew stretched out in a deckchair on the lawn, a blue floppy hat covering his face, and his feet in the paddling pool.

'Hey, you,' she shouted. 'If you're not too busy, would you like to come in here and make us some lunch? I've got all this washing to put out.'

'Okay, love. Won't be a minute!'

As Heather headed back to the kitchen, the phone rang. She hurried into the hall.

'Hello?'

'Is that Mrs Blundell?'

'It is.'

'Mrs Blundell, this is Janet Harty from Children's Services. Are you free to speak?'

'Oh, hi, Janet. Yes, yes, of course.'

'Mrs Blundell, I have a three-day-old baby boy by the name of James whom I'm looking to place with a family, and I've been given your name. I see from our records that you are happy to consider newborns.'

Heather resisted the urge to cry out. Instead, she restrained herself and attempted to remain professional. 'Oh, Janet, that's wonderful news,' she said. 'You've made my day. Can you tell me a little bit more about him?'

'Yes, certainly,' said Janet. 'James was earmarked for foster care before he was born. There is one matter I need to make you aware of: the doctors strongly suspect that he has fetal alcohol spectrum disorder. It's usually referred to as FASD.'

'I've heard of it, but it's not something I'm familiar with,' said Heather. 'How will that affect him going forward?'

'It depends on the severity,' said Janet. 'There are no specific tests for FASD and at this stage, the doctors can only go on certain indicators. It's known that his mother was drinking heavily during pregnancy, his birth weight was significantly low, and he has certain facial characteristics that point towards the condition. Potentially, there'll be some growth retardation; it's likely he'll look a little different, certainly until adulthood, and he may have some developmental issues. But he's had an MRI scan, and there are no obvious signs of any serious brain damage. Apart from affecting some of his features, currently, there are no other outward signs.'

'Personally, I don't see any of that being a problem,' said Heather, 'but let me just speak with my husband quickly.'

'Of course,' said Janet. 'I'll hold on.'

Heather put down the cordless phone on the hall table and returned to the kitchen, where there was no sign of Matthew. She walked through into the playroom. Again, no Matthew. She moved over to the double doors and looked out. Matthew was fighting to extract himself from the deckchair – the deckchair appeared to be winning.

'Matthew. I've got a social worker on the phone. They're offering us a three-day-old baby boy. He's got fetal alcohol spectrum disorder, but it doesn't sound like anything we can't cope with. What do you think?'

'If you're happy, I'm happy,' said Matthew, gripping the arms of the deckchair and pushing himself up. 'A baby in the house sounds wonderful.'

Heather grinned. 'Excellent. I'll say yes, then!'

She hurried back into the house and into the hallway. She picked up the phone. 'Janet? Hi. I've spoken with my husband, and he's as keen as I am. We'll be happy to give James a home.'

'Well, that's great news,' said Janet. 'You'll need to collect him later today, straight from the hospital, if that's okay. I'm James's social worker, so it's me you'll be dealing with. Can you meet me in the main reception area at St Mary's, Newport at, say, three o'clock?'

'Three o'clock is fine,' said Heather.

'Perfect,' said Janet. 'I'll take you up to the maternity ward. James's mother will be there with her social worker – but don't worry, you won't have to deal with her. Someone will bring James through, and we'll go through all the necessary paperwork before you take him home.'

'No problem, Janet,' said Heather. 'We'll be there.'

She rang off and punched the air. 'Yes – a placement! We're in business!'

Matthew poked his head out of the kitchen door. 'All done? Come in here, and you can tell me all about it. What do you want in your sandwich?'

'Forget lunch, Matthew.' Heather grabbed hold of his arm and ushered him towards the stairs. 'Go and get the Moses basket ready!'

That evening, Heather was in the lounge, sprawled among the cushions littering their oversized turquoise sofa. She had the laptop out and was reading through an online booklet outlining James's medical condition. James was asleep in a Moses basket on a stand next to her, having just had his ten o'clock feed, which he hadn't seemed particularly interested in. Matthew was in the kitchen sterilising and making up bottles for the night ahead. When he finished, he came into the lounge to join her.

'Making yourself comfortable, I see,' he said and flopped down next to her, losing himself in the soft, plump cushions.

'Yes, I'm just doing a bit of research and enjoying some quality time with the little man here.' Heather reached out and began adjusting the blanket covering James. 'It all seems so surreal,' she said. 'I can't believe we're sitting here with a newborn baby.'

Matthew grinned. 'I told you it would all work out. Our first foster child on the Isle of Wight, and I don't reckon it'll be long before we get more.'

'He seems content; but he's so small, Matthew, and he seems so frail.' She finished fussing over James's blanket and sat back. 'I've been reading more about FASD. Apparently, only ten per cent of people born with it have sentinel facial features, which is why it can be so difficult to detect until they're older. But you can definitely see James has got the thin top lip, and he hasn't got that groove above the lip and under the nose – the philtrum. And he has...' she referred to the laptop screen, '... "short palpebral fissures", which basically means he's got small eyes. And his head is noticeably smaller than usual, which is why they can be pretty sure he has FASD.'

'What else have you discovered?' said Matthew, stretching out.

'That he might not reach his milestones as quickly as the average child.'

'So, that's what they meant by "developmental issues"?' said Matthew.

'Yes,' Heather looked back at the laptop screen. 'It says here that his physical growth, motor skills, cognitive development and language development will almost certainly be affected. There's a good chance he'll be small for his age and that he'll probably move onto solid foods later than most infants.' She continued to refer to the screen. 'He might sit and crawl okay but walk later than most other toddlers, and it's likely his ability to speak will be delayed.' She turned to look at Matthew. 'The thing is that every case is different. No one can tell at this stage how severe any impact will be.'

Heather looked up at the clock on the wall, above the gas fire to the right of the lounge door. 'It's twenty past ten,' she said. 'I don't know about you, but the little man's fast asleep. He took a long while to settle down, but he's out like a light now. Shall we all go up to bed? You can read your book, and I'll carry on reading this.'

'Fine by me,' said Matthew. 'Let's finish up down here and then take him up.'

When they were done downstairs, Matthew carried the Moses basket up to their bedroom, and Heather followed him in with the stand. She placed it on Matthew's side of the bed. Matthew frowned as he secured the basket in place. 'You okay if I use the bathroom first?' was all he said.

'Of course. I'll just get another blanket for James. He seems to settle better when he's wrapped up.'

Matthew readied himself for bed and came back into the bedroom wearing his boxer shorts and an old 'Delicate Sound of Thunder' t-shirt.

'Okay, so how are we going to do this?' said Heather.

'Do what?'

'Well, James is going to require feeding in just over three hours...'

'I see...' Matthew slipped under the duvet and picked up his book from the bedside table. 'Well, why don't you tell me all about it in the morning?'

'Oh, what a wag you are, Mr Blundell. You're the night owl, so I suggest you feed him at two o'clock. I'm the lark, so I'll do the one at six.'

'I guess that explains what you're doing on my side of the bed, then, little man,' said Matthew, reaching out and touching the side of the Moses basket. 'Be warned, though – I don't want any nasty little surprises at two in the morning. You save all that smelly stuff for six o'clock.'

Monday, 5th September 2016

Ms Morton, dressed in her navy suit and carrying her matching briefcase, had placed herself in the armchair in the far corner by the window and was making herself comfortable, rearranging her skirt. Her bleached blonde coiffure barely reached the top of the cushioned headrest, and her feet barely touched the floor.

Heather opened her mouth to speak.

'If you're going to offer me a cup of tea or coffee, Mrs Blundell, I won't, thank you.'

Heather took her place next to Matthew on the four-seater sofa. James was asleep in his Moses basket at her feet, wrapped tightly in a white lattice swaddle blanket. Heather wet a finger and reached down to smooth a stray strand of his hair into place. She looked at him fondly and smiled. 'I can't believe it's been nearly a month since he arrived,' she said. She looked across at Ms Morton. 'Do you think he's changed since you first saw him?'

Ms Morton had called in a few days after James had arrived, as was protocol with any new placements. She hadn't stayed long, and it was noticeable that she hadn't fussed over him or paid him any real attention. She ignored Heather's question. 'So, your first placement,' she said. 'How's it going? I know you're not familiar with newborns. You haven't cared for one before or, of course, had children of your own.' She stared intensely at them through brown designer glasses that, as before, perfectly matched her eyeshadow.

'Everything's going really well... may I call you Sarah?' said Heather.

'If you must,' said Ms Morton. She pursed her violet lips. Matthew looked down at her shoes. Violet.

Heather smiled and continued. 'Well, Sarah, the health visitor came round last week. She measured his head circumference and commented on his beautiful head of blond hair.' She looked down at James, who was sleeping soundly, and smiled again. 'Sometimes, we have trouble feeding him. Occasionally at night, we have to wake him, and he's not always interested, but he's put on a bit of weight, which is the main thing. She was happy with that.'

'And his bowel movements are a little unpredictable, aren't they, my love?' Matthew chipped in.

'Yes, dear.' Heather smiled sweetly at him. She looked back at Sarah. 'Sometimes after we've woken him, it can take a while to get him back off to sleep. It's not always easy to settle him when we first put him down, either. But apparently, sleep and feeding issues are common symptoms of FASD, and something we need to monitor.'

'And we've dropped him off at the contact centre a couple of times now,' said Matthew, making an effort to be cordial. 'He's going there every Tuesday morning for supervised visits with his mum. The contact supervisor says there have been no issues...' He was distracted by Sarah running her fingers through her bleached blonde hair. She'd had her roots done, he noticed. Matthew shook his head as if to clear the distraction. What was this fascination with their supervising social worker's dubious fashion sense? Stop it.

'Sarah,' Heather was saying, 'there's something I've been wanting to ask. James came straight into care from birth...'

'Yes,' said Sarah, 'it's because his brother, Michael, was already in care. When Michael was born, there was no father on the scene, and his mother was an alcoholic and unfit to look after him. It's the same story now she's given birth to James – just a different father. What about it?'

'Yes, well, we were wondering: usually, they try to keep siblings together, so why isn't James with his brother?' said Heather.

Sarah seemed irritated. 'Because the carer who looks after Michael only takes one placement at a time.'

'We've got room to have him here...'

Sarah was forthright. 'No, Michael's settled. He's a delicate child. They wouldn't move him at this time. Maybe they'll be reunited when they're both a little older. Now, don't forget to note all James's sleeping and feeding patterns in your daily logs. Log all the feedback you receive from the contact supervisor on how he is with his mother and, going forward, note any progression with his development.'

'You mean like this?' Matthew stood and handed several sheets of paper to Sarah. 'Patronising bitch,' he mumbled inaudibly as he retook his seat.

Sarah glanced at the logs casually. 'Yes, something like that,' she said, '– although, I don't know which one of you is responsible for producing them, but the handwriting could certainly be improved.' She placed them on the floor next to her armchair.

At that moment, James woke. Heather lifted him out of his Moses basket and gave him a warm cuddle. As she sat back and cradled him, his distinctive blue eyes searched for her familiar face. They fixed on her. Heather laughed. 'Look, Matthew – his lips – he's trying to smile.'

'He's got wind,' said Sarah. 'Just give him a few pats on the back.'

Matthew snorted with laughter. 'Wind, my arse! I think you'll find he's trying out his new smile. He's been doing that since the weekend.' Sarah gave him a humourless look and again pursed her violet lips. Matthew couldn't resist: 'Is that you smiling there, Sarah, or have you just let one go?'

'Matthew!' Heather looked embarrassed.

'What? What's wrong with a little humour? I'm sure Sarah can see the funny side...'

'Moving swiftly on, Mr Blundell.' Sarah glared at him. 'Has James taken any steps towards his milestones in his first four weeks with you?'

'Yes,' said Matthew. 'He had his first driving lesson on Saturday morning.'

'Sorry, Sarah, he thinks he's funny.' Heather turned to Matthew. Behave, she mouthed. She turned back to Sarah. 'I know it's quite an advanced skill at this stage, but I'm convinced James is trying to smile. He's been cooing. Apart from that...'

Sarah once again assumed an air of professionalism. 'Well, not to worry, Mrs Blundell – the first month is not necessarily an indicator of his future development. Now, as I've said before, it's my job to make sure you are fully equipped with all you need to do your job effectively. With that in mind, I've booked you both on a refresher course. Clearly, with James being so young and adorable and the fact I can see you're already besotted with him, I've put your names down for the Attachment Theory course. Obviously, you can't leave him "home alone", so you'll have to attend on separate dates. I'll email you those when they're confirmed. If there are any problems, let me know.'

'Marvellous,' said Matthew.

'That's the spirit, Mr Blundell. I'm sure you'll find it as interesting as the first time – assuming you can remember anything about the first time, of course.'

'We had to take James for an MRI the week before last,' said Heather, hurriedly changing the subject. 'He had one at birth, but they wanted another look at his brain now that things have settled down. We had a phone call a few days ago, and there's nothing new to report. James's brain is under-developed but only time will tell exactly how it will affect him. We also met with a consultant paediatrician and discussed FASD and the impact it might have on his life.'

'Do you know much about FASD, Sarah?' asked Matthew. 'Only you didn't hang around long enough to discuss it after James arrived.' Sarah scowled. A moment's hesitation was all Matthew needed. 'I'll take that as a no, then,' he said. There was a mischievous glint in his eyes. 'FASD stands for Fetal Alcohol Spectrum Disorder. It's a neurodevelopmental condition that can lead to lifelong cognitive, emotional and behavioural challenges. It's all to do with the effects of prenatal alcohol exposure.' He frowned. 'I can't believe that with all your experience you're not familiar with it, Sarah.' He paused just long enough to gauge Sarah's reaction, but she sat poker-faced. 'Never mind. It's caused by the transfer of alcohol from the mother's blood to her baby's through the placenta. Apparently, a baby can't process alcohol as quickly as an adult, so it remains in their system for longer, causing damage to their developing brain and body – apparently, the brain is particularly vulnerable. But,' he stressed with a finger pointed at Sarah, 'fetal alcohol spectrum disorder is not technically a condition in itself. You have to think of it as an umbrella – as the name suggests, it covers a whole range of conditions on a spectrum. Over four hundred at the last count...'

'Matthew!' Heather hissed under her breath.

Sarah drummed her fingers on her knees. 'Oh, please, let him have his moment, Mrs Blundell. He's clearly very excited to have grasped the basics.'

'Well, far be it from me to patronise *you*, Sarah, but I'm merely laying the foundations for our future conversations concerning James's welfare. I take it you've familiarised yourself with his diagnosis, then?' He noticed the almost imperceptible flash of panic in Sarah's eyes. 'No?'

'Please...' Sarah indicated with a wave of her hand that he should continue. 'Enlighten me.'

'Well, let me presume, then, that you know all about sentinel facial features and microcephaly. The very fact that he has the three determining facial features and a small head circumference indicates he has fetal alcohol syndrome, which will almost certainly lead to some form of neurodevelopmental impairment. But no two cases are ever the same, and so, as my dear wife has already alluded to, no one can say at this stage exactly how it will manifest. In James's case, they've caught it early, which is essential. Now, with the appropriate support, we can monitor his development and mitigate any issues as they arise. The paediatrician said they'll look to put a more structured FASD management plan in place at some stage, but they won't be able to carry out a neurodevelopmental assessment until he's about eight years old, six at the earliest. Until then, he'll have routine appointments just to monitor his progress.'

‘Good news for now, then,’ said Sarah. ‘So, moving on. We’ve discussed James, and I have your daily logs – which reminds me – I also need to book you in on the Record Keeping course.’

Matthew looked at Heather and raised his eyebrows.

‘You know the routine,’ continued Sarah. ‘I’ll take the logs away, read through them and sign them off. I’ll type up anything of particular importance or relevance in them, together with a record of what we’ve discussed today, and next month, when we meet, I’ll return the logs to you and we’ll sign off my supervision notes together. Any questions before I go?’ She reached for her briefcase, then stood and looked at Matthew and Heather for a moment. ‘No? Good. In that case, I’ll show myself out.’ In a few strides, she had crossed the lounge and disappeared into the hall. ‘You know how to contact me if you need me.’ The front door closed behind her, and Matthew and Heather were left sitting in silence.

‘She doesn’t hang around, does she,’ said Heather.

‘No,’ said Matthew. ‘A bit like a fart, I suppose: a quick fanfare, a bad smell that lingers briefly and then wafts away.’

‘There seems to be a fascination with flatulence today – what with you and Sarah. What were you thinking, asking her if she’d let one go?’

‘Well, she was asking for it. Patronising us when we’ve been keeping daily logs for the past four years. And what’s with all those bloody courses? She’s only doing it to spite us.’

‘Well, you need to watch what you say to her,’ said Heather. ‘You sailed too close to the wind for my liking today. We need to keep things civil.’ She stood up, cradling James. ‘Maybe it’s a good thing she keeps these so-called “meetings” to the bare minimum,’ she said. ‘Here, take James. I need the loo.’

Matthew got up from the sofa and took James from Heather. ‘Well, at least “Mad Mandy” used to stay for a cup of tea, chat and play with the kids. She certainly was what you’d call a “social” worker, eh? As nutty as a fruitcake, but Morton could learn a thing or two from her.’

‘Somehow, I can’t see Sarah ever socialising with us,’ said Heather.

‘No, nor can I,’ said Matthew. ‘Honestly – I don’t know what’s worse: a supervising social worker who trains goldfish to swim through hoops in her spare time or one with all the hallmarks of a psychopath.’

Christmas Day, Sunday, 25th December 2016.

The sleepless nights had continued with the incumbent rounds of bottle feeding and nappy changing. Matthew and Heather tried to stick to a nighttime routine, but James tended to wake and feed only when he felt hungry, and so eventually they allowed themselves to be guided by him. At a routine check-up in September, the consultant paediatrician gave them some helpful feeding tips. As James had a high cleft palate and weak cheek muscles that appeared to be making it difficult for him to swallow, and he didn't seem to be responding well to the bottle's standard-sized teat in his mouth, he recommended some larger, textured teats for his bottles. That seemed to help. Gradually, James, and they, began to sleep for longer, although it could still be difficult to get him to settle.

Relief also came in the form of Tony and Barbara, who needed no excuse to visit over the festive period. Matthew was their only son, and a family Christmas was far preferable to spending it alone. They arrived on the Friday, and Barbara especially was a great help in looking after James. She also helped Heather on Christmas morning, as 'the girls' took responsibility for cooking Christmas dinner. But with the warm, rich smell of a roast turkey dinner still lingering in the air, it was the boys who cleared up afterwards, while Heather and Barbara retired to the lounge with an after-dinner sherry. Not long after, Matthew entered the lounge carrying a bottle and two glasses, with Tony trailing him.

'That was a thoroughly enjoyable meal, ladies,' said Tony. 'The dining room is clear, and the dishwasher is on. Time for that brandy, Son,' he said, turning to Matthew.

'Coming up,' said Matthew. He placed the glasses on top of a nest of tables next to the four-seater sofa in the corner nearest the lounge door. He poured two generous measures of brandy and handed one to Tony. 'Cheers,' he said. 'Here's to family. It's great to have you here with us.'

'Cheers,' said Barbara, rising from the far end of the sofa, where she was sitting next to Heather. She raised her glass.

Matthew sat down between Heather and the brandy, while Tony made himself comfortable in the armchair in the corner next to the window.

'James loves his play gym,' said Heather. 'You picked a really nice one.'

'Yes,' said Barbara, 'we got it from Argos.'

Attention turned to an animated James, who was lying on his back on an activity play mat, staring up at the two padded arches that crossed perpendicular to each other directly above his head. From the arches hung various tactile, detachable toys.

'I like the fact that all the toys are so different,' said Heather. 'He'll lose interest quickly sometimes, so it's great we can switch them around. He always seems to respond well to a toy with a new texture or sound. It's almost like he's never seen it before, he gets so excited.'

'He seems a little rough with them,' said Barbara, watching as James reached out, and opened and closed his fists before slapping at a large yellow star hanging over him. When he made contact, it answered back with a jaunty electronic jingle, which made him gurgle in delight.

'All this is evidence that he's developing some of his basic motor skills,' said Heather. 'He's already learning how to track objects and respond to sound. It's pretty much what you'd expect from a boy his age, so he's on track with his early milestones.'

'Speaking of rough, he certainly enjoyed his bath last night,' said Barbara. 'He was kicking his legs and splashing around. It was all I could do to hold him still.'

Matthew laughed. 'Oh, he loves his bath. That's the highlight of his day. Watch this...' Matthew got down onto the floor and rolled James over onto his stomach. Everyone waited expectantly.

'He'll do it in a moment,' said Heather.

James lifted his head.

'Bravo,' said Tony. 'He's certainly coming on.'

'He's been practising every day,' said Heather proudly. 'It's called "tummy time". It's helping him build up his neck muscles. He practises sitting and rolling, too. His muscles are quite weak, so it all helps him grow stronger.'

Matthew rolled James onto his back and then retook his seat on the sofa next to Heather. 'His social worker, Janet, comes to check up on him every month,' he said, 'and she's really pleased with his progress.'

'He seems to have settled in well with you, that's for sure,' said Tony. He lifted his glass. 'Here's to James!' He took a large sip of brandy, and everyone raised their glasses.

'It's hard to imagine life without him,' said Heather.

'Well, don't,' said Barbara. 'Just make the most of the time you have with him and cross that bridge when you get to it. You've always dealt with it in the past.'

'I admire you. It must be very difficult to rein in your emotions and not get too attached,' said Tony.

Heather fell silent, and the conversation carried on around her. She looked down at James, lying on his back on his mat, absorbed in his own little world. She wondered what the future held in store for him. Whatever it was, she already knew that she wanted to be a part of it. She wanted to be there for him, to support him in whatever struggles he might face. He needed her. She needed him. Matthew laughed beside her; something about Tony behaving himself while he was sitting in Morton's armchair. One step at a time, she thought. Who knows what the new year has in store.

The new year kicked off with fireworks. And so did Grace.

7

Grace

Thursday, 5th January 2017

Grace had arrived the previous day. She was eleven months old – a wilful child with an enormous temper. Catch her in the right mood, though, and she could be very affectionate. She had come into care simply because her mother was no longer deemed fit to look after her, after Grace's father had walked out. Her social worker was Janet, which was convenient, as she was already familiar with Matthew and Heather through James.

Grace was standing, imprisoned, clinging to the top rail of the playpen in the window bay in the lounge, having just been brought downstairs after her afternoon sleep. Her dark brown hair was tousled. She was shouting. Nothing comprehensible, but making a noise loud enough to get everyone's attention. James was in his cot, which stood in the corner between the sofa and the door to the room they used as an office at the back of the lounge. He was sleeping through it all.

'Hello, Grace,' said Sarah, as she entered the room. Grace raised her chubby arms, her brown eyes gazing expectantly upwards, anticipating being lifted from behind the bars of her prison. She promptly lost her balance and plopped on her nappy-clad backside before rolling over. She sat up bawling. Sarah ignored her and took a seat next to the playpen in her usual armchair in the corner by the window, shuffling as she pulled out the creases in her skirt, which had ridden up. She was wearing the usual navy skirt suit and had placed her matching leather briefcase by the side of the chair.

Heather followed Sarah in. She walked over to the playpen. 'Let's get you out of there, madam,' she said, 'otherwise we won't be able to hear ourselves speak and you'll wake James.' She strained as she lifted Grace from the playpen and carried her over to the sofa, where she sat down and cradled her on her lap.

Matthew entered the room, having opened the front door and watched Sarah hang her coat in the porch before breezing past him without a word. He took his place next to Heather, and they waited expectantly.

It was Sarah's first introduction to Grace. Her usual practice of visiting soon after a new child's arrival had coincided with January's supervision meeting, which had been delayed due to New Year. 'So, first things first: how's it going with Grace?' she said.

'Well, she's arrived,' said Matthew, looking across and clocking Sarah's chosen shade of blue eyeshadow through the lenses of her blue-rimmed glasses.

'She's certainly got plenty to say for herself. Quite a determined young lady, aren't you?' said Heather, ruffling Grace's hair. 'Fearless.'

'Headstrong, that's for sure.' Matthew's eyes had moved down from Sarah's mauve lipstick to her mauve shoes. He shuddered. Hideous.

'She sounds just like her mother,' Sarah was saying. 'If she wants something, then there's no stopping her.'

Heather tickled Grace playfully under her arms. Grace squirmed and hit out, catching Heather on the chin. 'You won't cause us any trouble, will you, young lady...' Heather rubbed her chin and looked back at Sarah. 'Do you have any more background information? Janet just said her mother wasn't fit to look after her and there'll be no contact visits with her for the foreseeable future. Apparently, they're arranging for her to see her grandad every Friday afternoon.'

'All I know at this stage is that after Grace's father walked out, her mother went off the rails and was out most nights, drinking, taking drugs and palming Grace off on different babysitters. I believe she even took Grace to parties and stuck her in a spare room. Vile woman.'

'Poor Grace. That explains why you don't like being left in that cot once you're awake, doesn't it,' said Matthew.

'So, now you have two placements,' continued Sarah, 'you'll have two sets of daily logs to complete, two sets of contact visits, and all the medical, health visitor and haircut appointments, etc., etc. Are you both happy you'll be able to cope with all that?'

'We'll be fine – thank you,' said Matthew.

Sarah looked across at them through her eyeshadow-matching blue glasses. 'Well, you know my standards by now. I won't be making any allowances for the fact you have the extra workload. I'll still expect everything to be done by the book and completed in a timely fashion. Remember, the welfare of the children takes priority over everything.'

'Your standards are a constant source of inspiration to us, Sarah – aren't they, dear?' said Matthew, looking sideways at Heather. 'In fact, I'd like to take this opportunity to thank you for keeping us on our toes. I think it's fair to say that had we had any other supervising social worker, we wouldn't have had this unique opportunity to better ourselves as carers. If it weren't for your shining example, I shudder...'

'Matthew, would you be a sweetheart and get the daily logs? I think I left them on the desk in the office.' Grace was now straining to extricate herself from Heather's clutches, so Heather lowered her to the floor. 'Sarah, forgive me. I forgot to offer you a cup of tea or coffee.'

'No, no, Mrs Blundell. I haven't got time for tea or coffee.'

'Please, call me Heather.'

Matthew, who had ducked out of the room to retrieve the logs, walked back in, avoiding Grace, who was crawling towards a pile of building blocks in the corner by the television. 'Here you go, Sarah. I hope these meet with your approval.'

Sarah stared blankly at Matthew. 'Thank you.' She placed the pages on the arm of the chair. 'So, to the next item on our agenda. Grace will turn one next month, and she's going to need all her immunisations. When you register her with the local GP, you'll need to book them all in. Government guidelines suggest she has four injections: MenB, Hib/MenC, PCV13 and MMR, which cover measles, mumps and rubella.'

'No problem,' said Heather, smiling politely. 'We've taken one-year-olds for their jabs before – but we've yet to leave with a dry pair of eyes!'

'And that includes the children,' said Matthew. 'Boom, boom.'

'Indeed,' said Sarah. 'And while we're on the subject of Grace's birthday – when you get paid this month, there will be a little extra in your allowance from Children's Services. It's to buy Grace a present. You're not to spend it on anything else. I'm sure I can trust you to take care of that. Have you got any plans for the day? You should take her somewhere.'

'That might be a little tricky, seeing as we have a supervision meeting with you – and given your habit of scheduling them smack-bang in the middle of the day,' said Matthew.

'A problem easily solved,' said Sarah. 'I'll make an exception and get to you first thing – shall we say nine o'clock? You can set your alarm a little earlier that day, I'm sure, Mr Blundell.'

'A six o'clock alarm it is, Sarah.'

Heather gave Matthew a discreet warning nudge and forced another smile. She too was growing weary of Sarah Morton's condescending attitude – part of her wanted to be as brazen as Matthew and slap her off her high horse – but someone had to remain professional; though she was clinging to the last shreds of civility. 'We'll think of something, Sarah,' she said as she looked across at Grace, who had gripped the edge of the slimline television and was attempting to stand. 'Obviously, it's her first birthday – it's a special occasion. We'll get her some presents, and I'll make her a cake; that goes without saying.' She nudged Matthew again, nodded in Grace's direction and moved on quickly. 'Potentially, there's a big milestone approaching. The next time we see you, I think Grace might be walking.'

'And as you've no doubt noted, the stair gates are already in place,' said Matthew, hurrying over to Grace, grabbing her and placing her back among the building blocks. He retook his seat on the sofa.

'Talking of milestones,' said Sarah, 'has James reached any recently?'

Heather brightened. 'Oh, James is doing really well. I would say he's about the same as an average five-month-old, which, considering his diagnosis, is brilliant. Let's see... he can lie on his tummy and lift his head, and we encourage him to roll over. He can sit if we prop him up with cushions, and he constantly plays with his feet. There doesn't seem to be too much wrong with his hearing – he responds to sounds. His feeding is still a little hit and miss, but he gained a pound in December, so that's positive. Oh, and he seems to want to put everything in his mouth. I don't suppose it'll be too long before we try him on solid food.' She looked at Matthew and smiled. 'We're both really proud of him, aren't we, love?'

'Excellent!' said Sarah. 'Well done, James.' She ran her fingers through her bleached blonde hair and caught Matthew staring at her. She stared back. Matthew resisted the temptation to point out that her roots would soon need doing. 'I was just admiring your highlights,' he said instead. 'They're an interesting shade of blue...'

Sarah glared at him.

'Oh,' continued Heather hurriedly, 'and we're due to take James back to the consultant paediatrician at the end of the month for another routine check-up. Hopefully, there'll be no issues.'

'I'm sure everything will be fine,' said Sarah, her irritation with Matthew still evident. 'Now, before I forget, I've put you on a GDPR course.'

'Fantastic,' said Matthew. 'Just when I thought life couldn't get any better.'

'For a moment there, Mr Blundell, I thought I detected a hint of sarcasm. Do you know what GDPR stands for?'

'General Data Protection Regulation,' said Matthew.

'Excellent. Ten out of ten, Mr Blundell. It sounds as if you have a keen interest in the subject. You should have an enjoyable day out!'

Matthew grunted.

'Now, is there anything else you wish to discuss with me before I go? Anything else I can help you with? Otherwise, I have places to be, people to see.'

Heather glanced at Matthew, who shook his head. 'I don't think so, Sarah,' she said. 'There's not much more to add. We've given you our daily logs, which cover all the day-to-day stuff. We know what's coming up and what we're doing... I'd say that's about it.'

'Right. Well, I'll give you a few minutes to read November's supervision notes. As usual, if you're happy with them, just sign both copies and keep one for yourself. I'll put the other one in your file at the office. I'll pop to the ladies' room while you're doing that.' She rose briskly from the armchair and handed over the supervision notes as she walked past Heather and left the room.

By the time she returned, Matthew and Heather had scanned the notes and signed both copies.

'All done,' said Matthew, getting up from the sofa and handing the notes to her as she gathered her briefcase. 'I suppose you'll be wanting to get off now.'

'Indeed. We're all done here. I'll take these daily logs with me...' She opened the briefcase, placed all her paperwork inside, closed it again and secured the catches. 'Now, don't forget Grace's birthday, and I expect you to record in detail how she settles in. No need to see me to the door. I know my way out.'

8

Stairgate

Wednesday, 8th March 2017

'Heather, come and look at this.'

Heather had just emerged from the kitchen and was in the hallway. She poked her head around the door to the lounge. Matthew was sitting in the middle of the room on the cream-coloured carpet, puffing up the large turquoise cushions from the back of the sofa, smacking them with both hands. James was sitting next to him, joining in, thumping the cushions, gurgling in glee.

She walked in and stood next to them. 'Oh, he's such a sweetheart, Matthew.' She smiled as she watched. 'I can't imagine our life without him.'

'Well, don't get too attached, love – circumstances change – you know that as well as I do.'

'Yes, but James is special. You feel the same way; I know you do. Maybe we should consider adopting him?'

'Whoa.' Matthew looked up. 'We've only just started the fostering, and we need the income. Let's just see how things go before we entertain ideas like that.'

Heather's gaze lingered on James a little longer. 'Well, it's so good to see him showing such an interest in things. Just look how happy he is. You would never see Emily play like that when she was his age.' Then she turned and disappeared back into the kitchen, where she was tidying up. She was listening to Isle of Wight Radio and didn't want to wake Grace, who was asleep upstairs, so she closed the door behind her.

Soon after her first birthday, Grace had learnt to walk. It seemed she was impatient to get up and at it, as if driven by some restless, mischievous spirit, hell-bent on destruction. Now, she woke from her afternoon sleep in a strop, screeching over the baby monitor. Matthew left James playing, got up and opened the stair gate barring the doorway to the lounge. He closed it behind him and crossed the hall. He opened the stair gate at the bottom of the stairs and bounded up them, taking them two at a time. As he turned the corner at the top and reached the landing, Grace's room was the first on the right, the doorway barred by yet another stair gate.

'What's all this noise about? Come on, let's get you downstairs and get you dressed.'

Grace was standing up against the inside of the cot in just a nappy and t shirt, clutching the cuddly pink elephant that she took everywhere with her. Matthew grabbed a small pile of her clothes, lifted her out and took her down to the lounge, closing all the stair gates behind him. James was happily playing on his own. He had managed to crawl a short distance towards the door and was now sitting, holding his toy drum, which he was banging enthusiastically. Matthew put Grace down on the floor and sat between her and James. He turned her trousers and jumper the right way out. As Matthew was dressing Grace, James struggled onto his hands and knees and crawled forward. He paused frequently, seemingly to steady himself, and after a short distance, he toppled onto his side. He got back onto his knees and carried on. As he reached the lounge door, he picked up Grace's pink elephant, which she had dropped. Grace clearly wasn't impressed. She screamed her anguish. As Matthew finished dressing her, she wriggled out of his grasp, rocked to her feet and gave chase. She caught up with James as he was reaching out to grab the bars of the stair gate barring the way to the hall. She planted a hand firmly on the back of his head and pushed him face-first into the metal frame.

Matthew cursed under his breath. 'Grace! That's it, I've had enough of your bullying!'

He caught up with her and grabbed a handful of her trousers and the back of her nappy. She dangled, flailing and screaming, as he strode across the room, propelling her like an aeroplane, and plonked her into the playpen. In the meantime, James had picked himself up and carried on as if nothing had happened. Matthew hurried over to him.

'Come on, little man. Let's take a look at you.'

A red mark was showing on James's forehead. It was faint, no blood, just mildly inflamed. Matthew picked him up, opened the stair gate and carried him into the hallway, stroking James's silky blond hair as he walked towards the closed kitchen door.

'What do you make of this?' he said to Heather, indicating James's forehead as he entered the room. 'Grace just pushed him into the stair gate. You know what Social Services are like. Every scratch and bruise has to be recorded.'

Heather turned down the radio and came over. 'Well, he's obviously taken a knock,' she said, stroking James's forehead. His skin was warm to the touch. 'What do you think? Should we take him to the hospital?'

'Hospital? Why? Okay, it was hard enough to cause that little lump and mark, but he doesn't seem bothered at all.' James's bright blue eyes stared calmly at Heather through the narrow openings between his eyelids.

'Let me put an ice-cold flannel on it for a while,' said Heather, 'and we'll see what it looks like in ten minutes.'

Heather moved over to the sink and ran the tap. After letting it run cold, she wet a flannel and took a little ice from the freezer. Matthew reached for his phone and took a photo of James's face for reference. Then Heather took James from him, sat down at the kitchen table and held a flannel to his forehead. She held him tight, and he curled up in her arms and seemed to enjoy the warmth and affection.

'Look, it's going down already,' said Heather after a few minutes. 'What do you think?'

'I can't see any point in going all the way to A&E when there's nothing to show them except a red mark. It's not even broken the skin or caused any bleeding. The first thing they'll ask is how he is, and we both know he's fine. Look at him.'

'Well, we'd better keep a close eye on him for the next few hours. I'll just write the incident up in his daily log.'

The next day, there was no swelling, and the redness on James's face had all but disappeared.

'See, it was nothing to worry about,' said Matthew. 'Just a bit of practical common sense, and everything's fine.'

Monday, 3rd April 2017

Sarah Morton didn't quite see it that way. On her scheduled visit in April, she was reading James's daily log.

'What's this? I'm surprised at you – you should know better! I've outlined the council's policy on injuries, including marks and bruising, and yet you've failed to act accordingly. You should have phoned me immediately, and James should have been taken to hospital. What have you got to say for yourself, Mrs Blundell?'

Heather looked at Matthew as if to say, 'Why me?'

'Oh, come on, Sarah,' said Matthew. 'It was only a bump. It went down after ten minutes – all he had was a red mark. We applied common sense. It's not like he took a blow to the top of the head – there was absolutely no sign of concussion. The doctors would have thought we were mad carting him up to A&E.'

'May I remind you that this is a foster child we are dealing with here – the rules are different.'

'What rules?' Matthew glared at her. 'There are no set rules, and I don't recall you ever outlining any council "policy" on injuries! If you're referring to The Bruising Protocol, it relates to babies and children who are non-mobile. James is crawling. And who has day-to-day responsibility here, anyway? It's down to us to decide what's appropriate, and I'm telling you that there is no way James required hospital treatment.'

'And I'm telling you, as your supervising social worker, that you should have phoned me immediately, and I would certainly have advised you to take him to the hospital to be checked over. Now, is it too much to expect that you took a photograph of his injuries?'

'Of course I took a bloody photograph – on my phone! What do you take me for?'

'It's probably best I don't answer that. Right, I need you to attach that to an email and send it to me. Then I need you to delete the original and the sent email; you should not be keeping that kind of thing on your phone.'

Matthew called up his one photograph and sent it to Sarah via email. Then, he deleted the image and the email in his 'Sent' folder. 'There,' he said. 'Done!'

'Excellent! Now go to your "Deleted Items" folder and delete it permanently.'

'Done!'

'Good. You can be sure I'll be writing up this episode in this month's supervision notes. Now let's move on...'

Matthew's mobile rang at 6:45 PM

'Yes?'

'Mr Blundell. It's Sarah Morton.'

'I know who it is. Bit late in the day for you, isn't it? You must be doing some overtime.'

'Mr Blundell. I've just come off the phone to St Mary's. You need to take James for a check-up with a paediatrician. Now.'

'Check-up, my arse! What does he need a check-up for? And why now? Couldn't you have arranged it earlier? It's coming up to seven o'clock – he's had his bath, and he goes to bed soon. You know his routine and how hard it can be to get him to settle down.'

'Now, Mr Blundell. They're expecting you within the next half an hour. Someone from our team will meet you there.'

'I'll ask you again: why does he need a check-up? Is this to do with him bumping his head? That was a month ago, and you saw him today – he's fine!'

'Just do as I ask.'

'I don't see the point – it's a waste of time. There's nothing wrong with him.'

'Are you refusing to take him? Am I going to have to make a note in your records saying you declined an official medical request?'

Matthew saw where Sarah was going with this, so, once again making his extreme displeasure known, he acceded to her demands.

'Heather. That was Morton. She wants me to take James to the hospital so someone can examine him. Don't bother getting him dressed again; he can go in his pyjamas. I'll just grab his coat.'

'At this time of night? What on earth for?'

'I haven't a clue. But when I find out, you'll be the first to know.'

Inevitably, James fell asleep on the way. It wasn't unusual for him to sleep in the car at night, so long as he was screened from the distractions of the streetlights and passing cars, and Matthew often resorted to driving him around the block of an evening in an effort to get him to drop off.

On arrival at the hospital's North pay and display car park twenty minutes later, Matthew lifted James from the car, still in his car seat; tucked up and sound asleep. A young lady, Felicity, from Social Services was waiting in the North Entrance lobby together with the familiar pungent smell of disinfectant. Her seemingly pointless role was to escort him to Children's Outpatients, adjacent to the lobby on the ground floor, and then wait for him. A female paediatrician and a nurse were waiting in a small consultation room.

'Thank you for coming in at short notice, Mr Blundell. I'm one of the paediatricians here. We just need to give James a full examination – I'm sure your supervising social worker explained everything to you.'

'Like hell she did. Well, good luck with that. He's fast asleep, as he usually is at this time of night. I don't see why we couldn't have done all this in the morning.'

'Social services have asked us to do it now. We don't question it. It won't take more than half an hour, and then you'll be on your way. If you can lift him out of his car seat and take his coat and babygrow off.'

Matthew attempted to undress James without disturbing him too much, and as he lay half asleep on a padded baby mat, the paediatrician gave him a visual check from head to toe. His face was a particular source of attention.

'This is a farce.' Matthew had lost what little composure he had retained by this stage. 'Bloody ridiculous. He bumped his head a month ago!'

The paediatrician ignored him and continued, checking the movement of James's arms and legs. The nurse then helped her weigh him, measure his height and spine, and finally, they noted the circumference of his head.

After a few probing questions about James's diet, demeanour and any other injuries sustained, Matthew was allowed to redress him and settle him back into his car seat; although, by this time, James was fully awake.

'So, what's your prognosis?' said Matthew.

'I'm happy to say there's nothing to report,' said the paediatrician. 'As far as I can see, he's fine and you can take him home.'

'That's what I told my supervising social worker. I said there was nothing wrong with him. A waste of your time and mine.'

'We're just doing our job, Mr Blundell. If social services ask us to examine a child, then we examine that child. At least he's got the all-clear.'

Matthew bypassed Felicity, who was dozing in a chair off to his right, as he strode out through the North Entrance lobby. Another twenty-minute drive and he arrived back at the house. He came in through the front door fuming, with a wide-awake James in his arms.

'Guess what? There was nothing wrong with him! An hour-and-a-half round trip for bugger all.'

'Close the front door quietly, why don't you! For goodness' sake, you'll wake Grace.' James squirmed restlessly as Heather took him from Matthew and carried him upstairs to his cot in their room.'

'So, what was all that about, then?' she said as she joined Matthew in the lounge some twenty-five minutes later.

'That was nothing more than jobsworth Sarah Morton on an ego trip, flexing a bit of muscle and attempting to show us who's boss.' Matthew sat on the sofa staring into a second generous measure of brandy. He raised the glass to his lips and swallowed a mouthful. It burned as it hit the back of his throat, and he grimaced.

Heather flopped down next to him. 'I've been trying to see things from her point of view,' she said, relaxing into the sofa, tilting her head back and staring up at the ceiling. 'She seems to have the children's best interests at heart, I'll give her that, and she clearly believes what she's saying is right; but she's so rigid and by the book.'

'To say nothing of pig-headed and rude. There are more tactful ways of getting your point across.'

Heather turned her head to look at him. 'I'm not sure you're qualified to be advising others on the subject of tact, Matthew. You're hardly helping matters by constantly provoking her.' When Matthew smirked and said nothing, she continued. 'I agree, though. Her attitude is inexcusable; it's starting to grate on me too. There's no need for it. Why does she have to be so objectionable?'

Matthew scoffed. 'Objectionable is putting it mildly. She seems to take great pleasure in trying to undermine us. Well, you'll have to try harder than that, Morton!'

Sarah also wasted no time in informing James's social worker, Janet, about 'Stairgate', as Matthew referred to it. Inevitably, it meant a visit from Janet to check up on him and to review the incident. She was at the door the following day.

'Good morning.'

'Hi, Janet,' said Heather. 'Come in and sit down. James is in the lounge playing on his mat.'

By now, Janet was a familiar face. She was medium-height and very thin, with curly, dark grey hair – surely nearing retirement age. The wrinkles were beginning to show. Although refined, a slightly raspy voice suggested a history of smoking. The ever-present scent of an intoxicating perfume possibly masked the smell of the odd sneaky fag – who knew. She wore expensive jewellery – nothing too flashy, but enough to show she had money and class. But unlike Sarah, Janet was friendly and approachable, which was a breath of fresh air.

'Hello, little man,' she said, as she crossed the room and crouched down beside James. 'How are you doing?'

Matthew came into the room. 'He's doing absolutely fine, Janet. No issues at all.'

'Ah, Matthew.' Janet looked up. 'You're right; he looks right as rain. Still, Sarah has referred the matter to me. I'll come straight out with it: she has concerns that, given the nature of the incident and the fact that James suffered a head wound, there were no steps taken to contact anyone in the Fostering Team. She says you didn't seek any medical advice either.'

‘Head wound?’ said Matthew. ‘I can only repeat what I said to Sarah, Janet. It was only a bump. It went down after ten minutes, and all he had was a red mark. We’ve been fostering for some years now, so we aren’t beginners who panic at the slightest knock. We applied common sense, and we supervised him closely for twenty-four hours. He was fine.’

Janet turned her attention back to James and handed him the teddy bear he had dropped. He began chewing its ear. ‘Well, as I said, he seems fine – whatever it was, it’s cleared up nicely. What’s done is done, I suppose, and I appreciate you know what you’re doing, but perhaps, if there is a next time, you might consider giving me a call – just to advise me what’s happened, however unimportant you think it is.’

Janet accepted the offer of a cup of tea and used the time to fuss over James. After about half an hour, she stood up to leave.

‘Well, I shan’t take up any more of your time. It’s always a pleasure seeing the little man – and you, of course.’

‘No problem,’ said Heather. ‘Thank you for popping in. I hope seeing James has put your mind at rest. If there are any more accidents, I promise we’ll let you know.’

‘Perfect. In that case, I shall leave you and Mr Adorable here and be on my way.’

‘Mr Adorable?’ said Matthew. ‘No one’s ever called me that before...’

9

Trouble at Tapnell

Easter Sunday, 16th April 2017

Matthew was unloading the dishwasher as Heather emerged from the utility room, which was off the kitchen on the opposite side to the playroom.

'That Tupperware never dries properly,' she said, looking over his shoulder. 'It'll all need a wipe.'

'Wipe, my arse! That lot can dry on the draining board.'

There was a crash from the playroom.

'Bloody hell – what's she done now? I thought you were supposed to be supervising them,' said Matthew, hurrying over, opening the stair gate and going into the playroom.

Grace was wriggling out from underneath her two-storey play kitchen, the contents of which had scattered across the floor. James was crawling unsteadily towards the door, seemingly beating a retreat.

'I think Grace might benefit from a day out,' he said as Heather joined him in the room. 'Perhaps that Tapnell Farm Park near Yarmouth? What do you think? She can run around a bit.'

'Well, they have that petting zoo,' said Heather. 'But do you think James will be okay with the crowds and all the animals?'

'We won't know until we take him, will we?' said Matthew. 'I think it will do us all good to get out of the house.'

'Well, the weather forecast is good for the rest of today.'

'Okay,' said Matthew. 'Decision made. Let's get all the stuff together and get going.'

Matthew and Heather slotted the buggies and bags into the boot of their new second-hand black Volkswagen Caravelle. They had bought it the week before, having decided now was the right time. Matthew had been complaining for a while that driving around in his beloved Citroën with both kids and all the shit that came with them was getting a bit much. Also, with the potential for more placements, it seemed to make sense. They kept Matthew's Citroën as a runaround for when the extra space wasn't needed. The purchase of the Caravelle had used up most of their remaining savings, which had already been depleted by the work on the house going over budget.

The traffic was light, and within half an hour they were in the car park unloading the boot. They strapped James into the double buggy, and put Grace straight into her harness, at least for the time being. Walking was still a novelty, and she was determined to be on her feet. Confining her to the buggy would be a last resort.

Once inside the park, Matthew made a note of the various animal feeding times and planned the best route. The map showed a series of paddocks surrounding the main activity areas and car park, something akin to the layout of a ranch. Tapnell Farm Park was a vast open space, with the distant hills as a backdrop. However, far from the gentle farmyard sounds of lowing cattle and bleating sheep and goats, the overriding soundtrack to Tapnell was the sound of people enjoying a day out as they milled around with music playing over a sound system. Matthew and Heather made their way outside to the paddocks.

'Grace, come and look at these donkeys,' said Heather. 'Aren't they lovely? Here, shall we put Elephant in the buggy and let him have a ride around?' She took Grace's pink elephant and placed it in the storage compartment underneath the seats. Then she led Grace up to a donkey that was leaning over a paddock fence and placed her hand on its neck. Grace delicately patted and stroked the animal and then gave it a hug. Matthew pushed the buggy closer and squatted next to James as the donkey nuzzled around him. James seemed unsure at first, but then he reached out and thumped his tiny, clenched fist on the donkey's nose. The donkey started and pulled its head back, snorting snot as it turned and moved away.

'Thanks for that, James.' Matthew pulled out a tissue and dabbed his face before wiping a few spots off the buggy. James twisted and turned in his seat as he thrust a hand in his mouth and started chewing on it.

In the next paddock were several alpacas, which Grace also gave her undivided attention as they passed, but they left the rest of the paddocks until later and made their way through to the 'Wallaby Walkabout', where it was feeding time. The wallabies were easily accessible, and one individual by the railings was so tame that Grace could stroke and hug that too. By this stage, she was straining on the harness.

'Just let her off,' said Matthew. 'She can have a run around.'

All the while, James had been sitting upright in his seat, reaching out and straining to touch everything he could see. He watched Grace with the wallaby in animated amusement, grinning and babbling to himself. Matthew pushed the buggy and took him to see the goats that occupied a nearby pen. Grace followed. As she bent over with her back to the fence, attempting to retrieve her pink elephant from the buggy, one of the larger goats stuck its head through and head-butted her in the backside. Its stunted horns snagged on her jeans and hooked under the pink, sparkly belt she was wearing. It tried to lift its head, couldn't, and suddenly Grace was being violently shaken as the animal tried to free itself.

'Matthew!' screamed Heather. 'Grace is impaled on one of the goats!'

'It had to be Grace,' said Matthew, hurrying over to her. He gripped the goat and pinned it in a headlock. 'Quick, I've got it. Lift her off.'

Heather released Grace from the goat's horns and, as a few amused bystanders dispersed, she checked her over. There was no damage done. Grace seemed more in shock than distress. Heather brushed her down, soothed her and gave her a reassuring cuddle, and then she was back in the harness for everyone's sanity. Next up, it was time to feed the ducks and geese.

'You wait with the kids,' said Matthew, 'and I'll get some bags of bird food. You might want to get James out of the buggy for this one – he can try to throw some.'

James sat on Heather's knee. She held onto him around his waist and showed him how to hold his palm out. Matthew gave him a pinch of food. Then Heather clenched his fist and helped him throw the contents towards the hungry flock at his feet. Most of the food ended up on James's lap, but a couple of the more alert ducks were able to claim whatever found its way to the floor. Meanwhile, Grace had wasted no time. She shoved her hand into her bag and flung large handfuls directly at the birds.

Matthew groaned. 'For Christ's sake... Heather, look at this, will you? She's not feeding the damn things; she's bloody stoning them!'

Heather grabbed Grace's wrist. 'Grace, stop! That's enough.'

Grace's response was predictable. She threw herself onto the floor, screaming. By the time Heather dragged her up from the ground, there were tears and snot running down her angry, red face. This time the onlookers were not so amused.

'Do you think now's a good time to have something to eat?' said Matthew. 'We can have an early lunch, before everyone else.'

The Cow Co. restaurant was a large building covered in slatted pine panels. Inside, the cavernous space, with its vaulted ceiling, gave the impression of being inside a church. Numerous cows' heads adorned the walls. Presumably fake, or else a local herd somewhere had taken a pummelling. The occasional clatter of plates and crockery and the metallic chinking of cutlery punctuated the hum of conversation.

'It says on the menu here that their burgers are award-winning,' said Heather.

'Best we try them out, then, and see for ourselves,' said Matthew. 'Shall I order and get us all some cold drinks?'

While Matthew queued, Heather settled James and managed to feed him a couple of spoonfuls from a jar of homemade purée baby food she had prepared, following advice from a specialist, as they tried to adapt his food to his nutritional needs. She then held him as he sucked intermittently on his bottle of milk, and when the food arrived, she placed him back in the buggy, tending to him frequently. Everyone was silent as they ate, and Grace made light work of a plate of chips and her favourite dessert: cake.

'So, what did you think of your award-winning burger?' said Heather, wiping her hands on a napkin. 'I enjoyed mine.'

'Bloody marvellous,' said Matthew, as he finished the last of his. 'Best burger I've had all day.'

'Ha, ha, such wit,' said Heather. 'What's next on the timetable?'

'Shall we brave the rabbits and guinea pigs?' said Matthew, wiping his mouth and then reaching for Grace's harness, which was hanging from the buggy. 'They get fed in about fifteen minutes. I'm sure James and Grace would love to have a go at holding them.'

'Yes – sounds good to me. I'd leave Grace's harness off if she's going to be petting the animals.'

As they approached the 'Meet the Animals' area in the Animal Barn, the familiar backdrop of conversation and laughter echoed around them, and there was a warm smell of fresh straw and sawdust. They saw the pens and hutches housing all the smaller animals, and in an enclosed area off to one side, there were several rows of kiddie-sized benches ready to accommodate groups of children, all eager to sit, cuddle and feed the various rabbits and guinea pigs on display. Immediately outside the area were more benches for parents to sit on and wait while their children were otherwise preoccupied.

'Let me take the buggy and bags and sit down over there while you take James and Grace in to see the animals,' said Matthew.

'Come on, you two, let's go see the guinea pigs,' said Heather.

She carried James and took Grace by the hand and made her way into the enclosed area. She sat on a bench with James on her lap and Grace to her right, with one arm around each. Eventually, a young man in a staff uniform appeared and began telling everyone about Pets' Corner. It wasn't long before James and Grace were each holding a guinea pig on their laps and feeding them carrots. Then, another member of staff brought over a couple of small rabbits. The guinea pigs were passed on to a couple of other children, who were patiently waiting their turn, and Grace and James got a rabbit each. James made a sudden grab for his rabbit's ears. The rabbit reacted in fright, twisted and turned and leapt off James's lap onto the floor. As it loped away, another young boy nearby scooped it up and began petting it. James began to cry, and despite Heather's reassuring cooing, would not stop.

She struggled to get up off the low bench as she held him tight to her. Grace was sitting quietly, stroking her rabbit, which was so docile it appeared to have fallen asleep. Heather looked around. 'Excuse me,' she said, approaching one member of staff, who was standing close by.

'Will it be alright if I quickly take my son back over to his dad and leave my daughter here – just for a moment? She's absolutely fine with that rabbit on her lap. I'll only be a second. If there's a problem, the name's Blundell.'

The member of staff, whose plastic name badge identified him as Roger, was accustomed to most children being unaccompanied, and he shrugged. 'That's fine,' he said. 'I'll keep half an eye on her.'

'Thank you,' said Heather gratefully. 'I'll be just over there.'

The surrounding scene seemed somewhat chaotic. Some children had put their animals on the floor and were playing with them. Heather, carrying and soothing James, picked her way around them, and looked around for Matthew. He was sitting on one of the peripheral benches, deep in conversation with an attractive young mother, who was sitting next to him rocking a newborn in its pram.

'Where's Grace?' he said, looking up as Heather hurried over.

'Don't panic,' said Heather. 'The man said it was alright for Grace to stay – he said he'll keep an eye on her. There are other children on their own in there too. I gave him our name just in case.'

'This is Grace we're talking about – do you think it's a good idea to leave her?' said Matthew.

'She'll be fine,' said Heather. 'She's having a lovely time.'

Matthew nodded, unconvinced. He looked at James, who was proving hard to settle. 'What happened in there?'

'They put a rabbit on his lap. He made a grab for it and scared it. I don't think it bit him, but it was startled and I think maybe it scratched him as it jumped off.'

Both Heather and Matthew were checking James over for bite marks and scratches.

There was a sharp howl of feedback, and a voice boomed over a tannoy. 'Would a Mrs Blundell make her way immediately to Pets' Corner. A Mrs Blundell to Pets' Corner.'

'What the hell has she done now?' said Matthew. 'Wait here with James; I'll see what the problem is.'

As Matthew approached the enclosed area, several children, some in tears, were leaving to be reunited with their parents. Inside, Matthew noticed a young man in uniform holding onto Grace's hand. Matthew hurried over to him.

'Afternoon...' Matthew eyed the member of staff's name badge, '... Roger. What's the problem?'

'I presume this is your child, sir?'

'Yes,' said Matthew, looking down at Grace, who was busy scuffing the shoe on her right foot in the dirt.

'Your daughter has just stamped on a guinea pig.'

'Stamped on a guinea pig?'

'Yes, sir, that's what I said. I saw her myself. Then she picked it up and brought it over to me to show me what she'd done.'

'Well, where is it?' said Matthew. 'Is it alright?'

'Er, no,' said Roger, 'it's far from alright, sir. It's dead.' He let go of Grace's hand and walked over to a nearby bench. He came back with a lifeless, long-haired ball of fluff in his hand, dangling it by its back legs. Blood had seeped from the rodent's nose and ears. Roger held it up. 'One deceased guinea pig. She stamped on its head.'

As Matthew looked down at Grace, he could see her t-shirt was blood-stained.

'Now hang on a minute,' said Matthew. 'What makes you think for one moment that my daughter intentionally stood on this thing?'

'This "thing", sir, had a name. Tinkerbell.'

'Well, Tinkerbell, whatever... Kids of that age don't go around stamping on animals. Obviously, it was an accident; she is quite a clumsy child.'

'I don't think you're listening to me, sir. I witnessed the assault. It was deliberate.'

'Okay, Roger, I do hear what you say, but I find it hard to believe.' Actually, Matthew found it quite easy to believe. 'Obviously, my wife and I are very sorry for the loss of Tinkerbell. What are we talking about here? Compensation?'

'I'll need you to come with me, sir. I'll write up an incident report, which I'll need you to sign. But at the very least, sir, we're looking at a ban.'

'A ban?'

'Yes, sir. Your daughter will be banned from ever stepping foot – excuse the pun, sir – in Pets' Corner again.'

'Right,' said Matthew. 'Well, let's step on it and get this over and done with, shall we? – excuse the pun, Roger. I'll just go and explain the situation to my wife.'

About half an hour later, Matthew emerged from the Farm Park office. He found Heather sitting on a bench near the donkeys, rocking James, who was almost asleep, in the buggy. Grace, firmly secured in her harness, was attached to the bench they were sitting on.

Heather looked up as Matthew arrived. 'All done?'

'Yes, but I never want to go through that again,' said Matthew. 'It was humiliating. The bloody head keeper started giving me a lecture on how to bring up children. I gave him a piece of my mind. Then he got shirty and asked me what I thought they should do with the remains – the sarcastic git. I told them to feed it to the bloody pigs!'

'Matthew! How many times have I told you to hold that tongue of yours? That was insensitive and out of order. You should have been apologising.'

Matthew looked away. 'She's the bloody Antichrist, I swear it.'

'Matthew! Okay, we're all upset. Let's put it behind us and move on to whatever's next on the schedule,' said Heather.

'We can't.'

'What do you mean, we can't?'

'Well, I told you they were going to ban Grace from Pets' Corner...'

'Yes, what of it? It's understandable in the circumstances.'

'They changed their minds.'

'I don't understand. Is Grace banned or not?'

'Yes, she is... Only, it's not just Grace they've banned. It's all of us.'

'Okay, so none of us can go into Pets' Corner again. Big deal.'

'It's not just Pets' Corner they've banned us from...'

Heather stared at him in disbelief. 'You what? Let me get this straight. Are you telling me you've gone in there, opened your big mouth, and now they've banned all of us from ever coming here again?'

'That's the long and short of it,' said Matthew. 'But,' he added, 'look on the bright side: they didn't say we had to leave immediately. Anyone for an ice cream?'

Heather screamed her frustration, startling a young mother with her two young daughters close by. 'Sorry,' she said, smiling apologetically, 'it's been one of those days.' She detached Grace's harness from the bench, and, scooping Grace up, headed off in the direction of the gift shop.

James had woken amid all the commotion and was now squirming restlessly in the buggy. Matthew squatted down beside him. 'Don't worry, little man,' he said. 'Heather will be fine. She can never stay mad at me for more than a few minutes.' He ruffled James's hair and stood before turning the buggy and trailing after Heather, keeping a discreet distance until he knew she'd calmed down.

They wandered around the gift shop and then back out to take a last look at the animals in the paddocks as they made their way towards the exit. Stopping at a section of wooden fencing, Matthew lifted James from the buggy.

'Look, little man, can you see all the animals? There's some sheep, and look, there's some pigs – three different ones. Wait a minute...' Matthew leant forward and stared intently. 'No... surely not?'

'What are you on about?' said Heather. 'Come on, let's go.'

'No, wait,' said Matthew. 'I swear there's something poking out of that one's mouth. It looks like a little foot to me...'

'Matthew. Don't!'

Heather jerked on Grace's reins and half dragged her off. The slow exit continued via the Straw Bale Adventure Barn until, finally, Matthew said, 'Time to go home. I'm shattered.'

'I think you had better carry Grace,' said Heather. 'She's exhausted.'

'Come on then, Miss Antichrist, let's be having you,' said Matthew, taking Grace from Heather. 'Well, I don't think that turned out too badly in the end.'

'Yeah, right,' scoffed Heather. 'Apart from Grace being skewered by a goat and murdering a guinea pig, it was a wonderful day out.'

'Don't forget the stoning of the birds,' said Matthew. 'Right, where's the exit?'

10

The Devil's Child

Saturday, 13th May 2017

The weekend: two days when the thoughts of many of the island's residents turned to DIY and playing sports. As this particular Saturday afternoon stretched into the evening, those injured in the pursuit of said leisure activities could still be found clogging up the system at St Mary's A&E in Newport, soon to be joined by the casualties of a nighttime's revelry on the streets of the town, as an element of the working masses vented the frustrations of a week spent slaving at the grindstone. Matthew and Heather avoided DIY and sport wherever possible, and usually vented their frustration while watching the Britain's Got Talent auditions on ITV after the kids had gone to bed, thereby avoiding the three-hour wait to be stitched or plastered up – or, for those nighttime revellers arriving already plastered, the dubious pleasure of having their stomach pumped.

It was approaching seven o'clock, and Matthew was sitting on the sofa combing Grace's hair, with half an eye on 'Tom & Jerry' on the television. He stopped combing and began parting her hair with his fingers, first in one place, then another, then another.

'What are you looking for? Nits?' asked Heather.

'Nits are the least of our worries. I'm looking for marks.'

'Marks? What marks?'

'You've seen "The Omen". The Antichrist, Damien Thorn, has a "666" mark on his head.'

'Matthew, stop it. She might understand and repeat everything you're saying. God help us if Sarah gets to hear of it.'

Grace slid off the sofa and toddled off to play. Matthew got up.

'Fancy a cup of tea?'

'No, I'm fine, thanks,' said Heather.

Heather was watching James as he tried valiantly to pull himself to his feet from his knees, using the sofa for support. At James's last routine appointment at St Mary's in April, the consultant had been assessing his motor skills. He had previously discussed with them one of the many conditions associated with FASD: Sensory Processing Disorder, or SPD. He explained how the nervous system receives messages from the senses and turns them into appropriate motor and behavioural responses, and how someone with SPD finds it difficult to process and act upon that information, which creates challenges in performing countless everyday tasks, including movement. It was early days, but there were signs that James's balance might be affected.

Heather reached for his baby walker, which was all the colours of the rainbow and solidly built around an electronic activity centre, and moved it beside him. She stood him up, turned him around, and placed his tiny hands on the green handlebar.

'You see,' said Matthew, as James took a couple of steps forward, 'what do those doctors know? Nine months old and he's on his feet just like any normal kid his age.' He disappeared, heading towards the kitchen and the kettle.

James continued to push his walker with faltering steps. He stumbled as he ran over Grace's foot. She screamed. James tried to steady himself, but plonked down as the walker rolled out of reach. He ended up sitting next to the game that Heather had just been playing with him. It had a red plastic base with a long see-through plastic tube rising out of it and was battery-operated. When switched on, it generated a current of air, and when Heather helped James push a large, lightweight plastic ball into a hole in the base, it shot up the tube and into the air, which James responded to with gurgling delight. Now, he slapped the hole the ball slotted into and giggled. Heather smiled as she watched him. His giggling stopped when Grace, who had retrieved his walker, trundled at speed and rammed him. The wheels missed him, but the side of the walker caught James on the right-hand side of his head. As he toppled and flung out an arm, his hand caught the purple button on the walker's activity centre and an electronic rendition of 'Humpty Dumpty' started up. James fell heavily onto his game, but rolled and sat up again, dazed, but seemingly unhurt, impervious to pain. A few moments later, Heather removed Grace, kicking and screaming, from the scene and left her raging inside her playpen.

'Matthew! We need a cold flannel. Grace has done it again...'

Matthew was running the tap in the kitchen and wetting a flannel as Heather hurried in with James. 'Bloody hell! What's got into that child!' he said.

'The devil,' said Heather, taking the flannel and pressing it on the right-hand side of James's head, under his hair, just above his ear. 'I think you're right about her.'

'Let me take a look.' Heather moved the flannel, and Matthew parted James's hair and examined him. 'It's just a bump. Same as before.'

'Exactly,' said Heather. 'Echoes of last time – and you know what happened then. We got dragged over the coals for not taking him to the hospital. I guess we don't have a choice this time.'

'You must be joking! On a Saturday night? Have you ever seen A&E on a Saturday night? We'll be there for hours, queuing behind the poor bastards who've been sitting there all afternoon. And then they'll be carting in all those fucking drunks and druggies – all that shouting and swearing. I'm not having the kids listen to all that. No way! What are they going to do with him anyway – stick him on a gurney and rush him into theatre?'

'I know, I know... but how are we going to explain blatantly ignoring everything Sarah told us last time?'

'Just don't record it in the log.'

'We have to. They need to know what kind of child we're dealing with. I'm sick of Grace's violent behaviour. It needs to be recorded.'

'Look, it's common sense – common, bloody sense! The kid's got a bump, like millions of kids before him. Again, he's not concussed – look at him. If you want to spend the night in the children's ward, then go ahead. Personally, I would just put in the log that Grace pushed him over; don't mention the walker, don't mention the bump and leave it at that.'

'Well, leave the recording to me – I know what's best. You can deal with Sarah when she starts throwing her weight around again.'

Monday, 5th June 2017

Matthew was doing his best.

'Mr Blundell, you and your wife have a duty of care here. How could you let a thing like this happen again?'

'Kids will be kids, Sarah. We can't have eyes on them every second; that's ridiculous. It's all part of growing up.'

'I find your couldn't-care-less attitude quite incredible, Mr Blundell. Your wife has recorded that Grace exhibited aggressive behaviour when she deliberately rammed James with a baby walker. As a result, he fell onto his game. Two collisions, but you make no mention of any injury. I put it to you that in a case like this, there would have been some bruising or some form of contusion – maybe even trauma. Did he hit his head in all this?'

Matthew inwardly cursed Heather.

Heather was wishing she had taken Matthew's advice and just recorded that Grace had deliberately pushed James over. She had to put a stop to this. 'No, he didn't hit his head, Sarah. The walker caught him on his arm, knocked him over, and he rolled onto his game. And if I had thought for a moment that he was badly hurt, I would have taken him to the hospital myself.'

Matthew glared at her. Heather reddened, feeling the weight of her dishonesty.

'*Badly* hurt? So, you admit he was hurt – that he sustained an injury?'

'We're admitting nothing of the sort,' said Matthew. 'If there had been any injury worth noting, we would have noted it.'

'So, there was an injury. You just felt it wasn't worth noting. I'm afraid I don't believe you,' said Sarah, 'and I shall be reflecting that opinion when I write up my supervision notes, which, I remind you, will remain on your file.'

'And which we won't be signing.'

'Which is your prerogative, Mr Blundell. Now, do you have a photograph to back up your claim?'

'No,' said Matthew. 'There was nothing worth taking a photo of.'

'Well, once again, Mr and Mrs Blundell, a violent incident has taken place, the nature of which, I believe, would surely have resulted in an injury to the child, and you have failed to contact the out-of-hours service, and you have failed to seek medical advice.'

'Well, once again, Ms Morton, I'll remind you that we have day-to-day responsibility for James, but thank you for your opinion; it has been duly noted.'

'You really don't want to push your luck with me, Mr Blundell...'

'Luck has got nothing to do with it, Ms Morton. We're in the right. You haven't got a leg to stand on, and you know it.'

Sarah Morton stood and left without a word.

Tuesday, 6th June 2017

'Hello again,' said Janet, in her slightly raspy voice.

'Best I put the kettle on, eh,' said Matthew. 'We've got some cake – we can have afternoon tea.'

'No, thank you, Matthew, I can't stop. I've just come to take a quick look at the little man.'

'Oh. Okay. Please, come in. Heather's in the lounge.' Matthew breathed in an overpowering lungful of an exotic, heady perfume as Janet walked in through the front door.

'How did his contact visit go this morning?' said Janet, making polite conversation as Matthew led her into the lounge.

'Yes, fine. By all accounts, he interacts well with his mum,' said Matthew. 'But, apparently, she's still drinking.'

Janet acknowledged Heather with a quick hello and a smile, then knelt and immediately began fussing over James, who wore a Tigger babygrow and was pushing around the pieces of a large, four-piece jigsaw on his play mat.

'I know what you're going to say, Janet,' Matthew cut in quickly as he sat down, 'but I think you'll find that our friend Sarah is making these incidents out to be something they're not. Kids will be kids; you know that. They're bound to run into each other or push each other around sometimes. Let's not pretend this is anything other than everyday rough-and-tumble. If we wrap these kids up in cotton wool, they'll grow up pampered and spineless.'

Janet looked up. 'I have to say, I'm disappointed in you, Matthew. And if I'm going to be candid, especially you, Heather.' She looked across at her. 'I thought we had an understanding. I believe I was more than reasonable last time we met. All I asked of you was a phone call if anything like this happened again, and you promised. And before you start up again, Matthew, I hear what you say and, maybe, I even agree with you, but that's not the point here. These are foster children, and there are procedures that need to be followed. We are under intense scrutiny these days. I'm sure I don't need to remind you of some of the high-profile cases that have been dominating the news in recent years.'

'I did promise you, Janet, and I know I've let you down. I'm sorry,' said Heather.

'Hang on a minute before you go apologising,' said Matthew, looking across at Heather. He looked back at Janet. 'We promised to let you know if there were any more accidents – in my book that's incidents involving "injuries", as you lot refer to every bump, scrape and scratch. There was no injury in this case. In fact, if it weren't for the fact that we felt we should record any instance of aggressive behaviour towards another child, in case it forms part of an ongoing pattern, we wouldn't have bothered putting it in the daily log at all. Let me tell you, Janet. I was a kid in the system, and the foster parents who were "caring" for me knocked me around for fun, and I could have done with someone like you looking out for me back then, believe me. But what I would not have expected you to do was run my foster parents over the coals just because my sister poked me in the eye – no matter how much I hated the bastards.'

'Goodbye, little man; see you soon,' said Janet. She got up and brushed down her skirt. 'Well, I think we've both made our point, Matthew. We'll leave it there.' She turned to Heather. 'I appreciate your understanding, Heather. Thank you. Don't worry, I'll see myself out.'

11

Emma

Wednesday, 19th July 2017

Tony and Barbara had visited in the last week of June for a "much-needed holiday", as Barbara referred to it. Heather wondered if retirement wasn't all it was cracked up to be, or, smiling to herself, whether the much-needed holiday was just a welcome break from the stress of living alone with a man like Tony. She could relate to that. For Matthew and Heather, Tony and Barbara's visit proved to be a welcome distraction from a fairly stressful few months. Life had settled back into routine after they left, but now, as Matthew and Heather sat in the lounge with James and Grace and saw a car pull up in front of the house, they braced themselves for the fact that life might well be about to get even more interesting. They had received an emergency call a few hours earlier and had rather hastily agreed to a third placement. Emma. Her social worker was Ann, whom Matthew and Heather had not met before. Through the net curtains, they saw Ann emerge from a blue Toyota Auris, attempting to shield herself with a small umbrella from a heavy shower of rain.

'Okay,' said Heather, 'so, you take James and Grace into the playroom and I'll form the welcome committee.'

'As agreed,' said Matthew. 'Come on, you two.' He scooped up James from the floor and took Grace by the hand. 'We don't want to scare Emma off before she's even got in the front door. The poor thing will be nervous enough.' He headed off to the playroom with the children, and Heather made her way to wait behind the front door. Through the frosted glass window, she could make out Ann holding the umbrella over Emma as she escorted her up the path, dwarfing her. They hurried into the porch, and Ann rang the doorbell. Heather waited a moment or two and then opened the door.

Ann was almost six feet tall and stocky with it. Heather guessed she was around forty – a similar age to them. She wore a long black trench coat and looked like something out of 'The Matrix'. By her side, her eyes lowered and staring at the doorstep, stood a ten-year-old girl dressed in a blue sweater over a white polo shirt and black trousers, which appeared to be her school uniform. At ten, she was older than the children Matthew and Heather usually cared for, and at first, they had been reluctant to take her on, not only because of her age but because she had a chronic medical condition. She was medium-height, slightly overweight and pale, with short, curly ginger hair and ginger freckles.

'Hello,' said Heather, beaming. 'You must be Ann. I'm Heather.' She acknowledged Ann briefly before crouching down. 'And you must be Emma,' she said, taking care not to invade Emma's personal space but making eye contact.

Emma smiled but seemed shy.

'Come in,' said Heather. She looked back at Ann. 'Can I help with any bags?'

'No, I'm fine, thanks,' said Ann. 'In you go, Emma.'

Heather stood and stepped to one side, and Emma moved past her and into the hallway. Ann hung up her wet trench coat in the porch and followed her in. She seemed to fill the doorway with her huge frame and all of Emma's belongings.

'Shall we take all your things straight upstairs?' said Heather, 'and I'll show you your room?'

Emma nodded, and Ann smiled.

Heather led the way. At the top of the stairs, Matthew and Heather's room was directly opposite. Emma's room was to the left, on the same side, between Matthew and Heather's room and the bathroom. The room was large enough to accommodate all three of them comfortably. The walls had been given a couple of coats of magnolia paint, and a new beige carpet kept everything neutral. However, the duvet cover and pillowcases on the bed were pink. Also in the room, all in white, were the existing built-in wardrobes, a chest of drawers and a bedside table, on which was a lamp that had a pink shade. Matthew and Heather had bought various sets of soft furnishings to mix and match, according to the occupant of the room, and, in Emma's case, the curtains were cream with a floral design in pastel pinks and greens, around which flew fairies in various guises.

Heather and Ann spent a while helping Emma to unpack and put away all her things, all the while talking to her and putting her at ease. By the time they had finished, Emma appeared to have lost some of her shyness and was a little more animated.

'Shall we go downstairs and you can meet Matthew?' said Heather, in a voice that made the prospect sound, perhaps, a little too exciting. 'He's in the playroom playing with James and Grace.'

Emma looked at Ann, who smiled back at her and said, 'The playroom sounds like fun.'

Heather led them downstairs, along the hallway, through the kitchen and into the playroom. Emma stopped at the door.

Whereas the rest of the house had been painted in a standard magnolia, Matthew and Heather had decided to go for something a little brighter in the playroom, and the walls were painted in an eye-catching sunshine yellow. There were three-storey storage units across the back wall, like oversized pigeonholes, each containing a large plastic box full of activity toys – one for soft toys, one for Lego blocks, one for board games and so on. In the centre of the room was an interactive 'Play City Rug' play mat, which took up most of the light oak laminate floor space. To the left, against the wall, was a small dresser, and at the far end there was a small, yellow plastic table with four chairs: orange, green, blue and purple – each child assigned a colour. No arguments.

'Come in,' said Matthew. 'We don't bite.' He looked at Grace. Well, some of us don't, he thought. He smiled at Emma. 'We're playing at being chefs. Do you want to join in?'

Emma walked over and sat down between James and Grace. Immediately, Matthew and Heather could see that she seemed more at ease with other children. Grace ignored her and continued putting a slice of plastic toast into a toaster and pushing a button to pop it up, and so Emma turned her attention to James and was soon helping him to prepare a pretend full English breakfast from the play kitchen. The adults watched for a while and then Ann crouched down by Emma's side.

'Emma, I need to have a quick word with Heather and Matthew. Are you happy to stay here and keep playing with James and Grace?'

'Okay,' said Emma. She continued playing, showing James how to slide a fried egg from a frying pan onto his plate. James took the spatula but seemed uncertain, so Emma patiently took his hand and showed him again.

Ann turned to Matthew and Heather. 'Shall we go into the lounge?' she said.

'Can I make you a tea or coffee first?' said Heather.

Ann smiled. 'That's kind. I'll have a black coffee, two sugars, please.'

'Coming up,' said Heather. She smiled at Matthew. 'Be a love...'

Heather and Ann headed for the lounge, while Matthew prepared the tea and coffee. Tea with just a splash of milk for Heather and his tea with milk and two sugars.

'Ah, we were just talking about you,' said Heather, as Matthew walked in.

'Something nice, I hope,' said Matthew. He put down his tray on top of the nest of tables and handed Ann a mug of black coffee.

'Thank you,' said Ann. 'Perfect.' She looked around to find somewhere to put it down.

'On here,' said Matthew, pulling out a small table from the nest, carrying it over to Ann in the armchair and putting a placemat on it.

Ann relieved herself of her mug. 'I thought I should take this opportunity to give you a bit more background information on Emma,' she said. 'I know our conversation this morning was brief and unexpected, and you had some initial reservations about taking her on, mainly due to her age and medical history.'

'Yes,' said Heather, 'it's just that when we originally applied here, one of the few preferences we had was for fostering pre-school children. Obviously, with Emma being at school, we were concerned that a school run might impact our morning routine. We have two pretty demanding toddlers already. As for her medical history, you mentioned she has myalgic encepha... encephalomy...' Heather smiled awkwardly. 'I can't say it...'

'Myalgic encephalomyelitis,' said Ann. 'But don't worry, you can refer to it as ME/CFS – the CFS stands for Chronic Fatigue Syndrome. Emma's condition is mild to moderate. Although she attends school, her daily activities are limited, and she frequently needs to rest.'

'Of course,' Heather smiled. 'I have a basic understanding of ME. They used to call it "Yuppie flu".' Ann nodded, and Heather continued. 'Well, you said it affects her energy levels, and we thought that, perhaps, living with James and Grace in a hectic household might be a bit too much for her.'

'Well, her condition is stable, but I'll go through her medication in a moment,' said Ann. 'You're right, though; you will need to be mindful of the fact that she mustn't overdo it.'

Matthew lowered his voice. 'We just wondered if she wouldn't be better off in a single-placement family, where she can receive dedicated care.'

'Well, unfortunately,' said Ann, 'things happened quickly this morning, and we had limited options. We are grateful that you agreed to take her on.' She leant down and picked up a small bag next to the armchair. 'Shall I run you through her medication?' She pulled out two bottles and placed them on the small table in front of her. She held one up. It was a small, dark amber glass bottle with a large prescription label. 'This is fluoxetine,' she said. 'It's an SSRI antidepressant. It's not usually recommended for children under eighteen, but in Emma's case, she suffers from severe major depressive episodes, so her doctor prescribed it. She's been taking it in an oral solution for about eight months. Apparently, a 10 mg dose has been effective and improved her mood, so he's kept her on that. She also had to attend weekly therapy sessions, but now she's stable, they're monthly, and I'll be attending those with her, so you won't need to worry. The doctor prescribes twenty-eight days' worth of solution in a 70 ml bottle like this. The contents expire after sixty days.' Ann reached back into the small bag. 'You administer it once a day, in the morning, in a 2.5 ml dose from this syringe.' She waved one around. 'There's a few in this medical cool bag. I'll leave the bag with you. She dropped the syringe back in. Any questions about the fluoxetine?'

Matthew glanced at Heather and raised his eyebrows. Heather looked across at Ann and shook her head. 'No, I don't think so. I've administered plenty of medication in the past.'

'Okay,' said Ann, putting down the fluoxetine and picking up a white plastic bottle, 'this is naproxen. It's a painkiller. She takes it for muscle and joint pain as and when required, which is most days, apparently. Again, it's an oral solution, and her maximum dose is 8 ml per day: 4 ml in the morning and 4 ml in the evening, with meals. Her prescription is for two 100 ml bottles, and that should last you approximately a month.' Ann returned the fluoxetine and naproxen bottles to the bag, stood and crossed the room. 'I'll leave this with you. She's only just had her new prescription, so there's plenty in there.' She handed the bag to Heather and returned to the armchair, where she picked up her mug of black coffee and took a few sips.

Heather put down her own mug. She looked at Matthew. 'Do you think we should check on the kids?' she said.

'We?' said Matthew. 'Do you mean me?'

'That'd be nice. If you wouldn't mind.'

Matthew rose from the sofa and left the room.

Heather watched him go, then turned back to Ann, who sat comfortably in the armchair, still drinking her coffee. 'Is there anything we should know about Emma's family background?' Heather asked.

Ann placed her mug back on the table. 'She's been living with her uncle. Apparently, he'd been under surveillance for quite a while as part of a police investigation. This morning, they arrested him for dealing in stolen cars. Initial enquiries have revealed he's also in the habit of leaving Emma home alone at night while he's out "working" and that he has a history of violence. For all those reasons, it's been decided to place Emma into care. Her father died years ago, and I understand she's never known her mother. She left one morning shortly after Emma's birth and never returned.'

'Poor child. But her uncle sounds like a right piece of work,' said Heather.

Ann leant forward slightly. 'From what I've heard, he's a very difficult man to deal with. By all accounts, he reacted very badly this morning and swore at his social worker and the police when they told him she was being placed with a foster family for the foreseeable future.' Ann hesitated.

'Is there something else we should know?' said Heather.

Ann seemed slightly cagey. 'Well, I suppose I should warn you that Emma appears to have inherited a few family characteristics. Apparently, on occasion, she has quite a temper. But "oppositional behaviour" is also one of the common side effects of fluoxetine in children, and no doubt you'll have encountered all that before,' she added hurriedly.

'It gets better,' said Heather, under her breath.

'I'm sure it's nothing to worry about,' said Ann, sensing Heather's mood.

Matthew appeared at the lounge door. 'What's not to worry about?' he said. He walked over to the sofa.

'We were talking about Emma's uncle,' said Heather, sinking in her seat, as Matthew sat down right next to her. 'Apparently, he's a nasty piece of work.'

Ann smiled at Matthew. 'How are the children getting along?'

'They didn't even notice me when I looked in,' said Matthew. 'Totally engrossed and playing nicely.'

'So, Ann,' said Heather, 'I know it's early days, but do you think it's likely that Emma will have any contact with her uncle going forward?'

'As you say, very early days,' said Ann, 'but usually in cases like this, they allow contact – that's assuming he makes bail, of course. I'm not privy to the exact nature of his crimes. However, if visits do take place, they will almost certainly be supervised at the contact centre in Newport at first. In the circumstances, I would be responsible for taking her to any contact visits and bringing her home. You wouldn't have to get involved.'

'Well, that's a relief,' said Heather.

'Oh, and don't worry, Emma won't be returning to school for the last two days of term, given the situation,' said Ann, 'so, for the time being, you won't have to go anywhere near her home or her uncle. Hopefully, by the time she goes back in September, things will have calmed down.'

'And where exactly does Emma live and go to school?' said Matthew.

'Shalfleet,' said Ann.

'Shalfleet?' Matthew drew in a deep breath. 'That's at least a forty-five-minute journey at that time of the morning. You're talking an hour-and-a-half round trip, twice a day. It seems we were right to be concerned about the school run. Three hours is pretty extreme.'

Heather rested a hand on Matthew's arm. 'Well, there are two of us, Matthew,' she said. 'We can take it in turns if need be. And we have two cars, so it'll be no problem when we have to run James and Grace to their contact visits on Tuesday and Friday mornings. We'll manage. Emma's here now, so, for her sake, I suggest we make the best of it.'

Matthew said nothing.

'Well, I think that wraps it up?' said Ann, leaning forward in the armchair. She looked expectantly from Matthew to Heather. 'Is there anything I've forgotten to mention that you need to know?'

Heather thought for a moment and then shook her head. 'No, I don't think so.'

'In that case...' Ann got up and brushed down her skirt. 'I'll leave you in peace. You can contact me through Sarah if need be. I imagine she'll be round in the next day or so, now Emma's arrived. Likewise, if there's anything else to report from my end, I'll let Sarah know. Good luck and, again, thank you for taking Emma on. Without you, we'd have had to place her with an outside agency, which is something we prefer not to do.'

'Yes, because it costs you more,' muttered Matthew. Then, clearly, he said, 'I'll show you out.' He indicated Ann should go first and then followed her to the front door.

Ann retrieved her black trench coat from the coat hooks in the porch, put it on and then turned to shake Matthew's hand. 'I imagine I'll be seeing you again at some stage,' she said.

It was still raining, and Matthew watched her as she hurried down the drive to her car. After she got in and drove away, he turned and went back into the house. Heather sat slumped back on the sofa. He joined her in the lounge and closed the door behind him. 'Well, what do you make of that, then?' he said.

'Perhaps we've taken on a little more than we were expecting,' said Heather. 'But it's a bit late to worry about that now. We're paid to do a job, and that's to care for children like Emma, who need us. I'm sure she'll fit in and we'll cope.'

'So long as she's not a square peg in a round hole. That wouldn't be fair on her either,' said Matthew.

Heather got up. 'Right, I'll go and see if the kids want something to eat,' she said. 'What are you going to do?'

'I think I'll crank up the laptop,' said Matthew. 'I've been meaning to start looking for ideas for James's birthday. Can you believe he's one next month?'

'Mad, isn't it?' Heather picked up their empty mugs and walked over to the armchair to retrieve Ann's. 'Have a look at swings,' she said. 'We could put one in the garden for him. He'd love that.'

'Good idea,' said Matthew. He disappeared into the office and came out carrying their laptop. 'On the bright side,' he said, 'Emma does seem to have taken an instant liking to James. Perhaps she will enjoy being part of a family.'

'We can but hope,' said Heather. She took one last look around the room. 'I'll leave you to it, then,' she said and headed off towards the kitchen, carrying the mugs.

As she approached the sink, she heard a commotion. 'Get off!' Emma was saying.

Heather put down the mugs and sidestepped into the playroom. James was playing happily, bashing a slice of plastic toast against the toaster. He was chuckling to himself. But in the corner, Grace, who had been scrawling with crayons on a piece of white paper, was clinging to the yellow plastic table, sitting rigid in her orange chair as Emma tried to remove her from it.

'My chair! My chair!' screamed Grace.

'No, I want to sit in the orange chair,' said Emma. 'You can sit in one of the other ones.' She yanked the chair backwards and Grace rolled out onto the floor, pulling the table over as she fell. She came up screaming, crying, flinging her arms wildly.

Heather hurried across the room. Leaving Grace to wind down of her own accord, she approached Emma. 'Emma, love,' she said. 'The orange chair is Grace's. Everyone has their own colour. The blue one is James's. You can have the green or the purple if you like.'

‘I want the orange one,’ said Emma, pulling the chair closer to her.

Heather crouched down and faced her. ‘The orange one is already taken,’ she said firmly over Grace’s continuing protestations. ‘It’s Grace’s. And you really shouldn’t be fighting over it. Now please, let her have it back and say sorry.’

Emma pushed the orange chair away from her, and it tipped onto its side. ‘There,’ she said. ‘She can have it.’

‘Okay, Emma. Thank you.’ Heather stood up. ‘Now, why don’t you go to your room and sort out a few more of your things? I’m about to make some dinner. I’ll call you when it’s ready.’

Emma stood, and without a word, she left the room. Heather heard her heavy footsteps on the stairs. She looked around the playroom. James was still chuckling happily to himself. Grace was lying face down on the floor, still crying, her fists pummelling the Play City Rug play mat.

‘Maybe you’re right, Matthew,’ said Heather, to no one in particular. ‘Perhaps Emma will enjoy being part of a family.’ She leant over and set the orange chair the right way up. ‘We can but hope.’

12

A Bitter Pill

Wednesday, 30th August 2017

Matthew returned home from a last-minute dash to B&Q that Wednesday evening to find Heather in the kitchen tending to the serving of a late supper. James and Grace were already safely tucked up in their cots upstairs. On his way back down the hall, he poked his head in through the lounge door and saw that Ann had already dropped Emma home from her first unsupervised contact visit with her uncle. She was lounging on the sofa, staring intently at a computer tablet. Her fingers and thumbs were frantically tapping on the touchscreen.

'What have you got there?' Matthew asked.

'Uncle Nick's tablet.'

'Are you playing something?'

'A game,' said Emma, without raising her head.

'And what game are you playing?'

'Grand Theft Auto.'

'What do you have to do in that, then?'

All the while, Emma had not taken her eyes off the screen. 'Drive round, run people over, shoot them, stab them, rob banks... stuff like that.'

That was all Matthew needed to know. He strode over, took the tablet from her and switched it off.

'Who said you could play that game, Emma? It's way too old for you.'

'Uncle Nick downloaded it. I was playing it at his house.'

'Well, I don't want to see you playing it while you're here with us. You shouldn't be playing it at all. It's not suitable for someone of your age. Is that clear?'

Emma crossed her arms and huffed loudly. 'Uncle Nick's right,' she said. 'You're arseholes.' She got up, stormed out of the lounge, and stomped off up the stairs and into her bedroom.

Matthew stood open-mouthed, unable to respond, which he realised was unusual for him. He decided against following her upstairs and instigating an immediate row – no, he'd give her a chance to calm down and have a rational conversation with her later. Instead, he retreated into the kitchen, where Heather was preparing mugs of hot chocolate and plates of cheese and crackers. He told her about the incident. 'I guess we should note it in her daily log,' he said.

'We should,' said Heather, 'but can you imagine Sarah's reaction?'

'Let me worry about Ms Morton. The way I'm feeling, I think I might quite enjoy another confrontation with her. In fact, stick her in that "Grand Theft Auto" game and I'd take great pleasure in mowing her down in the street.'

'Don't you think we've got enough black marks in her book without you antagonising her? I'll take this up to Emma and have a quiet word. You take yours into the lounge.'

Matthew took his mug and plate from Heather. 'Christ,' he muttered. 'She's only been here six weeks...'

Monday, 4th September 2017

Sarah Morton sat slumped in a wood-framed, low-slung canvas deckchair on the lawn, perspiring in her navy two-piece suit. The midday temperature had reached a balmy twenty-two degrees, and much to Sarah's chagrin, Matthew had insisted that month's supervision meeting take place in the garden. 'It's such beautiful weather,' he said. 'You never know; it might be the last chance we get.' Sarah had looked wistfully at her armchair in the corner as they bypassed the lounge, and she was escorted outside. All three children had been instructed to play nicely in the playroom, although it had taken some gentle persuasion to get James out of his garden swing. He had become very attached to his birthday present.

Sarah looked up from reading Matthew and Heather's daily log for August with beads of sweat glistening on her forehead and a thinly veiled look of disgust on her face. 'How on earth can a child bring a tablet loaded with an adult game into your home and you not know about it?'

'Easily,' said Matthew. The ice cubes in his glass clinked as he lounged in the deckchair opposite her and idly stirred his Dr Pepper with a straw. 'For a start, we're not in the habit of checking her bag every time she walks through the front door – it's not airport security – so we didn't know she'd brought anything home from her uncle's. Anyway, I wasn't here when she got back, and Heather was preparing something to eat and drink in the kitchen. We can't monitor her twenty-four hours a day.'

'May I remind you that this is a foster child we are dealing with here.' Sarah shifted uncomfortably, and the deckchair creaked in protest.

Heather was sitting next to Matthew. She had been contemplating the dead-heading of the rose bushes in the flowerbed under the kitchen window, which had once been the pond. She sighed. 'Oh, come on, Sarah. Don't you think you're being a little unreasonable? With all due respect, can't you see that your confrontational attitude is self-defeating? Emma having access to adult games is cause for concern, and we've recorded it in the daily log. You should be encouraging honesty and transparency, but all you do is use it as a stick to beat us with. We know these are foster children, but every parent has to deal with these issues. If we don't feel we can discuss them with you without you getting on our backs, then, well...'

'Mrs Blundell...' There was a faint sign of a grimace on Sarah Morton's flushed face. 'Heather...' She brushed at a bead of sweat and attempted a smile, but the gesture was so thinly disguised you could see straight through it like a glaze of ice masking the murky waters below. 'If I come across as a little too... passionate, then I am...' she swallowed. The word "sorry" never made it past her lips. 'What I mean to say is I shall attempt to be more grounded in my approach in future.'

'Well, that's the first time you've called me Heather, so that's a start. Thank you.' Heather smiled.

Sarah Morton gripped the arms of her deckchair and adjusted her position. 'I suppose what I am saying is that I would appreciate it if you could increase your level of vigilance in matters concerning the children.'

'You mean like a nanny state?' said Matthew.

'Mr Blun...' Sarah Morton forced another smile. 'Matthew. You are making this very difficult for me.'

'My apologies, Sarah. I suppose what I am saying is that, in principle, I feel these children deserve a degree of respect and privacy, without us unduly interfering every time they so much as blink. Surely that undermines their self-esteem? It's a form of abuse – an abuse of their right as a human being to a little dignity. Of course, we will keep our eyes on them and guide them, but I do not see my role as being that of a dictator. Nor can I police the actions of her uncle. What are your thoughts on that?'

'Well, Matthew, since you ask, my thoughts are these...' Sarah struggled to sit forward, but gave up and continued, reclined at sixty degrees. '... nowadays, we are under a microscope and we have to be seen to be faultless in our approach to managing these children. If there is any hint whatsoever of negligence, then we, as a collective, will get it in the neck and stand to lose our jobs. It's all very well for parents bringing up their own children; ordinarily, they have no one to answer to. We, however, are being scrutinised...'

'... as someone with a microscope studies creatures that swarm and multiply in a drop of water,' said Matthew. Two blank faces looked at him. The cackling cry of a seagull broke the silence as it carried across town from the beach. 'War of the Worlds?' he said. 'Richard Burton...? Never mind. Forget it. You're right, Sarah – we're just cogs in a machine, being programmed what to think, what to say, what to do – it's dehumanising us. But that doesn't excuse the likes of you and me for dehumanising those in our care. I was a foster kid. I suffered physical and mental abuse because the system neglected me. These days it's gone to the other extreme – this micromanagement of kids is a modern-day form of abuse.'

'Have you finished, Matthew?'

'Yes, darling.'

'Well, welcome to the machine, Mr...' Sarah Morton looked up at the sky and took a deep breath, '... Matthew. Like it or not, we are part of it, and if we are seen to be a faulty part, we will be replaced. I am not suggesting that you run this house as a dictatorship and control your subjects; merely exercise a little more diligence in observing them.'

'I think we can agree to do that, Sarah,' said Heather.

'Excellent. Hopefully, you will also agree when I suggest it might be the right time for you to attend the Online Safety course.'

Heather smiled graciously. 'Of course.'

'And, obviously, I shall have to write up this conversation in my supervision notes – it's another blot on your copybook, I'm afraid.'

Matthew scoffed. 'Have you any idea how ridiculous you sound?'

'Matthew – that's enough!' Heather cuffed him on the arm.

'No, I'm sorry,' said Matthew, 'I'm not having that. To expect that level of "diligence" is totally ridiculous. Blame Emma's uncle. As soon as I saw what she was doing, I took the tablet off her. You, Sarah Morton, are blowing this out of all proportion. Why? You enjoy making our life difficult – is that it?'

'I'm just doing my job, Mr Blundell. How many strikes do you want before you're out?'

Heather thrust out an arm, palm out-facing. 'Stop! Please! Can we move on? Sarah, we're thinking it would be nice to take the kids on a week's holiday. It's a bit of a snap decision, but we'd like to go around the end of September. I don't know what your thoughts are, but we feel it might be a bit too much for Emma, given her condition.'

'What kind of holiday are we talking about?' said Sarah. She fumbled for a handkerchief in her pocket and dabbed her forehead.

'Well, we usually like to stay active,' said Heather. 'We take the kids to all the local attractions, go on short walks – that kind of thing. Emma's doctor advised her against strenuous activity, and she can't walk far.'

'Well, James and Grace are hardly old enough to engage in any sustained strenuous activity, are they, Mrs Blundell?'

'Well, there you go again, being argumentative, Ms Morton,' said Matthew. 'James and Grace can go in the buggy – unfortunately, I don't think sitting in a buggy would do much for a ten-year-old's street cred, do you?'

'What I am trying to say, Mr Blundell, is can't you find a holiday that caters for everyone's needs?'

'You mean sit on a beach?'

'Well, something like that, yes.'

'It's not particularly stimulating for James and Grace to spend a week on a beach, though, is it, Ms Morton? They may be limited in what they can do, but they need to be constantly entertained. We don't feel that Emma is capable of any meaningful level of activity. And then, of course, we have to be mindful of post-exertional mayonnaise.'

Heather glared at him. 'He means post-exertional malaise, Sarah. PEM. If Emma overdoes it, then it can significantly exacerbate her symptoms.'

Matthew jumped back in. 'For Christ's sake, even that poor excuse for an uncle of hers is constantly bellyaching that we do too much with her; that every time he sees her, she's worn out and half asleep.'

'Isn't that what her medication's for – to help her lead a more normal life?'

'No,' said Heather. 'There is no cure for fatigue. She has to rest every half an hour or so, and even at school, she doesn't get involved in any aspect of physical education. And the naproxen only reduces her muscle and joint pain. All that does is help her move around and enable her to stay active to a degree. The last month has been particularly bad – she's had to take it every day, and I've had to pick up her new prescription early.' Heather turned to Matthew. 'Which reminds me, we need to throw away the old bottle of fluoxetine. It's still in the kitchen cupboard. There's some left, but don't worry, I picked up the new prescription this morning and we'll start using that.'

Matthew nodded. 'Okay.'

'So be it,' said Sarah. 'We'll put Emma in respite for the week. She can stay with the Floyds if they agree to it. Now, if you'll excuse me, I need to visit the ladies' room.'

'Of course,' said Matthew. 'You know where it is.'

Sarah gripped the frame of the deckchair and fought to extricate herself. After two failed attempts, Matthew smiled. 'Can I offer you a hand, Ms Morton? Awkward buggers to get out of, these things.'

'I'm fine, thank you, Mr Blundell...' Sarah strained and with one last monumental effort, heaved herself out of the deckchair and hobbled stiffly across the lawn towards the double doors that led into the playroom. She entered and disappeared into the kitchen, from where a door led to the utility room and a shower room with a toilet. She was gone quite a while before Matthew and Heather finally heard the toilet flush and the faint sound of the utility room door closing. They waited expectantly for what seemed an age.

'Are you alright in there?' called Matthew.

'Just fine, thank you, Mr Blundell.'

Heather looked at Matthew. 'What's she doing?' she mouthed.

Matthew shrugged. He got up as if to go and investigate, but at that moment, Sarah Morton came out through the doors into the garden.

'Sorry, just emptying some sweet wrappers and tissues from my pockets,' she said. 'I popped them in your bin. The children seem to be playing nicely in the playroom. Now, any last questions before I go?'

'Yes, there is something,' said Heather, leaning forward. 'If we can just take a few minutes more of your time...'

Sarah eyed the deckchair warily, as if she were contemplating a bear trap, and somewhat reluctantly lowered herself into the sagging canvas seat.

'I've been meaning to ask you,' continued Heather. 'We haven't had feedback from any of Emma's contact visits with her uncle. Obviously, after his release on bail, she had the four supervised visits at the Newport contact centre in August, and last week was her first unsupervised visit at home. Has Ann said anything to you? All we get from Emma is a grunt or "fine" when we ask her how they went.'

Sarah considered the question. 'Well, I suppose you'd describe the supervised visits as "eventful",' she said. 'We all know her uncle's feelings about the fact that Emma has been taken into care – his attitude is hostile, to say the least. I understand that on his first visit to the contact centre, he swore at the contact supervisor. He objected to being watched the whole time. I believe he said something along the lines that he felt like a fucking paedophile with all their beady eyes on him – his words, not mine.'

'So, who on earth decided that he was fit to have Emma unsupervised at home?' said Matthew.

'Well, despite his rather objectionable attitude,' said Sarah, 'they assessed his behaviour with Emma and deemed him no direct threat to her. The conclusion was that he can be relied upon to look after her for the few hours she'll be with him every Wednesday and that, for the time being, the need to see his niece appears to be taking priority over whatever dubious activity he's engaged in.'

'I suppose I should have been more specific,' said Heather. 'What I'm interested in is how Emma is finding the visits.'

Sarah brightened. 'Oh, Ann tells me she enjoys seeing her uncle. He's her actual family, after all,' she said, with a hint of relish. 'I believe she's always had a good relationship with him. I'm told he was never abusive towards her – it's just the thieving, the neglect and his tendency to put people in hospital that's caused the issues.' She looked pointedly at Matthew. 'So, you be careful, Mr Blundell. I'd hate to see you get into trouble...' She smiled. 'Otherwise, apparently, he's treated her well. Her clothes are all designer labels – I suppose in his line of work, he's not short of a bob or two. Which reminds me...' Sarah's smile returned. 'Twice, Ann says he's complained about the clothes Emma's been wearing. He says you're dressing her in cheap shit – again, his words.'

'At least we paid for what we bought her with hard-earned money from an honest day's work,' said Matthew. 'Who does the cheeky fuck think he is? Someone needs to have a word with him. He's a bad influence on her.'

'Well, unless that someone's going to be you, Mr Blundell, I suggest you'll just have to grin and bear it.'

'So, I take it these unsupervised visits are going to continue?' said Heather. 'What happens after Emma goes back to school tomorrow?'

'Ah, yes. Ann asked me to mention that. The intention is that Emma's uncle will pick Emma up after school on Wednesdays and take her home. Ann will continue to collect her from there at six o'clock and have her back here with you by seven, at the latest.'

'Well, that's a relief,' said Heather, looking at Matthew. 'I'm glad we don't have to go over there.'

Sarah laughed. 'Quite right. We need to protect your anonymity. We don't want him following you home and finding out where you live, do we? Although, I suppose there's nothing to stop him following you home from school one morning after you've dropped Emma off, or pressuring Emma into giving him your address...' She let the thought hang, then slapped her knees. 'Okay, so I think we're done here.' With steely determination, she hauled herself out of the deckchair. 'Now,' she said with an air of triumph, as she straightened her skirt, 'regarding the week's respite for Emma, I'll speak to the Floyds, see if they will oblige and ask what weeks they're available. I'll let you know.' She grabbed her navy briefcase and looked down at them. 'In the meantime, you sit there and enjoy the last of the summer sunshine. I'll see myself out.'

Sarah came back to them after a few days and said that the Floyds were happy to have Emma for the week commencing Saturday, the 23rd of September. Heather had to break the news to Emma and sat her down in the lounge one evening after school.

'At the end of the month, Matthew and I are going to take James and Grace on a short break away,' she said. She paused. Emma was not making eye contact. She had her head down and was picking at her fingernails. 'We spoke with Sarah and Ann, and they agree with us that some of the things we'll be doing will be too much for you. What do you think about staying with some other very nice foster carers, Mr and Mrs Floyd – just for a week?'

'I don't want to. I want to come on holiday with you,' said Emma. She carried on picking.

'But you know you can't, darling. We'll be very active, and you need to take it easy.'

'If I came with you, I wouldn't have to go to school.' Emma looked up at Heather. 'Where are you going?'

'We're going to Poole in Dorset. It's not too different from here, really, but we'll be on the move the whole time. You'd get tired, and you know how badly that can affect you. And yes, you have to go to school – James and Grace don't.'

'I don't want to go to the Floyds.'

'I'm sure the Floyds are very nice.' Heather tried to sound reassuring. 'They'll look after you and do some fun things with you. I'm sure they like board games. Why don't you take your Junior Scrabble with you? You like that, and it helps with your spelling.'

'It's not fair,' Emma huffed and turned away. 'James and Grace have all the fun.'

'Don't worry,' said Heather, her tone soothing. 'We'll make sure you have fun too – you'll be fine. You'll have all your favourite things with you, and I'll give them all your medication and explain what you need to take and when.'

'I don't want to go!' Emma covered her eyes, and Heather thought perhaps she was crying.

'Well, I'm afraid, young lady, that you don't have any choice in the matter. I'm sorry.'

'Yeah, you will be sorry.' Emma took her hands away from her face and glared at Heather. Her eyes were red, and she was welling up. 'You wait till I tell Uncle Nick...'

13

A Slippery Slope – Part One

Saturday, 30th September 2017

Matthew and Heather left their self-catering accommodation in Poole just after ten o'clock on Saturday morning and drove to Lymington in time to catch the midday Wightlink ferry to Yarmouth, where they had lunch. On their way home, they picked up Emma from the Floyds, who lived in Apse Heath.

It was now Saturday evening. All the children were in bed, and Matthew and Heather were relaxing in the lounge after a particularly tiring day. Heather had drawn the curtains across the bay window. She had made them in a turquoise fabric that matched their sofa. The only light came from the television in the corner, to the right of the window, which emitted ever-changing hues. Matthew was watching 'Strictly' while drinking a Guinness and helping himself to handfuls of Twiglets from a bowl on the small table in front of him. Heather was reading the Floyds' daily logs. Brian Conley was trying desperately not to step on Amy Dowden's toes.

'You see that?' said Matthew. 'I could do a bloody cha-cha better than that. Stick to comedy, Brian...'

'Matthew, look at this.' Heather shifted across the sofa towards him, her finger pointing at the page she held in her hand. 'The Floyds are suggesting that the fluoxetine we gave them for Emma was an old bottle. They say there wasn't enough in it to last them the week. They had to arrange an emergency prescription.'

'That's bullshit!' Matthew snatched the page from her and read it. 'They're saying the issue date on the bottle we gave them was the 9th of August? There's no way that's true. We gave them the one we were using, which was the one you collected in early September. There was over a week's worth left in it.'

'Well, it must be true; otherwise, why would the Floyds flag it?'

'It can't be – you threw the old bottle away after you collected the new one.'

'Did I? I don't remember doing it. I thought you'd thrown it away.'

Matthew frowned. 'I'm pretty sure I didn't.'

'Well, surely one of us did? I don't believe this... What if we left it in the kitchen cupboard and packed it by mistake?'

'Well, that cupboard is always so rammed, we wouldn't necessarily notice if there were two in there.'

Heather thought for a moment. 'You packed Emma's medicine. Did you check the bottle before you put it in the bag?'

'Why would I? As far as I was concerned, it was the new one we'd been using for the past three weeks.'

'So, it could have been the old one, then?'

'Well, if we gave the Floyds an old bottle, where's the current one we were using? It should still be in the cupboard if neither of us threw anything away.'

'I'll go and look.' Heather left the room. She returned just as Gemma Atkinson and Aljaž Škorjanec were waltzing around the Strictly ballroom floor to Josh Groban's 'Un Giorno Per Noi (A Time for Us)'.

'There's only one bottle in the cupboard, and the issue date is the 25th of September. It's obviously the one the pharmacy issued to the Floyds while Emma was there.'

'So, I say again: where's the bottle that you picked up in September?'

'I don't know.' Heather sat down again and buried her head in her hands. She groaned. 'What the hell is happening? We can't seem to do anything right. Sarah's going to have a field day.'

'Well, hang on. Where's this old bottle we supposedly gave the Floyds, anyway? I want to see it before I'm convinced.'

'Well, Sarah's due here on Monday. I can't believe she won't have heard about this. Maybe she'll bring it with her.'

'Maybe. Or maybe if we're lucky, the Floyds said nothing, put a note in their daily log, which no one but us will ever read, and all this will just go away.'

'You think so?'

Matthew reached for the Twiglets. 'Like hell.'

Monday, 2nd October 2017

'Before I go, I need to speak to you both about a delicate matter...' Sarah seemed to be attempting to mask the delight on her face. 'I've already reviewed a copy of the logs from Emma's stay with the Floyds, and they've highlighted the fact that the bottle of fluoxetine you gave them was almost empty.'

'I find that very hard to believe,' said Heather. 'I collected a new bottle from the pharmacy on the 4th of September, and we would have thrown the old bottle away.'

'Well, it appears you didn't,' said Sarah. 'It appears you gave it to the Floyds, who did what you obviously didn't do and checked the contents.'

'I think before we go any further, Ms Morton,' said Matthew, 'I'd like to see the offending bottle. Do you have it?'

Sarah smiled. 'I'm afraid that due to the seriousness of this matter, I've escalated it. I've handed over the bottle to my manager, Mr Chilwell.'

'Well, I'm not sure you should have done that without speaking with us first,' said Matthew. 'And what other crap have you been feeding him? Have you escalated all our other so-called "failings"?'

'No. Though I can if you wish?'

'I want to see that bottle, Ms Morton, so I suggest you ask Mr Chilwell for it back.'

'Take my word for it. I've seen the label myself. The issue date on the fluoxetine you gave the Floyds was the 9th of August. It had virtually nothing in it. You obviously didn't throw the old bottle away.'

'Well, as Matthews says, we'd like to see the bottle, in case there's been some mistake,' said Heather.

'There's been no mistake, I assure you. Don't think you're going to wriggle out of this one.' Sarah paused. 'However, I shall see if Mr Chilwell still has it in his possession.'

'Why wouldn't he still have it in his possession?' said Matthew. 'Who else would have it?'

'As I said, I'll speak to Mr Chilwell.'

'Well, I suggest you do,' said Matthew, 'because if you can't show us that bottle, then as far as I'm concerned, it's our word against the Floyds' and you have no evidence – and I, for one, am certainly not going to take your word for it, Ms Moron – I mean Morton. Show me the bottle, and then we'll talk about it.'

'As you wish, Mr Blundell. Now, I must go. Chris isn't feeling well – "man flu". I need to check in on him before I head off to my next appointment.'

Sarah made her usual abrupt exit and left Matthew and Heather sitting on the sofa watching James and Grace watching Peppa Pig on Nick Jr. They had been sitting quietly on the floor, transfixed, throughout the meeting. Matthew flopped back into a cushion and covered his face with his hands. He groaned and massaged his eyes. 'I swear, that woman will be the death of me.' He thought for a moment. 'And who's Chris when he's at home?'

'Didn't she tell us she'd remarried?' said Heather.

'Maybe. I can't remember. Frankly, I'm amazed anyone made it as far as the altar with her.'

'Well, they say there's someone for everyone.'

'One – maybe. But Sarah Morton? Two's stretching it.'

Thursday, 5th October 2017

It was seven-thirty in the evening. James and Grace were in bed, and Emma had bathed and was in her pyjamas reading in the lounge with Heather. Because of her illness, Emma had missed a lot of school and had already been held back a year, so Heather spent as much time as she could with her, helping her with extra studies.

'I've printed off your favourite photos from the holiday,' called Matthew from the office.

'Oh, you are a sweetheart – when you want to be,' said Heather.

'Well, I know how old-fashioned you are. Why don't you get your album and we can put them in.'

Heather got up from the sofa and joined him in the office. It was the width of the lounge, but like a narrow corridor. To the right, at the far end, was Heather's sewing table with a chair in front of a window that looked out over the front garden. As well as the curtains and cushions Heather had made for the lounge, she also made dresses for the kids and quilts and throws, among other things. To the left, against the wall, was a desk in front of another window, which looked out onto next door's fence. On the desk was a laptop, in front of which Matthew sat. Built into the far wall, beyond the desk, were light oak shelves holding books and folders containing daily logs, the children's medical records, etc. They did not allow the children in the room and always kept the door shut, but unlocked.

Heather walked over to the shelves, reached up and brought down a red faux-leather photo album. 'I think it's nice to have something you can physically look through,' she said. 'It's not the same looking at them on a computer screen.'

Emma appeared in the doorway. 'Can I see the photos?'

'Of course, you can,' said Heather. 'Let's go and sit in the lounge.' Heather took the photo album, returned to the lounge and sat on the sofa. She patted the seat next to her. 'Here, come and sit with me while I put them in the album.'

Matthew followed them in and sat on the arm of the sofa, next to Heather. He handed her a small set of photographs. 'They've come out well,' he said. 'I'm pleased with that new photo printer.'

'Is that the one you got from Argos with our Nectar points?'

'No, that was a scanner. I got the printer from that camera shop in Newport.'

'Oh, right...' Heather looked at the first photograph. 'Yes, they have come out well. Here, Emma, look at this one. It's James and Grace paddling in the sea on Sandbanks beach. The weather wasn't great that day – very overcast – but we decided to go anyway. It was funny; it turned so dark at one point, I thought we were having an eclipse. Fortunately, it didn't rain, though.' Heather handed Emma the photograph. 'And this one is James on a donkey. Doesn't he look sweet?' Heather laughed and passed the photo over.

Matthew was looking at Emma. She was tight-lipped, and her face was flushed. She was not really concentrating on the pictures in her hand. Then she erupted.

'Why didn't I get to go on that beach? I wanted to have a donkey ride and go paddling!'

She lurched forward and stood up. Holding the photographs out in front of her, she ripped them in half, tossed them to one side and stormed out of the room.

'I wanted to come on that holiday. It's not fair. I hate you both!' she shouted. They heard her stomping hard on every step on her way up the stairs. Her bedroom door slammed.

'Oh, for Christ's sake, she'll wake James and Grace,' said Matthew. He got off the arm of the sofa and walked over to the lounge door. He stuck his head out and listened.

'I imagine she'll go to bed and sulk if I know that young lady,' said Heather. 'I know she was upset that she couldn't come with us, but I didn't realise it had affected her that much.'

'Well, we both know she wouldn't have kept up with the pace,' said Matthew. Hearing nothing from upstairs, he returned to the sofa and sat down next to Heather. He reached for the remote and flicked on the TV. 'She'll get over it.'

Friday, 13th October 2017

Emma had been quiet and withdrawn, and Heather kept a wary eye on her. Emma seemed to resent the extra attention.

It was approaching one o'clock. Heather had returned from picking up Grace from her contact visit with her grandad and was now in the kitchen preparing lunch. She stood at the sink washing a few cherry tomatoes. Outside the window, it had started to rain. Emma was in the playroom with James, having complained that morning that she wasn't feeling well. Heather had erred on the side of caution and kept her at home, even though Emma was already well behind on her schoolwork. About ten minutes earlier, she had removed Grace from the playroom after Grace bit Emma's arm when Emma reached for a book Grace was ripping pages from. Emma pushed Grace, who then raised merry hell. Matthew had her in the lounge and was still trying every trick in the book to placate her.

Heather paused at the sink. 'It's very quiet in there. What are you two up to?'

Silence.

Heather dried her hands and proceeded into the playroom. Emma was sitting quietly with her doll on her lap. James was sitting in front of an electronic keyboard. When he saw Heather come into the room, he started banging it over and over. There was no sound other than the thumping of James's hands and the clacking of plastic keys.

'Is that switched on, James? Let me have a look.' Heather bent down and saw the switch was in the 'ON' position. 'Hmm, looks like you've worn the batteries out in that one, my little piano man.'

Heather rummaged through the top drawer of the dresser, where she kept a small screwdriver. It wasn't there.

'Emma, have you seen the screwdriver we keep in this drawer?'

'Yes, I've got it. I've just used it to change Annabel's batteries.' Annabel was a talking doll.

'Thank you, darling.' Heather walked over to her, and Emma handed over the screwdriver.

Heather unscrewed and removed the lid of the battery compartment on James's keyboard, only to find there were no batteries inside.

'No wonder it wasn't working, James. Why don't you play your drum kit while I sort this out?' Heather reached over and switched on the electronic drum kit. 'Strange... Shouldn't that little red light come on?' Heather removed the back panel to find an empty battery chamber. She picked up Grace's powered activity ball and removed the panel. No batteries.

'Emma. Can you do me a favour and tell Matthew lunch will be ready in ten minutes?'

Emma left the room. Quickly, before she returned, Heather searched the area where she had been sitting. She lifted the curtain. She picked up a child's pink pencil case. It was bulging and heavy. She tugged at the zip and discovered what she already knew. The case was full of batteries. Heather turned as Emma came back into the room.

'Matthew said okay.'

'Thank you, Emma,' said Heather. 'Now, what are all these doing in here?'

'None of them worked, so I took them all out.'

'Okay, well you won't mind if I check them, just to be sure.'

Heather fetched the battery tester from the top drawer, tipped the contents of the pencil case out onto the top of the dresser and, one by one, inserted the batteries. The meter showed green, 'VERY GOOD', for each one.

She turned. 'Well, young lady, they look fine to...'

Emma had already left the room.

Tuesday, 24th October 2017

Matthew had taken James with him for what was supposed to be a quick visit to Morrisons in Lake, the small village three miles down the road from Alverstone. He'd promised to have him back in time for his bath at six o'clock. It was now quarter past six. Heather had given up waiting and put Grace in the bath first. Matthew wasn't the only one to let her down that afternoon – she'd been expecting a call from James's consultant at four. At his last routine appointment the previous week, James had been given a PET-MRI scan to check on his brain development. Given that he wasn't due to be seen again for another three months, Heather had called the hospital that morning to ask about the results. The consultant hadn't called.

Heather had washed the muck of the day off Grace, who was now playing with her squeezy plastic toys. She held one under the water. She squeezed it and waited while it retook its form, sucking in bathwater through a hole the size of a pinprick. Then, she held it up and squeezed it again to squirt water everywhere. Heather sat on the bath mat, next to the bath, and watched her, wishing her enjoyment of life could be so simple.

The phone rang.

Heather was momentarily caught off guard. She thought of leaving it. She didn't have the cordless phone with her, which was in its cradle in the bedroom. Whoever it was could call back. Then it occurred to her it might be the hospital calling late. She looked at Grace sitting in the bath, playing contentedly.

'Emma, can you come and watch Grace?' she shouted. 'I must get that.' Heather gripped the side of the bath and pulled herself up.

Emma appeared at the door, having been in her bedroom next to the bathroom.

'Just keep an eye on her, please. She's playing quite happily.' Heather hurried out to answer the phone before whoever it was rang off.

Emma looked down at Grace, who was now splashing the water and making waves. 'Let's wash your hair...'

Grace, who quite liked having her hair washed, was compliant as Emma took the water jug down from the shelf, tipped Grace's head back and poured water through her hair. She repeated the process and reached for the shampoo.

'Okay,' she said, squirting a palmful of the glutinous green shampoo into her hand, 'hold still. We don't want this to get in your eyes, do we...?'

Grace slapped her hands on the surface of the water, creating more waves. 'Splish, splash, splish, splash,' she said.

'Are you pretending you're at the seaside?' said Emma, massaging the shampoo into Grace's hair. 'You like the seaside, don't you... I saw the photographs of you and James. I saw you laughing and having fun.' The handful of shampoo was building up quite a lather, and the excess was seeping onto Grace's neck and face.

Grace cooed happily and tried to flap her feet.

'Is Gracie trying to swim?'

Grace looked up at Emma, smiling.

Emma's hand slipped down over Grace's face, and she massaged soap into her eyes.

Predictably, Grace screamed.

'Oh, no, look what's happened...' Emma wiped Grace's face, making matters worse.

Grace was bawling now.

'I know,' said Emma, 'does Gracie want a swim-swim?' She tipped Grace backwards into the water and rolled her over so she was face down. Grace kicked and splashed. 'That's it. Have a swim and get all that nasty shampoo out of your eyes.'

'Emma! What are you doing? Get her up!'

Heather rushed into the bathroom, snatched Grace from Emma's grasp and lifted her from the tub. Water streamed onto the floor tiles. Heather reached for a towel and began dabbing Grace's eyes and face. Then she wrapped her in the towel and held her tight.

'Emma, what on earth do you think you were doing? You could have drowned her!'

'I was just helping,' said Emma. 'She got a bit of shampoo in her eyes, that's all.'

'That's all? You had her face down in the water. She couldn't breathe!'

'It's no different to if she was swimming.'

'Toddlers don't swim in baths, Emma. Now go to your room; I'll deal with you later.'

Emma glared at Heather.

'Now, Emma!'

Emma left the room. Heather heard Matthew coming up the stairs. He had arrived home in time to hear the commotion.

'I just caught Emma holding Grace's head under the water,' said Heather, as he appeared at the bathroom door, holding James.

'No, surely not,' he said. 'You're overreacting.'

'I tell you – I asked her to watch Grace for a minute so I could answer the phone and when I came back in here, she was holding Grace face down in the water.'

'Emma!' Matthew strode out of the bathroom, still carrying James, and into Emma's bedroom. 'Tell me what happened.'

Emma was crying. 'I was just trying to help. I was washing Grace's hair, and she got shampoo in her eyes. I was trying to wash it out, and she slipped.'

Matthew looked back at Heather, who had followed him in, still rocking and soothing Grace in her arms. 'It sounds reasonable to me.'

'We'll discuss this later, Matthew,' said Heather. 'For now, Emma, you'll stay in your room.'

Twenty minutes later, Heather was sitting on the sofa. Grace was curled up on her lap, quiet and sleepy. Matthew came in with James, having bathed him, and placed him on the floor to allow him a few minutes' play before bedtime. Then he sat in Sarah's armchair, opposite Heather.

'Are you sure Emma was deliberately holding Grace under the water?' said Matthew. 'She seems pretty upset by it all.'

'I'm telling you, that's what I saw. She wasn't trying to get Grace up out of the water; she was holding her there, and Grace was kicking and splashing.'

'But why? Why would she do it? We know she's got a temper – it runs in the family – but surely she wouldn't go that far?'

'She's not been the same since we got back off holiday – you've seen it for yourself. She's been moody, sulky and she's constantly antagonising James and Grace. Honestly – this afternoon, I caught her taking their toys away from them while they were playing, and hiding them around the house. She told me it was "just a game". It's getting too much.'

'Well, what do you want to do about it? I agree; she's not been herself, but to accuse her of deliberately holding Grace's head under the water...'

'I'll note it in the log.' Heather sighed. 'I know I'll get an earful from Sarah for leaving her with Emma in the first place, but I had to take that call.'

'I don't know why you didn't have the phone in the bathroom with you.'

'I didn't think. And to be honest, it had got so late that I really didn't think the consultant would ring.'

'Was it him? What did he say?'

'He said there's nothing we need to be concerned about at this stage.'

'Are you sure it's wise to put all this in the daily log?'

'We have to. If this behaviour continues and we can't deal with it, then something will have to be done about it.'

'Well, I'd choose your words very carefully this time...'

Wednesday, 25th October 2017

Matthew saw the headlights as Ann's blue Toyota Auris drew up outside, bringing Emma back from her uncle's. He got up from the sofa. As he crossed the lounge and reached the hallway, Heather was already halfway to the front door. He stood back and let her open it and then joined her in the porch. Through the window, they saw Ann getting out of the car, which was unusual unless there was something to report from Emma's evening visit with her uncle.

Heather groaned. 'I wonder what that junkie piece of trash has been moaning about this week. I still can't get over him bellyaching over what we put in her lunchbox.'

'Whatever he's said, we just ignore it – remember?' said Matthew. 'Don't let him get to you.'

Ann escorted Emma up the path. As she approached, Matthew saw her indicate to Heather that she would like to have a word, so he took Emma's coat, hung it in the porch and ushered her inside. Heather pulled the front door closed behind him and shut herself in the porch area to speak with Ann. After the usual pleasantries, Ann got to the point:

'I've been hearing Emma's version of an incident involving her and Grace while they were in the bathroom together.'

'Oh, yes... and what did Emma tell you?'

'Well, I asked her how things were going at home. I'm paraphrasing, of course, but she told me there'd been a misunderstanding yesterday while Grace was having a bath; that she'd seen that you had left Grace in the bath alone and had gone in to keep an eye on her. She says she tried to help by washing Grace's hair and that Grace was splashing around when she slipped backwards and her face went under the water. Emma was, in her words, rescuing Grace when you came in and started accusing her of trying to drown her. I have to say, Heather, that seems very harsh to me.'

'With all due respect, you weren't there, Ann. For a start, I didn't leave Grace alone in the bathroom – I asked Emma to come in and keep an eye on her for a moment. When I came back, Emma was holding Grace's head under the water.'

'I don't know,' said Ann, looking perplexed. 'Is it not also possible that when you returned to the bathroom, you heard all the commotion, panicked and were mistaken? It must all have happened so quickly.'

'I'm in no doubt what I saw, Ann.'

'Well, that's as may be, but you can imagine the effect that an accusation of that magnitude has on a sensitive child. Emma was really quite upset when she was telling me about it. She feels you are, and again I'm paraphrasing, victimising her. She feels you don't care about her and want to get rid of her.'

'And do you really believe that, Ann?'

'No, of course not. But I can see how Emma might feel that way. Regardless, I think lessons need to be learnt here, Heather. Emma should not have been alone with Grace in that situation. Given her age and background, she is not responsible enough to be in charge of a toddler in the bath. Children of that age can drown in a few inches of water – but you know that as much as anyone.'

'Yes, of course, but you have to understand it was an extremely important call regarding James's PET-MRI scan, and I had to take it. What worries me is that Emma has clearly been lying to you. I think that young lady has a very manipulative side you need to be aware of. I'm guessing she hasn't told you she lied to me when she removed all the batteries from James and Grace's toys the other week, claiming they were all dead? It wasn't just a childish prank, believe me. It was cold and calculated, and she didn't do it for laughs.'

'This all seems to stem from you not including her in your holiday plans,' said Ann.

'It does,' said Heather. 'She even ripped up some of the holiday photos we printed off after we got back. But you can understand why we didn't take her, can't you?'

'I can see it from both sides,' said Ann. 'Still, that's history now. Looking forward, I think we should see how the lead-up to Christmas goes and then review the situation in the new year. That's assuming, of course, you don't have any other issues with Emma in the meantime.'

'We're happy to go with whatever you think is best – after all, you are her social worker. But what happens if her disruptive behaviour continues?'

'Well, try to focus her mind on something positive. It sounds crazy, but December is only five weeks away. Maybe sow some festive seeds. You know, buy some Advent calendars, talk about all those presents... Perhaps, sometime soon, you could get her to start a list of what she would like for Christmas; it might distract her enough to forget the holiday.'

'Maybe you're right. Perhaps distraction is the answer.'

'Look, Heather, I want Emma to be happy here as much as you do. She's had a tough start in life, bless her, and she's bound to be unsettled and confused. I think we need to press the reset button and focus on giving her a stable and supportive home environment. It's been an unfortunate start, that's all.'

'Yes, well,' said Heather, ' "unfortunate" is putting it mildly. We've done the best we can juggling her very specific needs with the rest of the family. We can't always run our lives around her. I expressed my reservations at the start, if you recall.'

'You did. But I had no doubt then, and I have no doubt now, that with all your experience you can cope with the demands of such diversity.'

Heather just looked at Ann, not knowing what to say.

Ann smiled. 'It'll be fine, Heather. I'll leave you to discuss the matter with Sarah. Let's see what she says.'

Monday, 6th November 2017

'You did what?'

'I had to take that call, Sarah. I was only in the bedroom down the hall. I thought Emma was more than capable of minding a toddler for a few minutes.'

'Well, clearly, Mrs Blundell, you thought wrong. Clearly, a ten-year-old is not responsible enough to mind a child of twenty-one months – especially not when that child is in a bath!'

‘I appreciate that, Sarah, and I’m sorry. There were extenuating circumstances, and it won’t happen again. To be fair, I was within hearing range, and when I heard the commotion, I was there straight away.’

Sarah reflected briefly. ‘I suppose we all learn by our mistakes, Mrs Blundell...’ Her sideways glance at Matthew was barely perceptible. ‘Well, some of us do...’

Matthew almost took the bait. There was a hushed moment in the room while he composed himself and Heather sat in quiet reflection. ‘It’s extremely unlike you to be so forgiving, Ms Morton,’ he said. ‘Usually, you’re blowing things way out of proportion and throwing the book at us. Why the sudden change of heart?’

‘Because I agree with Ann, Mr Blundell. I think your wife misinterpreted what she saw and is making a big fuss about nothing.’

Given he’d had similar thoughts, Matthew kept quiet. Perhaps it was advisable to sound the retreat on this occasion. Perhaps if Sarah Morton felt this was all just a storm in a teacup and nothing more, they should accept it as a small mercy.

‘That’s not to say that her actions aren’t a further example of a regrettable lapse in judgement,’ Sarah continued, ‘which I shall be noting... But let’s move on, shall we, Mr Blundell?’

Heather reddened – a fusion of anger and embarrassment. She, too, resisted the urge to rise to the bait. ‘This behaviour started after we got back from holiday, Sarah,’ she said. ‘She’s jealous that James and Grace came with us and she didn’t. It’s been a downward spiral ever since she came back from the Floyds.’

‘I did warn you,’ said Sarah.

‘It’s concerning,’ said Heather. ‘Do you think if this behaviour continues, there’s a possibility she’ll have to be relocated?’

‘Relocated? It almost sounds as if you’re giving up on the child, Mrs Blundell. Let’s monitor the situation. When we next meet, we can review the matter. It’s a little early to be talking about relocation and besides, you don’t want to give the impression that you can’t cope, do you? I shall note your concerns.’

‘Moving on,’ said Matthew. ‘Have you got that medicine bottle back off Mr Chilwell?’

'I mentioned it to him last week, and it seems he's misplaced it,' said Sarah.

'Misplaced it?' said Matthew. 'Bollocks! It can't just have gone missing.'

'Well, it has, I'm afraid – and I suggest you don't use that language with me, Mr Blundell. It's been misplaced, and it can't be found. Mr Chilwell's looked everywhere.'

'Well, if you don't have the evidence anymore, that's it. It's your word against ours. You can't prove a thing – not that there was anything to prove. The bottle we gave the Floyds was the one we had been using and had enough in there to last over a week. End of story!'

'Not quite, Mr Blundell.'

'Oh, why's that?'

'I've arranged for you to go on the Safer Use of Medications course.'

14

Release

Monday, 20th November 2017

He sat alone in his cell. Waiting. A ten-by-six-foot space, sparsely furnished with a crude bed, a table and chair, a small wardrobe unit, a sink and a toilet. The letter in his hand had come exactly two weeks previously. Idly passing time, he read through it again. It contained the usual formal bullshit: "Following your recent parole hearing, the Board of Governors has decided, after careful consideration, that you be granted parole", blah, blah, blah... There were various "attendant conditions" applicable upon his release: "A probation officer will be appointed, to whom you must report once a week. Failure to do so will result in a recall to prison... You must inform your probation officer where you are living... All medical appointments must be attended... You must not travel outside the UK... Any criminal offence, regardless of its nature, will result in a recall to prison... Under no circumstances are you to contact any of the victims of your offences..." It concluded by informing him that his name would be added to the sex offenders register – indefinitely. The letter was signed by Eugene Clegg, Parole Officer, HMP Isle of Wight – Parkhurst Barracks.

Bollocks. He was no sex offender. He'd taken her back to his place after a night out drinking, and they'd spent the night shagging. In the cold, sober light of the morning after, she'd cried rape and attacked him. He'd defended himself.

The judge and jury believed *her*.

The court considered the harm caused to the victim and decreed it was a sustained incident involving abduction, prolonged detention and violence – multiple factors from a long list, but none "extreme" in nature, which classified him as 'Category 2'. They determined his culpability and concluded there had been a significant degree of planning, involving the use of alcohol, which classified him as 'Category A'. Category 2? Category A? Make your fucking mind up! Legal bullshit that made no sense at the time and still made no sense to him now; but they had used it together with other aggravating and mitigating factors to determine his sentence. Upshot was, he was branded a 'Category B' sex offender. Ten years, with earliest release after six.

He failed parole after the minimum six years and learnt from his mistakes. Now, two years later, he'd kept his nose clean and told them what they wanted to hear. His solicitor, the judge, the prison psychologist and the victim's liaison officer had all sat there and discussed his behaviour while in detention and his future plans. The outcome: eight years served, release on a two-year licence. Any misdemeanour: instant recall.

There were sounds from outside his cell. The moment he had been waiting for. He stuffed the letter into his pocket.

'Open cell four!'

The locking mechanism was deactivated.

'Step forward.'

'Free four! Free four!' The chant came from another prisoner somewhere down the line.

'Waters, you arsehole!' he yelled back as he stepped forward into the harsh light of the corridor.

His farewell journey was along the all too familiar corridors of Parkhurst. He glanced left and right at the cells, all with their blue doors, like rows of identical council houses. He had spent the last eight years of his life here. Eight years surrounded by all manner of sexual offenders: perverts, porn peddlers, rapists...

In the prison reception area, a prison officer handed him a plain bag with his few personal possessions. 'Check everything's there before you sign.'

'That's fine, Mr Barrett. I trust you.'

Barrett escorted him to the gate and rolled out his parting lines like a well-worn carpet. 'You're lucky they don't release prisoners on a Sunday,' he said.

'Why's that, Mr Barrett?'

'God rests on a Sunday – he'd have more time to keep an eye on you.'

'Very good, Mr Barrett.'

'You behave, son.'

'You know me, Mr Barrett...'

'Now get out of here and don't let me see you again!' Barrett closed the gate and left him standing there.

He stood for a moment on the threshold and breathed in a lungful of air. Then he stepped forward and into the free world once again.

15

A Slippery Slope – Part Two

Saturday, 25th November 2017

The bath incident had sent shock waves through the Blundell household. Emma was subjected to near-military-style discipline – she couldn't sniff without Heather casting an eye in her direction. Matthew spoke with Heather one evening after all the children were in bed.

'Don't you think it's time you eased off on Emma? It's been over a month since the bath incident with Grace, and she's been as good as gold. She's living in Arnold Layne, Alverstone, not Parkhurst.'

Heather took some convincing, but over the next few days, Matthew noticed her regime softened. So far as Matthew was concerned, the events of October were water under the bridge, and he was prepared to let bygones be bygones.

'Me and Grace are going to play hide and seek,' said Emma.

'It's Grace and I are going to play hide and seek,' said Matthew. 'I think you'll find Grace is a bit too young to understand that game.'

'If I go and hide, you can help Grace come and find me, then?'

'Okay,' said Matthew. 'But I can't be too long. I've got some important paperwork to do, and you've been on your feet since lunchtime, so you need to rest.'

'Okay.' Emma ran out of the lounge towards the rear of the house. 'Close your eyes!'

Matthew counted slowly from one, '... nine, ten. Coming, ready or not. Come on, Grace, let's go find Emma.'

Grace seemed to understand what was being asked of her as she held Matthew's hand and followed him to the kitchen.

'Where's Emma, Grace? Where's Emma? Can you see her?'

On their right, the door to the utility room giggled. Tiptoeing, Matthew led Grace towards it. He pointed at the door. 'Who's behind there, Grace?' he whispered. Grace reached out and pulled at the door. Emma screamed and laughed.

'Found you!' said Matthew.

Grace looked up at Emma, laughing, glee all over her face. '-gain, -gain,' she cried.

'Your turn, Grace,' said Emma. 'You go and hide.'

'Okay,' said Matthew, 'but no peeping.' He picked up Grace and hurried off with her as Emma started the count.

'... coming, ready or not!'

Emma, who had been counting behind the utility room door, scoured the kitchen – not that there was anywhere for Matthew and Grace to hide in there. She looked in the playroom, even though she was convinced they had gone out of the kitchen and into the hall, which was where she headed next. The dining room was on her left. The room was quiet. There was a large table with a cream PVC vinyl, wipe-clean tablecloth hanging low around it, surrounded by eight chairs. She pulled up the edge of the tablecloth and looked underneath the table. No one. At the far end of the room were two bookcases – one on either side of a window with beige curtains and with the same view of next door's fence as the office. There were beanbags in front of the bookshelves, where they sometimes sat and read quietly. Nowhere for anyone to hide there. Drawing a blank, she tried the lounge next door. No one. She opened the door to the office and entered, even though it was off-limits. No one. She opened the stair gate and ran up the stairs, having looked in the under-stairs cupboard first. She checked all four bedrooms, the bathroom and the airing cupboard, but there was no one in any of them. Frustration set in. She kicked out at the airing cupboard door, stormed down the stairs, through the stair gate and into the hall. 'I give up,' she screamed. 'I give up!' There was a moment's silence and then the front door opened. 'You cheats! You cheats!'

'How's that cheating?' said Matthew. 'We were hiding outside the front door, in the porch, weren't we, Grace?'

Emma stood seething.

'Right, I must get on,' said Matthew. He looked at Emma. She seemed to be calming down, perhaps a little embarrassed by her outburst. 'I've got some online forms that have to be filled in by tomorrow. Why don't you two go into the playroom and entertain yourselves there? Just take it easy for an hour or so. I'll be in the office if you need me. I don't know what time Heather will be back – she's out with her carer cronies for one of their get-togethers.' Matthew looked at his watch. 'She shouldn't be long.'

'Jammy, jammy,' said Grace.

Matthew smiled as he let go of her hand. 'James is with Heather. He'll be back soon, Grace. Now, off you go.' He watched as Emma took Grace's hand and led her off down the hall, into the kitchen and through to the playroom. He sighed and retreated gratefully into the sanctuary of his office. There, he eased himself into his chair and opened his laptop. All was quiet. That boded well; they were obviously settling down to play.

Five minutes later, it was too quiet.

Matthew eased himself out of his chair and headed towards the kitchen. He walked to the far end and poked his head around the playroom door. Emma was sitting on a beanbag.

'Where's Grace?' he said.

'She's hiding.'

'I told you; Grace doesn't know how to play hide and seek, and you're supposed to be relaxing. Where did she go?'

'I've taught her how to play.'

'Where did she go?'

'Into the kitchen.'

'Of course she went into the kitchen – she had to go into the kitchen to get out of here. Where did she go then?'

'How should I know? That's the whole point of hide and seek.'

'Don't give me your cheek, young lady. Now, come and help me look for her.'

Emma huffed, rolled off the beanbag and stood up.

'She's very quiet,' said Matthew. 'It's not like her to be that quiet.' He turned back into the kitchen. The utility room door was closed. He crossed the room, opened the door and entered. There wasn't really anywhere to hide, but there was a muffled sound and a slight movement caught his eye. It came from behind the door of the washing machine.

'Grace!'

Matthew rushed to release the catch, and the door swung open. He eased Grace carefully from the drum. She had barely been able to move. He turned sharply, holding Grace close to him. 'How the hell did she get in there?'

Emma stood staring and said nothing, seemingly in shock.

'I said, how did she get in there?'

'I don't know. She went to hide. I couldn't find her, so I gave up.'

'And how exactly would she be able to get in the washing machine on her own and close the door behind her?'

Emma just shook her head and looked at the floor.

'Emma, how could you...?' Matthew carried Grace out of the kitchen and into the lounge to check her over. He called over his shoulder. 'When Heather hears about this, she'll go spare. You'd better think of a bloody good explanation. Just be thankful that Grace is okay.'

'That's it. We can't leave her alone with James or Grace anymore; we can't trust her.'

Matthew sighed and stared at the TV screen. 'Strictly' was on mute. 'I can't believe we're having this conversation again. She's been good recently. I thought we'd turned a corner.'

'For Christ's sake, Matthew – how can you be so naïve? What on earth possessed you to leave those two alone together after everything that's happened?'

'I honestly thought that Emma was over all this holiday business.'

'I'm beginning to wonder if this doesn't go deeper than that. You say she flipped when she couldn't find you. I think she's got serious anger management issues, just like her uncle.'

'Well, she seemed to calm down quickly afterwards.'

'Seemed – exactly! That's probably exactly what she wanted you to think. I bet she was still fuming inside.'

'So, what – you think she was already plotting her revenge? Oh, come on, Heather.'

'Why not? She's already shown how manipulative she can be, and some of her recent behaviour is bordering on psychopathic. If we're starting to see signs of her uncle's tendency towards violence, then we've got a problem.'

'I don't know what to make of it,' said Matthew. 'The kid's only ten years old! But I don't see any other explanation. I mean, however unlikely, it is feasible that Grace went into the utility room, closed the door behind her and managed to squeeze into the washing machine – the drum's large enough. But surely, she wouldn't be able to close the door behind her, would she? That's got to be beyond her cognitive ability?'

'Which leaves only one other possibility: that Emma shut her in and left her there.'

'Agreed.'

'In which case, as I said, we can never leave James and Grace unsupervised while Emma is around.'

'But that's just not practical,' said Matthew. 'There's no way we can do that.'

'I'm going to log it,' said Heather, 'and we'll have the inevitable conversation with Sarah. Let her give us the benefit of her vast experience and wisdom.'

Monday, 4th December 2017

'My, my, Mrs Blundell, you seem to be getting unnecessarily worked up over this,' said Sarah with a wry smile. 'I have to say, I'm surprised. I would have thought with all your many years of experience, you'd be more than equipped to deal with a little unruliness – if indeed that's what it was – but it appears you're at your wits' end. If you can't deal with it, perhaps you'd like Ann and me to speak with her?'

'You know, it strikes me,' said Heather, her irritation showing, 'that we've had Emma over four months now and in all that time, Ann has only twice been here to have a one-to-one conversation with her – and that was only during the first month or so after Emma arrived. I know she speaks with her in the car on the way home from her uncle's, but surely she can't have a meaningful conversation while she's driving. Shouldn't she be doing more to support us by guiding and counselling her?'

'As you know, Mrs Blundell, Ann is involved in Emma's monthly therapy sessions. She takes the opportunity afterwards to discuss more formally any issues that need to be addressed. It gives Emma the opportunity to talk more openly.'

'Are you saying Emma doesn't feel able to speak freely to Ann here?' said Matthew.

'That was Ann's feeling, Mr Blundell,' said Sarah, 'and so now she arranges all her meetings with Emma in a neutral space. You know yourselves; Emma is a sensitive child and easily upset. Ann and I update each other regularly. I understand she's already spoken with you about this latest episode. What did she say?'

'It was Ann's opinion, having heard Emma's side of the story, that it was two children playing innocently,' said Matthew, 'and that there was no intention of any harm. Easy for her to say when she wasn't there.'

'I understand someone else wasn't there...'

Matthew took a measured breath. 'I'd been supervising them for some time, and they were playing nicely,' he said calmly. 'What have I said to you before about nanny states, Ms Morton? I can't be there breathing down their necks every second of the day. Now, I'm not necessarily saying that this was a malicious act on Emma's behalf, but I believe Emma was to blame for shutting Grace in the washing machine. Heather and I are both of the opinion that we can never leave Emma unsupervised with James or Grace again, which, in this household, creates a problem.'

'Again, Mr Blundell, this is pure speculation because you weren't there to witness it.'

Matthew sensed his blood pressure rising. 'I understand that, but the circumstantial evidence is compelling, wouldn't you agree? Yes, Grace could just about have climbed into that washing machine on her own, but she could not have shut the door behind her.'

'I sense you have a negative view of Emma. Is that true, Mr Blundell?'

'Well, this scenario hardly paints her in a glowing light, does it, Ms Morton? It's very hard to find anything positive to say in the circumstances.'

Heather stepped in. 'Okay, look, I can see we're getting nowhere here. Everything's been okay for the last week or so, and the countdown to Christmas has started. Maybe it's as Ann said a while back, that Christmas is the distraction Emma needs to put her bitterness behind her. We've already got them opening their Advent calendars every day.'

'And I see you've got the tree up nice and early,' said Sarah, indicating the large white Christmas tree that stood next to her in the bay window, with its ice-white snowflake lights. 'I usually go for a green tree myself, with a red, green and gold colour scheme – I'm not sure white, turquoise and pink is my thing.'

'You're not a fan, then?' said Matthew. 'Shame. Emma chose the colour scheme. She'll be most upset to hear you don't like her baubles.'

'Well, each to their own,' said Sarah. 'Now, back to the subject of Emma. Don't forget that this is her first Christmas away from her uncle, so that might affect her. Not that I want to add to your problems – just something to be aware of.'

'Yes, that's something we're painfully aware of,' said Heather. She grimaced. 'Anyway, we're all booked in to see Santa next week, and I know she's looking forward to that. I don't think she's ever been before, and she's been busy compiling a long list of presents.'

'There we go, then,' said Sarah, 'that'll keep her occupied. Now, I'll arrange a date for Ann and me to meet with Emma. I'm sure we'll be able to sort this out.'

'Well, let's hope so,' said Heather. 'I have grave concerns for James and Grace's safety, as you can well imagine.'

'And your concerns have been noted, Mrs Blundell. Never fear, I'll be sure to document everything we've discussed.'

'Well, just so long as you get your facts straight, Ms Morton,' said Matthew. 'You seem to be oblivious to the harm Emma could have caused.'

'Well, no harm was done, Mr Blundell – unlike previous occasions, where it was, and you chose to do nothing about it. And,' she continued firmly, 'again, I remind you that there is an element of doubt over Emma's ill intention or even if she was to blame. And in both recent cases, there was a degree of negligence...' She surveyed them, stony-faced, almost daring them to challenge her. 'You do realise that Emma tells her uncle about everything that goes on here – and I'm sure you don't need me to remind you of the strength of his feelings when it comes to your treatment of his niece. To quote him, minus the expletives, he feels it's likely the other children are provoking Emma and are just as much to blame for any disruption.'

'That man and his incessant moaning are the bane of my life,' said Heather. 'He's constantly seeking to undermine us. What does he know about bringing up kids? He drives me insane!'

'Mrs Blundell, clearly there has been some "rebellious" behaviour since you returned from your holiday, but nothing you shouldn't have been able to deal with. As you've been so keen to point out in the past, you do have many years of experience. The show must go on.'

'Well, once again, Ms Morton, your insight into the effective supervision of wayward children has been most inspiring and, motivated by your example, we shall strive to do better – won't we, my love?'

'Yes, Matthew.' Heather gave him an exasperated look. 'Sarah, there's something we want to raise with you. It's about James. Matthew and I have been discussing adopting him, but we're not sure of the process.'

'Really?' Sarah hesitated. 'Well, er, yes... I suppose James has been in your care for over a year, so there's nothing to stop you...' She looked down at the floor, paused, and then back up again. 'If all other options have been exhausted, and it's been decided that adoption is the way forward, James's permanence plan will have been finalised, outlining his long-term needs – I'd have to check with Janet on that. But adopting isn't the same as fostering, you know. You'd still need to undergo an assessment to be approved as prospective adopters, though it would be a fast-track assessment, given you're already approved foster carers. And

I warn you; you'd be assessed in competition with others who have already been approved and are looking to be matched with a suitable child. You wouldn't get any preferential treatment just because you care for him now; although if he's thrived here, that might go in your favour. Unfortunately, we've had our issues, haven't we...?'

'Matthew...' warned Heather, under her breath.

'How long does it take to be approved as prospective adopters?' said Matthew, biting back a retort.

'Well, there's no guarantee you would be approved, Mr Blundell, but fast-track assessments are usually completed in around four months. For some, it might only be a month or two. It all depends on the circumstances. With your track record, I dare say it might make some of the assessment decisions slightly easier... Ultimately, suitability and matching must go through an independent adoption panel and an Agency Decision Maker.'

'Do we lose all our allowances if we adopt?' said Matthew.

'Legally, James would be your responsibility, Mr Blundell; although we would conduct an adoption support needs assessment.'

'I see,' said Matthew. 'Something else to consider, then.'

'Well,' said Sarah, 'if you've quite finished, I have another appointment I need to get to.'

'Hang on,' said Matthew, as Sarah rose to leave. 'We haven't signed the supervision notes from the last meeting.'

'I'm afraid I haven't had a chance to type those up yet, Mr Blundell. Things are a little hectic back at the office. I'll get them to you as soon as possible.'

'Are you suggesting you can't cope with the demands of your role, Ms Morton? This is all highly irregular. What would your Mr Chilwell have to say if he found out?'

'Mr Chilwell is painfully aware of the current staff shortages, Mr Blundell.'

Matthew shook his head. 'A lot happened in October, and as you well know, we failed to agree on most of what we discussed at November's meeting. I want to see what you've put on record. I suggest you make our supervision notes a priority.'

‘Noted, Mr Blundell.’ Sarah leant down and picked up her briefcase.

Heather rose from the sofa. ‘I’ll show you out, Sarah.’

‘No need, Mrs Blundell; I know the way.’

16

Sliding Into Christmas

Christmas Day, Monday, 25th December 2017

Sarah and Ann had spoken with Emma the week after the supervision meeting. Matthew and Heather were not privy to everything that was said, but ultimately, it seemed to have had some effect in enhancing the growing sense of calm. Grace was Grace, of course, and so there had still been the odd disagreement and dispute to settle, but with Santa's help, the promise of Christmas worked its magic. Tony and Barbara had once again been invited to stay over the festive period. They arrived on Christmas Eve. The novelty of their presence on Christmas morning was an additional distraction for the three children, who seemed to be too caught up in the excitement of the festivities – the opening of presents and playing with their toys – to be concerned with antagonising one another.

The Christmas armistice lasted well into the afternoon. Christmas dinner was a memory and a faint lingering smell, as Heather and Barbara decided it was time to prepare the evening buffet and disappeared into the kitchen. They left Matthew dozing on the sofa in the lounge, sleeping off the effects of a double helping of dinner and far too much wine. Emma and Grace were playing with their presents separately and quietly on the floor, and Tony sat in the armchair with James on his lap. James was tugging at the stiff cardboard page of a farm animal book he had received from Santa that morning.

'What animal's this?' said Tony, pointing to a drawing on the page that James was pulling.

'-ig! -ig!'

'That's right,' said Tony. 'A pig. Now, push its head, James. Like this.' Tony took James's hand and helped him press a button on the pig's snout. 'Oink, oink,' said Tony loudly, repeating the sound from the book. James laughed and slapped the page. Tony laughed too and hugged him gently, mindful of the fact that James was still small and somewhat fragile. Then Tony tickled him under the arm, which sent James into a frenzy of cackling and screaming.

'What's all that noise?' said Matthew, groaning and sitting up.

'Oh, sorry – did we wake you?' said Tony. 'James and I were just having a bit of fun with this new book I bought him. I think it's safe to say it's gone down well.'

'You mean the book that Santa bought him...?'

'Ah, yes, Santa – sorry!'

Matthew groaned again. 'Christ, I think my bladder's about to burst,' he said, struggling to get up off the sofa. 'Back in a minute!'

He headed towards the kitchen and the toilet in the shower room. 'Coming through!' he said as he swerved past Heather, who was slicing cold turkey and putting it into sandwiches.

Barbara turned her head from the sink, where she was about to wash lettuce in a colander. 'Where are you off to in a hurry?' she said.

'Best you don't ask,' said Matthew and disappeared into the utility room. He darted through into the shower room and closed the door behind him.

There was a moment's silence.

'Crikey,' said Heather, as Matthew started up. 'We don't need sound effects.' She crossed the room and closed the utility room door, which reduced the indiscreet sound of Matthew's activity to a muffled cascade.

'Boys!' said Barbara. She turned back to the sink and turned on the tap.

Activity in the kitchen continued for a few moments more. Then two doors opened in quick succession, and Matthew's head appeared around the utility room door.

'Have you got a pair of rubber gloves?'

'Rubber gloves? Why?' said Heather.

'I've just flushed a finger of Fudge down the toilet, but the Curly Wurly's got stuck.'

'And there was me thinking you were just doing number ones,' said Heather. 'How the hell did they get down there?'

'I believe it can only be one of the two usual suspects,' said Matthew. 'And someone's missing two chocolate bars from their Santa Selection Box!'

'Emma!' called Heather, down the hallway. 'Can you come in here, please?'

Matthew was rummaging in the cupboard under the sink when Emma entered the kitchen. He came up holding a pair of yellow Marigolds. 'Ah, young lady,' he said. 'We were just wondering if you have any idea how two Cadbury chocolate bars ended up in the downstairs toilet?'

Emma looked confused. She hesitated, then said, 'I left my selection box with all my other presents in the dining room.' She turned and hurried out of the kitchen.

Matthew and Heather followed her into the dining room. Emma was on her knees in front of a pile of books and toys. She held up a box. It was torn. She stood, put it on the dining room table and pulled out the plastic tray. There were two empty compartments.

'How do you know that's not Grace's?' said Matthew.

'It's not,' said Heather. She walked over to the bookcase to the right of the window. 'I put Grace's up here, out of the way, so she couldn't get to it.' She reached up and brought down an unopened Cadbury Santa Selection Box.

'That cow,' screamed Emma. 'I'll kill her!' She turned and stormed towards the dining room door. Matthew stepped across the doorway and blocked her exit. 'Whoa, whoa,' he said. 'Where do you think you're going? There's no need for that. We'll sort this out.'

'Here,' said Heather, opening Grace's box, 'you can have these.' She handed Emma a finger of Fudge and a Curly Wurly. 'Put those in your box and hide it somewhere. Okay? Are we good?'

Emma nodded, but it was clear she was still fuming.

'Okay,' said Matthew, 'everyone back to the lounge. I'm going fishing for chocolate.' He pulled on his yellow Marigolds and made his way back into the kitchen.

In the lounge, Tony was on his hands and knees pretending to chase James, who, at sixteen months, was now trundling reasonably confidently around the lounge with his walker. Tony would almost catch up with him, then lunge theatrically, shouting "Gotcha!" as he dived. He would miss and end up rolling around on the floor, which resulted in James getting overexcited and cackling loudly as he evaded capture and trundled off.

Everyone laughed, and even Emma smiled.

'Right, I'm going back to the kitchen to help Barbara and check that my husband hasn't flushed himself down the toilet,' said Heather. 'Be ready to eat in fifteen minutes.'

By the time they'd finished the buffet, it was way past the children's bedtime – but it was Christmas, after all. Given all the activity and excitement, James had fallen asleep far quicker than usual, and Grace was safely tucked up in her cot. Barbara had taken it upon herself to read with Emma each night before lights out, and that evening, she spent longer with her than usual. When she came back down to the lounge, she reported that Emma had settled and seemed relaxed.

Matthew had brought out a couple of bottles of wine. Heather was two large glasses in already. Barbara took a seat next to her at the end of the sofa and immediately took a sip from the large glass that Matthew handed her. Matthew and Tony had a beer each, and there were plenty of nibbles still to eat, so there were bowls filled with Twiglets, ready salted crisps and dry-roasted peanuts. Heather had commandeered the CD player, and the mellow tones of Michael Bublé eased the lingering, late-afternoon tension as they listened to songs from his 2011 'Christmas' album. It was the first time they'd had an opportunity to sit down together and unwind since Tony and Barbara had arrived.

Tony stretched out in the armchair next to the Christmas tree, his long legs extending out in front of him. He looked across at Heather, who was draining the last drops from her second glass of red. 'Is that Merlot doing the trick?'

Heather smiled, her face slightly flushed. 'I'll let you know after the next one,' she said.

'Well, you've had a pretty stressful afternoon – you deserve a few drinks.'

'Stressful afternoon? I've had a pretty stressful year.' Heather reached for the open bottle of red wine and poured. The remnant was barely enough for a few swallows, so she reached for the second bottle. She filled her glass and looked at Barbara, sitting next to her. Barbara's first glass was still full, so Heather put the bottle back down on the small table in front of her.

'I know you've had a stressful year,' Tony was saying. 'Every week when Matthew calls us, there seems to be another drama.'

'It's been one thing after another,' said Heather. 'I swear 2017 has taken five years off my life. I'm a physical wreck. Mentally, I'm exhausted. I'm not sure how much more of this infighting I can take.'

'Do you have to record all these incidents?' said Barbara. 'Couldn't you save yourself some grief by not reporting everything to that ghastly Sarah woman?'

'What? – and miss the opportunity to tell Ms Morton how I found a finger of Fudge down the toilet,' said Matthew. 'Not on your nelly!'

'So you're going to log what happened this afternoon?' said Barbara, who couldn't understand why her comment caused Tony to splutter halfway through sipping his beer and Matthew to laugh until tears ran down his face.

'So, how is your relationship with Sarah at the moment, dare I ask?' Tony had regained his composure and reached out to place his beer glass on the small table next to him.

Matthew dried his eyes with his handkerchief and then stuffed it back into his pocket. 'Delicate, I'd say.' He shook his head. 'I still can't get my head round what's going on with her,' he said. 'Right from the off, without provocation, she gave us grief. It seemed to me every little thing we did, she pulled to pieces, just to antagonise us. She made a right song and dance over Emma playing that adult game on her tablet, but ever since then, she seems to be making light of all the trouble we've had.'

Heather was idly swilling the wine in her glass. She looked up. 'Now, it's *us* making mountains out of molehills,' she said. 'Can you believe it? She even has the cheek to question our ability to parent.'

'Have you heard any more about that old bottle of medicine she claimed you'd given those other carers?' said Tony.

'No,' said Matthew. 'I thought she would read us the riot act, but she didn't; she just said she'd escalated the matter to her manager. Then she said he'd lost the bottle, and we've heard nothing since. As far as I'm concerned, it's done and dusted.'

'Even though she's playing down all the trouble we've had with Emma, she still seems to take great pleasure in reminding us that she's recording everything that's happened and everything we say in her monthly reports,' said Heather. She knocked back some more wine.

'Again,' said Barbara, 'why don't you just keep all the Emma nonsense to yourselves? Why involve Sarah? You're just giving her ammo to fire back at you.'

'We have to log it,' said Heather. 'We've got James and Grace to think about. If we don't flag the potential danger that Emma poses to them, and one day she does something really serious and hurts them, I'd never forgive myself. At least this way, social services can step in before it's too late.'

'But you've already said that Sarah's not taking what you say seriously. If all she's noting is that you're complaining...'

Tony waved his arm dismissively. 'Let's talk about something else, shall we?' he said. 'How's James getting on? Has he seen the consultant recently?'

'His next three-month appointment is in January,' said Heather. 'You know he had a PET-MRI scan in October?'

Tony nodded. 'Yes, Matthew mentioned it. Is there any update on his development and how all this might affect him as he gets older?'

Heather swallowed some more of her wine and wiped her lips. 'Yes. Some of his behaviours are becoming more apparent now. Obviously, we've known about his sleep, feeding and balance issues for some time – did we tell you that his irregular feeding patterns are likely due to a lower sensitivity to the sensations of hunger and thirst?'

Matthew swallowed a mouthful of sweets. 'And what goes in irregularly at one end, unfortunately, comes out irregularly at the other,' he said. 'Anyone for a chocolate raisin?'

Heather ignored his comment. 'Well, this thing about being under-responsive to certain sensory input and over-responsive to other stimuli is becoming more of a theme.'

'I've noticed he's always touching things,' said Barbara.

Heather laughed. 'Oh, he's always playing with his feet, and he loves the toys on that activity play mat. His consultant is certain he's under-sensitive to touch, which is why he's quite rough – he has to be to feel things properly. He's constantly splashing in the bath and hitting his toys, and he seems to enjoy it when you cuddle him or wrap him tightly in a blanket.'

'That sounds like most kids to me,' said Tony. He nodded at Matthew. 'That one was a right vandal. Always bashing things. Usually, the other kids in the playground if they tried to steal his packed lunch. Nobody messed with our Matthew.'

'That's right, Dad. A right little street fighter, me. I grew up in the school of hard knocks.' Matthew grinned.

'Yes, well, I'm not suggesting for one minute that I'm going to let James grow up to be a thug like his father.'

'Father?' said Tony, laughing. 'What d'you mean?'

Heather looked uncertainly at Matthew. 'Well, that's our other news,' she said. 'Matthew and I are thinking of adopting James.'

Barbara squealed. 'Oh, congratulations, you two. That's wonderful!'

Tony looked less sure.

'I know what you're thinking, Dad,' said Matthew. 'It won't be easy – but we've given it a lot of thought. And Heather will be a great mother.'

'I don't doubt it,' said Tony. He reached for his glass of beer and raised it. 'Congratulations.' He took a gulp and rested the glass back on the table. 'Now, tell us more about our future grandson's prospects.'

Heather smiled. 'Well,' she said, 'the fact that it appears James is "under-sensitive" might also explain some of the behaviours we're seeing. It's still too early to say where all this might lead, but, I admit, he is likely to be a bit of a handful, bless him.'

Tony cast a glance at Matthew. He laughed. 'Isn't one handful enough?'

Heather smiled. 'Let's just put it this way. The consultant says he's likely to be hyperactive at times and have a limited attention span; probably a little clumsy, a little loud, but he'll tire easily, because his body is under-developed. It's all because he's compensating for a lack of sensory input.'

'Will he play nicely with other children?' said Barbara.

'Well, he was playing alright with me,' said Tony.

'Yes, but I'm not talking about your rough-and-tumble antics,' said Barbara. 'I mean, will he integrate okay with other children?'

'He might have difficulty,' said Matthew. 'Because of all the traits Heather's mentioned, he might be disruptive, and he might struggle with things like taking turns. And I don't know if you've noticed, but we never put too many toys in front of him at one time. He seems to get rattled when there's too much going on around him.'

'We're also finding,' said Heather, 'that he has difficulty remembering things we've shown him. It's like that game where he has to put the ball into the hole so it shoots out the tube. We've played that so many times, and yet there are days you'd think he'd never played with it before.'

'All this must be very frustrating for him,' said Barbara.

'I think as he gets older and more self-aware, it might be,' said Heather. 'At the moment, he's just a typical toddler, with his ups and downs. It doesn't necessarily mean that he won't be able to socialise, but it is possible that he might have trouble relating to and mixing with other kids as he gets older. It's also possible that he'll need routine and won't like change.'

Tony reached forward for his beer. 'It sounds as if you'll need to be very patient with him,' he said. 'But more to the point, how will James cope? Isn't there a chance that all this will affect his mental health?'

'There is,' said Heather. 'I guess it all depends on how pronounced any emotional and behavioural issues become, and if it significantly affects his ability to interact with others and his education; it's too early to say. All we can do is give him as normal an upbringing as we can and address any issues as they arise.'

'Well, I'm sure he's getting all the emotional support he needs from you,' said Barbara, 'and at least they've diagnosed it early so they're monitoring him.'

There was a moment's silence and then a shriek from Grace's room.

Matthew jumped up from the comfort of the sofa, almost taking out the table with the nibbles and Heather's wine, and raced up the stairs. As his head levelled with the landing floor, he thought he glimpsed Emma disappearing into the darkness of her room.

'What the hell is going on up here?'

He turned right at the top of the stairs, went into Grace's room and switched on the light. The first thing he noticed was a clump of Grace's dark hair on the light-coloured carpet in front of him.

Grace sat in her cot, holding her head and whimpering. When she looked up at Matthew, there were tears in her eyes. Matthew lifted her out and, gently moving her hand away from her scalp, he revealed a patch of missing hair. He massaged her head, soothing her, and pulled her close to him. When she had quietened down after a few minutes, he laid her back down and pulled the quilt over her.

'There you go, back to sleep now.'

Matthew waited for her to settle, then left the room and crossed the landing to Emma's bedroom.

'Emma, do you have any idea how a handful of Grace's hair got on her bedroom floor?'

Emma was curled up under her duvet, pretending, so far as Matthew was concerned, to be asleep. Her tousled, curly ginger hair was partially obscuring her face. She groaned and lifted her head slowly, squinting up at Matthew. 'What? What is it?'

'I asked you: do you have any idea how a handful of Grace's hair got on her bedroom floor?'

'No... I've been asleep,' said Emma.

'Well, when I came up the stairs, I'm pretty sure I saw you sneaking back into your room.'

'I wasn't sneaking! I went to the toilet.'

'Really?' Matthew had only caught a fleeting glimpse of Emma's back and couldn't be certain which room she was returning from. She might have been to the bathroom. 'So, you think Grace is in the habit of pulling out her own hair, then?'

'Maybe she had a bad dream?'

Matthew hesitated. The circumstantial evidence was strong. Still, he felt perhaps it would be unwise to accuse Emma of an outright lie and potentially ignite another powder keg – especially at this time of night. Equally, he couldn't allow such behaviour to go unchallenged. 'Well, listen, if I find out that you've been in her room and pulling her hair, there'll be trouble, young lady. Do you hear me?'

'I told you. I didn't do anything. Why don't you believe me?'

'Well, it wouldn't be the first time you've picked on Grace, would it? You've been good recently, so let's not start all that again. It's got to stop.'

Emma said nothing.

'Right. Well, good night then,' said Matthew. 'And think about what I've said.'

He made his way back downstairs and into the lounge. Heather, Tony and Barbara paused in conversation and looked at him enquiringly.

'Emma's just pulled out some of Grace's hair. She's denied it, but I know damn well it was her. If this is all kicking off again...'

'This constant bullying is getting beyond a joke, Matthew,' said Heather, getting up from the sofa. 'Who knows what she'll do next – one of these days it could be something really serious. And how long is it going to be before she picks on James? I'm going to have a word with her.'

'Well, it's Grace that seems to be taking the brunt of it.' Matthew reached out and took Heather by the arm. 'Please, sit down. You confronting her isn't going to help matters.'

Heather thought for a moment before retaking her seat. 'We need to catch her in the act,' she said. 'She's been clever so far.'

'Okay, so tomorrow I'll set up the spy camera in Grace's room,' said Matthew. 'If she does it again, we'll catch her at it – before Grace has no hair left.'

'I'm suddenly feeling quite relieved that we're leaving tomorrow,' said Barbara. 'I'd quite forgotten how demanding kids can be.'

'Me? Demanding?' said Matthew. 'I was a pussycat compared to this.'

The next day, Tony and Barbara left for home. Matthew fitted the spy camera in the afternoon while Emma was reading with Heather downstairs. It was wireless and the size of a playing card. It fitted discreetly into the folds of the pelmet above Grace's bedroom window and transmitted to Matthew's laptop, which would record the footage. The next few days revealed nothing out of the ordinary.

The omens for a peaceful New Year, however, were bad. On the morning of New Year's Eve, Grace stamped on the tablet belonging to Emma's uncle, which he had loaned Emma over Christmas. The force was enough to crack the screen in several places. Fortunately, Matthew was on hand to prevent a violent reaction, and Emma retreated to her bedroom in tears. Given that the tablet belonged to Emma's uncle, and given that Emma was due to spend New Year's Day with him and take it back with her, Matthew alerted Sarah Morton to the incident, who in turn alerted Ann. Matthew did not want Emma to have to be the one to break the news to her uncle, whose reaction was predictable. So, Ann contacted him in the hope that he would have the rest of New Year's Eve to calm down – probably with a copious amount of drink and something up his nose. He would no doubt spend New Year's Day with Emma, nursing a stonking hangover. Matthew half expected some retaliation from Emma that night and checked the camera footage while she was at her uncle's the next day. But Grace saw the new year in sleeping peacefully and woke with her hair intact.

17

New Year

Wednesday, 3rd January 2018

As the first Monday in the month was New Year's Day, January's supervision meeting with Sarah took place on the Wednesday. Sarah followed Heather into the lounge only to find Matthew sitting in her armchair. A flicker of a scowl betrayed her annoyance. He watched with wry amusement as she approached, her piercing, black-coffee-coloured eyes appraising him. She stopped in front of the chair and waited expectantly.

'New year, new seating arrangements, Ms Morton,' said Matthew. 'I fancied a change. Why don't you sit over there?' He indicated the end of the sofa nearest the office.

Sarah twitched, as if an icy droplet of water had meandered down the length of her spine. She glared at him and turned sharply, crossing the room to the sofa, where she took a seat, placed her briefcase on her lap and clicked it open. Heather looked curiously at Matthew before taking a seat at the other end of the sofa, nearest the lounge door, as Sarah organised herself. Matthew sat like a king upon his throne; his legs planted squarely in front of him, and his arms rested along the arms of the chair, gripping the edges.

'Where shall we start?' he said. He thought for a moment. 'Perhaps we should get the elephant out of the room – no offence intended, Ms Morton. I presume you've spoken with Ann. What did Emma's uncle have to say about the unfortunate demise of his tablet?'

Emma's uncle's reaction was as expected, and the language relayed to Matthew and Heather, through Sarah, whose mood brightened noticeably, was colourful, descriptive, and abusive.

'Water off a duck's back, as far as I'm concerned,' said Matthew. 'I'm not interested in the opinions of a sociopathic smackhead. He had his chance to prove himself in the school of parenting, and he blew it. Who's he to lecture us?'

Sarah sat back in the sofa. 'He's demanding you buy him a new tablet,' she said. 'As far as he's concerned, it was broken under your roof and therefore it's your responsibility.'

'Fat chance of that!' Matthew flicked his hand dismissively. 'I'm not prepared to discuss the matter anymore. He doesn't frighten me, but his constant demands and accusations are causing Heather too much stress. Enough's enough!' He looked across at Heather, who appeared to have zoned out.

'Well, he's offered to come and collect it,' said Sarah. 'He knows where you live.'

Heather sat up in alarm. 'How the hell does he know where we live?'

'Emma probably told him, or perhaps he followed you home from her school,' said Sarah, with far too much relish. 'I think you need to take responsibility, Mr Blundell. I suggest you replace the tablet before this situation gets out of hand.'

'I agree with Sarah,' said Heather. 'You need to stop being so pig-headed, Matthew. Just replace the tablet, and we'll ask Ann to give it to him next week. I don't want him turning up here demanding a new one when you're not around.' She looked at Sarah. 'If you speak with Ann, please let her know that we'll be in touch, and Emma's uncle will have a new tablet by next week.'

'Leave it with me,' said Matthew, when Heather turned to face him again. 'I'll sort it.'

They spent the next fifteen minutes dealing with the usual mundane formalities and going through the daily logs.

'Now, the last thing of note is an incident of hair-pulling we think you should be aware of.' Matthew relayed the events of Christmas Day.

‘Again,’ said Sarah, ‘circumstantial evidence. You did not see Emma pull out chunks of Grace’s hair, so you cannot categorically say that she did.’

Heather stared at Sarah in disbelief.

‘Well, how else did Grace’s hair end up on her bedroom floor?’ said Matthew. His voice was laced with sarcasm.

‘Trichotillomania.’

‘I’m not interested in your sexual exploits, Sarah.’

‘Funny, Mr Blundell. Grace could very well have pulled out her own hair. It can be a coping mechanism in times of stress. I recall a social worker I once worked with telling me about a case she had. Very hairy it was, too.’ Sarah chuckled.

‘Hairy, my arse! That’s ridiculous!’

‘Oh, I thought as puns go, it was quite good...’

‘And I thought trichotillomania was a compulsive disorder,’ said Heather. ‘Isn’t Grace a bit young?’

‘Well, it has to start somewhere, Mrs Blundell.’

Heather thought for a moment. ‘Well, Grace has certainly been placed under stress in recent months. It could be subconscious...’

‘Well, there you go,’ said Sarah.

‘Typical,’ said Matthew. ‘Again, we come to you with an issue that should be a cause for concern, and you just brush it off. Well, for your information, we’ve put up a camera in Grace’s room and we’re monitoring the situation. Move on! Have you brought the outstanding supervision notes for us to look over? Memory can be an issue when you get to your age – who knows what you’ve been dreaming up.’

Sarah didn’t react. ‘I’m afraid circumstances haven’t changed since the last time I saw you. We’ve had a record number of placement requests in the last couple of months,’ she said firmly. ‘We don’t have enough carers, so we’ve been advertising, interviewing and going through all the assessments, and we’re short-staffed; it’s been all hands on deck. I only had Christmas Day off. I’ve had to prioritise. And on the subject of time off, I’m going to be on annual leave for the next two weeks. Lord knows I need it after the few months I’ve had. If you have any issues, just ring them through to the office.’ She clicked her biro and straightened her papers. She reached down for her briefcase. 'Any more questions before we conclude this month's meeting?'

'Yes,' said Heather. 'We spoke briefly in December about the possibility of us adopting James. Matthew and I have agreed: we want to start the process so we can at least be assessed.'

'As I said then, and I'll say it again,' said Sarah, putting her papers away, 'if the Local Authority has decided that adoption is the way forward, it'll be in his permanence plan; though I doubt any final decision has been made yet. I do know his mother is due to start a parenting course in the next few weeks, and she'll be assessed to see if she's fit to have him and his brother Michael back on a permanent basis. Janet will know what stage they're at. I'll speak to her.'

'I seem to recall that's what you said last time,' said Matthew. 'Anyway, that's irrelevant. If there's any possibility that James will be put up for adoption, which, let's face it, is likely, then we want to be approved and in a position to be matched with him. Why's it taking so long to decide, anyway? I thought a child's future should be determined within a year of their being placed in care?'

'Ideally, yes, Mr Blundell. But, as you know, James is a special case. There's his FASD to consider. You don't need me to tell you that the assessment of his future needs is still in its very early stages and, clearly, all options to return him to his family have not yet been fully explored.'

'We get that,' said Heather. She clasped her hands. 'We just don't want to miss the opportunity if it arises.'

'Okay...' Sarah stood. 'I'll make enquiries. If an adoption social worker has been assigned to James's case, maybe we can arrange a viability meeting as part of the parallel planning.'

'And what's a viability meeting when it's at home?' said Matthew. He saw the look of exasperation in Sarah's eyes and smiled.

'A viability meeting, Mr Blundell, involves an adoption social worker, Janet and myself visiting you here and discussing the implications of your interest in adopting James. Following that, said adoption social worker would complete a viability assessment, and a whole raft of Local Authority professionals would then get together to decide if we felt you could potentially meet James's long-term permanency needs. *Should* we decide to give you our backing, then, and only then, would we agree to assess you formally as prospective adopters and send you a Registration of Interest form. Does that fully answer your question?'

'It does, Sarah. Most succinctly. Please...' Matthew gestured towards the lounge door, '...don't let us detain you any longer.'

Sarah took a few steps and then paused. 'Remember,' she said, turning back to face them, 'it's not a blind auction where the highest bidder takes home a toddler.' She stared at them through glasses framed in shimmering gold plastic. 'Now, if that's all, I have a lot of meetings to catch up on after the festive season. I must be going.'

'Of course,' said Matthew, 'but it would be rude to let you go without complimenting you on your impressive choice of festive make-up, Sarah. Despite the fact Christmas was over a week ago, I'm loving the sparkly gold glasses-eyeshadow combo, and the holly berry-red lipstick. And are those Christmas tree-green shoes?'

Thursday, 4th January 2018

It was Emma's first day back at school after the Christmas holidays. She had been noticeably touchy and agitated. After Sarah's visit the day before, Grace had been in one of her more boisterous moods, and a series of minor incidents had led to Heather keeping Emma under close surveillance. Heather had been so wound up by the end of the day that she took a couple of Nytol sleeping tablets and retired to bed early. Matthew had relaxed with a couple of beers, or four, before turning in himself.

Heather had volunteered to run Emma to school and so woke early, leaving Matthew, in his pyjamas, to look after James and Grace. When she returned, James and Grace were playing in the lounge. She saw Matthew, still in his pyjamas, sitting at the desk in the office. He was staring intently at the laptop screen. Before Heather could join him, the phone rang, and she took the call. It lasted a few minutes. As she replaced the handset in the cradle, Matthew called out to her. 'Heather, come and look at this.'

Heather hurried into the office.

'Caught her red-handed.'

Matthew clicked back on a video he'd been watching. It was footage from the spy camera in Grace's room. The time clock showed one-thirty-seven in the early hours of the morning. Heather watched the screen, which showed a black-and-white, wide-angled, night vision image of Grace's room, overlooking the cot, with the bedroom door in the background. She waited. Moments later, Emma entered Grace's room, walked over to the cot, reached through the bars, grabbed Grace by the hair and pulled repeatedly, banging Grace's head against the side. Then she scurried out of the room. Not more than thirty seconds passed before Heather saw herself enter the room, clearly half asleep and dosed up to the eyeballs on Nytol. She reached into the cot and with some effort, lifted out Grace, who had been sitting up crying. She knew she had spent several minutes comforting her before laying her back down, settling her and returning to bed.

'The little cow,' said Heather. 'I swear she's psychopathic.'

'Yeah. What are the chances of two antichrists in one house?'

'Matthew – this is no time for joking; this is serious. Why is she behaving like this?'

'Payback,' said Matthew. 'Grace has been winding Emma up. We've had the incident with the sweets; she bust Emma's tablet and now all the shenanigans yesterday. And dare I say, if Emma's a bit psycho, maybe she gets a kick out of it... I wonder if her uncle put her up to this. I wouldn't put it past him.'

'We have to show this to Sarah,' said Heather. 'She must realise now that this behaviour cannot be tolerated; something is going to have to be done about it. We can't discipline Emma, and we've tried reasoning with her. The fact is, she can't be trusted around other children. We have to put the matter firmly in Sarah's court. Let her make the necessary decision as to where we go from here.'

'I agree,' said Matthew. 'We'll unleash the dogs of war, but Morton needs to see this and act accordingly. And I'm going to show it to Emma, and I'll leave her in no doubt that if she doesn't stop, there will be serious consequences.'

'Good luck with that,' said Heather. 'Anyway, we have another decision to make. That was a social worker called Maggie on the phone. She's just taken a girl called Ruth into care. It seems her mother's been using her as an ashtray over New Year. Her PE teacher discovered cigarette burns on her arm on her first day back at school. She wants to know if we'll take her?'

Matthew laughed. 'Are you joking? One minute, Sarah's implying we can't cope with the kids we have, and now they're asking us to take another one. And what about you? Will you cope?'

'Maggie assured me it won't be for long, and I think they're desperate,' said Heather. 'It's just while they assess other family members who might take her on. She's roughly Emma's age. I suppose it might be good for Emma; give her someone her own age to play with – distract her.'

'Well, we've got the space, I suppose – and you're right, it might be a short-term answer to the problem.'

Heather took a deep breath and let it out slowly. 'Okay, I'll call Maggie back and say we'll take her. For now, just try not to let Emma and Grace out of your sight, and I'll keep James close to me.'

18

Ruth

Ruth arrived that afternoon.

Maggie took Matthew and Heather to one side and briefed them. She told them that Ruth was an immature child, needy and extremely hyperactive. 'Apparently,' she said, 'she can't sit still. It doesn't matter what she's doing, be it eating, watching television, or playing games; she fidgets constantly. It seems her attention span is about ten minutes at most.' Matthew and Heather listened patiently and realised, perhaps a little too late, that Ruth might not be the solution to their problem after all.

At dinnertime, Matthew and Heather were in the dining room, supervising as the kids ate their fish finger sandwiches with Smiley Faces and peas. James and Grace were safely in their highchairs. Technically, Grace could have been in a booster seat on a dining chair, but a highchair was still useful for ensuring that she remained at the table. Emma was eating quietly; still smarting from the ultimatum Matthew had given her over the hair-pulling. Ruth, a rangy child, was squirming restlessly in her chair.

'Are you alright, Ruth?' said Heather. 'Are you in pain?'

'My arm hurts.'

'What's wrong with it?' said Heather.

'It's where my mummy burnt me with her cigarette.'

Matthew leant over and whispered in Heather's ear. 'Do you think you should take her to the bathroom and check her over? I'll watch the kids while they finish their dinner.'

Heather pushed back her chair and stood. 'Ruth, come with me, love, and show me where it hurts.' Heather offered her hand to lead the way.

A few minutes later, they both returned. Emma watched them closely as they retook their seats at the dining table. Matthew was staring silently at James and Grace, who were both munching their way through their remaining food.

Heather sat down next to Matthew. 'There's some bruising around the arm,' she said, 'and I've put some aqueous cream on the burns – they're itchy, aren't they, Ruth?'

Ruth nodded. 'Mummy was angry with me.'

'Does she get angry often?' said Matthew.

'She gets angry when she drinks lots of wine. She says I pester her. I want too much attention. Sometimes, she says I drive her mad, and she gets angry.'

'Has she ever done anything like that before?' Matthew pointed at Ruth's arm.

'She's never burnt me before.'

Heather felt a familiar sadness as she watched Ruth staring vacantly at the fish finger sandwich still on her plate. Tears were welling up in Ruth's striking blue-green eyes. 'And is that what you told your teacher today?' said Heather gently.

Ruth looked up, her delicate features contorting as she tried to fight back the tears. 'My teacher saw me crying and asked me what was wrong. That's when someone went to speak to Mummy.' She sniffed and wiped the back of her hand across her eyes. 'Then a lady came and said I had to come and live here for a while. She said they were going to get some help for my mummy and then I could go back to her.' Ruth reached out and pushed her plate away. 'I don't want to go back to live with my mummy.'

'Is there anyone else you'd like to live with?' said Matthew. 'Do you have a grandma or grandad?'

Emma startled them. 'Why don't you leave her alone?' she cried. 'Don't you think it's bad enough she has to come and live here, without you asking her all these stupid questions? You're making her cry!' She glared at them.

'That's enough from you, young lady!' Matthew glared back at her. 'I suggest you take your dinner and finish it in the lounge.'

'You've never given a shit about my feelings!' Emma jumped up and flipped her plate over. It clattered on the wooden tabletop, and the peas she had left scattered over the cream vinyl tablecloth. She turned and stormed out of the room. They heard her heavy footsteps on the stairs and her bedroom door slammed.

Ruth was in tears. Her head hung low, her medium-length fair hair partly masking her face.

Heather pulled a sheet from the roll of kitchen towel on the table. 'Here,' she said, handing it to Ruth, 'dry your eyes.' Ruth took it, dabbed her eyes and then blew her nose.

'Pay no attention to Emma,' said Matthew. 'You were telling us that you don't want to go back to live with your mummy. Do you have any other family?'

'I love my grandma and grandad. I'd like to live with them. That's my mummy's mum and dad.'

Heather reached across and rested her hand on Ruth's. 'Okay, well, if you feel that way, mention it to Maggie, your social worker. Or we can mention it to her for you, if you like. Now, do you want me to see if I can get an appointment with the doctor tomorrow about your arm?'

Ruth shrugged her shoulders. 'I've been already. They said it will get better on its own. It's not so bad now.'

Heather stood up. 'Well, finish your dinner if you can, and I'll go and get you a treat for your pudding.' She stroked Ruth's hair as she walked past her.

Matthew and Heather had a great deal of sympathy for Ruth; but she was hard work for everyone. She proved to be very needy and flitted from person to person and was not capable of forming a meaningful relationship with Emma. They would play nicely for so long as Ruth was engaged, which wasn't for very long. But they bickered. A few weeks was all it took.

Saturday, 3rd February 2018

'Where are Emma and Ruth?'

'Playing upstairs in Ruth's room, the last time I checked,' said Heather, looking up from her book. She and Matthew were taking five and relaxing in the lounge. James was pushing the pieces of a nine-piece puzzle around the floor, and Grace was practising gymnastics, as best a child of nearly two can practise gymnastics.

'Shall I look in on them?'

'No, they should be fine,' said Heather. 'They seem to be getting on okay. Ruth seems quite taken with the idea of a dolls' tea party.'

Emma and Ruth had placed several dolls in a circle around an upturned cardboard box that served as a table. Each doll had a plate and a cup and saucer, and there was a large pot of tea in the middle to share.

'You pour the tea for everyone,' said Emma. 'I'll serve the sandwiches.'

The party was going well until Emma decided she wanted to clear away the sandwich plates to make way for serving some cake.

'My dolls haven't finished their sandwiches yet! Don't touch my ones!' said Ruth.

Emma ignored her and started emptying the plates, tipping the plastic food into the box it came from. Ruth retaliated.

'Give me my dolls' food back!'

'No, we're having cake now.'

With one swipe, Ruth knocked everything off their makeshift table.

'What did you do that for?' said Emma. 'I'm telling Heather of you.'

'I'm telling Heather of you first,' said Ruth.

Both got to their feet, pushing and shoving as they tried to get through the bedroom door first.

Matthew heard the commotion and rushed to the bottom of the stairs. 'What's going on up there?' The arguing continued as Emma and Ruth fought their way out of Ruth's bedroom door and emerged at the top of the stairs, fighting to get down first. 'No playing on the top of the stairs,' shouted Matthew, as he opened the stair gate and made his way up, 'it's dangerous.'

‘Emma’s pushing me.’

‘No, I’m not; you’re pushing me.’

‘Enough now!’ said Matthew, approaching the turn on the staircase, three-quarters of the way up. ‘Stop it before one of you gets hurt.’

Emma had her back against a small section of wall at the top of the stairs. She was gripping Ruth’s top with both hands, with Ruth straining to free herself. Suddenly, Emma let go, braced herself against the wall and kicked out. Ruth stumbled, pitched backwards and fell from the top step.

Ruth screamed.

With lightning reactions, Matthew leapt forward and caught Ruth under her flailing arms. He just managed to stay on his feet, preventing them both from ending up in a pile at the bottom of the stairs.

Emma was shut, sulking, in her bedroom. Ruth was in hers.

‘That’s it! When Sarah comes round on Monday, we’re giving notice on Emma,’ said Heather.

Matthew buried his head in his hands. ‘I agree with you, but Morton’s not going to like it,’ he said, his voice muffled. He raised his head. ‘This behaviour’s been escalating for months and apart from that one chat with Emma, she’s been totally dismissive. She’s been trying to avoid this moment. She knows how difficult it is to get carers to take children with health issues; that’s why. This will not go down well.’

‘Well, that’s not our problem. I’m not having a vicious child in the same house as James. And her bloody uncle – telling us how to do our job every week. I know it’s a tough decision, but I think it’s in everyone’s best interest.’

‘Yes, I know, but it does feel a little like we’re giving up. It’s like we’re admitting defeat. Abandon ship! Set the controls for the heart of the sun! You know what I mean?’

‘Yes. But I’d rather steer that course than live another day like this. She goes.’

Monday, 5th February 2018

Even Matthew, who usually relished the thought of a battle of wits with 'Morton', felt the tension in the air. He and Heather were sitting in the lounge. Waiting.

She made them wait. Sarah didn't arrive until twelve-thirty, which was half an hour past the usual time of midday. The doorbell rang.

'You get it,' said Matthew. Heather got up, proceeded into the hall and opened the door.

'Good morning, Mrs Blundell. How are we today? How lovely to see a bit of sunshine. It makes one feel so much better.'

'Good morning, Sarah...' If Heather was surprised by Sarah's attempt at a bright and breezy entrance, she didn't show it. She stepped back as Sarah pushed past and walked into the lounge, making for her usual armchair in the corner by the window. Heather didn't bother asking her if she would like a cup of tea or coffee. Sarah always refused. Heather supposed she had a weak bladder.

'Mr Blundell.' Sarah acknowledged Matthew with a curt nod. Matthew responded with something approaching a smile as Sarah sat down.

Heather returned to the room, and Sarah cleared her throat. 'Okay, what have we got this month?'

'Well, hopefully, Ms Morton, you have the supervision notes from our past three meetings for us to sign?'

'Sadly not, Mr Blundell. As you know, I was extremely busy over Christmas and into the New Year, and I've not long returned to the office after two weeks' annual leave. I'm afraid they're low priority.'

'They may be low priority to you, Ms Morton, but a lot's been going on over the last few months, and I want to ensure you've accurately recorded everything we've said.'

'The notes are just a formality, Mr Blundell.'

'It may be just a formality, Sarah, but we would like to have them for our records, just the same,' said Heather. 'Just to be quite clear, we're missing your supervision notes for October, November and December.'

'I shall get around to them as quickly as I can. Now, how have the children been getting on?'

'Don't change the subject,' said Matthew. 'It's unacceptable. How long is this going to go on?'

'We can argue about this all afternoon if you like, Mr Blundell. Or we can move on?'

'We've made our point,' said Heather, looking at Matthew. 'I suggest we move on.'

Matthew sat back and folded his arms. Summarising the children's activities and well-being was Heather's domain, and he listened as she gave Sarah the update.

'James has been no trouble,' she said. 'The usual ups and downs with his eating and sleeping. We saw the consultant the week before last, and there's nothing new to report. Obviously, we're continuing to record his development against his cognitive milestones. His next appointment is in April.' She looked down at James, who was sitting next to Grace. Both were watching a cartoon on the television, which was on mute. 'He's playing nicely,' she said. 'He needs help a lot of the time, but he's doing well. He's still not showing any signs of talking; he just mumbles rather than forming words.' Heather paused. 'I guess it's pointless asking if you've spoken with Janet about adoption...'

Sarah shook her head. 'That's also on the to-do list, I'm afraid.'

Heather thought for a moment. 'Grace has been better of late,' she continued. 'I think Emma's bullying over the last few months has "put her in her place", for want of a better phrase. All the run-of-the-mill stuff is recorded in her daily log. Ruth has settled in okay. We had hoped she'd be a calming influence on Emma, but she can't sit still for a minute. I'm sure doctors would diagnose her with ADHD if they assessed her.'

'I need to speak with you about Ruth,' said Sarah.

'Oh, yes. Why?' said Matthew, sitting forward.

'It's been reported that you interrogated her and made her cry.'

Matthew turned to look at Heather. 'Emma,' he said.

Sarah frowned. 'Emma, Mr Blundell? What's Emma got to do with this?'

Matthew turned back to face her. 'Interrogated, you say?' He scoffed. 'Ruth was complaining her arm hurt. We were trying to ascertain the cause.'

'That's fine, Mr Blundell, but then it appears you used it as an excuse to quiz Ruth about her mother?'

Matthew shook his head. 'I think in a situation like that,' he said, 'we need to know what we're dealing with to empathise and offer support – to ignore the issue would suggest that we don't care. If Ruth hadn't wanted to talk about it, then fine; but she volunteered the information about her mother's drinking and angry outbursts.'

'Even if that were the case, it appears you used it as an opportunity to probe her for more information. I'm told you even said she could go and live with her grandma and grandad.'

'We said no such thing,' said Heather. 'Ruth said she didn't want to go back to her mother. We merely asked her who else she might like to live with...'

Sarah gave a despairing look. 'Unbelievable! Regardless – if you'd wanted to know more about Ruth's background, then you should have gone through me, Mrs Blundell, not the child.'

Matthew glared at her. 'Well, that's another issue we'll just have to agree to disagree on, Ms Morton.' Sarah met Matthew's stare, her mouth fixed in tight-lipped defiance. 'And I object to that word "interrogate". I can't imagine anyone who witnessed our conversation with Ruth would describe it as an "interrogation" – so is that their interpretation, or yours, perhaps?'

Sarah bristled. 'I believe the events, as described to me, can correctly be interpreted as an interrogation, Mr Blundell.'

'Never a straight answer... Why can't you just say, "Those are my words, Mr Blundell." – as if I needed confirmation! Regardless, what took place between us and Ruth was a perfectly reasonable, sensitive and caring conversation. Now, we have more important matters to discuss. Emma.'

'Yes, Sarah, I'm afraid we do need to discuss Emma,' said Heather, butting in. 'You know the trouble we've been having. You've spoken to her, Matthew's spoken to her, but she's not listening. Matthew, show Sarah the video.'

Matthew reached down and picked up the laptop at his feet. He opened it and walked it over to Sarah. 'Watch this,' he said, clicking the play button and thrusting the laptop at her. Sarah took it and watched patiently as Emma launched her assault on Grace. 'Now do you believe us?'

'I'm not condoning it, but this seems to me to be the typical behaviour of an attention-seeking child, Mr Blundell,' said Sarah, handing the laptop back to him. 'It all started when you refused to include her in your holiday plans, which, if you recall, I warned you about.'

'Regardless of why you believe Emma is behaving this way, Ms Morton, the fact is that Emma has been, and continues to present, a very real threat to the safety of members of this family.' Matthew returned to the sofa.

'Sarah,' said Heather, 'this can't continue. Last week, Emma pushed Ruth down the stairs. If Matthew hadn't been there to catch her, then I dread to think what might have happened.'

'Quite the hero, Mr Blundell. Well done.'

'Hardly a time for humour, Ms Morton.'

'Something you always seem to find time for, Mr Blundell – not that your humour is to my taste.'

'Can we get back to the matter at hand, please!' Heather's voice quavered. 'Sarah, you have repeatedly brushed off the incidents we've reported to you. You've chosen to focus on the fact that we've not been present to witness these events; you've accused us of overreacting, questioned our competence, and given Emma the benefit of the doubt. You've wilfully ignored the warning signs. All you've ever done, in your own words, is "note our concerns" – although we've yet to see any evidence of that.' She took a deep breath before continuing. 'Yes, there's been an element of doubt; yes, there's been an element of kids will be kids, but you can't ignore this. We have video evidence, and Matthew witnessed Emma's attack on Ruth. Matthew and I have discussed it, and we don't feel that Emma can remain here. Clearly, she cannot be in a house with other children. We want her relocated.'

'Mrs Blundell. That's a last resort and has serious implications.'

'I realise that, Sarah, but I think we've reached that point.'

Matthew jumped in. 'Bugger the implications, Ms Morton! This is serious. I'm sure it can be handled delicately and with the necessary degree of compassion for those involved – but it has to be done, for everyone's sake!'

'Have you thought of the implications for yourselves, Mr Blundell?'

'You're stalling, Ms Morton. Emma has specific requirements that cannot be met within our family environment. She clearly demonstrates a capacity for violence that's a potential danger to other children, and that requires managing. The bottom line is that she needs relocating to a home where there are no other children and where the focus can be on giving her the attention she needs.'

'Are you suggesting you can't give her the attention she needs, Mr Blundell?'

'We give her all the attention we can, Ms Morton, but, as you well know, with four kids and without eyes in the back of our heads, we can't monitor her every second of the time she's with us – and we have young, vulnerable children to think of.'

'You do realise that she doesn't behave this way at school...'

'What has school got to do with anything?' said Heather. 'At school, she's with girls and boys of her own age, and she's hardly the biggest child in her year. Here, she bullies James and Grace because they can't fight back – though Grace has a bloody good go sometimes.'

Sarah took a deep breath. She looked at them and shook her head. 'Well, what else can I say? If you won't continue her care, then we have no alternative but to relocate her. I shudder to think what this is going to do to the confidence of an already emotionally afflicted young lady who, at ten years of age, has already had more of life's shit to deal with than many of us would care to encounter in a lifetime.'

'Is this your attempt at emotional blackmail, Ms Morton?'

'No, Mr Blundell. I'm just facing the reality.'

'As are we, Ms Morton. As are we...'

'And goodness only knows what her uncle will have to say about all this.'

'Fuck him!'

Sarah sighed. 'This might take a few days to arrange. It's likely that Emma will have to move to a temporary home while we find a long-term carer for her; though ideally, we'd like to avoid that – poor child.'

'Obviously, we're happy to keep Emma for as long as it takes to find the right home for her,' said Heather. 'We don't want to cause her any more suffering than necessary. But we're sure this will be better for everyone in the long run. It can't be much fun for her either, constantly arguing and battling with us and the other children. Maybe her own space and someone who can focus solely on her needs will be good for her.'

'Well,' said Sarah, 'your patience will be appreciated. You know how short of carers we are – especially ones who *can* cope with medical complications such as Emma's. Say nothing to Emma at this stage and I'll speak with Ann. I'm sure you'll do your best in the meantime.'

Heather also spoke with Ann that Wednesday, in the porch, when Ann returned Emma from her uncle's.

'I hope our request to relocate Emma hasn't caused you too many problems?'

Ann grimaced. 'Well, clearly, it's not ideal – both in terms of the difficulty of finding a suitable replacement but, more importantly, the impact this will undoubtedly have on Emma.'

'Who knows,' said Heather. 'Maybe, secretly, she'll be relieved.'

'Possibly.' Ann shrugged. 'But I can't help but worry that from her point of view, this is just another form of rejection. Once again, her life is being disrupted, and she will have to adjust. I dread to think of the psychological trauma that girl is experiencing.'

Heather looked down at the floor. 'We're painfully aware of that, Ann, and we'll no doubt carry that guilt for some time to come.' She looked up again. 'But we must look at the bigger picture. This can't continue.'

'Well,' said Ann, 'the decision is yours. I can't offer you any further advice. I appreciate that you've tried to cope with her in difficult circumstances, and any improvements have been short-lived. We'll just have to "bite the bullet", as they say.'

It took almost four weeks for a suitable home to be found for Emma. Ann felt it best to soften the blow. At first, Emma was told that two new carers were taking her on holiday for a week, as Matthew and Heather were unable to. As expected, after being spoilt rotten by a couple who gave all their attention to her, Emma seemed happy with the suggestion that she might like to remain with them. Matthew and Heather wished her well. Despite some serious ups and downs, Emma had been a part of the family for over seven months, and it was sad to see her go. And there was an element of guilt that they hadn't been able to give her enough of the love and attention she so clearly needed. She deserved to be happy – especially given her medical condition. Moreover, they were painfully aware of the sense of abandonment that so many children in care feel, and they felt that, in some way, they had failed her. Still, not every child's first placement met with success. Often, it took time to gauge a child's reaction to being in care. The responses of children torn from the familiarity of their home life were many and varied and just because a child presented in a certain way in a natural family environment, it didn't necessarily follow that they would show the same characteristics as part of a foster family. Emma had received precious little attention from her uncle, and now she craved it. She hadn't flourished in a larger family where she had to compete for it. Matthew and Heather took comfort in the fact that, hopefully, she would be happier now. Their pain was her gain; they could see that; surely Sarah could see that. Surely? However, at their March supervision meeting, a few days after Emma's departure, Sarah, strangely, had nothing to say on the matter. She appeared to have moved on, despite her opposition to the relocation, and focused routinely on James and Grace's progress. She still had no update on the council's plans for James's future and no supervision notes for signing off.

Two weeks later, Ruth also left, but under slightly happier circumstances. Her grandparents were assessed and found not to share their daughter's flaws, so Ruth moved in with them. She seemed happy. On the day she left, she thanked Matthew and Heather for looking after her and took the time to kiss James and Grace goodbye. It felt as if a storm had blown over. A noticeable calm returned to the household. The calm lingered for a few days and then came a rumble of thunder.

19

The Call

Thursday, 22nd March 2018

Matthew leant over and carefully strapped James and Grace into their car seats. They were both half asleep. He slid closed the rear door of the Caravelle, paused, took a deep breath and then manhandled the awkward double buggy into the boot, closing it gently. Heather had just popped into one last shop after an afternoon shopping marathon in Newport town centre. With spring on its way, the kids needed some new clothes and shoes for the warmer months ahead. Matthew slumped into the driver's seat, exhausted, and pulled the car door closed behind him. He looked in the rearview mirror. 'It won't be long now, kids, and then we can all go home for some dinner.'

There was no reply. He turned. James and Grace were both fast asleep. He glanced in his wing mirror at the view along the pavement to see if Heather was on her way back. She was nowhere in sight. Checking the pay and display ticket on the windscreen, he noticed their time was running out. He considered listening to some music, but he didn't want to wake the kids. He rarely got the chance to listen to the radio in the car – background noise, Heather called it. She preferred talking.

Matthew again glanced in the wing mirror and this time thought he saw Heather walking along the pavement towards them. As she materialised, he saw her answer her phone. She was listening intently. Clearly, from the expression developing on her face, she was troubled.

What's up with her? he thought as he monitored her progress. It was unlikely the caller was a family member – both her parents were dead, and she never spoke to her only brother. There was a good chance it was related to the children.

Heather reached the car and lingered a few minutes more, resting against the boot, still talking. The call ended abruptly. She opened the passenger door, got in and slammed it behind her. Matthew had caught the tone of the conversation from inside the car.

'Are you alright – you look flustered? Who was that?'

'Sarah bloody Morton, that's who! We've been summoned to a meeting at eleven o'clock on Tuesday next week.'

'Calm down. Who wants us to go where on Tuesday?'

'Sarah says her manager, Andrew Chilwell, has called a meeting and I quote: "Our attendance is required." She won't say what it's about.'

'Just the two of us, or with the children?'

'Just us. Apparently, they've arranged for the children to stay with Margaret for the morning. She's going to take James to his contact visit.'

Margaret was another foster carer, part of the group, or cronies as Matthew referred to them, that met once a month for coffee mornings, or afternoon tea in Newport, or an evening meal at a local restaurant. They would swap ideas about fostering and gossip generically about what their respective placements had been up to.

'I don't like the sound of that,' said Matthew. 'We've been able to take them with us in the past. We've never had to leave them with anyone else.'

'Something's not right. Why wouldn't she tell me what they want to speak to us about?'

'Well, maybe we shouldn't worry unnecessarily. It's probably just something routine.'

Heather shook her head. 'I'm not convinced. Sarah was so vague. Why would you invite someone to a meeting and not tell them what it's about if it wasn't something serious?'

'It does seem strange.'

Tuesday, 27th March 2018

They both woke early on Tuesday morning.

'Time to face the music,' said Matthew.

Heather lay on her back, staring at the ceiling, trying to muster the energy to drag herself out of bed. 'Can we fast forward twenty-four hours?' she said. 'I'm not sure I can go through with this.'

'We've got no choice,' said Matthew. 'Come on, up you get.'

'I'm worried about how James will handle being at Margaret's,' said Heather. 'He doesn't really know her – he might not cope very well.'

'You worry too much,' said Matthew. 'Come on, we'd better get the kids dressed and pack their bags for this morning. We don't want to be late if Margaret's got to get James to the contact centre by ten.'

'Sarah told me to put in some lunch and a change of clothes for them. I'll prepare the food; you sort out the clothes,' said Heather.

'Can't Margaret feed them?'

'Apparently not.'

Heather made a packed lunch for James and Grace and put it in their rucksacks, together with the change of clothes. When the kids were ready, they put on their coats and shoes.

'Now, you two, Matthew and I have to go and see Sarah and some people from work, so we're dropping you off at a friend's house until we've finished. We'll be back to pick you up after lunch,' said Heather.

James and Grace seemed oblivious.

No one spoke on the short journey to Margaret's house, which was in Blackwater, just south of Newport.

'This is it,' said Matthew, checking the satnav.

Matthew carried James to the front door of a white, pebble-dashed, semi-detached property, set well back from the road, while Grace toddled confidently, under her own steam, up the garden path. Heather followed, carrying their bags. Matthew rang the bell, and a familiar face answered the door.

'Hello,' said Margaret. 'Come in.'

Heather smiled. 'Hi Margaret, how are you?'

‘Fine, thanks, Heather. It’s very quiet here now that Harry’s been adopted. Still, it won’t be for long: he only left last Thursday, and they’ve already contacted me about my next placement. Apparently, they’re short of carers...’ Her voice trailed off, and she quickly showed them in. Heather placed the bags she was carrying in the hallway.

‘Margaret,’ she said, ‘we’ve been summoned to a meeting with Sarah Morton and Andrew Chilwell at County Hall this morning. They won’t tell us what it’s about. Did anyone mention to you why they’ve asked you to look after James and Grace?’

‘No, not really. I... I just had a phone call asking me if I’d be prepared to look after them for the morning. They said you’d drop them off around half nine with a packed lunch. I’m sorry, I really can’t tell you much more than that.’

Grace had already made her way into the lounge. Matthew put James down on the floor. James looked up at Margaret and began to cry. He crawled over to Heather and clasped her leg.

‘Don’t worry, little man,’ said Heather, picking him up. ‘We won’t be long.’ She gave him a hug and kissed him on the nose. Then she handed him to Margaret. James reached back towards Heather, crying.

‘Come on, James. Let’s see what toys we’ve got for you in the living room,’ said Margaret. ‘Do you like Thomas the Tank Engine?’ She mouthed to Heather, I’ll take it from here.

‘We’d better go then,’ said Heather, hustling Matthew towards the door. ‘We’ll see you later, Margaret. I don’t know how long we’ll be at County Hall, but we’ll pick these two up on the way home.’

Margaret closed the door behind them, and Matthew and Heather made their way down the path.

‘I get the feeling Margaret knows a little bit more than she’s letting on,’ said Matthew as he got back into the car.

‘I don’t know what to think,’ said Heather. ‘I’ve got a bad feeling about all this. I’ll be glad when it’s over.’

Ten minutes later, Matthew and Heather arrived at County Hall in Newport. The car park rarely had any empty spaces, so they’d been assigned a visitor parking bay. They found it over by the wall of the main building and parked up. Matthew checked his watch. As they were an hour early for the meeting, he suggested they wander down

High Street. About halfway down, they turned left into St James' Street and sat in Costa Coffee for half an hour before heading back to County Hall. There, they made their way to reception and announced themselves at the front desk.

'Take a seat; someone will be down shortly,' said the receptionist as she put down the phone receiver.

Five slow minutes passed until the lift on their right pinged. The doors opened and revealed a young lady in a tailored jacket and skirt. She moved in their direction.

'Here we go,' said Matthew, breathing deeply.

'Good morning,' said the young lady. 'I'm Deborah, Mr Chilwell's secretary. They're in meeting room two. I'll take you up.'

Matthew and Heather stepped into the lift. The doors closed, and the mechanism whirred into action. Matthew stared up at the ceiling and Heather at her shoes. No one spoke. The lift shuddered and came to a stop on the second floor. The doors opened, and Deborah ushered them out and towards a room across the corridor. She opened the door, smiled nervously and indicated they should enter. Matthew and Heather stepped inside, and Deborah closed the door behind them. Matthew felt Heather's hand reaching for his, and he gave it a reassuring squeeze. They stared defiantly ahead and took in their new surroundings. The room was small, claustrophobic. No window. Two vacant seats waited before them – ordinary office chairs, but with all the dark appeal of 'Old Sparky' greeting the condemned...

20

Aftermath

Sarah escorted them back down the corridor and into the lift. Matthew and Heather had lapsed into a numb incomprehension. Heather clutched Andrew Chilwell's letter detailing the impending investigation and advising them that James... She swallowed hard. She couldn't bear the thought. No one spoke until they reached the exit door to the car park. Sarah held it open.

'I'm sorry about all this,' she said. Her words lacked any sincerity. 'It must be extremely difficult for you both.' In fact, she looked to be relishing the moment. 'Try not to worry...'

'Try not to worry? You patronising bitch. Since when have you ever given a toss about our feelings?' said Matthew. 'You've manufactured all this bullshit...' Matthew stalled as Heather crumpled beside him and began sobbing.

'I suggest you look after Heather, Matthew. She seems very upset.' Sarah turned abruptly and retreated into the building.

'Come on,' said Matthew, supporting Heather, 'let's get back to the car.'

Heather held on to Matthew's arm as they walked. 'I refuse to believe we'll never see James or Grace again...' Her voice broke once more, strained with emotion. 'So much for our dream of making James a permanent part of our family.'

'I know, sweetheart, but I think we're going to have to get used to the idea that they're gone – at least for now,' said Matthew. 'The only hope we have of getting them back is if we fight this tooth and nail. And I promise you we will.'

'That conniving bitch,' said Heather, forcing back the tears. She suddenly felt nauseous and stopped, thinking she would throw up.

Matthew looked at her. 'Are you okay?'

Heather took a moment to compose herself. 'It's relocating Emma that's started all this. Sarah was pissed off – I know she was.'

'Well, she didn't seem too concerned at our last supervision meeting,' said Matthew. 'I got the impression she was over it. And don't forget, she agreed to the relocation – albeit reluctantly. I think she realised Emma had to be moved to somewhere she wouldn't pose a threat to other children. She knew if she didn't and someone ended up getting hurt, it would be more than her job's worth.'

'That's obviously what she wanted us to think,' said Heather as Matthew steered her across the car park. 'So far as she's concerned, we were just palming Emma off on someone else, making her someone else's problem. This is her way of getting back at us.'

'I agree, but I think there's more to it than that,' said Matthew. 'She's been gunning for us since Day One.'

They reached the Caravelle. Matthew unlocked it with the key fob and ushered Heather into the passenger seat. Then he rounded the front, opened the driver's door and slid in.

'What makes me mad,' he said, 'is that all the issues raised in that letter are either just a difference of opinion or twisted lies.'

'Well, Chilwell has obviously bought them,' said Heather, fumbling with her seatbelt.

Matthew turned the key and started the engine. 'I doubt that spineless amoeba has got the balls to stand up to her; he's just swallowed them whole to make his life easier. I mean the lies, not his...'

'I know full well what you meant, Matthew. This is no time for levity.'

Matthew lapsed into silence as he reversed the car out of the parking bay and drove towards the exit.

Heather sat, numb, staring out through the windscreen. 'When we get home, I'm going to review all the supervision notes and daily logs we have,' she said finally.

'I can't go back home yet,' said Matthew. 'Not to an empty house without James and Grace. It'll be far too quiet and depressing.'

'I'm going to find what evidence I can to refute their allegations. That's the only way we're going to get James and Grace back. And we're going to insist that Sarah produces the outstanding supervision notes. We need those. They're a record of what's been said.'

'They're Sarah's record of what's been said.'

'You really think she's twisted everything?'

'Why else do you think she's been holding off producing them? It all makes sense now. She's fed us a line. All the while she was fobbing us off, she'd already written them. She'll have fashioned them to suit her own purpose. All that bollocks about being too busy.'

'Even more reason to insist we get copies.'

'You heard Chilwell. No comments, no questions until the investigation meeting. He'll come along with some bullshit excuse.'

Matthew was driving slowly towards home. They reached Apse Heath. 'Shall we have a walk along the front?' he said, turning to Heather.

She nodded, and so Matthew continued straight ahead. When he reached the Sandown Road, he turned right and further on turned left into Hope Road. The view of the sea opened up as they reached the top of Hope Hill, which wound down steeply through a right-hand chicane before joining the Esplanade.

He parked up on the left, opposite the Pirates Cove crazy golf. They got out of the car, emerging into the weak, early-spring sunshine. There were a few people strolling along the promenade, which stretched into the distance against the backdrop of Luccombe and the cliffs jutting out into Sandown Bay. It would be Easter this coming weekend, and the number of tourists would swell. But for now, it was quiet and pleasantly warm for the time of year, though there was a slight chill on the breeze. Matthew held Heather's hand. She was still processing the meeting.

She looked up at him. 'If Emma's relocation isn't the only trigger for all this, then what's Sarah's motive for feeding Chilwell all that "incriminating evidence"?' Her eyes were bloodshot and glazed.

'I've no idea,' said Matthew, 'but if we can't prove it's all a crock of shit, we're finished as foster carers. We need to find some answers, and pretty sharpish.'

'I told you. I'm going to go through all the supervision notes and daily logs.' Matthew felt her grip on his hand tighten. 'We need to be prepared when Chilwell walks through our front door. And I intend to be.' She sounded positive, but her voice lacked conviction.

They continued to wander, with the sea and the sandy Shanklin beach to their left. To their right, they passed more crazy golf, the Summer Arcade and the Victorian Cliff Lift before entering a stretch of gift shops, hotels and cafes. It was just after midday, and Matthew realised they hadn't eaten.

'Do you want to stop for lunch?' he said to Heather. 'You only had a slice of toast for breakfast.'

'I'm not sure I can face eating anything.'

Matthew turned to face her. 'Me neither. I guess we're just wasting time here, then. We'd better bite the bullet and head home.'

They were nearing the end of the Esplanade and turned around just before the small flowerbed roundabout and the narrow road leading steeply up towards Shanklin Chine. They retraced their steps along the promenade back to the car; neither in any hurry to get there.

The lounge had all the life and soul of a mausoleum.

Matthew picked up the remote control from the arm of the sofa. 'I'm going to put the TV on; it's far too quiet in here. I don't know about you, but I think a bit of background noise might help.'

Heather walked towards the office. 'You can watch TV if you want, but I certainly can't afford to sit around here thinking and getting depressed. I'm going to start pulling out our records.'

'I wasn't actually planning on watching the TV...'

Heather looked back at him. 'Why don't you phone your mum and dad?' she said. Her voice was devoid of emotion. 'They'll be wanting to know what the meeting was all about. I'm surprised Barbara hasn't been on the phone already.'

Matthew pulled a face. 'I'm not sure I can face it right now. We've not been in long. Let's have a cup of tea and then I'll call them.'

'Well, I'm going to get started.' Heather disappeared into the office. 'We haven't done six years of fostering with an unblemished record just for those fuckers to stitch us up,' she shouted back at him. 'We need to start writing some responses to the points in that letter.'

'That's better,' said Matthew. 'Fighting talk. I like it.'

But Heather knew her resolve was a thin veneer, nothing more than an attempt at bravado. Her words felt hollow. A year of fighting had taken its toll, and losing James was a hammer blow that had floored her. She had hit the canvas, and she wasn't sure she had the strength to get back up. The spectres of Sarah Morton and Andrew Chilwell were looming over her, counting... She came out of the office with an armful of empty ring binders and dumped them on the sofa.

Matthew looked at her. 'Surely, you don't need that many? Just pick one – any colour you like.'

'I'll use the fiery red one – it matches my blood boiling over.'

Matthew paused. 'Before we start, Heather, I've been thinking about our finances. They've said our allowances will continue to be paid, but they'll decrease over time. This could drag on for months, and we'll end up with no income. I'm thinking I should try to find some other work. There are plenty of landscaping jobs about at this time of year. I've seen plenty of adverts in the paper. I used to enjoy landscaping as a lad.'

'Well, I guess that makes sense.' Heather walked back towards the office. 'Now, go and put the kettle on while I sort this lot out.'

When Matthew returned with two steaming mugs of tea and a packet of Hobnobs, Heather was on her knees, rummaging through some paperwork. 'I've been thinking,' she said without looking up, 'those missing supervision notes from October 2017 through to February this year...' She sat back on her haunches. 'If Sarah's still preparing them to suit her version of events, shouldn't we be demanding to see them now, before she can do any more damage?'

'She's already prepared her case,' said Matthew, putting down the tea and biscuits. 'Any "damage" has already been done. If I'm right and she's been stalling deliberately, then she's been planning this since at least October last year.'

'Planning? Why? Planning what?'

'I've no idea.' Matthew pushed aside the unwanted ring binders and sat down on the sofa. 'But if she's concocted a load of bullshit in those notes, then it's pointless us challenging her on what's been said or done since October. A few weeks after a supervision meeting, yes – but five months down the line?' He shook his head. 'She's been clever. Whose version of events is Chilwell going to believe – our recollections or notes made "at the time" by his own supervising social worker?'

'But what about our daily logs? She can't alter those.'

Matthew reached for his tea. 'If she's been planning this, do you really think we're going to see those logs again?'

Heather stared at the papers on the floor. 'Chilwell's visit is in two weeks,' she said. 'We need to see those notes now. We'll go up to the council offices and demand to see them. If they give us some bullshit, we'll threaten to go higher.'

Matthew looked dubious. 'I don't like our chances. They'll just close ranks. It's us and them now.'

'Well, we have to do something,' said Heather.

Matthew took a sip of his tea and put his mug down on a side table. 'Who needs supervision notes and daily logs, anyway? We know what happened and what was said. Whatever Morton says, we'll refute it. I suggest we do as Chilwell says and leave it all until the investigation meeting. She's already failed to deliver five months' worth of supervision notes – that's suspicious in itself, if not downright incompetent. If Chilwell fails to produce them, or that medicine bottle, we'll turn the screw on him too.'

21

The Cradle Rocks

Tuesday, 10th April 2018

'Good morning, Mr and Mrs Blundell.'

'Morning, Mr Chilwell. Come in and take a seat in the lounge.' Heather felt nauseous as she faked a smile. 'Can I get you a tea or a coffee?'

'Tea with milk, no sugar, thank you. And, please, call me Andrew.'

'I think Chilwell will be fine in the circumstances,' said Matthew.

Heather glared at him. 'I'll get the tea...'

Chilwell opted to sit in Sarah Morton's armchair in the far corner by the window, placing himself at a forty-five-degree angle to Matthew, who sat on the sofa. Though immaculately presented and the image of a professional in his grey wool suit, white shirt and pink tie, Andrew Chilwell was, for all his dressing, a comical-looking man: not much over five feet, portly and with a shiny crown, banded by a circlet of grey hair. His facial expression oozed pomposity: a firm-set mouth, and stern eyes peering over his half-moon glasses. However, curiously, he had one ear noticeably higher than the other, which detracted from the potency of his disdainful appraisal of those around him. Matthew was taken by the way Chilwell's half-moon glasses sloped across his face, running down from his lofty left protuberance, across his nose, to his lower, right ear.

Heather soon returned with three mugs, and Matthew stood and pulled two tables from the nest of three. He placed one next to

Chilwell's armchair and the other in front of the sofa for Heather to put them on.

'Thank you,' said Chilwell.

'Don't thank us,' said Matthew, 'it's laced with strychnine.'

Chilwell chose to ignore the comment.

If I had some, thought Matthew, I'd bloody well be tempted. Pompous prick. He placed himself at the end of the sofa closest to Chilwell.

Chilwell took a laptop from the briefcase he had brought with him. He propped it on his knees and opened it – it was already running. He cleared his throat. 'Before we start, may I confirm that you have decided against independent representation?' He looked from Matthew to Heather.

'Correct,' said Matthew.

'Okay, noted.' Chilwell cleared his throat again. 'So, the purpose of today's meeting, as you know, is to go through the issues raised in our letter, which I gave you the last time we met. They're set out chronologically, so we'll go through them in order. I'll elaborate on our concerns, answer any questions I can and make a note of your responses. Then, having spoken to you...'

'I remember once being told that you don't speak *to* someone, Chilwell,' said Matthew, 'you speak *with* them. If you speak *to* someone, it suggests you're lecturing them.'

'Having spoken *with* you,' continued Chilwell, his face flushing, 'and all the other parties involved, I'll then detail everything, including my own findings and recommendations, in a report to the panel. A copy of the report will be sent to you. The review panel sits on the last Monday of each month, so in order not to prolong your ordeal, I shall hurry this through as a matter of priority, and we'll aim for the panel meeting on the 30th of April. The sooner the matter is decided, the better. I'm sure you'll agree. We have quite a bit to get through – it's possible that I'll need to come back again next week to continue this investigation. So, if we can start at the top. Refusing to...'

'Before we start, Chilwell, we're still missing five months' worth of supervision notes. Where are they?' said Matthew.

'Ah, yes, the supervision notes.' Chilwell looked at Matthew over the top of his half-moon glasses. 'Sarah mentioned an issue with those. I thought she said she's now forwarded copies to you?'

'No, she certainly has not,' said Heather, with a hint of anger. Hairline cracks were already forming across the thin shell of her composed façade. 'Are you aware, Mr Chilwell, that she's deliberately been withholding our supervision notes and daily logs for the last five months? Why do you think that is? She's denied us our opportunity to review and query them, and who's going to believe us now if we challenge them after all this time? She's given us excuses about staff shortages, dealing with a record number of placements, her holidays, etc., etc., but given all the crap she's come out with now, it's clear she's been stalling and manipulating them to suit her own version of events. Lord knows what she's added or left out.'

'That sounds rather like an unfounded and unwise allegation to me,' said Chilwell. 'But I agree, certainly, you should have been provided with a copy of each month's supervision notes in a timely fashion, and your daily logs should have been returned, signed by Sarah. I have spoken with her.' He looked pointedly at Matthew and smirked. 'And though I do find the time elapsed excessive, I believe there are some mitigating factors. Sarah is one of our more experienced supervising social workers and, as such, often has responsibility for more carers than other SSWs in our employ. This has been exacerbated by the fact that a couple of SSWs have left in recent months, and we are struggling to replace them. I'm not making excuses, but Sarah has taken on a lot of the extra work. And she is not exaggerating when she says that we have been seeing an increased number of children coming into care. It's a very unfortunate situation, and finding suitable carers is not always easy. You know the poor thing had very little time off over Christmas and New Year.'

Matthew laughed derisively. 'That's all very well, Chilwell, but it's clear that you knew nothing about this until recently. Your "poor thing" has failed to escalate the fact that she was not coping with her workload, and you've clearly failed to appreciate and address the situation as her line manager.'

A flicker of embarrassment ruffled Chilwell's otherwise self-assured mien, but he remained calm. 'I think we can agree, Mr Blundell, that in the grand scheme of things and in the circumstances, the preparation of formal supervision notes was low on the list of priorities.'

'I *don't* agree, Chilwell,' said Matthew, 'perhaps an inconsequential formality in the grand scheme of things – until you find yourself in the situation we do now. Now, they have become of paramount importance, wouldn't you agree? Now, in the circumstances, your failure to produce the notes that my wife and I require for reference and to challenge where we feel there are discrepancies casts a shadow on Sarah Morton's and your competence.'

'I don't believe competence enters into it,' said Chilwell. 'As I've already said, from our perspective, they were low priority and managed accordingly. Sarah provided me with the notes when she submitted her recent report. I'll ensure you receive copies. I can only apologise for the delay, and I have explained the mitigating circumstances. Now, can we move on?'

'Maybe after you provide evidence of the old medicine bottle you claim we gave to the Floyds.'

'Chronologically, I said, Mr Blundell. We will deal with that issue at the appropriate time.' He looked Matthew in the eye. 'Now, can we move on?'

'We can, Chilwell, but you haven't heard the last of this, believe me.' Matthew watched as Chilwell picked up his mug and took a sip of his tea.

'Noted, Mr Blundell,' said Chilwell. He returned his mug to the table. 'Now, if we can discuss the first issue in the letter: "refusing to take a child to hospital after a violent incident and their having sustained an injury and failing to report this incident immediately to Ms Morton." What's your position on that?'

'Firstly, we didn't refuse to take James to hospital,' snapped Heather, before Matthew had a chance to formulate his own response. 'We chose not to.' She jabbed a finger at a note she had made in her red folder. 'Grace pushed him into the stair gate and – I quote from our daily log – "he sustained a slight bump on his forehead. We applied a cold flannel, and it went down quickly" – in fact, it almost disappeared. All that was left was a red mark, which we decided wasn't a significant enough "injury", as you refer to it, to waste time over in A&E.'

'But don't you consider that if a child under one has hit their head, and it's produced a lump, you should be having it checked?' Chilwell raised his eyebrows.

'We considered it,' said Matthew. 'We considered it a waste of time! How exactly do you think a triage nurse is going to treat a red mark? And as you well know, Chilwell, we've undertaken three days of intensive first-aid training and two days of paediatric first-aid training as part of qualifying to become foster carers – that's the equivalent of an NVQ. We know how to check for signs of concussion without putting further strain on the NHS's precious resources, *and* we have six years' experience with children and all their little mishaps.'

Chilwell shook his head. 'I don't believe taking a child to hospital after a head injury is a waste of time,' he said.

'You're overplaying the "head injury" part,' said Heather, staring coldly at him, her hands clenched. 'It wasn't exactly a seventy-mile-an-hour motorcycle collision; it was a knock against a stair gate.'

'I hear what you say, Mrs Blundell,' said Chilwell, 'but I think you'll find that policy and procedure dictates seeking medical advice after a child has had an accident.'

Something in Heather snapped. 'Have you read James and Grace's care plans, Mr Chilwell?' She was spitting blood now. 'We have, sorry, *had* delegated responsibility for day-to-day decision-making, including anything medical. Not that any of that matters now you've taken James from us. Stick that in your report!'

'And for your information, Chilwell, no one has ever shown us the accident policy and procedures you refer to. I'm not even sure they exist,' said Matthew. 'And as I seem to recall telling Ms Morton at the time, if you're referring to The Bruising Protocol, it's irrelevant because James was mobile.'

'Hmm... well, Mrs Blundell, let's say you're right about day-to-day responsibility. I think what we're calling into question here is your judgement in this matter.'

'Our judgement was sound, Chilwell,' said Matthew. 'That's evidenced by the fact that James is no doubt sitting somewhere, playing happily, without a care in the world – or a headache!'

'Okay, your comments are noted,' said Chilwell, noting nothing at all on his laptop. 'Let's move on, shall we?'

Matthew felt Heather slump back into the sofa. He turned to look at her. She seemed exhausted, and her eyes were closed. He rested a reassuring hand on her knee and looked back towards Chilwell.

Chilwell had produced an A4-sized envelope and was taking out the contents.

'I have here a blown-up photograph of the injury, taken from the image that you took on the day of the incident. It doesn't look like just a bump to me.' He held it out.

Matthew took the photograph from Chilwell and studied it. It showed a bump on James's forehead. It also showed a cut.

'That's not the photo I took,' said Matthew. He turned. Heather was still sitting back, her eyes closed. He prodded her. 'Does that look like the photo I took to you, Heather?'

Heather opened her eyes and looked for a moment. She shook her head, but she seemed detached from the conversation – her mind elsewhere.

'In which case, can you show me the original?' said Chilwell.

'I can't,' said Matthew, turning back to look at him. 'I deleted it.'

'Deleted it?'

'Ms Morton insisted. Something to do with GDPR, I guess – not keeping sensitive images on my phone.'

'Yes, of course, and she was right to do so...' Chilwell paused. 'Well,' he said, 'what you have there was produced by Sarah and submitted with her report. It's taken from the original image that you sent to her, which she has transferred to a memory stick and passed to me.'

Chilwell retrieved a memory stick from his briefcase and inserted it into a USB slot on the side of his laptop. He brought the picture up on his screen and crossed the room to show it to Matthew. The bump and cut in the two pictures matched exactly.

'I'll have a copy of that, if I may,' said Matthew.

'Well, as we've already established,' said Chilwell, 'that would be inappropriate.'

He took the blown-up photograph from Matthew and returned to his armchair. He removed the memory stick from his laptop and placed it, together with the photograph and the envelope, on the arm of his chair.

'You want my opinion, Chilwell?' said Matthew, leaning forward and pointing. 'That's been altered. I don't know why she's done it or how she's done it, but that's been altered. She's manipulated the evidence.'

'Just for the record,' said Chilwell, 'I presume by "she" you are referring to Sarah Morton?'

'Too bloody right, I am.'

Chilwell removed his glasses and rubbed his eyes. 'I have to say, Mr Blundell, I find your accusations unfounded, highly unlikely and, quite frankly, insulting. I do not believe for one minute that Sarah would have any reason to manipulate a photograph. Your comments are noted, but I'd think twice before you go throwing around any more wild accusations – I don't think they'll sit well with the panel.' He replaced his glasses.

Matthew flopped back in the sofa beside Heather. 'I'll say it as I see it, Chilwell. Panel be damned.' He folded his arms.

'Right, well, if you've finished, we'll move on to issue number two: "not seeking medical advice for a trauma sustained in a further violent incident and failing to phone the Out of Hours Service to report this incident." What's your view on this one?'

'Trauma, my arse!' said Matthew. 'James was knocked over by a bloody baby walker. There was nothing to notify Out of Hours about. No mark, no lump, no blood. We have a clear case of exaggeration here. We noted the event in his log, just to highlight Grace's violent behaviour. There was no injury, nothing else to record, so we got on with our job.'

Matthew sat up and turned to Heather. 'Do you have the relevant page there, my love?' Heather stirred and absent-mindedly flicked through the pages in her red folder. She unclipped the rings and handed Matthew a copy of a page from their daily log. He passed it to Chilwell. 'There – no mention of any injury.'

'Quite. No injury, you say?' said Chilwell, taking the page that Matthew offered him. 'And on this occasion, no photograph was taken; is that correct?'

'On this occasion, we had nothing to take a photograph of,' said Matthew.

Chilwell gauged Matthew's defiant stare. 'Sarah seems to think you are hiding something.'

'Well, she would, wouldn't she...'

'Now who's making wild accusations?' Heather's voice trembled, and she fell silent again.

Chilwell took a deep breath. 'What I am suggesting, Mrs Blundell – and what I'll be noting in my report – is that given your previous decision not to refer James to a medical practitioner and having had that judgement questioned by Sarah, it is not unreasonable to suggest that on a subsequent occasion you might have made the same decision and conveniently "overlooked" a similar injury to avoid further repercussions.'

'Well, as my wife has just said, Chilwell, now who's making wild accusations?' Matthew jabbed a finger. 'And you can be sure I'll be noting that in *my* report.'

'Well, maybe a photograph to prove that there was no injury on this occasion might have been a good idea, given previous events...' Chilwell looked pointedly at Matthew.

'Maybe it would, maybe it wouldn't,' said Matthew, holding Chilwell's stare. 'You have no proof of anything. It's our word against your speculation. There's no impartiality here, Chilwell. It's clear you've already made your mind up and conveniently taken Morton's side; you're just building your so-called case against us, brick by brick.'

Chilwell looked away. 'Well, in my view, Mr Blundell, the circumstances are suspicious. I draw your attention to the fact that you, Mrs Blundell, recorded that, having been knocked over by the baby walker, James collided with a game on the floor. The two incidents are almost identical, and yet one resulted in a head injury, as we've seen in the photograph here...' Chilwell indicated the A4-sized photograph on the arm of his chair, 'and the other resulted in no injury whatsoever. I find that hard to believe – there must have been some kind of injury, minor or otherwise, and the fact you have chosen to deny the obvious suggests deceit and brings into question your trustworthiness. I'm sorry, but I'm going to have to record that as my considered opinion on the matter.'

Matthew scoffed. 'You do that, Chilwell, you do that – it's just another brick in the wall.'

Chilwell paused to make notes. 'I'll just be a few minutes,' he said. 'It might be a good time for a comfort break – or another cup of tea?' He looked hopefully past Matthew at Heather, who turned her head away.

'Yes, I think I could do with a comfort break,' said Matthew, pushing himself up out of his seat on the sofa. 'Given that you're going out of your way to make me feel so *un*comfortable.'

He crossed the room to retrieve Chilwell's mug and brushed past the armchair, knocking the precariously placed evidence of James's head wound into the gap between the arm of the chair and the seat cushion.

'My apologies! Let me get that for you.' Matthew reached down and replaced the photograph and envelope on the arm of the chair.

'Oh, thank you,' said Chilwell, with a sideways glance. He looked back and continued tapping away on his laptop.

A few minutes later, Chilwell looked up as Matthew's return to the room broke the uncomfortable silence. If he registered that Matthew had returned empty-handed, he didn't betray his disappointment at being denied a fresh mug of tea. 'Ah, good timing,' was all he said. 'Shall we get on?'

'Mr Chilwell, before we carry on...' Heather paused as Matthew sat down next to her, nervously playing with her hands, mustering the composure to speak. The conversation so far had evoked overwhelming memories of James, and she had withdrawn – allowing herself to become a silent witness to the war of words between Chilwell and her husband, who was rapidly turning the meeting into a slanging match. She breathed in deeply. 'I know you side with Sarah when you say that we've fallen short of what you expect of us as foster carers, but please, we've tried to explain it from our point of view. We loved James and cared for him. Are you not even prepared to consider the fact that Sarah might be trying to undermine us?'

Chilwell sighed. 'I'm purely looking at the evidence, Mrs Blundell, and weighing up the balance of probability where there is doubt. I have to say, from all that I've seen and heard during my investigation, I can fully understand Sarah's misgivings. I don't think she's undermining you at all. I believe she's raised some legitimate concerns.'

'But she's been on our backs since Day One,' said Heather. 'She never even gave us a chance. We never had a single complaint when we fostered children in Kent.' Her voice wavered as the last fragments of her composure threatened to disintegrate.

Chilwell shook his head. 'I don't believe for one second that Sarah hasn't got your best interests at heart. Perhaps it's a case of we do things differently over here.'

Heather's hands trembled. 'I know we were expected to document any incidents,' she said, 'but no one said that every time a child had a mishap, we were to call Sarah or Out of Hours.'

'But didn't it occur to you, Mrs Blundell, that it might be a good idea to let someone know when these things happen? Sarah is there to support you.'

Matthew moved closer to his wife's side. 'And what the bloody hell use is she going to be when we've already got everything in hand?' he said. 'Can't you see what this is doing to my wife?'

Chilwell's voice hardened. 'Mrs Blundell's discomfort is a very unfortunate consequence of these proceedings,' he said, 'but I can't let it distract me from performing my duty.'

'Performing your duty?' Matthew snorted. 'Can you hear yourself, you pompous... Why are you so keen on defending Morton anyway? Anyone would think you two were...' He paused with a gleam in his eye. 'Maybe you are...'

Chilwell spluttered. 'That's enough, Mr Blundell! This may be your home, but how dare you speak to me in that manner. I won't tolerate it! If it weren't for the fact that this process must be brought to a swift conclusion, I would leave now. I've warned you before that you are doing yourself no favours by behaving this way. I shall note your outburst in my report; of that you can be sure. Now, let's move on swiftly. It's our belief that you have had a negative opinion of some of the children in your care.'

Heather feared Matthew might fire back a volley of abuse. 'Who exactly are we supposed to have had a negative opinion of?' she asked wearily.

'Your interpretation of Grace's behaviour is frequently negative when you speak of the trouble she's caused, as documented in your daily logs,' said Chilwell. 'More recently, your negative opinion of Emma led you to ask for her to be removed from your care. But we'll discuss Emma's situation in more detail later.'

'Mr Chilwell...' Heather faltered. She took a deep breath, and Matthew once again put a reassuring hand on her knee. 'We are asked to document everything a child gets up to on a daily basis, which includes behavioural traits, good and bad. I can't see how recording Grace and Emma's disruptive actions can be seen as having a negative opinion.'

'Maybe not – it depends how it's written.'

'It also depends how it's interpreted,' snapped Matthew.

'Mr Chilwell,' said Heather. She pointed to the red folder on her lap. 'I've got months' worth of daily logs in here, and most are very positive about the children.'

'Since you've brought up the subject of disruptive behaviour,' said Chilwell, ignoring her, 'it's been noted that it was a persistent issue throughout Grace and Emma's time with you. It occurs to me that with all the training and experience you often refer to, you should have been able to cope with more challenging children, such as those with Grace and Emma's history, and put a stop to it.'

'How would you have any idea what caring for Grace and Emma was like on a daily basis, Chilwell?' Matthew struggled to keep his voice low. 'You never spent one minute with them in this house. Grace was a toddler you couldn't reason with, and Emma was just like her uncle – a loose cannon.'

Chilwell steepled his hands and smiled. 'It seems to me, Mr Blundell, that you are intent on being the architect of your own demise. The panel will laugh you out of the room. Comparing a ten-year-old girl to a violent man; a man not afraid to use his fists and with a criminal record.'

'All I'm saying is, like uncle, like niece – there's nothing derogatory in that.'

'Nothing derogatory in that, Mr Blundell?' Chilwell laughed. 'If loose cannon's not a slur on the character of a vulnerable child, constituting a negative opinion, I don't know what is.'

'What Matthew is trying to say is that Emma exhibited the same violent behavioural traits as her uncle.' Heather's eyes were filling with tears. 'It's not uncommon for such behaviour to run in families. But I think you know that, Mr Chilwell.' Heather buried her head in her hands.

Chilwell turned his attention to his laptop. 'As much as I should very much like to applaud the psychological insights of your husband, Mrs

Blundell, I have reason to doubt his ability to interpret the behaviour of children. I have here a note of something that Sarah has recorded in her supervision notes for December 2017. Apparently, you, Mr Blundell, referred to Grace, and I quote, as "the Antichrist". Do you think that's appropriate?'

'It might have been something I said in jest,' said Matthew, wondering how on earth Sarah would have got to hear about his "Antichrist" references. Had he inadvertently joked about it in front of her? Surely Grace hadn't repeated the word. It had to be something that Emma had overheard and repeated. Shit! Sarah and Ann had spoken with Emma in December... 'Anyway,' he continued, 'Sarah never raised the issue with us, so why would it be in her supervision notes? Notes, may I remind you, that never materialised and that we never formally signed off.'

'Regardless, if it's in her supervision notes, then I'm sure it would have been discussed, Mr Blundell. These defamatory remarks you made about Grace. Do you deny them?'

'I've told you – anything I've said was said in jest and certainly not in front of the children.'

'Well, in this reported case, it most certainly was...' Chilwell paused to type some notes, while Matthew cursed inwardly. 'Do you have anything else you want to add?'

'Well, I guess it's pointless trying to discuss humour with you, Chilwell. Do you seriously believe I think Grace is the Antichrist? Is there any evidence that I've treated her any differently from the other children? No, I think we've said all we have to say on that one. So far as our daily logs are concerned, we've recorded factual information on the behaviour of two children in our care. Anything else reported to you has either been fabricated or taken out of context and twisted to suit a pack of lies – but we can't comment on that, because you and your vindictive minion have failed to provide us with a record of what's been said over the last five months.' Matthew pointed at Chilwell. 'Morton's allegations are clearly flawed, and you don't appear to have the competence or the courage to challenge their veracity. Does she have some kind of hold over you? Are you spineless? *You* may think the panel's verdict is a foregone conclusion – if it is, it'll be down to your pitiful attempt at an impartial investigation of the facts.'

Chilwell snapped his laptop shut. 'I think this would be a good point to finish today,' he said firmly. Tight-lipped, he returned his various papers and his laptop to his briefcase and closed it. He composed himself before turning to look at them. 'Emotions are clearly running high again,' he said. 'We'll end this meeting before you add to the many things you're already going to regret you've said, Mr Blundell. If the facts don't speak for themselves, I think the panel will arrive at the correct conclusion based on your attitude alone. Let's all reflect on this morning and meet at the same time next week to clear up the remainder of the issues.'

'No problem,' said Matthew. 'See you next Tuesday.'

22

Photo Shop

Wednesday, 11th April 2018

Matthew pulled on his coat and put his head around the lounge door. 'I've copied the photo of James from Chilwell's memory stick onto one of ours.'

'Are you sure we'll be able to use it as evidence if they accuse us of stealing it from him?' Heather was curled up on the sofa with her head buried in a large cushion. She hadn't slept well and was tiring as the day wore on.

'I told you, we didn't steal it,' said Matthew. 'Chilwell left it here – well, with a little help from me and the armchair. Anyway, if they ask, I'll just tell them we got it from an "internal source" who wishes to remain anonymous.'

Heather smiled weakly. 'Have you decided what to do with it?'

'I'm taking it to that camera shop in Newport – the one where I got the printer. They do all sorts of digital imaging and restoration work. I'm sure they'll have someone who can take a look at it. What time are you leaving to go to the doctor's?'

'In about fifteen minutes. My appointment's at two.'

'Are you okay to walk? You don't want me to drop you off?'

'No, you go. The walk will do me good.'

'Now, be honest with them, Heather. Tell them how you're feeling.

I don't like seeing you like this. Maybe they'll give you something to help you sleep.'

Heather struggled into a sitting position. 'Don't worry, love, I will,' she said. She looked and sounded weary. 'Now you get going and I'll see you later.'

The camera shop nestled between a convenience store and a Chinese takeaway. A metal sign standing on the pavement outside the shop advertised a digital imaging service, which sounded promising. Inside, the shelves were loaded with a mind-boggling array of photographic equipment: cameras, lenses, tripods, flash soft boxes, umbrellas, carry bags... Matthew was distracted when he saw, on sale at half price, the same photo printer he'd bought only late last year. Bloody typical! Movement alerted him to the approach of someone from his left-hand side. He had no problem identifying the shop assistant, a young lad who had adopted the unusual practice of attaching his name badge to the knot of his tie.

'Is sir interested in that printer? It's the last one.'

'Er, not now, John, thank you.'

''Ow can I 'elp you then, sir?'

'Well,' said Matthew. 'An unusual request, maybe. I'm wondering if you've got someone here who can take a look at this for me.' He produced the memory stick from his pocket. 'I want to know if the photo on it has been Photoshopped.'

John looked and smelt like he knew more about public houses than cameras. Matthew tried hard not to stereotype or let the stink of booze and cigarettes put him off. He handed the memory stick over to John, who took it between two fingers and attempted to focus on it. 'Er, I dunno. I'll check with the boss man.' He turned, walked a few paces and disappeared through a small curtain in the doorway behind the counter. A few moments passed before he returned, swatting at the curtain, which got caught up around him.

'He says we can do it, but we'll 'ave to send it to 'ead office. They got the expertise up there.' He winked at Matthew. 'We don't know nuffin 'ere.' He seemed to appreciate his own peculiar brand of humour.

Matthew smiled patiently. 'And how long does the, er, boss man think it will take?'

'Well, he says 'ead office 'ave got a bit of a backlog at the moment, so it'll be anything up to two weeks.'

Matthew did a bit of mental arithmetic. Two weeks still left him a few days before the panel review on the 30th of April – enough time to prepare the evidence for the meeting.

'Yep, that's fine. If they can do it as soon as possible, I'll be grateful.' He winked at John. 'And maybe there'll be a pint in it for you...'

John grinned. 'Okay, sir. Well, we'll let you know when it's back.'

'There's one other thing,' said Matthew. 'The photograph on there is of a very sensitive nature. Under no circumstances should it be copied from the memory stick, and definitely don't attach it to an email. If you can arrange for it to be sent to your head office, signed for, with clear instructions that it's only to be shared with the person analysing it, I'd be grateful. It's nothing illegal, but it is sensitive, so I'd appreciate your discretion.'

'No problem,' said John. He looked slightly puzzled when Matthew didn't move to leave. 'Is there anything else I can 'elp you with, sir?'

'Would you like to take my name and number, John, so you can call me when it's ready?'

23

The Cradle Falls

Tuesday, 17th April 2018

Chilwell was again seated in the armchair. No tea. No biscuits.

'First things first,' he said. 'As promised, here are the supervision notes you're missing. October 2017 to February 2018, I believe. Now, I have spoken to – yes, Mr Blundell, *to* – Sarah, and she has apologised for the delay and any inconvenience caused.'

'Delay, my arse! More like deliberate procrastination!' said Matthew, taking the sheaf of paper that Chilwell handed him. 'And what about our daily logs?'

'Mr Blundell. I hope we're not going to have a repeat of our last unfortunate meeting?'

'It depends on what you have to say.'

'The daily logs, I'm afraid to say, have been lost.' Chilwell continued hurriedly to deflect the storm of protest he knew was imminent. 'Now I know what you're about to say, Mr Blundell, and I suggest you cast no more of your aspersions and wild accusations in Sarah's direction. These things happen. Apparently, the team secretary shredded them in error. Obviously, as they are handwritten documents, I realise they are irreplaceable; but Sarah assures me that all the salient points have been recorded in her supervision notes.'

'Un-bloody-believable, Chilwell. And you bought that?'

'I spoke with the secretary as part of my investigation, Mr Blundell. She was understandably upset and most apologetic. She doesn't understand how the mix-up occurred, but having discussed the matter with Sarah, she's accepted responsibility. Somehow, the two of them got their wires crossed.'

'What did I tell you?' said Matthew, turning to look at Heather.

Heather was pale and withdrawn. 'It means we can't challenge anything that appears in Sarah's supervision notes,' she said, almost to herself. Her voice was laboured. 'It's too late for that now. She can say what she likes, and we have none of our notes to back up our version of events.'

'It's a most unfortunate situation,' said Chilwell, 'and one for which Sarah will receive a reprimand.'

'What good's a bloody slap on the wrist?' said Matthew. 'The damage is done!'

Chilwell looked down at his knees and remained silent.

'Well, now that you've brushed another worrying example of Ms Morton's incompetence under the carpet, Chilwell,' said Matthew, 'what can we expect next in this farcical charade of yours?'

Chilwell looked up. 'We need to move on, Mr Blundell. Let's discuss the next issue detailed in my letter: "Allowing a child access to adult games rated 18+ on their tablet". This relates to Emma. While under your supervision, she was playing a game...' Chilwell looked at his notes. '... "Grand Theft Auto", I believe, which is rated eighteen and over.'

'We do not have eyes in the back of our heads, Mr Chilwell,' said Heather. She looked across at him with a glazed stare. 'We cannot possibly monitor the children in our care every minute of every day.' She fell silent.

Matthew took her hand and looked across at Chilwell. 'Look, Chilwell. This was the first time that Emma had visited her uncle, and we were unaware that he had a tablet, let alone that he'd downloaded an adult game and let her play it. We certainly didn't know that he'd allowed her to take the tablet away with her that day. As for her playing it after she got home, when I realised what she was doing, I confiscated the tablet immediately.'

'I don't think it's unreasonable to suggest that you should have made it your business to know what Emma brought back from her uncle's and, knowing she'd brought home the tablet, that you should have supervised her while using it.'

'Okay, so perhaps we should have patted her down and run her rucksack through the x-ray machine in our hallway, but I'm sorry, we didn't. I don't think such a thing would occur to the average parent every time their child walks through the front door.'

'This is not your child, Mr Blundell; this is a foster child.'

'Any child,' said Matthew.

'So, having got past security, how was she afforded the opportunity to be playing with it unsupervised?'

Matthew sighed. 'I was out when Emma got home, and Heather was busy in the kitchen. Not for one minute did either of us suspect that while our backs were turned, she would be playing adult games on her uncle's tablet.'

'I appreciate that monitoring what children play and watch is not easy, but with Emma's family history, I feel you should have been more vigilant. And, as you alluded to at our last meeting, her uncle is not exactly the greatest role model an impressionable young girl could have,' said Chilwell.

'Okay, well, as usual, I disagree with you, but having taken our rap on the knuckles, I would appreciate it if we could move on to an issue that I find more concerning,' said Matthew. 'Emma's fluoxetine.'

'Of course,' said Chilwell. 'The sooner this is over and done, the better. So, Emma was on her respite week, and her carers, the Floyds, discovered that the medication you had supplied was an old bottle, the contents of which were insufficient to last her for the week. A rather unprofessional and embarrassing oversight, don't you think?'

'Mr Chilwell,' said Heather. She breathed in deeply and slowly exhaled. 'I picked up Emma's new medication from the pharmacy on the 4th of September, and I threw away the old bottles of naproxen and fluoxetine. When she went on her respite, I checked everything, and the medication was fine.'

Matthew butted in. 'We understand that you've mislaid the evidence anyway, Chilwell. Rather unprofessional and embarrassing, wouldn't you say? If you can't produce it, then who's to say the bottle was an old one?'

Chilwell looked puzzled. 'Who told you I'd mislaid it?'

'Morton, of course,' said Matthew. 'In our November 2017 meeting, when we reviewed the events of October. She said she'd given it to you and you'd lost it. But of course, we've only been given the October 2017 notes today.'

'Well, I don't recall reading about any such conversation,' said Chilwell.

'I'm not surprised,' said Matthew. 'When we signed off September's notes, she hadn't deemed it necessary to mention that she'd escalated the matter to you, so I doubt she's recorded her claim that you subsequently mislaid it in her notes for October.'

Chilwell retrieved his briefcase from the side of his armchair and reached into it. He produced a small, dark amber glass bottle. 'Regardless, Sarah was the last person to have this, but she passed it on to me to bring today. I've checked the issue date myself, and she's quite correct: it was an old bottle of fluoxetine dispensed on the 9th of August, not the bottle you say you collected from the pharmacy on the 4th of September. The Floyds used the last of it, so the bottle is empty. They say there were only three doses left in it – clearly not enough to last the week.'

'Can I see that, Chilwell?'

Chilwell passed the bottle to Matthew.

Matthew looked at the label carefully, then passed it to Heather. Heather looked at it, shook her head and passed it back to him.

'Satisfied, Mr Blundell? Now, do you have anything further you would like me to record on this matter? For me, it's a cut-and-dried case.'

'I think my wife has stated quite clearly that we checked the bottle we gave to the Floyds, and it was the one that we were using, collected on the 4th of September. I don't know where this bottle's come from, but it's not the bottle we would have given the Floyds. I can't prove anything at this stage, but don't think you've heard the last about this one.'

'Well, as I said, Mr and Mrs Blundell, I think from our perspective it's quite a clear-cut case. This is the bottle that the Floyds handed to Sarah Morton, and, clearly, it's an old bottle, which contained an insufficient amount of fluoxetine to last Emma the week. I don't see what other conclusion I can draw.'

'Another brick, Mr Chilwell, another brick...'

'Okay then. That brings us to the inappropriate questioning of a child in your care who had sustained injuries at her mother's hands. Mrs Blundell, I believe you were mostly responsible for questioning the child, Ruth.' Whether or not it was true, Chilwell did not feel inclined to involve Matthew any more than he had to. 'Do you feel up to giving me your version of events?'

Heather nodded. 'Ruth was sitting at the dinner table complaining that her arm hurt. The first thing I did was ask her what was causing the pain. You'd do that with any child, whether it was your own or a foster child.' Heather paused and gathered herself. She took a deep breath. 'When she told us her mum had burnt her with a cigarette, I felt I needed to check her over before I could decide on the appropriate course of action.'

Matthew jumped in. 'It was Ruth who then volunteered the information about her mother's drinking and anger management issues and not wanting to return home. Of course we asked the odd question. What were we supposed to do? Show no interest? Ignore her?'

'Ah, yes. I understand you told Ruth that she could go and live with her grandparents?'

'We certainly did not! Listen, Chilwell: it doesn't take a genius to work out who reported this, and – I'll choose my words carefully – it doesn't surprise me that the recollections of a certain ten-year-old girl got a little "muddled". In fact, it's clear from this farce of an investigation that certain so-called professional adults also suffer with selective memory!'

'Mrs Blundell,' said Chilwell, pointedly ignoring Matthew. 'Need I remind you that many of the reasons these children come into care are sensitive. Ruth's mother is an alcoholic, which is something you should not be discussing in front of her. It's something for her social worker to deal with. It's as it says in our letter: inappropriate questioning.'

'Rubbish!' said Matthew. 'But once again, our judgement counts for nothing.'

'Mr Blundell, before you start ranting and raving again, I'll give you one last warning: you may think you're skating nicely around what are serious allegations, but you're on thin ice, so I suggest you think before you speak.'

'Not as thin as the thin ice you're on, Chilwell.'

Heather continued, ignoring them both. 'Mr Chilwell. You're telling me that I have a child in pain and even though it's my responsibility to discover why and deal with it, I'm not allowed to listen to or comment on her explanation because it's a sensitive subject?' Heather's hands were shaking. 'How the hell am I going to care for someone if I can't speak with them?' Heather sank back into the sofa and covered her face with her hands. She seemed to be sobbing.

'Are you alright, Mrs Blundell?' said Chilwell.

Matthew couldn't tell if Chilwell's concern was genuine or faked.

Heather removed her hands and looked up at the ceiling.

Matthew stood. 'Heather, do you need to go and lie down?'

'I'm alright; I just need a glass of water,' said Heather.

Chilwell sat silent. Matthew hurried to the kitchen and returned with a glass of water, which he handed to Heather. Then he retook his seat on the sofa next to her.

'Chilwell. I shall say this calmly and plainly. My wife has been under a lot of stress over the last few weeks, as you can imagine. We've been carers for many years, and we certainly never expected to be in this situation. She's not coping with these visits very well. In fact, she's been to the doctor, and he's prescribed some strong sedatives.'

'I'm sorry to hear that,' said Chilwell. 'How are you feeling now, Mrs Blundell?'

'Numb.'

'Well, there's only one matter left to discuss. Are you okay if we continue? I think, for all our sakes, we should try to remain calm and civilised.'

'Let's just get on with it, shall we, Chilwell?' said Matthew, slumping back in the sofa.

'Okay.' Chilwell paused, preparing himself for what he was about to say. 'So, the final issue we've raised is this whole business around the relocation of Emma. And I'd appreciate it if you'd hear me out with no interruptions.' He paused again before continuing. 'We've documented several instances where we believe you have demonstrated – how can I put this sensitively – an "inability" to cope with what you have claimed to be unruly and violent behaviour by Emma. Now, I'm not suggesting the child was a saint – no doubt some of her behaviour was a little "rebellious" – but whatever mischief occurred was certainly triggered by your decision not to include her on a family holiday: something Sarah warned you about. Did you think about how Emma would react to that? No, Mr Blundell, hear me out... Here we have a young child already painfully aware of her limitations; a child who sees her friends leading a "normal" life that she knows she'll never have. She has never experienced a mother's love; her uncle neglects her, and so what life she has is taken from her and she is placed in care. If you ask me, the one thing that child feels more than anything is rejection. Your decision not to include her on the family holiday would have exacerbated that. And then, when the inevitable happens and your relationship deteriorates, you repeatedly sought to paint her in a negative light. You exaggerated certain events, shifted the blame onto her, and denied your own negligence and culpability.' Chilwell seemed to be enjoying his coup de grâce. 'You admitted yourselves, on more than one occasion, that you couldn't cope with her, and you sought to make the problem somebody else's.'

'That's enough!' Matthew's voice cracked, and he rose like an angered grizzly bear from the sofa. Heather grabbed his sleeve roughly and pulled him back down. 'You've gone too far this time, Chilwell! How dare you question our integrity! How dare you suggest we couldn't cope! Everything you say about Emma is true, and no one can be more painfully aware of her misfortune than us – we lived with her. But you should know that we shared our reservations with Ann and Sarah at the start, given Emma's age and medical condition.'

'There you go shifting the blame again, Mr Blundell.'

'You listen to me, Chilwell!' Matthew rose again, and again, Heather pulled him back. 'We had two young children to care for. It was never going to be possible to give Emma our undivided attention. And as for the holiday... For a start, Emma was at school, and the fact was, like it or not, that her needs were very different from James and Grace's, and we couldn't cater for everyone. I'd have expected you to understand that and support us in managing the situation. Yes, Sarah arranged for her to stay with the Floyds, but I doubt she or Ann counselled Emma in any way.' Matthew took a deep breath and steadied himself. 'You said that we admitted we couldn't cope with her behaviour. That's a lie, Chilwell. If that's what Sarah has recorded, then, so far as I'm concerned, it's just further proof that she's held the supervision notes back in order to manipulate them. There is no way we would've signed any supervision notes that said that. Emma's behaviour was challenging, for sure, and we dealt with it as best we could in the circumstances. Yes, we sought Sarah's support – as you've reminded us before, that's what she's there for. But the painful truth is that Emma needed care tailored to her particular circumstances – those circumstances you so eloquently described a moment ago. She wasn't going to get that as part of a large family – that much became obvious. Given your acute insight into the needs of disadvantaged children such as Emma, Chilwell, perhaps that should have been obvious to you from the start?'

'Mr Blundell. All I'm hearing is more evidence that you are denying any culpability for what happened. In your meeting with Sarah on the 5th of February this year, you said, and I quote: "Emma has particular requirements that we are not equipped to deal with. She clearly demonstrates a capacity for violence that's a potential danger to other children, and we cannot cope with her behaviour."'

'That is not what Matthew said, Mr Chilwell,' said Heather.

'Then what did Mr Blundell say, Mrs Blundell?'

'I don't recall his exact words, but his meaning was that it had become obvious that Emma did not fit into a family environment and, therefore, we were not able to cater for her needs. Sarah has twisted his words.'

'I'm afraid that your repeated accusation that Sarah has altered the notes she made at your meetings just doesn't wash with me, Mrs Blundell. What possible reason does Sarah have to do that? She is wholly and, I might say, passionately focused on the welfare of the children in our care, and if she feels that this is being compromised, she will act accordingly. No, I'm afraid it's as Sarah has detailed in her report to me. You avoided taking Emma on holiday with you because you could not cope with her being there. You then demonstrated repeatedly that you could not cope with the alleged incidents that occurred, resulting in Sarah and Ann being called in to deal with the situation. But by then it was too late; the damage had been done, and having continued to struggle with her behaviour, you requested Emma's relocation. This inability to cope is a common theme, wouldn't you say?'

Heather looked stunned.

Matthew fumed.

'And I'm afraid to say,' continued Chilwell, 'it's the straw that's broken the camel's back. We have already covered the prior incidents Sarah has raised. Not only do they call into question your judgement, but equally, I believe, they demonstrate you are unable to cope with the demands of caring for foster children. I feel sure that the panel will reach the same conclusion. Is there anything else you wish to say?'

Matthew cracked. 'Look, we've tried to reason with you, Chilwell. We've implored you to use common sense. You bang on about our judgement being questionable, but the fact remains: we had day-to-day responsibility for all the children in question, and we had the authority to decide what was in their best interests. So far as I know, no harm has come to any child in our care, and all your accusations are therefore irrelevant and serve no purpose other than to irritate us and embarrass yourself. You haven't heard the last of this, and you will regret the day that you engaged in this pointless exercise. No, we have nothing further to say, because nothing we say really matters to you.'

'I'm pleased to see that you're still taking this seriously, Mr Blundell.' Chilwell smirked. 'I think in that case we will conclude matters. As I outlined in our first meeting, I shall write up what has been discussed here today and last week,' he paused, pointedly looking Matthew in the eye, 'and the manner in which it has been discussed.' He sat forward. 'I'm still aiming for the panel meeting on the 30th of April – I'm a day or so past the deadline for submitting my report, but I've been given a little leeway. The sooner this matter is decided, the better; I'm sure you'll agree.'

'It's the first thing we've agreed on,' said Matthew.

'Oh, by the way,' said Chilwell. 'Did I leave my memory stick here last week?'

'Not that I saw,' said Matthew. 'Where did you last have it?'

‘I remember placing it on the arm of the chair, together with the blown-up photograph of James’s injury that I showed you.’

‘Well, maybe it dropped down the side of the chair?’

Chilwell stood and lifted the cushion he’d been sitting on. ‘Ah, yes, here it is.’ He pocketed the stick and retrieved his briefcase. ‘Well, if we’ve covered everything, you’ll be hearing from me by the end of this week to confirm arrangements for the panel meeting. I’m sorry to say this, but if I were you, I’d prepare myself for the worst.’

24

Questions

Wednesday, 18th April 2018

Matthew slept poorly, partly because the events of the day were playing over in his mind and partly because Heather had taken an extra sedative and her snoring kept him awake. In the morning, having slept well, she surfaced with renewed vigour.

'The first thing we're going to do is pay the Floyds a visit,' she said. 'If that bottle was an old one, I want to hear it from the horse's mouth.'

Matthew was slumped, forehead on the breakfast table, cradling his head. 'It can't harm, I suppose,' he mumbled. 'They might let something slip that we can use. God, I'm tired.'

'That's settled then. I'll give them a call and see when we can go round there. You'd best jump in the shower and wake yourself up.'

'What reason are you going to give for wanting to visit them?'

'I'll just say we'd like to discuss Emma's respite stay.'

Matthew yawned long and hard and sat up. 'Well, sooner rather than later, we need to go through the supervision notes Chilwell gave us. We should make a note of anything that Morton's missed out, anything she's added, anything she's twisted.'

'Are we really going to remember everything we discussed over those five months?'

'I think so. If anything sounds off, I think we'll know.'

'It all seems so pointless – it's just going to be her word against ours – and we know Chilwell isn't interested in anything we say.'

'Heather, I won't sleep until I've nailed that patronising, manipulative bitch to the wall.' Matthew thumped the tabletop with a clenched fist.

'Thinking back,' said Heather, ignoring his violent display, 'how the hell did we put up with all her constant nit-picking, negativity and rudeness?'

'Maybe, one of these days, I'll have the pleasure of tying her to a chair in a basement somewhere and extracting the answers.' Matthew thumped the table again. 'Oh, Morton, I'm going to spend many a happy hour dreaming up ways to make you suffer.'

'Which does highlight the fact that you've hardly been "diplomatic" in your dealings with her. It's probably fair to say that half our problems have been caused by you rubbing her up the wrong way. To say nothing of your antagonism towards Chilwell.' Heather shuddered. 'I suggest you make it a cold shower and, for Christ's sake, calm down. Now, get upstairs, and I'll phone the Floyds while you sort yourself out.' She sounded a little weary again.

Matthew pushed back in his chair and stood up. He felt a new energy pulsing through him. Diplomacy? Antagonism? Bollocks! Up till now, he'd played nice – too nice. As he climbed the stairs, he clenched his fists. In his head, his hands were around Morton's throat, and he was squeezing the pitiful life out of her BMI-busting body. It felt good. Matthew laughed.

The Floyds' modest semi-detached house in Apse Heath was immaculate. The small garden was immaculate: shrubs pruned and shaped, the borders weed-free, the driveway swept and the car on it polished to a shine. The house was freshly painted white, and the windows gleamed. Obsessive attention to detail. The Floyds were not the kind of people who overlooked things. Not the kind of people who didn't know a spent bottle of fluoxetine when they saw one.

Matthew rang the bell. 'God Save The Queen' chimed somewhere in the house.

Through the frosted glass panel in the front door, he saw a figure walking briskly down the hallway towards him. The door opened. Mrs Floyd smiled.

'How lovely to see you again, Mr and Mrs Blundell. Please, come on in.'

'Thank you for agreeing to see us this afternoon,' said Heather, 'we'll try not to take up much of your time.'

'Oh, that's okay, dear. We were expecting you, of course. The kettle's on.'

She showed them into the lounge: a spacious room with a lush carpet, a comfy sofa and armchairs, carefully spaced ornaments and photographs in frames adorning the flat surfaces and magnolia-painted walls. It looked like a show home.

'Take a seat. Syd will be in with the tea shortly.'

Tea turned out to be afternoon tea, with full tea service and a cake stand displaying miniature sandwiches with the crusts removed and cakes of varying descriptions.

Matthew's eyes lit up and even Heather, who had been finding it hard to show much appreciation for anything lately, couldn't help but admire the effort the Floyds had gone to.

As Syd played 'Mother' and poured the tea, Mrs Floyd said, 'So, we understand you want to talk to us about the time Emma spent with us on respite?'

'Yes, if that's okay,' said Heather. 'There are just a few questions we'd like to ask.' It had been agreed that it was probably best that Heather do the talking – tact had been mentioned when Matthew and Heather discussed it.

'Well, please, fire away.' Mrs Floyd smiled politely.

'Well, actually,' said Heather, 'our first question relates to the medicine bottle containing Emma's fluoxetine. Apparently, you discovered it was an old one issued back in August and there wasn't enough in it to last the week she was with you.'

'Oh yes, that. It's a mistake that anyone could make, I'm sure. But we had to report it in our notes. I'm sure you understand.'

'Quite,' said Heather, 'but,' – she felt the question was tantamount to an insult in the Floyd's case – 'without wishing to offend you, are you absolutely sure that the bottle we gave you was issued in August and not September? We're convinced the bottle we gave you was the

September one we were using. It had over a week's worth left in it. We just can't understand how this mix-up could have occurred.'

'Absolutely sure,' said Mrs Floyd. 'We double-checked, didn't we, Syd?'

Syd nodded. Like Matthew, he had been sitting comfortably, nibbling on a smoked salmon sandwich and saying nothing.

'Well, I... I had to ask,' said Heather.

Mrs Floyd smiled patiently. 'Fortunately, we noticed it when we were going through Emma's medicine bag. I specifically remember that because it was not long after Sarah left.'

'What do you mean, Sarah left?' said Matthew. Heather immediately shot him a warning glance.

'Well, she came round shortly after you left – to check that everything was okay.'

'Why would she do that?' said Heather.

'Well, why wouldn't she?' said Mrs Floyd. 'Sarah is very thorough and professional. It's her job to make sure everything is as it should be. I don't think she was checking up on you, as such. She said she was just passing and thought she'd drop in to see that we had everything we needed.'

'Did she ask to see the medicine bag?' said Matthew.

'Not as I recall,' said Mrs Floyd, looking puzzled. 'We hadn't had a chance to unpack anything. It was all still in Emma's room. She just had a quick chat and a cup of tea with us, used the bathroom and left.'

'And where exactly did she go to use the bathroom?' said Matthew.

'That's an odd question, Mr Blundell. The bathroom's upstairs. We don't have a downstairs toilet.'

'And was Emma upstairs in her room?'

'No, she was down here with us in the lounge.' Mrs Floyd looked confused.

Matthew glanced at Heather, who raised her eyebrows. 'Well,' he said, 'we're sure that the bottle we put in the medicine bag was the one issued in September. Do you think it's possible that Sarah could have swapped it for the old bottle while she was upstairs?'

'Why, what a thing to suggest, Mr Blundell. Why on earth would Sarah do a thing like that? I'm not sure I want to be party to what you're suggesting here. Can we change the subject, please?'

They spent the rest of the time in pleasant enough polite conversation. Matthew and Heather asked whether the Floyds thought Emma had enjoyed her stay. Had they sensed any resentment that she had not been able to go on holiday with Matthew and Heather? Had she seemed depressed at any stage? They talked until everyone had drunk enough tea and they had eaten all the sandwiches and cake.

'Well, thank you,' said Heather as they left. 'That was an amazing tea, and it's been lovely talking with you. I'm sorry if you felt my husband's questioning was a little harsh – he's not known for subtlety. We're just confused how you ended up with an old bottle of fluoxetine when we're sure we gave you the one we were using. It's a mystery. He didn't mean to cast aspersions on Sarah, I'm sure.'

'Well, the less said about it, the better,' said Mrs Floyd. 'Likewise, it's been a pleasure seeing you again. Do take care.' She closed the door behind them.

'Well,' said Matthew to Heather, 'what a fucking revelation that was! Morton must have removed the old bottle from our kitchen and swapped bottles. But how the fuck do we prove it?'

Matthew walked into the lounge to find Heather watching 'The Simpsons' on TV. After returning from the Floyds, she had said she needed to rest.

'Do you feel like going through those supervision notes now?' he said.

'I told you; I don't see the point – well, I do, but there's no rush, is there? It won't make any difference to the panel meeting. We can't prove anything. All we can do is continue to stress that Sarah failed in her duty to sign them off monthly.'

'Well, I think we should make a start now,' said Matthew, reaching for the remote to the TV. 'Let's switch this off. I'll have a tea if you're making one. Then we can sit down and look through them. I'll make a start.'

Heather took her sweet time but eventually brought in two mugs of tea. Matthew had been flicking through Sarah's supervision notes from October 2017 to February 2018 and making his own notes on a loose leaf of paper.

'How are you getting on?' Heather placed the mugs down on two coasters on the smallest table from the nest of three.

'Well, I've skimmed through them, and I've made a note of everything that's immediately jumped out at me.'

Heather looked over at his illegible scrawl. 'Shall I crank up the laptop, and we'll type them up neatly in a Word document?'

'Good idea,' said Matthew. 'You can tell me what you think as we go through them.'

Heather reached for the laptop on top of the nest of tables and started it up. When it had completed all its start-up procedures, which seemed to take longer and longer the older it got, she looked at Matthew.

'Hit me with it,' she said.

'Okay, so I've noticed incidents and other matters we raised at various times that she hasn't recorded.'

'Like what?'

'Well, starting in October, apart from the battery incident, she's not recorded any of the other "minor" instances of Emma's bad behaviour we told her about. They're important because they're further early indications of Emma's vindictiveness and temper. Obviously, she's had to record the later ones because Ann was made aware of them, but she's twisted what we recorded in our daily log and the conversations we had with her.'

'Okay, but give me some specific examples.'

'I'm getting to that... She's not recorded anything about Emma taking the kids' toys while they were playing with them and hiding them... anything we said about Emma's tantrum at the dinner table when she threw a plateful of food at Grace. She's not recorded...'

'Hang on, hang on, I can't type that fast.'

'Well, just get the bare bones down. You can tart it up later.'

'Okay, carry on.'

'She's not recorded the incident where Emma threw James's train engine at Grace's head. That could have been nasty – thank Christ she missed. Then there are all the occasions we raised our concerns re: the unwarranted criticism and abuse we received from Emma's uncle – nothing! And, as we suspected, she's not recorded the conversation where she told us Chilwell had mislaid the old medicine bottle she'd given him, which was clearly all nonsense. Nothing about the two discussions we had with her about adopting James.'

'Okay, let me get that down...'

'That's what I can see she's missed out so far – there could be more. When it comes to what she *has* recorded about incidents involving Emma, she's omitted or twisted our version of events and our concerns, and she's continued to play down Emma's responsibility for what occurred. Listen to this: the battery incident. She quotes you as saying in the daily log, "Emma's behaviour bears all the hallmarks of a psychopath: cold, calculated, deceitful and without a shred of remorse." As we know, Sarah just put the whole thing down to a harmless, childish prank, but here, she's added that she expressed her concern that we were vilifying Emma over such a petty incident and warned us not to allow our feelings towards Emma to become clouded.'

Heather looked up from the keyboard. 'A psychopath? Nonsense.' She gave a wry smile. 'I didn't refer to her being psychopathic until much later...'

Matthew laughed. 'Yeah, but thankfully you said that to me, not Sarah.'

Heather frowned. 'I remember telling Ann that Emma's behaviour was cold and calculated and that she lied about the batteries being dead. But that was at the time of the bath incident, to show that she could be manipulative and economical with the truth when it suited her.'

'Ah, yes. The bath incident. You want to hear what she has to say about that one! She's recorded that you totally overreacted and accused Emma outright of trying to drown Grace. That you said if you hadn't returned, Grace might no longer be with us.'

'You're joking?' Heather looked stunned. 'That may well have been Emma's version of events, but it certainly wasn't mine. I only ever said that she was holding Grace's head under the water. Wait while I get this down.'

Matthew waited patiently, consulting his notes, while Heather tapped furiously at the keys.

'What next?' she said.

'Sarah's opinion that you panicked and mistook what you saw in all the confusion – that, in fact, Emma was likely assisting Grace. However, she goes on to claim that, even though you admitted negligence, you furthered your accusations to suggest that Emma was out of control, said that we couldn't cope with her and, ultimately, that she should be relocated.'

'Twisted lies,' fumed Heather as she typed. She lapsed into silence.

When Matthew thought she was ready, he continued. 'When she refers to the washing machine incident, she fails to say that the washing machine door was closed behind Grace, which is the proof that she couldn't have climbed in alone. Again, her opinion, which she claims to have discussed with us, is that even though Emma may have played some part in it, we were exaggerating the whole incident to portray her in a negative light and using it as yet another opportunity to claim she was beyond redemption and a danger to James and Grace, because in reality, we couldn't cope with her. Oh, and she accuses me of negligence...'

Heather shook her head. 'And she says all this safe in the knowledge that we have no daily logs showing what we actually documented at the time and no witnesses to our conversations in the supervision meetings.'

'You spoke with Ann after the bath and washing machine incidents,' said Matthew. 'Wouldn't she confirm what you told her and what you did or didn't say?'

'Ann was as sceptical as Sarah on both occasions,' said Heather. 'And I didn't go into much detail with her. She received most of her information second-hand from Sarah and Emma. Even so, she couldn't comment on what was or wasn't said in our daily logs and supervision meetings.' She lowered her head and continued typing.

Matthew reached for his tea, which was going cold. Heather hadn't touched hers. He took a gulp and then placed his mug back on the coaster.

Eventually, Heather looked up. 'I'm guessing the next warped recollections are of the hair-pulling incident?' she said.

‘Yep,’ said Matthew. ‘She highlights the extraordinary lengths we went to with the video camera, just to capture Emma in a “one-off example of tit-for-tat behaviour”, in an attempt to further justify our demand that Emma be relocated. When it comes to Emma pushing Ruth down the stairs, she says it was established that Ruth was wearing socks and likely slipped – where did she get that from?’

Heather tapped away on the laptop keyboard. ‘... wearing socks and likely slipped.’

Matthew flopped back into the cushioned embrace of the sofa and covered his eyes with his hands. ‘We’ve said it before, and Chilwell more or less confirmed it. It’s the fact that we gave notice re: Emma that has triggered this whole investigation. Morton’s seen it as an opportunity to get us struck off by claiming we can’t cope.’

‘Yes,’ said Heather, ‘but, as you’ve said before, Sarah’s had it in for us since Day One. She’s dredged up all those other incidents from the past – she could have manipulated and used those at the time to claim we couldn’t cope. If her aim is to get us struck off, why wait until now?’

‘She’s like a demented serial killer; she enjoys torturing her victims and watching them suffer before she bangs the final nail in the coffin. She’s been toying with us, playing the waiting game!’

‘A little overstated, as usual. But let’s say there’s something in that. Why? What motive could she possibly have?’

‘I have no idea.’

‘Nor do I.’ Heather shook her head. ‘Did you find anything else?’

Matthew looked back down at his notes. ‘Well, no surprise, in January 2018, she’s failed to note we said it was Ruth who volunteered the information that her mother had burnt her arm, was an alcoholic, had anger management issues and that she didn’t want to return home. Sarah’s notes just refer to Ruth saying she had complained her arm hurt, whereupon we immediately asked her if her mother often burnt her with cigarettes, and then interrogated her and suggested she might like to live with her grandparents.’

‘Anything else?’

‘There’s her reference to my pet name for Grace.’

‘The Antichrist. What the hell were you thinking, Matthew? How many times did I tell you not to call her that!’

'I was only teasing. Obviously, she's not the Antichrist... Anyway, the point is Morton never once raised it as an issue with us; we didn't discuss it; therefore, it shouldn't even be in her notes.'

'Is that it?'

Matthew smiled. 'Oh, no – she's saved the best till last. You'll like this one. In February 2018, she noted that I am "foul-mouthed and argumentative" and that she had insisted that I need to address it.'

'And what do you have to say about that?'

'It's a load of bollocks!' said Matthew.

'Well, there you have it, then,' said Heather. 'The sum of Sarah's manipulation. On top of all her accusations from earlier in 2017, she's claiming that we had no reason to request Emma's removal, apart from the fact we couldn't cope with her; that we interrogated Ruth; that you believe Grace to be the daughter of the Devil and, worst of all, Matthew, that you are of questionable temperament and need to wash your mouth out with soap...'

'You may laugh,' said Matthew. 'So, what have we got? A load of discrepancies and lies in five months' worth of supervision notes that Sarah has held back and not submitted to us for verification and signature. All our daily logs destroyed, so that we have nothing to contradict her with. It's going to be her word against ours regarding the content. But we can have her up for her negligence, at least.'

'Yes, but Chilwell already knows about the delay and Sarah's reasons for it, and he'll have had to note it in his report, so the panel will already be aware of it. It's nothing we can stand up and shout about.'

Matthew scoffed. 'As things stand, we've got nothing we can stand up and shout about; that's the problem. The panel is only going to consider fresh evidence if it alters the fact. Everything we have so far is circumstantial and/or conjecture. We're as sure as we can be that we gave the Floyds the bottle of fluoxetine we were using, issued in September. Morton turns up soon after and, bugger me, the Floyds discover the August bottle in the medicine bag. But we can't prove she stole the old bottle from us, or that she swapped them over. Chilwell produces a photograph allegedly printed from the original digital file we supplied to Morton. It shows a cut on James's forehead. We know it wasn't on the original, but we don't have a copy of the original because I stupidly deleted it. Our best hope is that we have a copy of an image that I'm pretty damned sure Morton Photoshopped and gave to Chilwell. But unless we get something positive back from the camera shop, we can't prove the file's been altered.'

'When will you hear back from them?'

'They said it could take up to two weeks, so if I haven't heard anything by next week, I'll call them.'

'So, in the meantime, we do what? Just sit here and sweat?'

'What else can we do? When it comes to the panel meeting, I think Chilwell's right: maybe we should prepare ourselves for the worst.'

'Well, it can't get any worse than this.'

Friday, 27th April 2018

The phone rang.

Matthew emerged from the bathroom and, hearing no movement from downstairs, hurried into the bedroom to answer it.

'Hello?'

'Is that Mr Blundell?'

'Yes, it is.'

'Hello, Mr Blundell, it's Stanley Wright at the photo shop. I got your messages.'

'Ah, Mr Wright – at last! I've called you every day this week and this morning, but there was just the answerphone. I drove all the way to Newport yesterday, just to find the shop was closed.'

'Ah, yes, I'm so sorry, Mr Blundell. I was called away suddenly on a family emergency over on the mainland. I had to close the shop for a few days.'

'But what about John? Could he not hold the fort?'

'Please don't talk to me about John, Mr Blundell. I'm afraid there's been a problem at this end.'

'Oh. And what kind of problem is that?'

'A problem that went by the name of John, I'm afraid. I found your memory stick this morning underneath the counter here. It has your name and number on a Post-it note, with details of your query, but I'm afraid my ex-employee never got around to filling out the necessary form and sending it to head office.'

Silence.

'I'm ever so sorry, Mr Blundell. Obviously, I'll arrange for a courier, and I'll mark it up as a priority.'

'I need that information for an important meeting on Monday,' said Matthew. 'Without it, I'm screwed.'

'I'm afraid there's not a cat in hell's chance I'll have it back by then, Mr Blundell. Given your image is of a sensitive nature, I'll have to arrange for the delivery to be signed for. Head Office isn't open over the weekend, so that'll be Monday morning. I'll ask them to look at it immediately and return it by overnight courier. I should have a report and your memory stick back here on Tuesday morning.'

Matthew fumed as he paced the lounge and relayed the news to Heather, who was lounging on the sofa. But she had already resigned herself to their fate and didn't react to his repeated outbursts. Her head remained firmly in her magazine.

'It's not even as if we can insist they push the panel meeting back a month,' he said. 'What do we tell them? That we believe Morton has tampered with evidence? They'll side with Chilwell. Wild accusations! Why on earth would she do that?' He sighed as Heather continued to ignore him. 'There is some good news, though,' he said. 'I got an email while you were out shopping. I meant to tell you earlier, but I got distracted.'

'Really. What's that?' Heather carried on reading without looking up.

'I've got my first landscaping job.'

'Great.'

'Well, I expected a more positive reaction than that,' said Matthew. He paced over to the sofa and sat down next to her. 'I'm worried about you, Heather. Are you okay? You've not been yourself this last week.' He put his arm around her. 'We always made such a good team. Now you're distant. It's like you're... I don't know... on the dark side of the moon.'

'Sorry,' said Heather, lowering her magazine. 'I'm listening.'

‘I’m going to be part of a small team working in the grounds of an old folks’ home in Newport. I saw the advert in the paper.’

Heather looked up at him. ‘Well, we’ll certainly need the money.’

‘Well, it won’t be much,’ said Matthew, ‘but it’s better than nothing. We’re entitled to full pay from the council for another two months, but it’ll supplement our income when that phases out. That’s assuming we lose on Monday, of course – but even then, there’ll be the opportunity to appeal, and we could be reinstated. Hopefully, it won’t get to the stage where we have to dip into our remaining savings.’

‘You know as well as I do,’ said Heather, ‘that our future isn’t looking bright. This isn’t a full-time job, then?’

‘Not at the moment,’ said Matthew, ‘but if I fit in well, I’m sure they’ll give me more work on their bigger jobs – and I can always try to pick up the odd bit of work on my own.’

‘When do you start?’

‘They’re finishing off another job next week, so we’re kicking off at the old folks’ home on the Tuesday after the bank holiday.’

‘Well, at least you’ve made an effort, I suppose.’ Heather raised her magazine and carried on reading.

25

Revelations

Monday, 30th April 2018

Armed with nothing other than words and conjecture, Matthew and Heather were shown into the same room where, two years previously, they had sat before the panel and been successful in their application to become foster carers. The meeting began with the usual introductions, starting with the Chair of the panel, who was a full-time female employee of the council and well versed in the mechanics of such meetings. The introductions then ran through the twelve "jurors" and finished with Sarah Morton and Andrew Chilwell. Chilwell had completed his report and submitted it, and each member of the panel had read and digested it. What followed was a verbal run-through highlighting the pertinent issues, with the opportunity for questions to be raised and points clarified.

Chilwell spoke first. He explained the concerns the department had regarding Matthew and Heather's judgement and other failures in matters pertaining to the children in their care. He spoke for some considerable time, referencing the accusations that were listed on the original letter and the questions and answers discussed at the two face-to-face investigation meetings with them. Naturally, when questioned, Sarah corroborated everything Chilwell said, most of which stemmed from her own report, anyway. Janet, Ann and others were not in attendance. They had been interviewed, and their evidence and opinions were read out. At each stage, Matthew and Heather had ample opportunity to defend themselves. Heather had been preparing mentally for this moment, masking her emotions in an attempt to present their defence in a calm and rational manner. Despite being totally deflated and resigned to their fate, she was the self-nominated spokesperson, for obvious reasons. She tactfully rephrased their "confusion" and "concerns" regarding the copy of the photograph of James's injury and the bottles of fluoxetine, without directly accusing Sarah. She also clearly stated their objection to Sarah's having "inadvertently" destroyed their daily logs and to the five-month delay in producing the supervision notes – for which, she noted, Sarah would undoubtedly receive a half-hearted "slap on the wrist". Finally, she contested the various anomalies in the supervision notes. Matthew, at this stage, could not contain his frustration any longer. He finally scratched the itch, eyeballing members of the panel and stating his belief that, for reasons unknown, Sarah had deliberately manipulated and left out elements of their discussions. Whether the panel took these accusations seriously or whether it deemed them to be unsubstantiated, inflammatory and ultimately counterproductive was unclear in the stunned silence. Inevitably, Matthew almost lost his temper, struggling as he was to present himself as the antithesis of the character painted by Chilwell. On meek reflection, he acknowledged that his outburst may have overshadowed Heather's attempts to adopt a more subdued manner, hoping a less argumentative approach would show them in a better light and somehow improve the outcome. And then it was over. Matthew and Heather were shown into a small office just down the corridor to await the panel's decision.

Heather took a seat against the far wall. 'Did you see the way Sarah kept looking over at us? She was loving it.'

Matthew sat next to her and looked over at the door, as if expecting Sarah to walk in at any moment. 'If she were in here, I'd probably bloody murder her.'

Heather fidgeted in her chair. 'I hope they don't keep us waiting too long.'

Matthew hung his head. 'This is what it must be like being on death row...'

'That's a bit bloody dramatic!' said Heather.

'What I mean is it's like we're sitting here, waiting to find out if our life is over.'

'I think it's obvious that our life, as we know it, is over. I just hope they don't take too long to put us out of our misery.'

'Well, thank Christ we're not on death row – those fuckers can wait years!' Matthew sighed. 'I don't know what's more depressing: the thought of waiting for a lethal cocktail of drugs or knowing that my last meal's been a bowl of Rice Krispies.'

'I'm surprised you managed that this morning,' said Heather. 'I felt so sick, I couldn't eat anything.'

'I'll tell you what's sickening,' said Matthew, 'it's when two people in cahoots have the power to pull the wool over the eyes of a panel of so-called professionals.'

'Oh, for Christ's sake,' said Heather, 'just get this over and done with.'

What seemed like an age later, there was a knock at the door and the Chair of the panel stepped into the room.

'Thank you for being so patient,' she said.

'I guess you've reached a decision, then?' said Matthew.

'Unanimous, I'm afraid. I hate to be the bearer of bad news, but the panel has recommended that you be removed from the carer register with immediate effect; though the final decision rests with the Agency Decision Maker. She'll write to you within the next ten days, and of course, you'll have the right to appeal the decision by providing her with written representation within twenty-eight days. You'll be given the option of an independent reviewer – he or she will review the case with you and, if appropriate, submit the paperwork on your behalf. If the ADM determines that you have reasonable grounds for requesting an appeal hearing, your case will be reviewed by another fostering panel, and your independent reviewer will attend the meeting to support you and ensure your case receives a fair hearing.'

'Well, we've clearly been pretty stupid,' said Matthew, 'because if we'd accepted the offer of an independent reviewer in the first place, then we wouldn't have witnessed this farce here today! What you've just heard was a series of accusations manipulated by Sarah Morton for reasons we can't fathom!'

'You know as well as I do, Mr Blundell, that I can't comment on that. What I will say is that you have had "your day in court", so to speak; your case has been heard before a panel, and it has ruled accordingly. If you decide to launch an appeal and take up the offer of an independent reviewer, you'll need to speak with Andrew Chilwell, and he'll arrange for one to be appointed.'

'It'll probably be his brother or sister, knowing our luck,' mumbled Matthew.

'Right. I'll leave you here to gather your thoughts and your belongings,' said the Chair. 'I believe you know the way out.' With that, she left the room.

Heather turned to Matthew. 'Well, that's it. The trial is over. They've administered the lethal injection, and it looks as if your last meal was Rice Krispies after all.' She fell into his arms and sobbed uncontrollably.

Sarah Morton popped her head in at the door.

'You should know that no one is sorrier than I am about the verdict today,' she said. She shook her head and sighed. 'I firmly believe that had you worked more closely with me, rather than against me, it wouldn't have come to this. It's a sorry state of affairs.' Then she smiled. 'Now, I know the decision hasn't been rubber-stamped, but I'd like to pop by after lunch to collect the last of the children's belongings. Will you be in?'

'Yes, we'll fucking well be in, Morton!' Matthew stood up and pointed at her, stabbing his finger aggressively. 'We'll be planning our appeal. And next time we'll be better prepared. Next time, the panel will get to hear the truth. The truth about how an old bottle of fluoxetine came to be in the medicine bag we gave to the Floyds; the truth about a photo of James that you tampered with.'

'I don't know what you're talking about, Mr Blundell. You gave the Floyds that medicine bottle, and the photograph of James was a print from the original you gave me.'

'You finally caught up with your backlog of work, then,' said Heather angrily, wiping the tears from her face. 'Now I know why you held the supervision notes back till the last minute: you've twisted everything to fit the "facts" you presented in your report and left us without a leg to stand on. Very clever. You bitch!'

Sarah Morton remained silent for a moment, staring hard at them. 'What goes around, comes around,' she said finally. She turned sharply and closed the door behind her.

'What goes around...? What the fuck did she mean by that?'

'I don't know,' sobbed Heather, falling back into Matthew's arms.

Matthew and Heather had gone straight home and were now sitting together on the sofa, mugs of tea in hand, staring blankly through the net curtains at the hazy world outside their window.

Heather welled up as her thoughts turned to what they would do next. Their days as foster carers were over. The years of training, the move to a bigger house, the dream of both working from home doing what they enjoyed most. It was all over. But worst of all, they'd lost the opportunity to adopt James. Beautiful James. The boy they had come to love as if he were their own. Matthew had said not to worry, that it would all be fine. But it wasn't all fine; it was a living nightmare.

'What time did Ms Backstabber say she was coming round to pick up the rest of James and Grace's belongings?' said Matthew, eventually.

'After lunch. She'll be here around two o'clock, I guess.'

It was around three that Sarah rang the doorbell. Heather opened the door, while Matthew remained slumped on the sofa. 'Can I come in?' he heard Sarah say.

'If you must.' Heather was in no mood for pleasantries. 'We've put all the remaining things in boxes. They're here.' She pointed to a stack of boxes waiting by the front door as Sarah bustled past her and into the hallway.

'Do you think someone might give me a hand loading them into the car?'

Matthew rose from the sofa. 'If it helps get you out of here quicker, I'll do it,' he said, appearing at the lounge door.

'The boot's open,' said Sarah. 'I took the liberty of parking on your drive.'

'You would.'

'Well, I thought it made sense, what with carrying things to the car.'

'I meant you would take liberties!' snapped Matthew, grabbing the first box.

'Let's try not to make this more painful than it has to be,' said Sarah, covering her mouth with her hand to mask a fake cough. 'I have a favour to ask. James and Grace's temporary carers don't usually take on younger children. They borrowed a couple of car seats, but they've had to return them. Would you be willing to lend them the two you were using? As you won't be needing them,' she added.

'Have James and Grace settled with their new carers?' said Heather. 'Where are they living now?'

Sarah smiled. 'Tut, tut, Mrs Blundell. You know as well as I do that I cannot divulge that kind of information. You've been forbidden to have any contact with them. The current arrangement is temporary. They'll be moving on to another couple soon. They're new on our books – no one you know – and James and Grace will be far from here. But I will say that James in particular is thriving in his new environment. And,' she looked pointedly at Matthew and smirked, 'after the exorcism, Grace is a model child. Now, back to the car seats...'

Heather looked at Matthew. Matthew looked straight back, saying nothing.

'I don't see why not,' said Heather finally. 'For James and Grace's sake. It'll give them something to remember us by. You can return the seats with them after we win the appeal. They're in the playroom. I'll get them.'

Matthew, clutching the first box, turned abruptly and started towards Sarah's car.

Heather turned to make her way towards the kitchen, her anger rising, and found Sarah in her way. Sarah held her ground, forcing Heather to back up a step. Now she was fuming. 'Why don't you get out of my face and get out of my house, Morton!'

'Oh, I shall,' said Sarah, smiling. 'Once you get me those car seats.'

'You're a bitch, you know that? Ever since you came round here for that first home visit, you've been nothing but hostile towards us. Why? I've always tried to show you respect, and all you've ever done is throw it back in my face. No matter how many times I've asked you to, you've never even had the common courtesy to call me by my name!'

'Oh, I really couldn't face calling you Heather, Mrs Blundell.'

'I'll tell you, Sarah: frankly, you're a nit-picking, belligerent... cantankerous... pig-headed bitch. What you need is a damn good shag!

Go home, get that husband of yours to whip his cock out and give you a bloody good seeing to!'

Sarah gave Heather a look of mock shock and horror and then smiled. 'For a start, Mrs Blundell, Chris isn't my husband. I've had one of those.' She shuddered. 'Never again! And if I may be frank with *you*. I don't know how you put up with yours. He's a monstrosity of a man. And just for the record, Chris isn't strictly a "he" – he doesn't have a cock to "whip out", as you so politely put it – although there's a lot to be said for a strap-on... No, Chris is Christine, not that he'd thank you for calling him that. Christine is transgender – identifies as a man. And we're not married because, frankly, I'm not having him get his grubby hands on my money when I die.'

Heather glared and then pushed past her. She headed through the kitchen and into the playroom.

Matthew was staring into the small boot of Sarah's red Fiat Panda Cross. It was a 2017 model, very sporty, with tinted windows and heavily highlighted with black trim. Sarah hadn't prepared it for the number of boxes that James and Grace's belongings had filled. There were several items littering the bottom. Matthew scooped aside a picnic rug and lowered the box he was holding in its place. He returned to the house to find no one in the hallway. He poked his head around the lounge door and saw Sarah sitting comfortably in the armchair.

'Don't strain yourself,' said Matthew. 'Aren't you going to give me a hand with these?'

'I'm afraid I have something of a bad back, Mr Blundell,' she said. 'My doctor has advised me against lifting heavy items.'

'Oh, well, you make yourself comfortable, you poor thing, while I knacker my back instead.' He swore under his breath and lifted the next box. 'Good job you sent me on that manual handling course, eh?'

He took the second box to the car, shoved a few more items to one side and placed it next to the first. He repeated the exercise with boxes three and four, placing them on top of the first two. When he tried to close the boot, it wouldn't quite shut.

'Right, out you come,' he muttered, lifting the boxes back out. He laid the picnic rug on the ground and started tossing the clutter from Sarah's boot onto it. Out went an electronic tyre inflator. He heard the cheap plastic casing crack as it landed, and he smiled. He held up a worn pair of trainers, sniffed and grimaced, quickly tossing them aside. A similar sweaty odour emanated from a linen duffel bag. Matthew pushed aside the thought of a sweat-soaked Sarah down at the gym as the bag hit the pile. He needed to push the boxes right to the back, and so he reached for the remaining items wedged up against the rear of the back seat. Out went a first-aid kit, a can of de-icer and an ice scraper. He reached in for the last item – an old box of Kleenex tissues, almost empty. As he lifted it, he felt something shift. He tilted the box, and an object rolled into view. A small, dark amber glass bottle. Matthew pulled it out of the oval hole. Hang on. Emma's fluoxetine. For a fraction of a second, he wondered what Morton was doing with a bottle of Emma's fluoxetine in her car. His almost immediate realisation was that he knew exactly why Morton had a bottle of Emma's fluoxetine in her car. The fucking bitch! His fourth, more considered, thought was: gotcha! His mind raced. He remained hunched under the raised lid of the boot, repeatedly and unconsciously tapping the bottle on the top of the plastic casing of the car's rear light. His mind made up, he took out his phone and took a close-up picture of the bottle in the tissue box, placed where he had found it in the boot of Sarah Morton's car. Then he took a picture standing further back, having rested the bottle in the tissue box on the edge of the boot over the rear bumper, with the registration plate in the frame. Finally, he slipped the bottle into the right pocket of his trousers, triumphantly patted it twice and reloaded the boxes. He stuffed all of Sarah's clutter, including the tissue box, into the remaining gaps, slammed the boot and made his way back up the drive. He poked his head into the lounge. 'Okay in there?'

'Fine, thank you, Mr Blundell. You?'

'I'm certainly feeling a lot better than I did five minutes ago, Ms Morton – thank you for asking.'

'Are you nearly done?'

'Yes, almost. Where's Heather with the car seats? She's taking her sweet time.' He looked down the hallway towards the kitchen. 'Ah, here she is. Perfect timing. I'll take those love and pop them in the back seat of Ms Morton's car. You can see our guest out. As usual, I'm sure she's got other places to be, other people to see.'

Matthew was just closing the rear door of the car as Sarah emerged through the front door and into the sunshine, with Heather close behind.

'It's turned out nice, hasn't it?' said Matthew, grinning. 'Better than I expected.'

'If you say so, Mr Blundell. This must be a very worrying time for you. I do hope you'll get back on your feet, eventually. I dare say we won't be seeing each other again anytime soon.' She squeezed between Matthew and the row of thorny rose bushes lining the driveway.

'I wish that were the case, Ms Morton, but don't forget there's the appeal. We'll be seeing you soon enough.'

'Well, I wouldn't get your hopes up on that score.' Sarah smiled as she reached for the car door handle. She got in, started the engine, reversed down the drive and into the road. She scraped the gear into first and drove off.

Matthew turned to Heather. 'I think perhaps we ought to go inside, make some tea and open a celebratory pack of chocolate Hobnobs.'

'Are you mad? What have we got to celebrate?'

'Make me a cup of tea and I'll show you.'

'Mad,' said Heather. 'Our lives are in tatters and all you're interested in is tea and Hobnob biscuits.'

'Chocolate Hobnob biscuits. We're celebrating, remember.'

'In the words of Victor Meldrew: I don't believe it!' Matthew paraded the bottle around the lounge like a championship trophy. 'She left the evidence in her fucking boot. What stupid bitch does that?'

'I don't know,' said Heather, picking up her mug of tea before Matthew knocked it over. 'Perhaps she forgot about it, thought she'd already thrown it away, or lost it. Who cares? The fact is, we have it.'

'I took pictures: the tissue box I found it in, her car, her registration – all timed and dated.'

Heather took the bottle from Matthew and studied it. 'Well, this is the bottle I collected on the 4th of September. If Sarah had it, then it *is* the one we gave to the Floyds, and she's replaced it with the old August bottle.' She frowned. 'It's as we suspected; she must have taken that from our kitchen at some point, the thieving...' She handed the bottle back to Matthew and thought for a moment. 'This must have been premeditated. When we requested Emma's respite, she must have seen that as an opportunity and taken the old bottle from the kitchen. She's a quick-thinking, devious bitch, I'll give her that.'

'But what I still don't understand,' said Matthew, 'is why is she doing this? What reason would she have for swapping the bottles over and setting us up?'

Heather shook her head. 'Your guess is as good as mine. By all accounts, she doesn't treat her other carers the way she treated us.'

Matthew reached for his tea. 'At first, I thought it was just her way: blunt, to the point, verging on rudeness.'

'Well, you certainly matched her in that department, Matthew.'

'But she was so antagonistic. Always negative. She never once paid us a compliment that I recall. It's no wonder I gave as good as I got. But this situation with the photo and the medicine bottle is taking it to a whole new level. This isn't just sheer bloody-mindedness; this is insane. Surely, we didn't piss her off that much?' Matthew sipped his tea.

'When did you say we'll get the results back on the photo?' said Heather.

'It should be tomorrow,' said Matthew, taking another sip of his tea. 'Mr Wright, the manager at the shop, said he'd send it by courier and mark it as priority. Head Office should have received and dealt with it today. They're due to return it to the shop overnight.' He reached for a chocolate Hobnob. 'I'm positive Sarah's messed with it. We both know that's not the picture I took of James's face.'

'Well, the sooner we have all the evidence, the sooner we can lodge a request for an appeal and present it to our "independent reviewer" – whoever he or she might be. There's no way a review panel can ignore all this. They'll have to reinstate us, and Sarah will be the one struck off. They should prosecute her for fraud.'

'Well, let's just see what transpires first, shall we? Did Sarah have anything of interest to say while I was loading her car?'

'Just the usual patronising bullshit... Oh, but get this! It turns out she's not married after all. It seems the Chris we thought was her husband is actually Christine.'

'But she refers to "Christine" as a "he"?' Matthew took a moment. 'Oh, I see...' He shrugged his shoulders. 'That's okay – I'm cool with all this latest gender and sexual minority stuff.'

'And,' Heather continued, 'she's not married "him" because, in her words, "I'm not having him get his grubby hands on my money when I die". Typical.'

'So, Morton isn't her married name from a second marriage. Perhaps it's her maiden name – or her old married name.'

'Oh, I doubt she'd have kept her old married name,' said Heather. 'She was hardly complimentary about her last husband. Maybe we should do a little digging into her past. It might prove interesting.'

'A complete waste of time,' said Matthew. 'We've got better things to do than worry about Morton's sordid sex life. Who cares who married whom?'

'But you never know what dirt we might find.'

'Her past is of no relevance to us. But she's a grubby little tart, I'll give you that.'

Heather laughed, despite Matthew's scorn. The discovery of the bottle had given her a glimmer of hope. It had been a while since she'd felt any light relief, and it felt good.

Matthew sat on the sofa and gazed around the room. In that moment, he felt a sense of calm return, and he welcomed it. For all his surface belligerence and bravado, an undercurrent of doom had pervaded and darkened every day for many weeks now. He was relieved to be rid of it. After so many losing hands, it now felt as if they'd finally been dealt some winning cards. His gaze came to rest on an envelope, propped up against a vase on the windowsill, next to the armchair in the corner. 'What's that?' he said.

'What's what?'

'That envelope over there.' Matthew pointed, and Heather retrieved it, standing in front of Matthew as she studied it.

'It says Mr and Mrs Blundell.'

'It can only be from Sarah,' said Matthew. 'No one else has been here. I don't suppose it's a "Thank You" card full of Argos vouchers...'

Heather opened the envelope. It was a 'With Sympathy' card.

Matthew snorted. 'She's got a nerve. Read it out.'

Heather frowned as she opened the card and read it.

'What does it say?' said Matthew impatiently.

'I don't understand it. It just says: "It was fate". And it's signed "Sarah XXXXX".'

'Fate? Five kisses? What the fuck's that supposed to mean?'

Heather shook her head and remained silent.

Matthew stood and walked towards the lounge door. 'Fate, my arse,' he said.

26

Answers

Tuesday, 1st May 2018

'Get up.'

'What?'

'I said, get up. We're going into Newport.' Heather moved past the bed, over to the window and pulled back the curtains.

Matthew groaned and manoeuvred himself into a sitting position. 'Newport? What do you need to go to Newport for?'

'I'm coming with you. You're going into that photo shop to see if the results are back and, if not, make a nuisance of yourself. I'm popping into the library.'

'The library?'

'Yes. Will you stop repeating everything I say and get your backside into that bathroom. I want to make the bed.'

'Just five more minutes...' Matthew flopped sideways and buried his head into Heather's pillow. 'Man, I feel a little spaced out.'

'What's got into you, Matthew? I thought you were celebrating with a couple of beers last night, not jacking up on smack.'

'Smack, my arse!' He raised himself onto one elbow. 'I could do with an aspirin, though.'

'Aspirin, I can do,' said Heather. 'But your arse is going into that bathroom!'

Matthew grumbled and groaned as he threw back the covers, swung his legs over the edge of the bed and planted his feet firmly on the carpet. 'What do you need to go to the library for?'

'It's the first Tuesday of the month. I thought I might pop into the "Dying Matters Café" – what's it to you?'

'You what? Isn't that some kind of therapy group they run? What d'you want to go there for? Are you thinking of calling it quits? What's this – goodbye cruel world?'

'What's with all the questions? Can't I pop into the library if I want to? Maybe I want to borrow a book.'

'I guess so – if you think reading the latest Danielle Steele is the most appropriate way of passing the time right now.'

'Maybe I need a bit of Danielle Steele to take my mind off things.'

'Maybe you do, Little Miss Tetchy. Well, the library is only just round the corner from the photo place, so while I'm in there, you can ponder meeting your maker. But I warn you: death by Danielle Steele is not a pretty way to go.'

'Hilarious, as ever. Now get a move on!'

'I'm going, I'm going. I think I might pop into Maccy D's, get a late breakfast, if you're going to be in there a while.'

'You can stay for lunch too, if you like.'

'Maybe I shall. Death by double cheeseburger. Now you're talking!'

They parked in the Chapel Street short-stay car park and parted outside the photo shop in St James' Street. Heather took a left into Orchard Street and followed it round until she reached the Lord Louis Library, opposite the bus station. She found the quiet area with several computers on desks. She took a seat at one, logged in with her library membership number, as prompted, and then sat staring at the screen. A member of staff must have seen her looking bewildered and came over.

'Do you need some help with something?'

'Er, yes, thank you,' said Heather. 'I want to use Find My Past – you get free access here, is that right?'

'Yes, that's right. Do you have an account with them?'

'No, it's not something I've used before.'

Connie, as Heather gleaned from her name badge, talked her through setting up an account. Once registered, it was just a case of using her account on the library's computer, which acted as a gateway to the free services.

'Is there anything in particular you're looking for?' asked Connie.

'I don't know,' said Heather. 'I just wanted a play around, really. I've just found out I have a distant cousin I've never met, and I wanted to see if I could find out anything about her.'

'Well, this is the main search screen.' Connie clicked on "Search" at the top of the screen, and a drop-down list appeared. 'You can see all the various searches you can do. "Births, marriages and deaths" is a good place to start. It's all quite intuitive. You've also got access to...' She moved the cursor over to the right of the drop-down box and clicked on "Newspapers and periodicals", '... British Newspapers. You never know; she might be famous – or she might just have won first prize in the church raffle. It depends what paper you find her in.' Connie smiled. 'There, I'll leave you to have a play, and if there's anything you need any help with, just let me know. I'll be at the desk over there.'

'Thanks for all your help,' said Heather. 'I'll give it a go.'

Heather clicked on "Births, marriages and deaths" and brought up a new screen. "Civil Marriage & Divorce" appeared in the list of options on the left-hand side. If Morton's her maiden name... Heather filled in the first name, Sarah, surname, Morton, and deselected "Name variants". She then looked at the next box, which was under the heading "When". The box was labelled "Year". Presumably year of marriage. The next box was "Year of Birth". Matthew and she had discussed this. Heather could almost hear their conversation. How old do you think she is, she had asked Matthew.

'She's at least sixty!' Matthew said without hesitation.

'In her sixties? No way. She's somewhere in her mid-fifties.'

'Come on, I told you, she's mutton dressed as lamb.'

Heather frowned. That was back when they first met her in 2016. She made a generous allowance each way: in 2016 she was no younger than 50 and no older than 65, which meant she was born somewhere between... 1951 and 1966. Surely, she wouldn't have married earlier than 18, and surely not later than, say, 40. Heather did some more calculations and opted for a marriage date of 1987 and set "Give or take" at 20 years to cover all eventualities. She left "Where" as "Britain". Already the screen bid her to "View 81 Results". Heather clicked, and a new screen appeared with a long list, seemingly in random order. One heading was "Location". Heather recalled Sarah mentioning that she had lived with her husband in Essex – it seemed like a good place to start. She scrolled down the list until, about halfway down, an Essex entry appeared. There was an icon on the right, which was a sheet of paper with lines on it and a folded top right-hand corner. She hovered the cursor over it, and "View transcript" appeared. She clicked. Sarah Morton, Marriage quarter: 1, Marriage year: 1986, District: Barking & Dagenham. And there, highlighted in gold, it said: MarriageFinder™ Sarah Morton married one of these people... Heather didn't need to look any further. She now knew everything she needed to know about Sarah Morton.

A bell tinkled as Matthew pushed open the door to the photo shop. He was halfway over to the counter when a man he presumed to be Stanley Wright emerged from behind the curtain pulled across the doorway to the back room.

'Good morning, sir. How may I help you?'

'I'm Matthew Blundell. I believe it was you I spoke with on the phone on Friday.'

'Ah, yes. Mr Blundell.' The man immediately looked sheepish. 'That's right, it was. I'm Stanley Wright. How are we today?'

'I'll be honest with you, Mr Wright. I've been better.'

'Yes, yes. I can understand that.' Stanley Wright wrung his hands. 'I can only apologise most sincerely, Mr Blundell. I just wish it had been me that had served you. Dare I ask? How did that meeting go yesterday?'

'Not great, I'm afraid,' said Matthew. 'Yesterday, my wife and I were officially struck off the council's foster carer register.'

Mr Wright seemed to pale. 'And was that in any way due to...?'

'Well, let's just say, Mr Wright, that if the findings from your head office are what I'm expecting, then it might have thrown a whole new light on proceedings. Do you have the results back?'

'I'm pleased to say I do, Mr Blundell.' Stanley Wright's mood brightened. 'Would you like to take a seat at that table over there and I'll just go and grab the report? Can I get you a tea or coffee?'

Matthew thought of his double sausage and egg McMuffin with hash browns and a McCafé flat white. 'I'm fine, thank you, Mr Wright,' he said. 'I'm going to grab a late breakfast after this.'

'Right, you are...' Stanley Wright moved off in the direction of the counter and disappeared into the back room, while Matthew went over to a small round table with two chairs and sat down. He was straight back out, waving some papers in his hand. 'If you'll forgive me for saying – purely from my perspective, you understand – the bad news is that it *is* good news. Will you be able to appeal?'

'Thankfully, yes,' said Matthew. 'If you can run me through what you've found – and, please, bear in mind, I'm a bit of a technophobe.'

'Right. I'll do my best.' Stanley Wright sat down next to Matthew. 'Let me show you what we've discovered.' He flipped over the title page of the report and pointed at a print of the photograph on the second page. 'There have been two distinct alterations made. The first is that the mark on the forehead, here, has been enlarged, approximately by a factor of three.'

'Yes, it looked bigger than I remember,' said Matthew.

'This central darker area has been expanded, and there's been some very subtle and clever shading of the surrounding area. Whoever did this certainly did a good job.'

'And second?'

'Well, this laceration is artificial. It's been added over the top of the lump. I'm no expert either, Mr Blundell, but this has either been lifted from another photograph and blended in, or it's been created from scratch. Either way, very impressive, but it was never going to fool our expert. In fact, that's what surprises me: whoever did this knows their stuff and surely must know that manipulation can be relatively easily detected.'

'I'm guessing he or she was paid to do it and getting paid was all that mattered,' said Matthew. 'And I doubt it even occurred to the "client", shall we say, that I would ever get my hands on this image again. My wife and I both knew there was never a cut; it was just a case of proving it.' Matthew leant forward across the table. 'So, in layman's terms, how can you tell the image has been altered? I'm going to need some kind of explanation for the appeal.'

Stanley Wright leant back in his chair. 'I'm not sure there are any layman's terms, Mr Blundell. This is where it gets complicated, I'm afraid. I won't attempt to explain the technical terms – it's all in this report – but these days, you've got software such as Amped Authenticate, FotoForensics, Ghiro, etc., that use Error Level Analysis, metadata analysis – EXIF files and such like – and looks at things like JPEG compression. With the right know-how, even something that looks great visually is relatively easily exposed. As I say, though, the technical details are all in here if you need them, and it's all on official paper.'

'That sounds perfect,' said Matthew. 'I just wish it had come in time for the panel meeting. Still, there's no point crying over spilt milk,' he added, noticing Stanley Wright's obvious discomfort.

'Again, I am so sorry, Mr Blundell. Obviously, there's no charge for this in the circumstances...' He handed Matthew the report. 'Oh, and here's your memory stick.'

'Thank you, Mr Wright. I appreciate that. I guess there's always the appeal – it's only a temporary setback. I'm just pleased we got the right result in the end.'

'Well, for my part, Mr Blundell, I appreciate your understanding. Not all folk would be as reasonable as you've been in the circumstances. If ever you're in the market for any camera equipment, come and see me and I'll do you an exceptionally good deal.'

'I might take you up on that one day – thank you,' said Matthew, getting up from his seat. 'And now, McDonald's beckons.'

'Well, enjoy that,' said Stanley Wright. 'And I hope whoever fudged that photograph gets what's coming to them. They sound like a nasty piece of work.'

'You can say that again, Mr Wright. You can say that again.'

Matthew wiped his hands on his napkin and dabbed at his mouth, just in case any brown sauce had gone AWOL. He pulled out his phone and typed a text message to Heather: "Just finished breakfast; not sure I can face a Happy Meal right now. Are you ready?" A minute later, Heather replied: “Leaving in 5. Meet you at the car?” Matthew acknowledged, got up and took his tray and rubbish to the bins. He looked wistfully at the Crème Egg McFlurry advertised on a poster as he left.

Matthew was waiting in the car when Heather arrived. ‘So, come on then. What news?’ she said as she opened the passenger door and got in.

‘It’s as we expected,’ said Matthew, turning in his seat to face her. ‘The conniving bitch has gone to great lengths to make the photo look authentic. It seems she’s paid some “professional” to alter it for her. Fortunately for us, these days there’s software out there that can detect stuff like that. I would go into the technical detail, but I’m not sure you’d be able to get your head around it.’

‘Right. And you can of course...’

‘Of course. Stan and I had quite an in-depth conversation about it. Error Analysis, EXIT files – stuff like that. Anyway, it’s all in the report he gave me, on headed paper, from a qualified, professional photographer-cum-computer expert. It’s proof, if proof were needed, that the photo Sarah presented as the original has been altered. I had a quick look at the report in McDonald’s. They can even determine the date of the changes from the metadata.’

‘So that’s it? We’ve got her?’

‘Yes. We just don’t know why she’s done it.’

Heather was silent for a moment. Then she said, ‘Except now I do know why she’s done it.’

‘Really? You’re joking?’ Matthew stared at her. ‘One visit to the library, a near death experience and a chapter of Danielle Steele and all has been revealed?’

‘I think we should wait until we get home. I’ll tell you all about it when we’re sitting comfortably. It’s not the kind of thing I want to discuss in the car.’

Matthew looked ahead thoughtfully. ‘Right... This sounds ominous.’

27

Confession

The mood in the lounge was subdued.

Matthew waited as Heather composed herself. Eventually, she spoke.

'Fourteen years I've been trying to forget this and put it all behind me. Fourteen years. I guess there's no getting away from your past.'

'Are you talking about what happened at Barking & Dagenham?'

'Yes.'

'Well, I know it's a sensitive subject and I've never pushed you to tell me about it before, but if Sarah Morton's involved somehow, I think you owe me an explanation.'

'I know. I'm trying...'

Matthew waited, drumming his fingers impatiently.

When Heather spoke again, her voice was calm and measured. 'When I was at Barking & Dagenham, I taught computer science and ICT to Year 10 and 11 students. They were all aged between fifteen and sixteen and preparing to take their GCSEs.' She paused. 'In September 2003, a boy called Dylan Dumas started in Year 11. He'd just moved to Barking & Dagenham, right in the middle of his GCSE studies, which was not ideal, obviously. We were told he'd had troubles at his previous school, though we were never told exactly what those troubles were.' She paused again to reflect. 'At first, he was very quiet, kept his head down and seemed okay, but when it came to his mock exams in December, he failed most of them miserably. He seemed to be more of what I'd call the "creative type". He did better in English, art and drama but struggled with subjects like maths, physics and chemistry. I couldn't help feeling responsible for the fact that he did particularly badly in computer science. After his mock results in January, he hung around after our classes and even after school, asking questions about stuff he didn't understand. At first, I had no problem with that – unless he or I had another lesson to get to. In fact, I found it admirable that he cared enough to come and see me...'

'And?'

'Well, it seemed to become habitual, and it was time-consuming. It got to the point where I suggested it might be better if we spent some time after school, once a week, going over things. I guess I was naïve, but I saw him as a challenge. I guess I wanted the satisfaction of helping a student, who was clearly struggling and almost guaranteed to fail his GCSE exam, to pass with flying colours. That's the sense of fulfilment you crave as a teacher. So, we met each week on a Tuesday for a few weeks, and his progress encouraged me...' Heather looked away from Matthew and up at the ceiling. It was a moment longer before she spoke. 'The problems started when we returned after the February half-term. On the Monday, he suggested we meet outside of school that week – somewhere more private.'

'Yes, well, that certainly should have started some alarm bells ringing,' said Matthew.

'Of course, it did!' She turned sharply to look at him. 'I said no, it wasn't appropriate, and the next day, we met in the classroom as usual. But it was only then that I really woke up to what was happening. As I said, I was naïve. Yes, I'd been teaching for over five years, but I was still only in my twenties...' She reached for a cushion, pulled it onto her lap and held it there. 'I began to notice the way he looked at me, the odd things he said. I tried to put the brakes on it. At the end of the study session, I told him that the following week, I wouldn't be able to see him at all, as I had other commitments. His response was totally irrational. His tone was aggressive. He said he would deliberately fail his GCSE if I didn't meet with him and that the extra coaching was the only reason he was getting better grades. That was when I bit the bullet and told him that, really, it was inappropriate for a teacher to be spending so much time with one pupil and that maybe a private tutor would be a better option, if his parents agreed.'

'What did he say to that?'

'He said he didn't want a private tutor. He said...' Heather brought the cushion up to her face and buried her head in it.

'Take your time,' said Matthew. He rested a hand on her knee.

Heather lowered the cushion and clutched it to her chest. She took a moment. 'He said he was in love with me and that he knew I felt the same way too.'

Matthew was silent. He didn't know what to say. He could see that Heather was reliving the moment, and that it was painful. She was clutching the cushion and staring at the floor. He imagined her sense of panic as the gravity of the situation gripped her.

'What did you say to him?' he said finally.

Heather looked up and stared across the room at the lounge door. 'I said exactly what you'd expect me to say. I told him: my only interest in you is to help you and see you do well – nothing more. I said that I would do the same for any other pupil that came to me for help.'

'And what did he say?'

Heather scoffed. 'He started spouting a load of poetic nonsense. He likened "our love" to a burning sun, obscured by clouds.'

Matthew looked puzzled. 'You know poetry's never been my thing,' he said.

Heather continued to look away. 'He was referring to the illicit nature of a teacher-student relationship. In his twisted mind, when he left school, "the clouds would part". Sickening, poetic nonsense! I told him that the sun was setting on "our love" right here and now and that, in light of his inappropriate behaviour, he should now confine any questions he had to the classroom.'

'And obviously that wasn't the last of it?'

'No,' said Heather. 'For the rest of that week, I tried to treat him like any other student, but that became increasingly difficult. Effectively, he stalked me. He would hang around and try to strike up casual conversation. I'd catch him peering through classroom windows at me. I'd see him watching me as I crossed the playground and walked to my car after school.'

'Did you mention any of this to anyone?'

Heather finally turned back to look at Matthew. Her expression exposed the burden she had carried all these years; her eyes betrayed her torment. 'Not at first,' she said. 'I was too embarrassed and afraid of what the reaction might be. I thought perhaps he'd get tired and give up. Despite how he was making me feel, I felt I had it under control.'

'So, when did it get out of control?'

'The following week, he handed me a poem.'

'A poem?'

'Yes. A declaration of our love.' Again, Heather unconsciously gripped her cushion.

'Jesus,' said Matthew.

Heather reached over to the arm of the sofa. 'I've got it here to show you,' she said. 'I kept a copy, together with all the other documents relating to the inquiry.' She handed Matthew a single folded sheet of lined A4 paper.

In the depths of darkness, you found me
Your eager hands reached out, unbound me
I let those same hands guide me
From perpetual night, into the light
And there you did embrace me.
A love I'd never known.
A moth, I came, your flame ensnared me
A planet around your sun, you claimed me
And yet, dark clouds obscure me
You captured my heart, the clouds will part
And then you can reveal me.
For all the world to see.

'Very good, considering his age,' said Matthew.

'We're not here to judge the quality of it, Matthew.' Heather snatched the paper back. 'He may have been bad at computer science, but he knew how to manipulate words.' She tossed the poem to one side. 'He was a loner. The kind of boy who spent all his time in his room – probably doing drugs and immersing himself in all kinds of weird shit.'

'A bit like a young Bob Dylan, then?'

Heather stared blankly at him. 'If you say so.'

Matthew looked down. 'Sorry...'

Heather shook her head. 'Everything he wrote in that poem pointed to me initiating the "relationship".' She reached out and grabbed the A4 sheet of paper. 'Look at the words he's used: I guided him, embraced him, ensnared him... It smacks of me grooming him!' She tossed the paper to one side again, and it fell to the floor. 'I should have gone to the headmaster straight away – but I didn't. That was my mistake. Again, I was naïve. I was too afraid of what people might think and the repercussions. He made a point of giving me the poem on the Tuesday we'd have been due to meet, if I recall, and to my enduring regret, I spent the rest of that week and the weekend trying to summon the courage to report it. Finally, I came to my senses and first thing on the Monday morning, I showed it to the headmaster, Mr Gilmour. I hoped he would speak with Dylan and deal with it in-house. Unfortunately, he immediately summoned Dylan's mother to the school for a meeting the next day.'

'And Dylan's mother was?' Matthew suspected he already knew the answer.

'Sarah Dumas. But in conversation, we only really ever referred to her as Mrs Dumas.'

'Sarah Morton's married name?'

'Yes, she was still married at the time.'

'So, did you meet her?'

'No, Gilmour didn't include me in any of the meetings. Given the implications, he didn't want me anywhere near her.'

'What about at parents' evenings?'

Heather thought for a moment. 'No. I was off sick the week they held the autumn term parents' evenings, and by the time the spring term ones came around, all this had kicked off and I'd been suspended, pending inquiry. Anyway, even if I had met her briefly, it was fourteen years ago; I wouldn't recognise her. I'm not good with faces.'

'So, did "Mrs Dumas" kick off?'

'I think we can refer to her as Sarah now, can't we?'

'Okay,' said Matthew, 'so did Sarah kick off?'

'No, not at first. The situation was explained to her, and she was shown a copy of the poem. I think she already knew about the extra tuition I'd given Dylan, but the poem must have raised a lot of questions in her mind. She took it home and said she'd speak to him.'

'And then what?'

'And then it kicked off.' Abruptly, Heather got up from the sofa and walked over to the window. She gripped the sill and leant against it.

Matthew waited as she stood, her back to him, looking out. 'And?' he said finally. Heather's arms shook slightly. Matthew noticed the movement as it travelled to her shoulders. When Heather spoke, her voice was broken.

'Sarah confronted Dylan with the poem...' She sucked in a lungful of air. 'The upshot of it all was that he accused me of sexually assaulting him.'

'Christ, Heather...' Matthew got up from the sofa and moved towards her. 'To be honest, I always suspected it was something like that. Why did you never talk to me about it?'

'Because I've spent years trying to forget it, Matthew.' Heather crumpled and pressed her forehead against the windowsill. As Matthew reached her, she was sobbing. 'NatWest, meeting you, getting married... it was supposed to be a new life.'

Matthew bent down beside her and put an arm around her shaking body. 'Why don't we take a break?' he said. He led her back to the sofa and eased her down into the cushions. She sat forward, with her head in her hands.

'I'll make us a cup of tea.'

'Yes – sorry,' said Heather, looking up. 'Just give me a moment. I'll be fine.'

Matthew gave Heather a little time before returning with the tea. He didn't suppose she'd be in the mood for a biscuit, so he resisted the urge for a Hobnob. Heather was sitting up and seemed calmer. The poem was still on the floor and so, after placing the mugs on a table, Matthew picked it up and put it on the sofa, between them, as he sat down.

'How are you feeling?' he said. 'Are you okay to carry on?'

Heather nodded. 'I'm sorry, Matthew. Talking about it is even harder than I thought it would be.'

'That's okay,' said Matthew. 'In your own time... So, what happened after he accused you of...?' He reached for his tea.

Heather reached for her mug and cupped it in her hands. 'Sarah demanded another meeting and lodged an official complaint with Gilmour,' she said. 'I guess, as any parent would, she believed what her son told her. They made accusations that the school was obliged to take seriously. Gilmour reported the matter; they set up an inquiry and suspended me.' She blew on her tea and then took a sip.

Matthew frowned. 'But what was Dylan's story? One minute he's writing you a love poem and the next minute he's claiming he's the victim of a sex pest. It doesn't make sense.'

Heather lowered her mug and, again, clasped it in her hands. 'Dylan only used the word "love" once, and that referred to the "love" I had shown him. When Gilmour asked him what the poem meant, Dylan claimed it was an innocent expression of appreciation. He twisted the meaning of everything he'd written in that poem to that effect. He said that I'd deliberately taken it the wrong way and taken advantage of him – that he was in a dark place, vulnerable, and I'd exploited that. "Eager hands" reaching out, remember?'

Matthew waited as Heather slipped into a moment's reflection.

She continued. 'He said I used the fact that he was struggling in class as an opportunity to get him alone after school and that, thinking back, he'd felt uncomfortable at times and accused me of making suggestive remarks and even touching him inappropriately once or twice. But, he said, he was blinded by the fact that someone had shown an interest in him and that his grades were improving.'

Matthew picked up the poem. 'But he's echoed here what he said to you: dark clouds obscuring your love, but that the clouds would part and your love would be revealed?'

'Yes, that's what he *said* to me, but he doesn't refer to love in the poem.' Heather paused, thinking back. 'If I remember, his explanation was that the dark clouds obscuring him referred to the fact that he was still struggling – a work in progress – but eventually the clouds would part and he'd be revealed as my "star student" when he had passed all his exams.'

'But you'd captured his heart. If that's not an expression of love, I don't know what is.'

'Easily twisted,' said Heather. 'A way of saying that I had inspired him, given him a sense of belief and determination...'

'And the assault? How was that supposed to have happened?'

Heather stared at her tea. Matthew feared another meltdown, but she held it together. 'According to Dylan,' she said, 'the day after he had given me the poem, he went to the toilets before going home. He accused me of following him in and accosting him. Apparently, I then made persistent, aggressive, sexual advances, but he fought me off and managed to escape.'

'So, why didn't he report it at the time?' said Matthew.

'The usual reasons abused children don't report sexual abuse: they're too embarrassed, they don't think anyone will believe them, etc... All totally understandable in genuine cases.'

Matthew absent-mindedly massaged the stubble on his chin. 'I can see why the school had to hold an inquiry,' he said. 'Quite frankly, those are serious and believable allegations. It's frightening how easily things can be twisted.'

Heather hung her head. 'How could I have been so naïve? I should have seen it coming. Yes, I did reach out to him after he came to me for help, and of course, that could be misinterpreted. I should never have put myself in the position where I was alone with him. And if I hadn't delayed taking his poem to Gilmour, if I'd taken it to Gilmour immediately, the subsequent alleged assault could never have taken place.'

'Well, hindsight and all that,' said Matthew, 'but at the end of the day, you were acting with good intentions. Surely, Gilmour realised that?'

Heather finally put down her mug of tea. 'Well, as I said, I was suspended pending inquiry; but my integrity was beyond question. No one doubted me. But we had to prove to the authorities and Dylan's parents that Dylan was lying.'

Matthew sat back. 'Well, from the little you've told me, I know you were exonerated, so obviously he was found out somehow?'

'Yes. He made two mistakes. First, when Sarah confronted him, he should have just dumbed down the meaning of his poem to an "innocent expression of appreciation" and left it at that. No one knows why he decided to accuse me of sexual assault – it was totally irrational. All he did was dig himself a massive hole and spark an investigation. And because he fabricated the story on the spot, he didn't have too much time to think it through, which was his second mistake: the school had CCTV. Either he'd forgotten it was there, or he thought he would have been out of range, but the camera at the far end captured the whole length of the corridor, including the entrance to the gents' toilets that he had supposedly visited on the afternoon in question. Needless to say, neither he nor I appeared on any CCTV footage that afternoon – or any other afternoon that week, if he claimed he'd got his days wrong. Once that side of his story collapsed, so did the believability of the rest of it. Add to that the fact that I had a structured plan for his extra tuition and examples of his work – it all counted towards my professionalism. And then there were all the character references and the psychiatric report...'

Matthew couldn't resist it. 'They sent you for psychiatric evaluation?'

Heather managed a smile. 'Stupid. They recommended that Dylan undergo a psychiatric evaluation. He hadn't attended school since he made the accusation, claiming he was suffering from post-traumatic stress. And when his story was disproved and my version of events was accepted, the impulsive nature of his suggestions, fabrications, manipulations – call them what you will – suggested there were possibly signs of sociopathy. Gilmour said it threw up the possibility that his actions might have been calculated at every stage; that he used his difficulties in class to get closer to me; that he fantasised about developing a sexual relationship with me; that maybe he wasn't quite able to distinguish that fantasy from reality. And I don't know what troubles he had at his previous school, but I was told that they were deemed relevant in the circumstances. There was also the possibility that eventually it might have been *him* sexually assaulting *me*...'

The thought hung in a moment of heavy silence.

'So, what was the psychiatrist's view? Do you know?'

Heather seemed a little more relaxed now. She sat back and tucked her legs up beside her. 'Only from what Gilmour let slip.' She gave a wry smile. 'Which was quite a lot.' She shifted to get comfortable. 'Apparently, Dylan stuck by his story, but the psychiatrist concluded that there were clear signs of an antisocial personality disorder. Dylan understood that a teacher-student relationship was inappropriate. He agreed that if someone lied with the deliberate intention of getting someone else into trouble, that was wrong. And yet, he couldn't, or wouldn't, apply any of it to his own actions, despite being caught in lie after lie. He countered with retractions and the manipulation of facts so many times that the psychiatrist said he clearly showed an inability to distinguish fact from fiction and little remorse for the distress he had caused to others.' Heather was silent for a moment. 'I think this sexual fantasy, which deep down he knew to be wrong, had become so real to him that when he was confronted, he panicked. He could have made it appear like an innocent schoolboy crush, but I think in his head the crime was as good as committed, and so he tried to make it somebody else's.'

'So, what happened to him?' said Matthew.

'They sent him to a "special needs" school,' said Heather, 'one that specialised in teaching young adults with mental disorders, in the hope that they could arrest the development of any abnormal behaviour. It set back his education because he certainly didn't sit his GCSEs that year.'

'And what of "Mrs Dumas"?'

'Again, only what I was told. She refused to accept that her son was lying. She accused me of sexual abuse and the school of a cover-up. Apparently, she couldn't let it go. The school received letters of complaint pretty much every week, I heard. In her eyes, I had effectively had her son expelled, ruined his education, and I think she found it hard to deal with the stigma of him being admitted to a special needs school. Knowing now what we do about Sarah, I wouldn't mind betting her obsession with it was what killed her marriage. What I don't know is how she came to be here on the Isle of Wight...'

'Or, how the fuck she came to be our supervising social worker! Has she always worked in fostering?'

'I don't know.'

The shift of focus onto Sarah had riled Matthew. 'So, you were reinstated. Why did you leave Barking & Dagenham, exactly? Was it because of her? I can't believe you didn't meet her in all this. Didn't she confront you?'

'There was no way I wanted a confrontation with Dylan's mother. I did everything I could to avoid one. Dylan wasn't at school, and I was at home, suspended pending inquiry, and the school was hardly going to give her my address. I was renting at the time, and I always opted out of the electoral register and suchlike. And remember, Dylan hadn't been at the school long, so I doubt she knew anyone well enough to ask and expect an answer. I just kept my head down. Of course, afterwards, I was worried about her confronting me, especially when it became obvious she wasn't prepared to let it go. Maybe that did have something to do with my decision to leave, but mainly it was what I heard Dylan's mates and other kids saying around the school...' Heather could picture the school corridors and small groups of students laughing and looking across at her. Her mood soured again. 'When you have pupils who are supposed to look up to you asking you when Dylan's baby is due... in front of the whole class, hoping to get a laugh... I couldn't take it. I handed in my notice two weeks after being reinstated and moved away from the area.'

Matthew scowled. 'So, do you think Sarah has been plotting her revenge since 2004?'

Heather shook her head. 'I can't believe that. No, she would've had no idea where I'd gone after I left the school. But I bet she couldn't believe it when she saw the name Heather Matterface on our application. I bet she jumped at the opportunity to be appointed as our supervising social worker. Everything since has been a case of her toying with us. What was it you said recently? She's like a demented serial killer who enjoys torturing her victims and watching them suffer before she bangs the final nail in the coffin. I guess in her eyes, I destroyed her son's life and hers, and now she's done the same to us.'

Matthew looked across to the windowsill, where Sarah's card still stood. 'So, she's waited until now, until after we're deregistered, to leave her calling card.'

'Yes. And now those five kisses make sense,' said Heather. 'Sarah XXXXX is Sarah DUMAS.'

Matthew scoffed. 'Sarah Dumb Arse, you mean. Well, at least now we know the "why".'

'Well, we can let her think it's all over and she's won,' said Heather. 'What she doesn't know is what evidence we now have to take to our appeal.'

Matthew and Heather sat in silence, each dealing with their emotions, as the reality of the last two years sank in.

'Do you ever wonder what became of Dylan?' said Matthew.

'Once I started at the bank,' said Heather, 'I didn't really give it too much thought. I once heard from an old colleague that he struggled at his new school. Apparently, after he left, he failed to get a job and became an alcoholic.'

Matthew looked into his wife's eyes. 'This isn't your fault, Heather. I appreciate it wasn't easy bringing up all those old memories, and I'm sorry you had to go through all that.' He placed a hand on her knee. 'But thank you for being honest with me.' He stood up. 'We'll get through this. I'll speak to Chilwell now, and we'll get this appeal process started. Then we'll gather all the evidence we've got and get it ready for when the independent reviewer comes to see us. Does that sound like a plan?'

'I never wanted to have to think about any of this again.'

Matthew leant down and kissed her. 'I know, love. But it'll make a pretty compelling case to present at the appeal. Now we have motive!'

28

Appeal

Matthew banged down the cordless phone onto the hall table. 'Pompous prick!'

Heather had been leaning in, straining to hear Matthew's conversation with Chilwell. 'I didn't quite catch that,' she said. 'When will we be told who's reviewing our case?'

'He said that once the panel's decision has been ratified, he'll begin the process, and we'll receive notification in writing,' said Matthew. 'He has to go through his manager to arrange it.' He picked up the cordless phone and set it in its docking station.

'Well, how long's that going to take? Did he say? We've got new information. I just need someone to tell me it's going to make a difference.'

'I wouldn't worry, my love,' said Matthew, grinning. 'As far as I'm concerned, we have enough proof of Sarah's misconduct to get her sacked. In one day, we've turned this whole thing around. We've got proof the photo was doctored; we've got the actual bottle we gave the Floyds.' Matthew rearranged one of the artificial flowers in a vase on the hall table. 'All this puts everything in a new light. The appeal panel must surely question all the other accusations she's made and realise that nothing Sarah says can be taken at face value. The fact that she held back five months' worth of supervision notes is now going to look extremely suspicious. She'll have lost any trust they had in her as a professional. And then, of course, there's the motive.'

‘Okay. But how independent is this independent reviewer going to be?’ said Heather. She slapped Matthew’s hand away from the flowers. ‘How do we know that Morton or Chilwell aren’t buddy-buddy with them?’

Matthew shrugged. ‘I suppose we just have to have faith in the system,’ he said, watching Heather return the artificial orchid to its original position.

‘Well, I’ll make sure that everything in our case folder is in order, so we look as professional as we can.’ Heather was feeling a renewed sense of vigour and purpose. ‘Whoever this reviewer is,’ she said, rubbing her hands together, ‘we’ll be ready for them.’

Thursday, 10th May 2018

Matthew had started work in the grounds of the old people’s home on Tuesday, but by Thursday, it was tipping it down and he was at home. It was he who retrieved a letter delivered by a rather sodden postman. It was dated the 9th of May and advised them that their independent reviewer was to be Mrs Amanda Kennedy, the manager of the fostering department in Portsmouth.

‘She’ll be no pushover, then,’ said Matthew. He passed the letter to Heather. ‘She’s higher up the food chain than Chilwell. She’s coming in two weeks to discuss matters.’ He smirked. ‘And we’ll present her with a shitload of new evidence.’

Heather frowned. ‘Yes – well, I wouldn’t put it quite like that in front of her, if I were you.’

‘As if I would...’

Wednesday, 23rd May 2018

‘Good morning, Heather.’ Amanda Kennedy stretched out her hand. ‘It’s good to meet you.’ She paused. ‘And you must be Matthew?’

‘I know – you’ve heard a lot about me.’

‘Well, I’d be lying if I said I hadn’t.’ Amanda Kennedy winked at him.

Cheeky, thought Matthew. I might get along with you. He reached out and shook her hand. Amanda Kennedy was a no-frills kind of lady: probably in her forties, with dark wavy brown hair down to her shoulders. She was perhaps a little frumpy in jeans and a jumper, but she was well spoken and confident.

'Come in,' said Heather, showing her towards the lounge. 'Would you like a tea or coffee?'

'Coffee, black. Thank you.'

'Matthew. Be a love...'

'Yes, dear.'

'I must admit,' said Amanda, as Matthew headed towards the kitchen, 'I hadn't expected to find him this well-trained.'

'He has his moments – in the right hands.' Heather showed Amanda to the armchair in the corner by the window.

'I can still hear you,' called Matthew from the hallway. If this was Amanda Kennedy's way of breaking the ice, it was working. Matthew liked her already. He made Amanda's black coffee, a tea for himself and Heather and carried everything into the lounge on a tray.

'Service with a smile,' he said, setting the tray down on the small table Heather had put out and transferring Amanda's cup to a smaller table by the side of her armchair.

'Thank you,' said Amanda. 'Now, I believe we're ready to get started.'

'What? Before I've even offered you a biscuit?' Matthew affected a look of mock horror.

'Well, that depends on the biscuit, of course,' said Amanda. 'It'll have to be something a little fancier than a Rich Tea.'

'Well, we did have a packet of chocolate Hobnobs... but I'm afraid Heather and I were celebrating recently and ate them all. I can offer you a Jaffa Cake?'

'My favourite. I'll take two, if I may.'

Matthew waited as she removed two from the packet and then took his seat on the sofa next to Heather.

Amanda looked across at them purposefully. 'So, down to business. I've looked at everything pertaining to the investigation so far and the conclusions of the panel that sat on the 30th of April. Already in your favour, we have the evidence of Sarah Morton's failure to provide five months' worth of supervision notes in a timely fashion.'

Heather raised her hand. 'Regarding the supervision notes, we've prepared a document contesting their accuracy. I have it here.' Heather opened the red clip folder that was resting on her lap and removed three sheets of A4 paper.

Amanda nodded. 'Excellent. Hang on to those – we'll go through them later.' She looked almost apologetic. 'Although, as I'm sure you realise, it does all boil down to your word against hers, which is frustrating, I know.' She reached down and pulled a notepad and pen from her handbag. 'I think, to start though, I'd like to hear what other issues you have with the verdict. That's to say, do you feel that anything relevant was overlooked? Was anything misconstrued? Was anything a blatant untruth, in your opinion?'

Heather looked at Matthew. 'Are you still happy for me to go through this?'

'Of course,' said Matthew. 'It's what we agreed. I shall sit here quietly, behave myself and speak when spoken to.'

'Very good,' said Amanda. 'I'll make notes if that's okay with you?'

'Well, I hope you've got a sharp pencil,' said Matthew. 'There's a lot to write down.'

'Ready when you are...'

'I'm not ignoring your questions,' said Heather, 'but if it's okay with you, we'd like to start by sharing with you some new evidence that's come to light since the panel's verdict.'

'Any way you want to play it,' said Amanda, taking a sip of her coffee.

'It's just that once you've seen and heard what we've discovered, we believe it will shed a whole new light on what's been said already.'

'It's quite amazing, really,' said Matthew. 'We'd only been home from the panel meeting a few hours when Sarah came round and I found...'

Heather was staring at him, with a look of exasperation in her eyes. Amanda chewed silently on a Jaffa Cake.

'Sorry. I'll shut up,' he said.

Heather got up, walked over to Amanda and handed her a brown A4 envelope. 'I'm sure you noted,' she said, returning to her seat on the sofa, 'that one of the key pieces of evidence Sarah Morton and Andrew Chilwell presented was a purported copy of the photograph Matthew took of James's bump after Grace pushed him into the stair gate. The photograph they presented showed a laceration in addition to a large area of bruising.'

Amanda had removed the contents of the envelope and was studying them.

Heather continued. 'Clearly, Matthew and I knew the real extent of James's injury, and there was no laceration, just minor inflammation. What you have in your hands, Amanda, is a report that states the photographic evidence presented by Sarah Morton was a doctored version of the original. It's been professionally analysed, and the findings are incontrovertible.'

'Impressive work on your part,' said Amanda. 'And quite frankly, I'm astounded.'

'Well,' Matthew snickered, 'when you've heard the rest of what we have to say, I don't think you'll be in any doubt that Sarah had motive and malicious intent.'

'I can't wait,' said Amanda, raising her eyebrows and taking another sip of her coffee.

'I'll move on, then,' said Heather.

Matthew snorted. 'This is the best one, in my book,' he said, chewing on a mouthful of Jaffa Cake.

Heather slipped her hand into her pocket. 'Another key component of Sarah Morton's report was the suggestion that we gave an old bottle of fluoxetine to Mr and Mrs Floyd when Emma went on a week's respite.' She paused and looked across at Amanda.

Amanda nodded. 'Yes, I'm familiar with the circumstances. The old bottle was issued in August and contained insufficient medication.'

'Yes –' Heather nodded, 'but we were convinced we'd given them the bottle that I'd picked up from the pharmacy in September, which had plenty left in it. But doubt creeps in. Nothing made sense, so we took it upon ourselves to pay the Floyds a visit.'

'And they told us – get this,' said Matthew, 'that not long after we'd dropped Emma off, Sarah arrived under the pretence that she was checking we'd given the Floyds everything they needed. All very suspicious, don't you think?'

Amanda nodded while scribbling notes.

Heather picked up again. 'For us, it was obvious – after we requested Emma's respite, Sarah removed the old August bottle from our kitchen before we had a chance to throw it away, and when she visited the Floyds, she switched the bottles.'

Amanda stopped writing. She looked incredulous. 'Wait a minute. You're saying she planned this?'

'Oh, we know she did,' said Matthew.

'Well, I'm assuming you have proof? You're certainly going to need it.'

Heather nodded. 'Just humour us for a moment, Amanda. I know how it sounds – we couldn't believe it either. Why on earth would Sarah do that? But then you found the September bottle, which we *had* given to the Floyds, didn't you, Matthew?'

Matthew grinned.

Amanda began scribbling notes again.

'It was when Morton came to pick up the last of the kids' stuff...' he said.

Matthew told his tale with relish. When he'd finished, Heather pulled the bottle from her pocket and removed two photographs from a plastic wallet in her red clip folder. She crossed the room and handed everything to Amanda.

Amanda looked at the bottle and photographs and hesitated. 'You know what they'll say, though, don't you?'

Matthew smiled. 'They'll say I planted it in Sarah's boot.'

'Exactly.'

Matthew pushed on. 'Yes, we know there's a counterargument here. As far as Morton and Chilwell are concerned, we gave the Floyds the old August bottle, which is feasible, because it had some wastage left in it. That means *we* still had the September bottle that we should have given to the Floyds. They'll say we found it and, realising our mistake, concocted our story about Sarah switching bottles and planted it in Sarah's car at the first opportunity. But I suggest it's more likely that we'd have disposed of the incriminating evidence. And if our "devious" plan had been to stitch up Sarah, wouldn't we have planted the bottle *before* the panel meeting and then used it against her in our defence?'

'It depends,' said Amanda. 'You might not have had the opportunity, or you might only have found it at home after the panel meeting.'

Matthew hesitated. 'True. But don't forget there's the fact that Morton paid a visit to the Floyds after we left – the Floyds will testify to that. She had the opportunity. And, it's as I said, when you've heard the rest of what we have to tell you, you'll see that Morton also had motive and malicious intent.' He sat back, and Heather took the cue to continue.

'This is difficult for me, Amanda. I've only just realised the significance of an incident from my past, which has a bearing on this case. Until recently, I hadn't even discussed it with Matthew. It's something I'd tried to forget.'

'Well, take your time, Heather,' said Amanda. 'We're in no rush and I'm not here to judge you.' As if to emphasise the informality of the meeting, she reached for her coffee, took a few sips and then reached for her second Jaffa Cake.

And then Heather painstakingly repeated the story she had told Matthew.

'Well, that certainly sheds light on the question of why,' said Amanda.

'I just need to know it's going to make a difference,' said Heather.

Matthew sensed Heather's tension as she sat close beside him. He leant forward. 'It must do, surely? We have proof that Sarah presented the panel with a doctored photograph of James's face. And in light of what Heather has told you, whose version of events is the panel going to believe regarding the bottle of fluoxetine? Not only that, it sheds a whole new light on all the accusations Sarah's made. Most of the time, it's been her word against ours – her word is worth nothing now. Any credibility, any professional sway she had, has been destroyed.'

'To a large extent, yes...' said Amanda. 'But, on occasion, your judgement has been called into question, and the panel might still find validity in some of the concerns raised. That said, overwhelmingly, the motivation behind the persistent attempts to undermine you, the failure to produce what must now very likely be viewed as inaccurate records of conversations and events, will damage the integrity of the council's case.'

'To the point that they'll find in our favour?' Matthew looked at her expectantly.

Amanda paused only briefly. 'I have high hopes, Matthew. High hopes. What I will say is that there is no doubt whatsoever that you have a valid case for appeal, and that will be my recommendation to the Agency Decision Maker.'

Matthew sensed Heather's tension ease. 'In which case,' she said, 'there's one other thing we need to discuss.'

'Fire away,' said Amanda.

'James,' said Heather. 'At the panel meeting, I outlined the conversations we had with Sarah regarding our interest in adopting him. It should have been noted in the minutes.'

'Indeed,' said Amanda. 'You claimed she failed to record them in her supervision notes, and failed to respond formally, having committed to determining a way forward. Again, unfortunately, it's your word against hers that those conversations ever took place.'

'Quite,' said Heather, 'but I'm thinking of getting in contact with Janet to see if there's been a decision on his future yet. I heard on the grapevine that his mother failed her assessment a few weeks ago, and I'm worried they've already put him up for adoption.'

'I think in the circumstances, Heather, it might be best if you wait until after the appeal panel meeting. Reinstatement would strengthen your application.'

'I understand that.' Heather felt a flush of anxiety. 'But the appeal panel is likely to be at the end of June, and that's over four weeks away.'

'I don't think you have a choice,' said Amanda. 'You're going to have to be patient.'

'I just need reassurance that we're not too late,' said Heather, 'that if... *when* we're reinstated, he has the chance to be returned to the only real family he's ever known – that we'll be given the same consideration to adopt him as anyone else.'

'The Adoption Team is obliged to consider everyone, Heather, and don't forget, you also have the option of applying directly to the Court for an Adoption Order. As for being too late – quite rightly, they are clearly exploring every option before they go down the adoption route. That can take time. And James has a complex medical condition that will affect the understanding of his long-term placement needs. It could be a while before they finalise his permanence plan, and then they have to apply to the Court for a Placement Order.' Amanda smiled gently. 'Look. Let's see how the panel review goes, Heather. One step at a time. If all goes well, I'll do everything I can to support your application.'

Matthew reached out and took Heather's hand. 'Amanda's right, my love. Have faith in the system.'

Heather stared at him. 'You what? You mean the system that you're always pointing out has gone bloody mad?'

'Yes,' said Matthew. 'That system.'

29

A Day For Reckoning

Monday, 25th June 2018

A rather officious council representative led Matthew and Heather through the now-familiar corridors of power in the council offices and showed them into the waiting room next to the appeal panel's courtroom.

'Let battle commence...'

'What are you muttering about?' said Heather.

'How about this... We shall fight in the photo shops, we shall fight in the pharmacies, we shall fight with growing confidence and growing strength in our appeal, we shall defend our honour, whatever the cost may be. We shall never surrender!'

'Matthew, what are you prattling on about? This is serious.'

'House of Commons. The 4th of June 1940, following the evacuation of British and French forces from Dunkirk, as the Germans swept through France.'

Heather stared at him.

'Winston Churchill,' he added.

'No, Matthew. It's you being a prat. Shut up. This is no time for levity.'

'Just trying to lighten the mood...'

A knock at the door saved Heather from any more of Matthew's ramblings. It was Amanda.

'Morning, Heather, Matthew. I've just been next door, and they're nearly ready for us. How are you feeling?'

'Confident,' said Matthew. 'Looking forward to seeing Morton squirm.'

Amanda looked at Heather, who appeared pale. 'Try not to worry, Heather. You've got a much stronger case this time round. Be positive in front of the panel.'

A few minutes later, the Chair of the panel called everyone through. She was the same middle-aged lady that had overseen the previous panel meeting. Matthew and Heather followed Amanda into one of the largest rooms at the council offices, which was reserved for such meetings to accommodate the number of people present. Several tables had been pushed together to make one large one in the centre of the room. Jugs of water and glasses on a large tray formed the centrepiece. Matthew, Heather and Amanda took the three remaining seats and sat together among the twelve members of the panel. Andrew Chilwell and Sarah Morton sat across the table from them. Some of the panel were fresh faces. Each had in front of them a sheaf of paperwork, and proceedings began with the usual dreary introductions. Every member of the panel stated the public service department they represented: social workers, foster carers, police, teachers, NHS workers...

The Chair of the panel spoke. 'This appeal panel is considering the decision made on the 30th of April this year, in which Mr and Mrs Blundell were removed from the fostering register. I suggest we don't spend our time going over old ground unless there is a significant reason to do so. I suggest we focus on what has been submitted subsequently, much of which is new information.' She looked around at the faces, all focused on her, before continuing. 'I believe all members of the panel have had the opportunity to review the relevant case notes, the minutes from the initial panel meeting and the appeal submission by Amanda Kennedy on behalf of Mr and Mrs Blundell. No doubt this has raised some questions. If this panel will indulge me, may I start by addressing, Ms Morton, the issue that has concerned me most. Having read that there is clearly history, or "bad blood", between you and Mrs Blundell, why did you not flag this conflict of interest when you were assigned as her supervising social worker?'

Sarah Morton stared defiantly into the eyes of her cross-examiner. 'Until I read the document submitted by Mrs Kennedy, I had no idea who Heather Blundell was. Yes, I now appreciate who she is and, yes, we were both involved in an unsavoury incident concerning my son, but that has no bearing on this case.'

'Did you not recognise her as the same woman?'

'We never met. All our dealings went through the headmaster and the school.'

'Yet, it says here,' said the Chair, referring to a piece of paper in front of her, 'in a recollection by both Mr and Mrs Blundell, that when you conducted your first home visit, you mentioned noticing Mrs Blundell's maiden name, Matterface, on their application form, as it was an unusual name. Apparently, you also commented on the fact that she had been a teacher at Barking & Dagenham school, which you knew well, having resided in West Ham.' She looked across at Sarah Morton.

'As I've already said, when I was assigned as their supervising social worker, I had no idea who Heather Blundell was.'

The Chair took a measured breath. 'Ms Morton. Are you asking us to believe that after your son was expelled from school, subsequently deemed to have serious mental health issues, all of which disrupted his education and all of which you blamed on Heather Matterface, you didn't recognise the significance of Heather Blundell's maiden name or her association with Barking & Dagenham school?'

'Correct.'

'I have to say, Ms Morton, I find that very hard to believe. Mr Chilwell, what are your thoughts?'

Andrew Chilwell looked up from absent-mindedly picking at some minor bobbling on his jacket. 'Well, of course,' he said, 'had I known of this prior association and the nature of it, I would certainly have queried the wisdom of appointing Sarah as Mr and Mrs Blundell's supervising social worker. In fact, it might have prompted me to look more closely at Mrs Blundell's suitability as a foster carer...'

Matthew saw Sarah Morton's lips curl into a smile.

The Chair shuffled some papers. 'Mr Chilwell. Having read the due diligence notes carefully, Barking & Dagenham School unequivocally cleared Mrs Blundell of any blame in the matter.' She shifted in her seat.

'It is also quite clear, Ms Morton, that you did not accept this decision and repeatedly and vociferously made your displeasure known. I think it fair to say that you harboured considerable resentment towards Heather Matterface, as she was known at the time. One could be forgiven for suggesting that any future opportunity for redress would find you in a vengeful mood.'

Sarah Morton ignored the remark and looked over towards Andrew Chilwell, who, in turn, looked down at his paperwork. 'As you are aware, Madam Chairman,' he said, 'we deal with a large number of foster parents and have a limited number of support workers to supervise them all.'

'That's as may be, Mr Chilwell...' The Chair shifted her attention back to the panel. 'Members of the panel. Given the fact that Mrs Blundell's historical details were on the Blundells' application form and that Ms Morton would certainly have noted these, as evidenced by the Blundells' recollections of her comments to that effect, I believe it would be remiss of this panel not to acknowledge the possibility that Sarah Morton knew from the start who Mrs Blundell was and saw the opportunity to exact revenge. Does anyone have any thoughts to the contrary or any further questions in this regard?' She looked around.

Several nods and murmurs of agreement had accompanied her words, and a few now vocalised their support for her conclusion.

Sarah Morton's emotions flared. 'This is all speculation and lies.'

'Your comments are noted, Ms Morton.'

Heather raised her hand. 'I would also draw the panel's attention to the "sympathy" card that Sarah Morton left in our lounge after we were deregistered. I think it's clear now that she played her hand when she cryptically signed it Sarah followed by five Xs. As you'll have read, her married name at the time of the school incident was Dumas. There are five letters in Dumas,' she added hurriedly.

'Noted, Mrs Blundell. Thank you.' Again, the Chair looked around the room. 'Right, if there are no more questions,' she said, 'then we'll move on. I suggest we look at the new information in the order in which the relevant events occurred. Which means we start with the photographic evidence supplied by the council at the first panel meeting, showing an injury to the face of the child, James, sustained while in the care of Mr and Mrs Blundell. The council claimed, "a worrying degree of negligence", saying the injury warranted a hospital visit, which the Blundells, "displaying a clear lack of judgement", did not deem necessary. This was a view that the original panel upheld; however, it is not this decision that we are being asked to consider today; it is the nature of the photographic evidence. Mrs Kennedy, do you want to take us through the pertinent points?'

Amanda leant forward and rested her arms on the table. 'You've all seen the professional analysis of the digital photograph used in evidence by Sarah Morton and Andrew Chilwell at the original panel meeting. First, I believe the fact that Matthew and Heather Blundell went to such lengths to obtain this report demonstrates their absolute belief in their case. Sadly, I also believe that this is just the first of a few instances that we'll be discussing today where Sarah Morton appears to have gone to extraordinary lengths to undermine their credibility as carers, by manipulation. Now, I'm a self-confessed technophobe, and I think most here would struggle to fully understand the technical aspects of this report – and it's probably beyond the remit of this panel to do so, anyway. So, let's keep things plain and simple. What's important here is a) it has been produced by a professional company that will testify as to its validity and b) the damning phrase in the summary, which reads: "This photograph has without doubt been altered from its original state". Which leads to some inevitable questions: first, why was it necessary to alter the original photographic evidence?' Amanda looked around at the members of the panel, who were listening intently. 'Surely, there is only one answer? The original photograph did not necessarily support the argument that James should have been referred to the hospital. Second, who altered it? Let's go back over the chain of events. Matthew Blundell took just the one photograph, which was the only evidence of the true nature of James's injury. When Sarah Morton learnt of the incident during a supervision visit almost a month later, she demanded Matthew forward the image to her and delete it from his phone and email account. The Blundells heard nothing more on the matter until Andrew Chilwell produced what we now know to be a doctored copy over a year later. Perhaps Ms Morton can tell us what she did with the image after she received it from Mr Blundell? And perhaps Mr Chilwell can tell us when he first became involved?'

Chilwell was clearly agitated. 'The first time I laid eyes on that photograph was when Sarah Morton submitted it to me as part of her report.'

A member of the panel spoke up. 'For clarity, Mr Chilwell, was this report you refer to one that Sarah Morton produced around the time of the incident, or the recent report she filed that triggered the investigation into the Blundells' suitability as foster parents?' Matthew looked to his right at the young lady who had posed the question. Her name badge identified her as Jessica. Her dress and demeanour suggested she was a no-nonsense high flyer.

'The recent report,' said Chilwell. 'She didn't escalate the incident at the time.'

Jessica frowned. 'Is that usual?'

'Is what usual?'

'For one of your direct reports not to flag a serious case of negligence?'

Chilwell bristled. 'Given the alleged significance of the injury, she certainly should have raised it with me, which is something I discussed with her when I read her recent report.'

'And what reason...' Jessica's voice trailed off, and she looked over at the Chair. 'Apologies, Madam Chairman. Am I overstepping the mark?'

'No, you go right ahead, Jessica. The more discussion, the better.'

'Thank you, Madam Chairman.' Jessica turned her attention back to Chilwell. 'Mr Chilwell, what reason did Ms Morton give you for not escalating the incident at the time?'

'I'm really not sure where you're going with this...'

'I'm just trying to understand how an alleged case of serious negligence can be seemingly overlooked and then brought before a panel over a year later.'

'Because,' Sarah Morton interjected, 'I took responsibility and concluded the matter satisfactorily at the time. Ultimately, James seemed fine. The hospital checked him over, and after visiting James at the Blundells' home, Janet Harty, James's social worker, was satisfied. And I received assurances from the Blundells that in the event of any future incidents they would inform me.'

'I get that,' said Jessica, 'but, regardless, if this was a case of serious negligence, as you claimed in your report a year later, surely you failed in your duty to escalate it?'

'Look,' said Sarah Morton, 'this wasn't raised at the previous panel meeting. They obviously didn't consider it to be an issue.'

'I can't speak for the members of the original panel,' said Jessica, 'but I have noted it and I do consider it to be an issue worthy of discussion. I believe your decision not to escalate might have a bearing on this case.'

Sarah Morton said nothing, prompting Jessica to continue.

'Ms Morton. The first you knew of the incident was nearly a month after it occurred. Any superficial injury would pretty much have cleared up by the time you and Janet Harty assessed James. So really, when it came to assessing the Blundells' judgement at the time of the incident, all you had to go on was Mr Blundell's photograph. It suggests to me that if that original photograph evidenced the significant injury highlighted in your report, you failed in your duty to escalate a serious case of negligence; or, it's as Mrs Kennedy has already suggested...'

Sarah remained silent. Amanda shifted in her chair and waited a few moments. When it became clear that Jessica was not going to elaborate, she said, 'I think what Jessica is, perhaps, reluctant to articulate, Ms Morton, is my previous suggestion that the original photograph showed nothing more than a bump, which meant there was no case of serious negligence to escalate and your only immediate satisfaction was to read the Blundells the riot act.'

Sarah Morton could no longer contain herself. 'Absolutely not. I dealt with the matter. The original photograph showed a cut on James's forehead, but the cut had healed nicely and he seemed no worse for wear. Therefore, I was prepared to give the Blundells a second chance.'

'Or perhaps,' continued Amanda, 'you saw an opportunity and stayed your hand? Perhaps this incident sowed the germ of an idea: a means to exact revenge by the persistent undermining of Matthew and Heather's credibility until you felt you had enough damning evidence to petition for their dismissal? I suggest to you that the subsequent manipulation of the original photograph was an attempt by you to strengthen your case in this instance and ensure that the accusations in your final report were indisputable. That's for this panel to decide once it's addressed further examples of your alleged deceit.'

A middle-aged man with salt-and-pepper hair half raised his hand. 'If I can come back to you, Mr Chilwell. What are your thoughts on the report detailing the alterations made to the photograph of James and, in light of its findings, who do you believe was responsible for the alteration?'

Chilwell cleared his throat. 'First off, I want to know how Mr Blundell came to be in possession of a copy of this photograph. He told Ms Morton he'd deleted it.'

'I deleted the original, Mr Chilwell. This is not the original, and it doesn't matter where I got it from,' said Matthew. 'What matters is that I managed to get hold of a copy and have exposed a blatant act of fraud, which has had serious ramifications.'

'I think the means by which Mr Blundell acquired the image can be overlooked in the circumstances,' said the Chair. 'I think we need to get back to the question of who was responsible for altering it. Continue, Mr Chilwell. I'd like to hear your thoughts on that.'

Chilwell cleared his throat again. 'When Sarah Morton came to me with her report,' he said, 'the image was on a memory stick. I viewed the image and during my investigation, presented Mr and Mrs Blundell with a printed copy and queried why, given the condition of James's face, they had not taken him to hospital to have him checked over. I admit the Blundells' response was that the image had been tampered with, but at the time the accusation seemed ludicrous. Obviously, now, with the benefit of hindsight, that certainly appears to have been the case, and it seems that I was misled and acted on false information. The image must have been altered before it came into my possession. If you are asking me who altered it, then I can only conclude that it must have been Sarah. It had been in her possession ever since she took it from Mr Blundell.'

Matthew began a slow handclap. 'Oh, well done, Chilwell. Have a cigar!'

'Now, now, Mr Blundell, let's keep this civil,' said the Chair. She turned her attention to Sarah Morton. 'Ms Morton. Mr Chilwell has suggested that you were the sole custodian of the image, which suggests that you were likely to have been involved in its alteration. I'm sure this panel would like to hear your side of the story.'

Sarah Morton responded immediately. 'Yes, I retained the image and, yes, I suppose I must take responsibility if an unauthorised third party, unbeknownst to me, has gained access to it and made alterations for reasons unknown. There is, however, one other person who had the opportunity and possibly a motive for altering it...'

'Go on...'

'When I handed the memory stick to Andrew Chilwell with my report, I hadn't looked at it since the time of the incident. Is it not possible that it was he who felt the need to enhance the image to strengthen a case of negligence?'

'That's preposterous!' Chilwell spat back a half-taken sip of coffee into his cup. 'How dare you question my integrity. I merely printed a copy of an image on a memory stick that had been in your possession since Day One!'

'I'm deeply concerned,' said the Chair. 'A photograph was taken of a young child with an injury that may or may not have required medical attention. You, Ms Morton, state that it did, and that you resolved an incident you now claim to have been a serious act of negligence. If that's the case, then it should have been escalated to senior management. No question. However, in light of a report from a professional, we now know that the image, for which you were responsible and subsequently presented as evidence of your claim, has been manipulated to exaggerate the nature of the injury; and yet, apart from accusing each other, neither you nor Andrew Chilwell have any idea how it was tampered with. Whichever way you look at it, there have been some serious failings here. In my opinion, we also have to consider this matter in the context of your previous, toxic relationship with Heather Blundell and the motive it presents in a chain of events that you have controlled from the outset. Plenty for the panel to deliberate over.'

'Well, we don't need Sherlock Holmes to work out who's responsible, do we?' said Matthew. 'Sarah Morton is up to her neck in this fraud.'

'Something for the panel to decide, Mr Blundell,' said the Chair. 'And I'm not sure that such comments are particularly helpful. We should move on. There have been considerable developments in the matter of the old bottle of fluoxetine, issued in August 2017 and containing insufficient medicine, which was allegedly given by the Blundells to respite carers, the Floyds. They reported the issue to Sarah Morton, after which the said bottle disappeared and then reappeared. Quite the story. You will note from Mrs Kennedy's appeal submission that the bottle of fluoxetine issued in September, that the Blundells assert was the bottle they gave to the Floyds, has also now surfaced – allegedly found hidden in the boot of Sarah Morton's car by Matthew Blundell. I've done enough talking. Does someone else wish to take the lead on this one?'

A gentleman across the table from Matthew and Heather, whose name badge was illegible, cleared his throat and addressed the room. 'Well, Madam Chairman, for the record, I've noted, as I'm sure my fellow panel members have also, that there are now, clearly, two sides to this story. Previously, the facts seemed to speak for themselves – a case of negligence; however, my understanding is that in light of Mr Blundell's discovery and what we've heard regarding the history between Sarah Morton and Heather Blundell, we are now being asked to consider two additional scenarios: First, the possibility that Sarah Morton switched the bottles in order to discredit the Blundells; second, that the Blundells discovered the bottle they should have given to the Floyds and, to cover up their mistake, planted it in the boot of Sarah Morton's car. I believe it would assist our deliberations if we heard from both parties involved and their interpretation of events. Would either Mr or Mrs Blundell care to start?'

Matthew leapt straight in. 'I'll say with no hesitation that we have always known, without a shadow of a doubt, that we gave the Floyds a bottle of fluoxetine that was issued in September 2017 and contained enough medicine to last the duration of Emma's stay. However, at the last panel meeting, we were also acutely aware, as you have already alluded to, sir, that the facts seemed to speak for themselves: namely, we gave the Floyds the dregs of an old bottle of fluoxetine that was issued in August 2017. How could we contest that without calling Sarah Morton a liar? How could we contest that without suggesting that Sarah Morton had procured an old bottle from our kitchen and switched the bottles – even with the Floyd's information that she had visited them shortly after we dropped Emma off and, I suggest, had the opportunity to do so? "Why on earth would she want to do that?" would have been the response – a question we couldn't have hoped to answer without seeming to be desperately clutching at straws. Better to say nothing than to demean ourselves, wouldn't you say? But now, and I think you'll agree with me, we are seeing this matter in a whole new light. Sarah Morton had a clear motive for switching the bottles. Yes, I could have planted that bottle in her boot at the first given opportunity, but I ask you, given all the other evidence you've heard, which scenario do you think is most likely?'

'So, for the record, Mr Blundell, you are stating that you did not place the bottle of fluoxetine, issued in September 2017, in Ms Morton's car?'

'Correct.'

The nameless gentleman turned his head and looked at Sarah Morton, seated to his right. 'So, Ms Morton, how did the bottle of medication come to be in the boot of your car?'

Sarah Morton scowled. 'I don't think there's much more to be said. Clearly, after they were deregistered, the Blundells discovered the bottle they should have sent to the Floyds with Emma and were trying to cover up their mistake by planting it in the boot of my car and concocting this ridiculous story.'

Identifiable by his name badge, another member of the panel, Paul, asked, 'Ms Morton, did you see Mr Blundell put the bottle in your boot?'

'No, but it certainly wasn't there before I arrived.'

There was a moment or two of silence.

'It's just an observation, really,' said Paul, addressing his fellow panel members. 'When I was reviewing the minutes of the panel meeting on the 30th of April, I noted the Blundells asserted they had been told by Sarah Morton, when the fluoxetine issue was first raised in early October 2017, that the matter had been escalated to Mr Chilwell. Subsequently, they were told that the bottle in contention had gone missing. They said Sarah Morton claimed that having passed it on to Andrew Chilwell, he had mislaid it, denying them the opportunity to examine the evidence. However, when Andrew Chilwell brought the bottle to his second investigation meeting with the Blundells in April 2018, he claimed Sarah Morton had only recently given it to him and denied ever having it or mislaying it.' Paul paused and flicked to the next page of the paperwork in front of him. 'Quoting the panel's response from the minutes: "As neither of the alleged conversations between Sarah Morton and Matthew and Heather Blundell was formally recorded in the relevant supervision notes, this is possibly an unfortunate misunderstanding, which, in any case, appears to have no bearing on the facts of this matter".' He looked up. 'However, re-evaluating this "misunderstanding" in the context of Ms Morton's enduring resentment towards Mrs Blundell alters one's view to something a little more sinister. It conveniently prevented the Blundells from viewing the bottle themselves and, believing the evidence lost, led them to assume the matter was closed.' He looked across at Amanda. 'Possibly, as Mrs Kennedy has already alluded to, another example of you, Ms Morton, staying your hand until you were ready to deliver the final coup de grâce.'

'Do you have anything to add, Mr Chilwell?' asked the Chair.

Chilwell eyed Sarah Morton distastefully. 'I can only reiterate what I've said all along. Having prepared her report highlighting the repeated failings of the Blundells in their duty of care to the children, Sarah Morton presented me with the offending bottle of medication, which she said had been given to her by the Floyds. That was the first time I saw the bottle in question.'

'It was also the first time you were made aware of the issue, is that correct?' said the man with salt-and-pepper hair.

'It was.'

'So, as I say, potentially, another example of you deliberately stalling the escalation of an incident involving the Blundells, Ms Morton,' said Paul. 'And again, you've opened yourself up to accusations of failing to escalate a serious case of negligence.'

'I'll tell you why if I may, Madam Chairman.' Matthew continued regardless of consent. 'Control. She had to be in control. She wanted us to know that our future was in *her* hands. At every opportunity, she was undermining us, antagonising us and then lulling us into a false sense of security when we thought everything had died down and gone away with no further action being taken. All the while she was building this case against us, manipulating the evidence, the facts and the supervision notes to fit her version of events. She was prepared to take risks by not escalating immediately. Better to ask for forgiveness, if you get my drift.'

The Chair took control of the meeting again. 'And now that the bottle of medicine the Blundells claim to be the one they actually gave to the Floyds has been found in the boot of Sarah Morton's car, what is your assessment of the situation, Mr Chilwell?'

'I had always assumed that if the Blundells gave the Floyds the wrong bottle, they would still be in possession of the "right" one. Therefore, it's feasible that they could have planted it in Sarah Morton's boot...' He hesitated and looked around him. '... but I'm really not convinced the Blundells would do such a thing,' he added rather hurriedly.

'Oh, but you're convinced that I could have done such a thing as switch the bottles, Mr Chilwell?' Sarah Morton seemed to be losing her composure.

'Madam Chairman,' said Chilwell. 'All I can say is that if Sarah Morton switched the bottles, then she had us all fooled.'

The Chair looked around. 'Does anyone have any other points they'd like to raise – anything they'd like to clarify?' Most shook their heads. 'In which case, there is just one last point to consider before we ask the parties involved to leave the panel to its deliberations. It is the matter of the supervision notes. The previous panel has already established and noted the purported reasons for the delay in producing five months' worth of supervision notes. What we need to address here is the claim by the appellants that the new information pertaining to Sarah Morton's past association with Heather Blundell strengthens their assertion that they were deliberately denied the opportunity to review and query said notes over a five-month period, because they had been manipulated and did not provide an accurate record of events.'

Matthew leant over and whispered in Heather's ear. 'How do you think it's going so far?'

'Not bad, but I need a stiff drink to calm my nerves.'

Matthew reached out and took her hand. It was cold and clammy. 'I think it's going well,' he said. 'Surely, at least, they have reasonable doubt now.'

'Does anyone have any questions or thoughts they'd like to put to either party?' the Chair was saying.

'I think we have all the information we need,' said the nameless gentleman. 'As you say, it's just a matter for the panel to discuss whether the new information about the prior relationship between Ms Morton and Mrs Blundell affects our view on the matter.'

'Well, if that's the general consensus, then I would like to bring the first part of this meeting to a close,' said the Chair.

No one spoke. Heather raised her hand.

'Mrs Blundell?'

'Madam Chairman. When we were first called into the council offices and handed the letter detailing the various allegations against us, Mr Chilwell informed us that all the children in our care were to be fostered elsewhere with immediate effect. It was common knowledge, or so we believed, that we were considering adopting James at the time. I'm not looking to prejudge the decision of this panel meeting here today, but if we are reinstated, will the panel state it has no objection to us pursuing our interest in adopting James?'

'That is certainly something we can discuss and factor into our recommendation, Mrs Blundell; but ultimately, there are formal processes in place for foster carers wishing to adopt. If you are reinstated on the register, you can certainly express your interest and explore your options.'

'Thank you,' said Heather.

'That just leaves me to thank everyone for attending. Mr and Mrs Blundell and Mrs Kennedy, if you could once again wait in the room next door. Or, feel free to exit the building and have some lunch. I'll call you, Mrs Kennedy, when the panel has come to a decision. We're having lunch too, so we'll be at least an hour.'

As Matthew stood, he couldn't help but look over at Morton and Chilwell, who were also vacating their seats. He could almost feel the chill from the ice that had formed between them as Chilwell hurried out, eventually followed by Sarah Morton, who held back, glaring at his back as she allowed him a head start.

'McDonald's, anyone?'

'For Christ's sake, Matthew. How can you think of your stomach at a time like this?' Heather stood wearily. 'Anyway, maybe Amanda would prefer a wine bar or something. That's if she wants to go out at all.'

'It's a bit early to be celebrating,' said Matthew, 'but I'm up for a drink if anyone else is.'

‘It’s a tempting offer. I could murder a Big Mac.’ Amanda winked at Matthew. ‘But I’ve got some phone calls I have to make. You two go on if you wish. If you’re not back when we’re called, then I’ll ring you on your mobile, Heather.’

Matthew took Heather’s hand as they emerged from the council offices into a pleasant twenty-two-degree heat and sunshine and wandered down High Street from County Hall. She had made it clear that she did not wish to walk all the way to McDonald’s, especially as she could not face eating anything, so Matthew suggested the ‘Slug & Lettuce’ opposite, which had opened earlier in the year. It occupied the site of the old 1930s Medina cinema, and the décor was contemporary, quirky and glitzy. Not Matthew’s usual taste, but he contented himself with a decent burger and a beer, while Heather nervously knocked back a couple of glasses of wine.

‘I don’t know how you can eat at a time like this,’ she said, watching her husband stretch his mouth around a burger in a bun crammed with lettuce, tomatoes and a relish that dripped and found its way onto his chin. ‘I actually find it quite repulsive.’

Matthew’s eyes widened as he bit and chewed.

‘Honestly,’ said Heather, ‘I swear there’s something wrong with you.’ She stood and disappeared in the direction of the toilets. By the time she reappeared, Matthew had finished and his plate had been cleared away.

They whiled away another uneasy half an hour or so before Heather’s phone rang and Amanda advised them that the panel had finished its deliberations and was just having an informal chat over sandwiches.

‘If you head back now, they should have finished up by the time you get here,’ she said.

Matthew and Heather retraced their steps from the Slug & Lettuce in half the time it had taken them to get there.

‘Hi Amanda, have we kept them waiting?’ said a breathless Heather as they arrived back in the waiting room.

‘No, not at all,’ said Amanda, closing her laptop and looking up. ‘The Chair popped her head round the door earlier and said there was no rush. I’ll let her know you’re back.’ She stood, arched her back, winced and smiled weakly. ‘Just the usual aches and pains.’ She moved slowly towards the door. By the time she reached it, her stiffness had eased.

'I don't think I can take another "guilty" verdict,' said Heather, looking despairingly at Matthew. She slumped heavily into a cheap yellow faux-leather sofa against one wall.

'You won't have to. We've got this.' Matthew joined her.

Amanda came back with the Chair and both sat down opposite them.

'Okay, well, I'll come straight to the point,' said the Chair. 'I can imagine what a nightmare this must have been for you these past few months.'

'It's driven me to the edge, if I'm honest,' said Heather. 'I feel sick.'

The Chair looked mildly alarmed.

'I'll be okay,' said Heather. 'I just can't take much more of this.'

'Well, it's good news, Mrs Blundell.' The Chair smiled gently. 'It's the panel's recommendation that you be reinstated. Of course, it's down to the Agency Decision Maker to ratify that, and you'll be advised of her decision by letter within the next ten days, but I'd be very surprised if she challenges the panel's decision. However, we are recommending some conditions.'

'What conditions?' Matthew's face clouded over.

'I'll explain. I just wanted to reassure you, Mrs Blundell, that you've no need to worry.'

The relief flowing through Heather was palpable, and Matthew gave her a hug. 'I told you everything would be okay.'

The Chair continued. 'I probably shouldn't say some of what I'm about to, but you've been through the mill and, frankly, I think you're owed an honest explanation. I'll say first off that, given the information they had at the time, it's felt the original panel probably came to the correct conclusion. However, the fresh evidence has raised considerable concerns over Sarah Morton's conduct and integrity; though I'm sure you'll appreciate that at this stage, there is little that can be proved. The panel has recommended a full internal investigation. If the council has made mistakes, then it needs to learn from them. And here's the bit I'd ask you to keep to yourselves, though you'd probably find out anyway. Sarah Morton has been suspended pending the outcome of said investigation.'

Heather stiffened. 'It's the very least she deserves. I hope if the council finds evidence against her, she'll be prosecuted for fraud.'

‘Okay, Heather, let’s listen to what the Chairlady has to say.’ Matthew still had his arm around her and squeezed her gently.

The Chair continued. ‘Circumstantially, the evidence is overwhelming, but she claims she didn’t recognise you. She also claims that though the digital image was in her possession, she wasn’t the one who altered it; that you planted the medicine bottle in her car and, partially backed by Andrew Chilwell, that there were legitimate reasons why she struggled to produce the supervision notes. She insists they’re an accurate reflection of events and the discussions between you. Anything to the contrary needs proving. Some of it may never be proved. But there’s enough there to warrant her suspension. Rest assured, if the council finds enough evidence against her, it will refer the matter to the police.’

‘And what about Chilwell?’ said Matthew. ‘Surely, his incompetence can’t go unpunished? He backed Morton all the way. He never once stopped to challenge anything she said; if he had, we might not be in this mess.’

‘I’m afraid I can’t comment on Mr Chilwell,’ said the Chair. ‘Now, those conditions...’

Heather paled. ‘Does this have anything to do with our adopting James?’

‘I’ll get to that, if I may, Mrs Blundell. No, the conditions have nothing to do with James. This panel upholds the original concern that your judgement in some instances was questionable. Nothing of serious concern; certainly not the negligence that Sarah Morton claimed, but enough that it feels more comfortable recommending that you be reinstated on a phased basis. It’s been suggested that you be limited to just the one placement to begin with, and we’ll see how it goes.’

‘And James?’ said Heather.

‘The panel sees no reason why, if its recommendation is accepted, you cannot continue to pursue your interest in adopting James. Quite the contrary. It can often be difficult to place children with complex medical conditions, and your commitment to providing James with security as part of a loving family is not to be underestimated. I wish you every success. All being well, you can start the ball rolling with your new supervising social worker.’

'When will we get to meet this new supervising social worker?' said Heather.

'Andrew Chilwell will inform you who it will be once the Agency Decision Maker has ratified our recommendation.'

'Oh, not Chilwell again.' Matthew groaned.

'I think Mr Chilwell will be quite keen to ensure things run more smoothly this time round,' said the Chair. 'He's the only manager dealing with the supervising support workers, and he's a busy man, which, fortunately for him, amounts to a mitigating factor in his case.'

'So, is that it?' said Matthew. 'Reinstated. Do we get an apology?'

'Well, let's not pre-empt the ADM's final decision, but, as I've said, Mr Blundell, I can imagine what a nightmare this has been for you. Personally, I am very sorry that you've had to go through all this – all very unpleasant. As for an official apology... You might have to wait some time for that. I'm sure if the investigation highlights that you were victims in some way, you will be entitled to some redress. I can't possibly comment at this stage.'

'Well, thank you anyway,' said Heather. 'It's one step in the right direction, at least. I doubt we'll have to wait too long for a new placement given the current situation, so that'll take our minds off things. Hopefully, we can get back to normal as quickly as possible.'

'I hope so too, Mrs Blundell. Mr Chilwell will be in touch, I'm sure. Any other questions?'

'I don't think so,' said Matthew. 'I think it could be time for another glass of wine. Will you join us, Amanda?'

30

Antisocial

Saturday, 17th November 2018

The door of the gents swung closed behind him. He double-checked his flies and gravitated back towards the bar. The moody red lighting in the place seemed to emanate from the blood-red maelstrom raging in his head. Elton John's 'Saturday Night's Alright for Fighting' was playing, which he thought was appropriate given the stinking mood he was in. He checked his look in a wall mirror, carelessly pushing past a couple standing talking, drinks in hand.

'Watch it, mate!'

He momentarily clocked the guy who had spoken. A large bunch of keys hung from his belt. Perhaps the landlord. Or a caretaker. He moved on. Too early for trouble. Leave it. For now...

'The Moulin Rouge'. A tacky red neon sign hung above the bar. What a shithole. Crimson curtains pulled across the windows, and the disco lights predominantly the same colour. He'd been here a few times in recent months. He didn't know why. And if he'd known tonight was eighties night... The place had a social club feel to it, and the atmosphere reminded him of evenings spent as a young boy with his parents in a nightclub at a holiday camp in Great Yarmouth. Maybe it was some sort of comfort thing, then – not that anything was comfortable these days. And not that he was looking for comfort now. Not after four pints of snakebite and a line of coke in a cubicle in the gents. If anyone so much as looked at him the wrong way tonight... He removed his grey hoodie from where he had left it draped over a stool at the far end of the bar and waited what seemed like an age to attract the barman's attention. He ordered a fifth pint of snakebite and looked around him. There were two old fuckers on the dance floor, writhing around on their backs, riffing on plastic guitars to 'Burning Bridges' by Status Quo. Fuck knows where they'd found those. At their age, they should know better. He couldn't fault their taste in music – but he preferred Quo's earlier stuff.

An irritatingly chirpy DJ came on the mic. 'That's the Clifford and Eric medley. Well done, lads!' The men rose from the floor, took a smattering of applause and returned to their pints on a table somewhere in the gloom.

'And now, "Fade to Grey". Visage.' The DJ's irritating voice grated.

Clutching his hoodie, he handed over a fiver and necked half his snakebite before the twat behind the bar had even made it halfway to the till to get his change. That was a lousy one-pound coin, which he stuffed into his pocket as he moved towards an empty table in a corner, away from the dance floor and out of the light. Four quid for a fucking pint! He needed money. In an ideal world, he needed a job. But he'd had his fill of work coaches, resettlement workers, employment support groups – all of them were fucking useless. He knew the stats. Less than ten per cent of ex-offenders found work within six weeks and only a few per cent more within six months... Fact was, he'd never find a job. Unskilled and untrustworthy. Antisocial Personality Disorder – that didn't help either. He had to face it: no one was ever going to give him anything. He'd have to take it from the bastards. Settling in a chair in the corner, facing the dance floor, he supped his pint. Thirty-one fucking years old and still living with his mother – the bitter, twisted old cunt. He'd been sitting pretty, living rent-free until she'd lost her job. Now, she was demanding he move out and stand on his own two feet. And he knew who was responsible for that. He was sick of listening to her bitch about it. He knocked back more of his pint and belched. Fucking little Miss Matterface – Heather Blundell, now. The teacher who had fucked him over. He hated her almost as much as he hated his mother. All that hate. It was fucking with his brain. He had to get away. Away from this godforsaken island. But he needed money. He idly swilled his pint glass. Perhaps the Blundells were loaded. Perhaps he could do what his mother failed to do and fuck *them* over. Take their money and run. No one was ever going to give him anything; he'd have to take it from the bastards. It was worth thinking about...

He looked out onto the dance floor. Christ, he felt horny. It had been a long time since he'd had a woman, and he liked the ladies. Probably too much. That had got him into trouble in the past. The cocktail of coke and alcohol in his veins fuelled his desire – the fear of ending up back inside numbed it. His mood continued to darken. It didn't help that there were a couple of young tarts on the dance floor who had forgotten to dress. They were asking for it. He watched them gyrate, grinding their bodies against any hot-blooded male who had the balls to approach them, as if trying to seduce them in some erotic mating ritual. Something snapped. Moving onto the dance floor, he cut some shapes until he was up close to them. He smelt the warmth of their perfume, felt the heat of their bodies. He pushed right up behind one of them, feeling her arse grinding into his crotch as he writhed with her in a snake-like dance. Sliding his hands over her hips, he clasped her to him. He leant in and nuzzled into her ear, her hair, and breathed in the scent of her. He explored her neck with his lips, kissing her warm skin gently. She turned sharply.

'Fuck off!'

She faced him, square on. 'Fucking pervert!' And then she turned and moved off with her mate, who looked back at him and cast one final look of disgust.

He stood, silent, raging inside, watching them as they resumed their dancing in front of the DJ's decks. The DJ once again came on to the mic and in a camp voice that raked and abraded, announced Queen's 'I Want to Break Free'. Then he put down the mic, sidled out from behind the clutter of record decks, speakers and disco lights on stands and approached the two girls. The DJ leant in and spoke to them, casually looking across the dance floor in his direction. Unheard, his words and concern were nonetheless obvious.

A violent impulse, like a disease, caused him to move towards them. But he checked and turned away. Fuming, he retreated and lost himself among the dancers, again surrendering himself to the dark isolation of the corner. There he stayed for a while. Let them think he'd left; moved on. Time passed. He caged his rage – left it prowling and snarling – always conscious of it. He had two more pints and paid one more visit to the gents, always keeping a low profile, moving in the shadows on the periphery. Biding his time.

Just before midnight, before the lights came up and the punters started to leave, he donned his grey hoodie and pulled the hood over his head. He slipped unnoticed out of the Moulin Rouge like a ghostly phantom and into the shadows on the corner of a narrow passageway alongside the club. There he waited, his breath condensing in the cold night air. People spilled through the doors and onto the street. Good-timers, some sober, some drunk, untangled like threads and drifted off into the night. He saw Clifford and Eric, arms around each other, singing. 'I... I... I... have become... comfortably numb...' They were heading towards the kebab shop. Still, he waited.

And then, the two girls emerged. The centre of attention in a crowd of young bucks. In its cage, his rage roared. He watched as the group turned left and made their way up the street, away from him. A car pulled up alongside the kerb. The girls fobbed off their lustful admirers with a few hurried kisses and then got into the back seat. The car promptly moved away. Frustrated, the males jostled and argued among themselves, then turned and carried on up the street. His distorted rage flared again, railing against his earlier rejection. It clamoured for violent expression. He fought it down. Not with those two tarts. It was too soon to be courting that kind of trouble. His card was marked. His would be the first door they'd be knocking on. He focused his rage on another avenue of expression. He knew he might have to wait a while.

And finally, he came, struggling with two large black vinyl cases. A voice from the front entrance bade him goodnight, and the front doors slammed shut.

He watched from the corner of the passageway. He felt like a leopard lying in ambush for an unsuspecting antelope. The antelope hobbled towards him on unsteady legs, straining under the weight of its burden. The passageway led to a small car park behind the club. The leopard had made its calculations. He retreated and secreted himself behind some large commercial dustbins at the far end. The antelope was a big one and should give him a good fight. The leopard was pumped. Bring it on.

The antelope came on, unaware, and the leopard struck.

'What the...' He knocked the wind out of the DJ as his shoulder rammed hard into his midriff. The cases hit the floor with a heavy thud and tumbled. A catch popped and LPs slid out across the tarmac. The DJ stumbled and fell. He looked up, panic in his eyes. 'What are you doing?'

'Get up!'

'What do you want? Money? Here, take it.' The DJ fumbled in a pocket of his black cargo pants.

'I don't want your fucking money. Get up!'

The DJ looked confused.

'I want to spill your blood, you irritating, interfering fuck! Now fight me!'

'You're mad. Look, I've got a wife and kids to go home to...'

'Shut up and get up!'

'No, I'm not fighting you. Just piss off!'

The blood-red maelstrom in his head turned supernova. He struck again, and the DJ felt the full force of a right boot to the head. He threw his weight on top of the DJ's helpless form and landed blow after blow to his face. Left after right, left after right... Bone cracked and blood spilt from the DJ's nose. And then he stopped and stood over the DJ's twitching body. It was as if a switch had been flicked off. He felt a calm sense of satisfaction. He stared at the inert form.

Dead or alive?

The thought flashed through his subconscious. It resonated. Dead or alive? He laughed, tilted his head back and half sang, half roared:

'You spin me right 'round, baby, right 'round, like a record, baby...'

He howled with delight.

'Stick that in your eighties playlist.'

The DJ groaned.

He gave him one last kick in the head and walked off into the cold night, singing.

31

Cloud Nine

Wednesday, 21st November 2018

'Hi, Dad.'

'Hello, Matthew. Is it good news?'

'Didn't Mum tell you?'

'No, I've just come in from the garden. Bloody next door's cat's been digging in the borders again. It's taken to shitting in my winter pansies! Your mother just handed me the phone and said she'd let you tell me.'

'Well, I'm not sure I can trump the headline "Cat Shits In Prize-winning Pansies", but even so, it's pretty exciting... We've just got back from the adoption panel meeting. They're recommending us as a match for James. The decision just needs to be rubber-stamped by the Agency Decision Maker, and we're good to go.'

'That's wonderful news. I'm so pleased for both of you. Have they given you a date when he'll move back in with you?'

'Not an exact date, but it'll probably be a week or so after we receive the ADM's letter. He'll be here for Christmas.'

'I bet Heather's ecstatic.'

'That's an understatement. It's a shame you and Mum are off on your Christmas cruise this year, of all years.'

'Well, if we'd known... But it's too late to cancel it now, and your mother would skin me alive. We'll sort something out when we get back. It'll give James a chance to settle in. How do you think Noah will feel about having a younger brother?'

'I think he'll be great with James,' said Matthew. 'He's that little bit older, and you can tell he's a nurturer. He's settled in so well – such a gentle soul.'

'It's amazing, isn't it, when you think what the poor lad went through?'

'Well, his mum had severe mental health issues, but I'm not aware that she mistreated him – she just couldn't cope with his daily needs. You should see him playing with his toys. He really takes care of them. I think he'll be protective of James, just like a big brother.'

'How's he getting on at school?'

'He's doing well. First term and making lots of new friends already.'

'Excellent. And have you heard anything about Grace? Is she still with James? If she is, I imagine she'll miss him when he goes.'

'Well, you know how hot they are on GDPR, Dad. We're not supposed to know anything about Grace's whereabouts. But putting two and two together, I think they must still be under the same roof. Even though we've been approved, we've been told we're not allowed to visit him. That can only be because Grace is there. If that's the case then, yes, I'm sure she'll miss him. They've been together almost two years. But I don't imagine it'll be too long before she gets another brother or sister; although, given her family background, I expect she'll end up being adopted.'

'And how about you? Did you secure that landscaping job you mentioned last week?'

'Yes, I started that last Friday. It's going well. I think I'll be finished by the end of this week, and then I'll wind down for the winter and James's arrival. It'll be nice to spend some quality time with him.'

'Excellent. It seems your life is returning to normal at last, then. I'm pleased. You've been through enough shit recently.'

'Talking of shit, I'd better let you get back to your pansies. When we know the exact date James is arriving, I'll let you know.'

'Yes, please do. As for that cat, I'm going to put some black pepper down. Let the bastard get a nostril full of that. I'll put your mother back on. She's loitering with intent. Speak soon, son.'

Monday, 3rd December 2018

Heather walked into the lounge with a tray of tea and biscuits. Matthew was laughing loudly.

'What's so funny, you two?'

'David was just telling me a joke.'

'Well, let's hear it then.'

David blushed. 'Well, it's not particularly PC, Heather. I wouldn't want to offend your sensibilities. I'm not sure, as your supervising social worker, I should be...'

'No, but it was bloody funny, though,' snorted Matthew. 'Tell her.'

'Ah, what the hell,' said David. 'Comedians get away with murder these days. Just don't you go repeating it to my superiors.'

'As if...' Matthew laughed.

'Okay, Heather... so, there was this poor young lad who was placed with a foster family. Unfortunately, the father beat the family dog every day, which upset the boy.'

'Understandably,' said Heather.

'When he told his social worker about it, the boy was sent to live with another family. Unfortunately, in the second family, the father beat the wife every day, so the boy was moved again. In the third family, the father got drunk most nights and beat the boy. At that point, the boy thought he would never find a safe foster home. At Christmas, he was taken to see Santa, and Santa asked him what he wanted for Christmas. "Santa," he said, "I want to be adopted by my local football team." Confused, Santa asked him why he would want to be adopted by his local football team. The boy said: "Because they never beat anybody..."'

Heather looked at David, stony-faced. David looked uncertain and looked at Matthew. Matthew shrugged.

'Only joking,' said Heather. 'Hilarious. Now, who's for a cup of tea?'

David's relief was palpable, and Heather smiled. Things really couldn't have worked out better after their reinstatement. It was almost as if the council had gone all out to ensure a best fit, so far as their new supervising social worker was concerned. David was the very antithesis of Sarah: warm, relaxed, fair and even Heather felt comfortable enough in his company to tease him. David was one of only two male members of the council's fostering team. He was a similar age to Matthew and Heather, which they'd hoped might mean they'd have more in common. They did. David shared Matthew's sardonic sense of humour for a start. He dressed casually, had an unkempt beard and long black hair tied back in a ponytail. There were no airs and graces. Take me as you find me. When they'd first met, shortly after David had been appointed as their new supervising social worker at the end of July, Heather had taken a cautious approach, but his first words had been reassuring.

'In the spirit of full disclosure,' he said, 'I should tell you I have been given full access to all the information in your file, so I know what's gone before. I guess you'd be surprised if I didn't... What I want you to know, though, is that so far as our relationship goes, all of it is irrelevant. And I don't believe it will *ever* be relevant. Because I sincerely believe that we will work well together as a team and that we'll earn each other's respect. I commit to doing my very best to support you. All I ask is that you help me to help you. Communication is the key, so keep talking!'

'A fresh start is exactly what we're looking for,' Heather had said.

'And you're right about respect,' said Matthew. 'It has to be earned. And it's a two-way street.'

From that sure foundation, the relationship had blossomed, and David continued the time-honoured tradition of visiting on the first Monday of every month. When Matthew and Heather had received news that their first placement was to be four-year-old Noah, David had been the first to congratulate them and send them flowers. A lovely touch, thought Heather. Noah arrived early in August, just before his fifth birthday in September. Now in December, it was their fourth meeting with David. All previous notes had been diligently typed up and signed off at the subsequent visit, which deserved respect right off the bat!

'Okay,' said David. 'Just the usual format today. If you want to run me through your daily logs – as opposed to running me through...'

'Now, if your name were Morton, I might be tempted to run you through,' said Matthew.

'Well, thankfully, he's not,' said Heather. 'That's fine, David. I have them all here. There's nothing to highlight from our end – just the usual daily routines. Noah continues to seem very settled. He plays quietly and happily. He's been interacting well with us. He's affectionate. His reading and writing have come on leaps and bounds since he started school – his teachers are very pleased with him.'

'It'll be interesting to see his end-of-term report,' said David.

Heather nodded. 'Well, he breaks up on Friday the 14th, so I guess we'll have that soon.'

'And is he excited at the thought of being a big brother? I understand you've been given a firm date for James's arrival?'

'The tenth of December.' Heather beamed. 'A week today.'

'That's fantastic news. Do you have everything ready? Is there anything you need from me?'

'I don't think so, David,' said Heather. 'Thank you. Janet is bringing him here first thing, and we plan to spend the day reacclimatising him. Noah will meet him when he gets home from school. He can't wait. He's got all his toys ready to show him. He's prepared a big banner saying, "Welcome Home, James".'

'And he tells me,' said Matthew, 'that he's going to teach him to read and write, just like he's learning to at school.'

'I'm liking the sound of this,' said David. 'Your notes are going to be very interesting to read at our January meeting. I can't wait to hear how they get on.'

'I think Noah is going to be good for James,' said Heather.

David nodded. 'Let's hope so. With all that's gone before, we want this adoption to be a success. If the powers that be can see that James is making progress, it'll be a feather in your cap – especially when it comes to the question of you taking on more foster kids.'

'We'll make it work,' said Heather. 'We adore James. He's going to get all the love and attention he needs here.'

'Okay.' David leant back in his chair. 'There's only one other thing we need to discuss, and that's Noah's contact with his mum last week. How did that go?'

'It took a while to arrange,' said Heather. 'At first, his mum's psychiatrist was concerned that seeing him might be detrimental to her health. As it turned out, she was fine. She was delighted to see him. When we arrived and Noah saw her, he ran straight into her arms.'

'Did you get any feedback afterwards from the contact supervisor?'

'Yes, she noticed that after the initial contact, he was a bit subdued, but that's not uncommon. Even though he understands that his mummy's not well and he's living with us so that she can get better, it's still going to be confusing for him seeing her again – especially in a place he doesn't know. Apparently, though, he ate all his packed lunch and there were no tears at any stage.'

'How many times a week have they offered his mum contact?'

'Initially, it's every Wednesday from ten till two. If all goes well, they'll add another day, but that won't be for some time yet.'

'And how has he been since Wednesday?'

'Absolutely fine, hasn't he, Matthew? Which is a relief, because it's important from our point of view that his visits with his mum don't upset him and unsettle him at home. As we've already said, Noah will play an important part in James's reacclimatisation and, hopefully, be a good influence on him.'

'Well, don't be afraid to grill the contact supervisor and share any concerns you have. I'll add this as a discussion point at our monthly meetings, and we'll keep tabs on it. That's it from me, unless anything else has cropped up that you want to discuss?'

'I think it's all been extraordinarily ordinary,' said Matthew. 'Obviously, we'll have lots more to discuss next month. Talking of extraordinarily ordinary, David, I see Portsmouth just about scraped through to the third round of the FA Cup yesterday. A lucky deflection in the 90th minute, wasn't it...?'

Monday, 10th December 2018

'What the fuck was that?!'

Matthew thought Heather must have fallen down the stairs and came rushing out of the bathroom with his trousers around his ankles, nearly pitching headlong down the top flight, as he grasped the bannister rail on the upstairs landing and saved himself.

'He's here!' screamed Heather. 'He's here!' The front door banged against the wall as it was flung back, and Heather ran through the porch and down the drive to meet Janet's car, which had just pulled up.

A few minutes later, Matthew had adjusted his clothing and was on his way downstairs as Heather was leading James by the hand in through the front door. Janet's slender figure trailed in behind her.

'In you come, James.' Heather squatted beside him and removed his little red puffer jacket. She handed it to Matthew as he reached the bottom of the stairs. 'Do you remember our house? We had lots of fun here, didn't we?'

James was still small for his age, but he had grown. His fair hair was longer, his eyes were still strikingly blue, and he seemed to be walking with more confidence, although Matthew noticed the odd wobble.

Heather took James's hand again. 'Now, if you come into the lounge, we've bought you a brand-new toy to play with.' She walked him in through the lounge door. 'Look! It's a garage and lots of cars.'

'Car, car, car, car, car!' James cried.

'Who let that crow in here?' laughed Matthew as he waited for Janet to pass before hanging James's coat in the porch. 'Hi Janet. Great to see you again.'

'Likewise, Matthew. I bet the little man's pleased to be home.' Janet's voice still rasped, and Matthew was enveloped in a familiar cloud of strong perfume as she walked past him, smiling. She followed Heather and James into the lounge.

'Now,' said Heather to James, 'you have a play with that while Matthew and I talk with Janet, and then I'll get you some juice and an iced bun I bought specially for you.'

James plonked in front of the garage and began playing happily; though he seemed more intent on ramming the cars into the garage walls and vocalising loud crashing sounds than motoring them up the winding ramps and into their parking spaces.

'They don't make cars like that anymore,' said Matthew, standing in the doorway. 'Not a dent or a scratch on them.'

'He drives about as well as you do,' said Heather.

Janet laughed. 'Not known for your no-claims bonuses then, Matthew?'

Matthew feigned a hurt expression. 'Me? My record is unblemished, I'll have you know.' Then he grinned. 'Mind you, I once gave an old lady a rather nasty scare on a zebra crossing...' He walked over to James and sat down next to him.

'Best I be careful when I'm out shopping, then,' said Janet, running a hand through her dark grey curls before perching on the edge of the sofa.

Heather crouched down next to Matthew. 'Did you notice how he's walking now? He seems much steadier on his feet. It's amazing the transformation in the nine months since he left. He looks well.' She reached out and rolled a car towards James.

Matthew turned to Janet. 'Can we offer you a cup of tea?'

'No, thank you,' said Janet. 'I can't stay. I just have a couple of things to give you, then we can bring James's things in from the car, and I'll leave you to get James settled – although it already looks as though he's never been away.' Janet smiled as James rolled a car into the car wash and started making loud sloshing noises as the brushes spun round.

'It seems so surreal,' said Heather, rising to her feet again. 'I can't believe James is here and officially our son.'

'Yes, he's all yours now.' Janet pulled a couple of items from her handbag. 'So, you've been brought up-to-date with his medical progress. All his routine information's been recorded in his red medical book – let me give you that.' Janet held out the book and Heather took it from her. 'As you can see,' Janet turned her attention back to James as he vroomed a car into Matthew's shin, 'he's quite a character these days. He's certainly getting louder and more boisterous.' She smiled as Matthew rubbed his leg. 'You'll be pleased to hear that his sleeping has improved, though.' Then she handed the second item in her hand to Heather. It was a sealed envelope. 'And here's a little something. Buy James something nice from me, please. A welcome-home present.'

'Oh, Janet, that's so sweet of you. Thank you.' Heather leant down and gave Janet a hug, which took her somewhat by surprise, but she responded with a quick squeeze. 'And thank you for dropping him off.'

'My pleasure.' Janet stood and looked down at Matthew. 'Will you be kind enough to help me with James's things from the car?'

'Of course,' said Matthew. He left the room with Janet, while

Heather sat on the floor next to James, picked up one of his cars and played with him. James didn't seem to mind.

In the afternoon, James tired. Heather took him upstairs for a nap, and indeed, he settled a lot quicker than she was used to. At the time they were fostering James, he'd been sleeping in with them. Now, however, despite his special needs, she and Matthew decided it would be best for him if he had his own room. Noah was occupying what had been Emma's bedroom, and so they had completely redecorated Grace's old room for James. Disney "Cars" wallpaper, with Lightning McQueen, Mater and Sally, together with a new bed, had transformed the room into James's own sanctuary. Heather had worried the décor was too fussy and that all the cars and characters on the wallpaper might be too much for him, but Matthew had reminded her: 'What did we say? A normal upbringing. If he doesn't like it, we'll change it.' Heather lowered James into his bed, where he buried his head in the pillow and closed his eyes. He opened them again and smiled. Heather turned as Matthew joined her, and they waited until he had settled. He looked the picture of contentment. He drifted off while they looked on – no doubt dreaming of cars, iced buns and his favourite chicken nuggets, which he'd had for lunch.

Heather sighed. 'Welcome home, James.'

'It's good to have you back, little man,' said Matthew, as he turned and left the room quietly.

Heather remained, her eyes firmly on the sleeping child, smiling.

Tuesday, 25th December 2018

'Why am I the one with my hand up a turkey's arse?'

'I'm sure we have this conversation every year, Matthew.'

'Okay, so technically, it's not its butthole – but it's as near as dammit.'

'Well, don't spend too long trying to find its G-spot; you've got potatoes to peel.'

Matthew huffed and spooned in some more sage and onion stuffing mixed with a little sausagemeat.

'When we've prepared everything, we'll see if James and Noah are awake and open some presents. I'm surprised they're not up already.'

'They've got more sense than us,' said Matthew, looking up at the clock. 'I'll rephrase my question: Why am I standing here with my hand up a turkey's arse at six-thirty in the morning?'

'You know once the kids are up, opening presents and playing, we won't have a moment's peace. Best we get everything prepared now, and then I can just pop it in the oven later.'

By the time Matthew and Heather had finished the food prep and brought the children downstairs with their Christmas stockings, it was eight o'clock. James had still been asleep, oblivious to the significance of the day. Noah, bless him, had been waiting quietly under his duvet to be summoned. Everyone sat on the floor in the middle of the lounge. When the two boys had opened the presents in their stockings, Matthew played Father Christmas and handed out some of the smaller gifts around the tree. The excitement levels grew with the pile of trashed wrapping paper that littered the lounge floor.

'Now, who's ready for their main present?' Matthew looked enquiringly at both boys. Noah's hand shot up, and James chuckled happily.

Matthew stepped into the office and dragged out a huge box wrapped in colourful Christmas wrapping paper. 'This one's for James...' He stepped back into the office and emerged dragging something akin to an elongated pyramid, also wrapped in garish wrapping paper.

'Who's going first?'

'James can go first,' said Noah.

'Ah, that's nice of you, Noah,' said Heather. 'Here you go, James. Shall Mummy help you unwrap this?'

James looked up from tearing spent wrapping paper to shreds and crawled over to Heather. He knelt up and started pulling away the paper covering the box. He uncovered a wide, grinning mouth with a long row of uninterrupted pearly-white teeth.

Matthew pointed. 'Look, he's got no gaps between his teeth. I guess that means he doesn't have to floss.'

Heather gave Matthew a "really?" look and encouraged James to keep going.

Further ripping revealed the owner of the grin to be a sporty red car with a pair of blue eyes in the centre of a white windscreen.

'Who's that, James?' said Heather.

'Lightning...'

'That's it. Your favourite. Lightning McQueen!' Heather removed the last of the wrapping paper that clung to the box and looked up at Matthew. 'Do you want to get it out?'

'I certainly do. What's in here, then, little man?'

Matthew knelt, opened the box and then stood to lift out what was inside. Polystyrene protectors fell to the floor as he manhandled the object out of the box and looked for some floorspace to put it down.

'What's this, little man?'

'Car! Car!' James was animated. He crawled over and climbed inside a large electric toy car – Lightning McQueen. He took his seat and gripped the steering wheel. 'Vroom, vroom.' Dribble ran down his chin, and Heather wiped it away.

Matthew had already set up the car before wrapping it. Now, he flipped a switch and said to James, 'Watch this.' He reached down into the footwell and pushed the accelerator pedal. The car whirred into life and lurched forward. James giggled and started stamping his right foot down, stabbing at the pedal.

'Calm down, little man,' said Matthew, 'you'll break it. Now, you can only drive in it if you are with me or Mummy; otherwise, you'll have to pretend.'

'Are you sure this was a good idea?' said Heather, looking around at slender table legs, polished wooden surfaces and the slimline TV screen that suddenly looked very fragile.

Her words didn't appear to register, as Matthew prepared James for action. 'Come on then. Shall we go once around the room? Put your foot here.'

James, aided by Matthew, drove one circuit around the lounge.

'More later,' said Matthew, switching off the car. 'You sit in there, and we'll let Noah open his present now.'

Noah seemed to have been getting as much enjoyment from the electric car as James, but now his eyes lit up even more as he scrutinised the strange-looking shape before him.

'What is it?' he said.

'That's what you need to find out,' said Matthew. 'Why don't you open it?'

'I've never had a present this big.'

'Well, it's a special present for a special boy,' said Heather.

Noah, somewhat gingerly, began to peel off the paper. After what seemed like an age, he had revealed what appeared to be a cardboard tent.

'What is it?'

'Keep going,' said Matthew. He peeled away some of the Sellotape holding two of the cardboard sections together. Noah took over and ripped off one side. Inside the tent was a brand-new bicycle with stabilisers. Noah's mouth opened wide.

'Wow!'

'Have you ever ridden a bike before?' said Heather.

'No. Is it hard?'

'We'll go outside later and you can test it,' said Matthew. 'In the meantime, shall we go once around the room?' He winked at Noah, who didn't need to be asked twice and climbed on. Matthew reached down to push him, but Noah's legs were already working the pedals and he trundled forward, wobbling the handlebars as he navigated his way around the room.

'Well done!' Heather clapped. 'You're a natural!'

Noah smiled and, when he had completed his lap, got off. 'Thank you,' he said. 'It's amazing.'

Matthew and Heather both smiled.

'Right, well if you boys want to stay in here and have a play, I'll go and get our Christmas dinner started.'

'Need any help?' said Matthew.

'That's fine,' said Heather. 'You can stay in here and supervise.'

Matthew looked ever so slightly relieved, and Heather headed for the kitchen.

It was around an hour and a half later. The kitchen was filling with steam, and condensation was appearing on the windows. Heather had checked on the turkey and was just closing the oven. She stood up and winced as she felt a sharp twinge in her back. Rubbing at it, she walked over to the sink, absent-mindedly watching rivulets of water negotiate their way down the kitchen window. She caught movement out of the corner of her eye. At first, she thought it was a drop of water starting on its journey down the inside of the glass. But as she looked through the window, she saw what appeared to be a head appear over the fence to her left. Along the left side of their back garden was an alleyway that ran between their house and next door's, connecting the roads that ran in front of and behind the house. Someone had pulled themselves up and was looking over. Heather pulled back out of sight. The head seemed to be looking in her direction, surveying the back of the house.

'Matthew,' she called.

There was no response from the lounge, just human-made sounds of honking horns and then a crash.

Heather moved into the hall and called again. This time, more urgently. 'Matthew!'

Matthew's head peered around the lounge door.

'There's someone in the alleyway looking over the fence into our garden. They're wearing a hoodie.'

'What do you want me to do about it?'

'Go and see what they want.'

'Maybe the divine smell of your cooking has permeated the neighbourhood and people are coming to get a noseful?'

'Matthew.'

'Okay, okay...'

Matthew opened the front door and made his way across the drive to the alleyway entrance. He peered around the corner.

'Excuse me. Can I help you?'

What Heather had taken for a hoodie was in fact a knee-length parka jacket. The wearer had the hood pulled over their head. Stepping down from the back rail on the fence panel, the figure turned to face Matthew. The zip was fully fastened on the hood, leaving only a small, shadowy aperture in front of the face. Matthew couldn't make out any features. He had the feeling he was being eyeballed by the Grim Reaper. Assessed. But then the Grim Reaper wasn't known for wearing a parka jacket. The stand-off lasted a few seconds and then the figure turned and walked away. Slowly, as if to say, I dare you. Matthew thought about following. But it was Christmas Day, dinner was about to be served, and he didn't feel in the mood for confrontation. Better to leave it be. The figure reached the end of the alley. It stopped. Turned back to face Matthew. In a few moments, it turned again, left, and disappeared from view.

32

Thunderclouds

Friday, 11th January 2019

'They're back, Noah,' said Matthew. 'Let's give Heather and James a hand with the shopping. Are you going to help me put it away again?'

'Okay,' said Noah, looking up from a book he was reading on the lounge sofa and smiling. He jumped off and followed Matthew to the front door.

The porch was full of bulging bags containing the weekly grocery shop. Coming up the drive were Heather and James with the last of the items; James carrying a loaf of thickly sliced bread and looking very pleased with himself. Noah heaved one of the lighter bags into the kitchen, and Matthew followed him, groaning under the weight of two bags that must surely contain all the tins and bottles that Heather had bought.

'Why don't you spread the load and put a few tins in each bag? These two weigh a tonne!'

'You know the speed they chuck everything at you,' said Heather. 'I have to throw everything in the bags just to keep up with them. Stop your moaning and get unpacking.'

Matthew and Heather began to put everything away, while Noah and James were given the job of stacking tins and matching up the labels – at least, Noah did the stacking, while James sat by playing with a tin of baked beans and "supervising".

'Call me paranoid,' said Heather, 'but I'm sure I was being followed around Morrisons this morning.'

'Who by?'

'I didn't actually see anyone. I just had that feeling, you know?'

'Isn't that the very nature of shopping in a big supermarket: everyone trundling after everyone else, up and down the aisles?'

'Maybe...'

'Where are these two air fresheners going?'

'I bought one for the lounge and one for the bathroom.' Heather winked at Noah, who was listening intently. 'Someone keeps making some nasty smells in there, don't they?'

Noah laughed. 'Not me!'

'And it's not me and it's not James,' said Heather.

'Well, who the hell is it?' said Matthew, 'cos it sure ain't me!'

'Must be a ghost,' said Heather.

Noah giggled. 'Or a phantom farter.'

'Do they teach you that kind of language at school, young man?' said Matthew in mock horror.

'Everyone says "fart" these days,' said Noah. 'Even Miss Lomax.'

'Oh, I guess that's alright then...'

'Right, who's for a cup of tea?' said Heather. 'I'm gasping.'

'I'll make it,' said Matthew. 'You put the last of those tins away and then go and put your feet up. Did you buy any decent biscuits?'

'We've got those Rich Tea to finish up.'

'Rich Tea? Boring. I meant nice biscuits.'

'Well, look in the cupboard and you'll see what I got. Oh, and make the kids a drink while you're at it, will you?'

'Consider it done!'

Heather put the last tins of soup away and headed for the lounge, taking James and Noah with her. Matthew made some juice for the boys and then looked in the treats cupboard as he waited for the kettle to boil.

'Ah, Jammie Dodgers. They'll do nicely.'

He put some on a plate, added it to the tray already loaded with two mugs and two plastic cups of juice and then stood waiting for the kettle.

'Matthew!'

'What?'

'It's that nosy parka again.'

'You what? You're joking?'

Matthew hurried from the kitchen to the lounge. He crossed to the window and pulled the net curtain to one side. A figure stood on the pavement across the street. Medium-height. Blue parka coat down to the knees. Hood up. Matthew couldn't see a face.

'Right, that's it. No goodwill at Christmas this time. I'll go and have a word.' The net curtain fell back into place as he turned.

'Matthew, be careful. They may have a knife.'

'Good point.' Matthew stopped and looked back through the window. Through the hazy screen of the net curtain, he saw the figure was already moving away. 'They obviously saw me,' he said, 'and decided not to mess with Matthew.' He turned and faked a karate chop at Noah.

'Pow!' Noah chopped back and kicked out, somewhat expertly, landing a slipper-clad foot squarely on Matthew's shin.

'Ow! You've been watching too much Bruce Lee on television,' said Matthew, rubbing his leg.

'Bruce who?' said Noah. He kicked again, and Matthew jumped out of the way.

'That's enough now, Noah, thank you.' Matthew hurried back into the kitchen and finished making the tea, which he brought into the lounge on the tray.

'What are we going to do?' said Heather. 'Shall I call the police?'

'And say what?' said Matthew. 'That we've spotted an individual checking out the house a couple of times. You know what they'll say: we can't do anything unless an actual crime's been committed.'

'I don't like it, Matthew. What do they want?'

'I don't know. Probably it's nothing. Maybe they used to live here or knew somebody who did.'

'But they look suspicious with that hood up.'

'Well, it is bloody cold out there. Here, drink your tea and have a Jammie Dodger.'

Heather smiled. 'What would I do without you?'

'You'd be lost and lonely,' said Matthew. 'But I'm not going anywhere.'

Friday, 18th January 2019

'James, can you hold Mummy's shopping list while she gets some flour? I'm doing a lot of baking this week.'

James, who was sitting in the trolley strapped in, clutched the piece of paper in both hands and stared at it as if he could read everything on it.

'There we go,' said Heather. 'Now, what else do we need?' She looked at the list in James's hand. 'Right. Next aisle. Deodorant for Daddy.'

She moved on and turned left as she wheeled the trolley around the corner and into the next aisle. As she paused to scan the shelves ahead, James leant over and grabbed a pack of sanitary towels off the shelf. He lost his grip, and it fell to the floor.

'Nappies,' he said.

'No, darling, not nappies. Those aren't for you. You don't know how lucky you are being a boy...' Heather picked them up and put them back on the shelf. She looked ahead. There were several shoppers with trolleys milling around, blocking the aisle. 'Okay, stay there a moment, James, and wait for Mummy. The deodorant's just up there.' Heather negotiated the maze of shoppers and scanned the deodorants on the shelf. She found the one that Matthew used and took two, as they were on special offer. She turned to make her way back down the aisle and looked towards the trolley. James was sitting there, stretching once again for the sanitary towels. He couldn't quite reach them. Heather returned to him and put the deodorant in with the other shopping. 'Let's go and get you some nappies then, little man, and you can put them in the trolley.' She did an about-turn, crossed the arterial aisle that ran from one side of the store to the other, and entered the aisle directly across from them, heading in the direction of the tills. James burbled happily to himself as he grabbed the nappies Heather gave him, twisted and half-threw, half-dropped them in among the shopping behind him.

'Good boy,' said Heather. 'Now, jams and marmalades...'

They moved on and turned left around the next corner, opposite the tills, and headed up the aisle displaying a vast array of condiments. Heather searched for Matthew's favourite brand of marmalade. 'He loves this one,' she said to James, showing him a jar of Rose's lime marmalade, 'but he has to pick out all the rind because he doesn't like it. He ends up with a sticky mess on his plate. Silly Daddy.'

'Silly... Daddy,' James repeated several times.

Heather walked along and stopped at the jams. She placed a jar of strawberry and a jar of raspberry into the trolley. 'Raspberry is Mummy's favourite,' she said to James. She rolled the trolley on, politely excusing herself as she eased past two couples with trolleys who had stopped to chat, right in the middle of the aisle, and turned right around the next corner into the aisle with all the cereals, which was empty. She gazed absent-mindedly at the jar of strawberry jam and noticed it had a crack in it. 'I'm sure we didn't do that,' she said. 'I'll just pop back and get another one, and we'll give this broken one to the person at the till when we get there. Now, wait there a moment. I won't be a second...'

Heather walked around the corner, weaving past the two couples, who were still talking, and back to the jam. She had to wait briefly. A lady was blocking the way and took a few moments to move on. Heather grabbed another jar of strawberry jam and hurried back. She turned the corner.

'There we go,' she said.

She froze.

The seat in the trolley where James had been sitting was empty, and James was nowhere to be seen. Her shopping list was on the floor by the wheels. She panicked. Had James somehow managed to climb out? Impossible. She had strapped him in securely. Frantically, she started looking up and down the aisle for him, calling his name.

'James!'

She ran.

'James!'

She ran up and down the adjacent aisles, pushing past shoppers as they got in her way, calling out to no one in particular. 'Excuse me, have you seen a small boy – a two-year-old in a red coat, jeans and white trainers?'

Some people shook their heads, some seemed confused, some slightly irritated. A few good Samaritans showed concern.

'Where did you last see him?'

'In the aisle with the cereals. James! James!'

James was nowhere to be seen.

Some shoppers offered to help search, and some just drifted off. One middle-aged man said he would get the manager and set off at pace.

Heather stopped running momentarily and stood, turning one way then the other in the middle of the aisle, feeling helpless. Hopeless.

'Don't worry, love,' said an elderly lady, gently squeezing Heather's elbow, 'there's lots of people looking for him now and that man's gone to get the manager. I'm sure he's just wandered off.'

'He couldn't have just wandered off...' Heather's eyes reddened and tears formed. 'He was strapped in. Somebody must have taken him.' She felt like screaming.

'Will all available staff come to the manager's office immediately.' The tannoy announcement was firm but calm.

Heather was already running towards the main entrance. She reached the area around the entrance and exit doors. Nothing. Heather rushed up to the lottery and cigarette kiosk, but it had been busy and no one there remembered seeing a child matching James's description. She turned swiftly to run out into the car park. Her thoughts were racing, her head pounding. And then she collapsed. The stress overwhelmed her. Her mind blanked momentarily, her legs buckled, and she ended up on the cold, hard resin floor. Several people rushed over to see what was wrong. Someone scurried off and fetched a chair for her, and a couple of young lads helped her back onto her feet and sat her down.

'What's the matter, my love?' said an elderly lady. 'Are you pregnant?'

Heather stared at the floor. Dazed. Numb.

'Speak to me, love. Are you okay?'

'No. I lost my child.' Heather tried to stand.

'Oh, you poor thing.' The lady reached out to steady her. 'My eldest had a miscarriage.'

'No, someone's got my son.' Heather staggered a step forward. 'Someone's taken him. You've got to stop them, please.'

'She's saying someone's taken her child,' said one onlooker. 'Someone better get the manager or call the police.'

'I need to call my husband,' said Heather. She fumbled in her shoulder bag, looking for her mobile phone.

A lady in a green polo shirt and black trousers hurried up, with an entourage of employees behind her. 'Are you the lady who's lost her child?' Her name badge said Caroline, Manager.

'Please. Someone's taken him. You need to call the police.' Heather reached out to grasp Caroline's left arm.

Caroline sidestepped and indicated a short, stocky man in uniform to her left. 'This is our security guard, Jim. He's been on the door. Can you describe... is it your son?'

'Yes, yes. My son,' said Heather, steadying herself. 'He's nearly two and a half. Fair hair, blue eyes. He's wearing a red winter coat – a puffer jacket kind of thing – jeans, and he's got white trainers on.'

'A red puffer jacket... I remember seeing it,' said Jim, running his hands through his ginger beard. 'I didn't see the child's face, though. Someone was carrying him out with the child pulled close to their chest.'

'Who was carrying him out?' Heather felt her panic rising again.

'I didn't see their face. They had a coat on with the hood up. I think it was blue – possibly black. I thought it was odd inside the store, but they were heading outside, hands full, carrying a child, so I let them go. I didn't challenge them.'

'I think we *had* better call the police,' said Caroline. 'I'll do it. Jim, if you take Jake and Amy and search the car park, please. Russell, Tim, you double-check around the store, just in case the child Jim saw was not this lady's son.' Caroline turned to Heather. 'Sorry, what is your name?'

'Heather. Heather Blundell.'

'If you come with me, Heather.'

Caroline took Heather to her office and sat her down while she called 999. After giving a few details, she put down the phone.

'They'll be here in a few minutes. I'm so sorry. This must be agonising for you.'

'You have no idea...' Heather was clutching her phone. 'Sorry, I must speak to my husband.'

She rang Matthew's mobile.

Matthew picked up. 'Hello, darling. How's your shopping trip?'

'Matthew... someone's taken James.' Her voice broke.

'Say that again?'

'Someone's taken James.' Heather was sobbing uncontrollably again.

'What do you mean someone's taken James?'

'James was in the trolley and I took my eye off him – not for long. When I got back, he was gone. I think someone's run off with him, Matthew. He couldn't have got out himself. Even if he could, he wouldn't get far. I've searched the store. I can't find him anywhere. The security man saw someone carrying out a child in a red coat just like James's. The manager has called the police. They'll be here any minute.'

'Alright, alright. Calm down. I'm trying to think.'

'What the hell do I do now?'

'Just try to stay calm. I'm on my way.'

Matthew arrived just before the police. Caroline and Heather were waiting outside the main entrance. Heather ran to Matthew and flung her arms around him, sobbing freely as she buried her head in his shoulder. A few moments later, a police car pulled up and two officers got out.

'PC Davis,' said one, referring to himself, 'and PC Roth,' he indicated the other. 'We understand there's a missing child?'

Caroline greeted them, gave quick introductions and led everyone back to her office.

'Do you have CCTV?' was the first thing that PC Davis asked.

'Yes, yes, over here,' said Caroline. 'We had the system upgraded to 4K last year, so we should get a clear image.' She sat down and tapped away on the keyboard in front of a computer screen and pulled up some folders. She clicked her way through to a folder containing video files and double-clicked on one. 'What's the time?' she asked.

'Ten-forty,' said PC Roth, checking his mobile phone.

Caroline scrolled through the video. 'I'll go back to ten o'clock and fast forward through. We're looking for someone in a dark blue coat with their hood up, carrying a small child in a red coat.' She continued scrolling through. 'Here we go...' She hit fast forward.

The screen showed the main entrance. Shoppers raced in and out, reminiscent of characters in a Benny Hill show. Jim was visible, standing in the space between the entrance and exit doors. His arms moved up, down and around in quick animation as he scratched his nose, smoothed his hair, picked fluff off his uniform and generally shifted about uncomfortably.

'Stop! There they are.' PC Davis leant in towards the screen. The time showed ten-sixteen. 'Mrs Blundell, does that look like your son?'

'That's James. Definitely. Oh, my god!' She turned and threw herself into Matthew's arms.

'We've seen this person before,' said Matthew, 'twice, hanging around our house. That knee-length parka jacket is unmistakable.'

'The hood covers the face. I can't make anything out,' said PC Davis. 'From the build, I can't even tell if they're male or female. And it's not necessarily an adult – it could even be a teenager. Do you have footage from the car park, Caroline?' PC Davis seemed to be the one taking charge. PC Roth stood back and observed.

'Yes, give me a moment and I'll pull it up.'

Caroline spent a few moments locating the relevant file and advancing to the point where James was taken from the store. When she played the video, they saw the same figure carrying James into the car park. James seemed to be struggling but was being pulled tightly into his abductor's chest to restrict his movement. Again, the hood obscured all features, and deep shadow hid the face. The figure carried James out of shot.

'We need to see the car they leave in. They must have a car. Do you have other cameras?'

'Yes,' said Caroline. 'Bear with...'

The next video was from a camera further away from the entrance and showed a wider area. The figure was moving towards a row of cars.

It stopped by a black Ford Fiesta. The Fiesta's indicator lights flashed as the key fob was activated, and James was bundled unceremoniously into the boot, which was then slammed shut. The figure got into the car, reversed out and drove away.

'The fucking bastard!' Matthew could barely contain himself. But he knew there was nothing he could do.

PC Davis turned to his colleague. 'Andy, if you take that registration number and radio it through, we'll try to put a trace on the vehicle.'

'Okay.' PC Roth, with notebook already in hand, approached the screen as Caroline scrolled back through the footage. He made a few quick notes and then left the room.

'Okay, Mr and Mrs Blundell,' said PC Davis, 'I'll run you to the station and we'll take a written statement and a description of James. Do you have a photograph of him on your phone?' He turned to Caroline. 'PC Roth will stay here and take statements from any witnesses, and we'll need a copy of that CCTV footage, Caroline, if that's okay.'

'I'll run it by head office, but I'm sure it'll be no problem.'

'Thank you. Okay, Mr and Mrs Blundell, come with me, please.'

PC Davis led Matthew and Heather out of the office, and they made their way across the shop floor, negotiating the aisles on their way to the exit. Matthew was conscious of the shoppers who were staring in their direction as they tailed their police escort, no doubt thinking they'd been caught shoplifting. As they emerged from the exit into the bright light of the morning, they met PC Roth hurrying back in. 'The car was reported stolen first thing this morning,' he said to PC Davis. 'Apparently taken from outside a house in Wroxall sometime in the early hours.'

'To be expected, I guess,' said PC Davis. 'Only an idiot would drive away from here in their own car.' He pulled out a set of keys. 'Andy, are you okay to take care of business here if I take Mr and Mrs Blundell to the station?'

'No problem, Dougie. You'll have to send another car to pick me up, though.'

'Come off it, Andy, you can get the bus.' PC Davis winked at him and then showed Matthew and Heather into the back seat of the police car parked immediately outside the store entrance.

The police station in Newport was opposite the council offices on High Street. Matthew and Heather were in an interview room, seated opposite PC Davis and his supervising officer, Sergeant Mason. Heather had given her statement outlining the events leading up to James's abduction, and the police were now in possession of a photograph of James, which would be circulated internally and to the various authorities around the island who would potentially be involved in the search for him.

'Is there anyone you can think of who might have a reason to want to take James?' said Sergeant Mason.

Heather looked at Matthew. 'You don't think Sarah has anything to do with this, do you?'

'I wouldn't put anything past her. We know what she's capable of.'

'I'm sorry,' said Sergeant Mason, 'who is this Sarah?'

By the time Matthew and Heather had finished apprising him of the recent events involving Sarah Morton, Sergeant Mason had filled several pages of his notebook. PC Davis was also scribbling furiously.

'Thank you,' said Sergeant Mason, looking up. 'I think at the very least we need to consider Sarah Morton "a person of interest". I'll take PC Davis and we'll speak to her immediately and make some neighbourhood enquiries. It goes without saying that I'm designating this case as high risk. Our most senior officers have been informed, and if we need any specialist expertise, we can call that in from the mainland. In the meantime, Mr and Mrs Blundell, the best thing you can do is go home. It's possible that James's abductor might contact you with a ransom demand, in which case you need to let us know immediately. If anything else occurs to you, don't hesitate to call us, day or night.'

Sergeant Mason sat on a sofa with PC Davis uncomfortably seated beside him, opposite Sarah Morton, who looked very relaxed in her armchair. PC Davis marvelled at her somewhat eccentric dress sense. She wore pink designer glasses that matched her pink eyeshadow. Her lipstick was a deep fuchsia pink and matched her shoes, and she wore a white blouse, which was unbuttoned at the top and revealed just a little too much of her sagging breasts for PC Davis's liking. She was a small woman, a little rounded, with piercing eyes. PC Davis knew she was sixty-two. Mutton dressed as lamb sprang to mind.

‘Thank you for inviting us in, Ms Morton. We’ll try not to take up too much of your time,’ Sergeant Mason was saying.

Sarah Morton sat tight-lipped and said nothing.

‘I need to ask you, Ms Morton: where were you this morning?’

‘I was here.’

‘Can anyone corroborate that?’

‘My son. He was here with me.’

‘Your son... that would be Dylan? Dylan Dumas?’

‘That’s right.’

‘And I understand your son has been living here with you since his release from prison?’

‘That’s right. He’s still looking for work. He can’t afford a place of his own.’

‘And where is Dylan now, Ms Morton?’

‘He’s gone to the shop for some cigarettes. He’ll be back soon. What’s all this about? He’s done nothing wrong. I knew it wouldn’t be long before you lot would be back, sniffing around, trying to pin something on him. I tell you, he’s been here with me all morning.’

‘This is just a routine inquiry, Ms Morton. Nothing to worry about.’

‘A routine inquiry about what?’

‘A little boy was snatched from a local supermarket this morning.’

‘Why the hell would I know anything about that?’

‘Your name has come up regarding a recent dispute you had with the boy’s parents. We have to follow up on these things. I’m sure you understand.’

‘Matthew and Heather Blundell by any chance?’

‘That’s not something I can discuss, I’m afraid, Ms Morton. Your partner, Christine Patton. Is she still living here?’

‘No, *he* moved out. We’re not together anymore.’

‘I’m sorry to hear that.’

‘Not as sorry as he was that we had an ex-convict living with us and that I’d lost a forty-grand-a-year job.’

Sergeant Mason stalled.

PC Davis took over. 'Do either you or your son drive, Ms Morton?'

'Yes, we both do. If he needs to go out, he uses my car. I put him on the insurance. But he spends most of his time here. I can never get him off that damn Xbox of his.'

'What car do you drive, Ms Morton?'

'It's on the drive. The red Fiat Panda Cross.'

Sergeant Mason took the lead again. 'May we take a look around, Ms Morton?'

'I don't know what you expect to find.'

'It's just a box-ticking exercise, Ms Morton, so we can eliminate you and your son from our inquiries.'

'Well, neither of us has anything to hide. If it gets you off his back, search all you like. You won't find anything.'

Sergeant Mason and PC Davis got up from the sofa and left Sarah Morton sitting rigid in her armchair.

'We're looking for the knee-length blue parka or any of the clothing the boy was wearing,' said Sergeant Mason in a low voice as they stood in the hallway. 'And keep an eye open for any car keys that might belong to a Ford Fiesta. I'll take upstairs; you take down here.'

PC Davis looked back into the lounge, where a seething Sarah Morton sat. He then looked around him, taking in a simple dining room, a small kitchen and a downstairs toilet. I get all the glamorous jobs, he thought.

They came up empty-handed, but just as Sergeant Mason descended the stairs to rejoin PC Davis, Dylan Dumas arrived home. The front door opened, and a man in his early thirties walked into the hallway, bringing with him the stench of cigarette smoke. He was around five feet ten, dressed in a faded Disturbed 'Believe' hoodie and a pair of ripped black jeans. His black hair was cropped, and his eyes were dark and angry. He stopped as he registered PC Davis in the hallway and glowered at him.

'Ah, Mr Dumas, I presume. We're sorry to disturb you,' said Sergeant Mason, arriving at the bottom of the stairs.

'No bother. What can I do for you gentlemen?'

'We've just spoken with your mother. I'll ask you the same question I asked her: where were you this morning?'

Dylan Dumas looked past him and at his mother, who was staring at him, still seated in her armchair. 'I was here – with her.' He nodded towards the lounge.

'Okay,' said Sergeant Mason, 'well, that's it. No more questions. Thank you both for your time today.'

Dylan stepped aside as the two policemen left and the door clicked shut behind them.

'Okay, now for the neighbours,' said Sergeant Mason. 'Which do you want? Left or right?' PC Davis opted for the right.

He rang the doorbell and stood waiting for what seemed like an age before the door was opened. 'Good morning, Madam. PC Davis, Hampshire & Isle of Wight Constabulary.' He smiled engagingly and showed his identity. 'May I ask you a few quick questions?'

'Oh, my!' said a lady who was probably somewhere in her seventies. 'What have I done wrong?'

'Don't worry, Madam. I'm just making a few routine inquiries.'

'Of course. How can I help you?'

'May I just take your name?'

'Yes, it's Mrs Warrington. My husband's dead, though.'

'I'm sorry to hear that. May I ask your whereabouts this morning, Mrs Warrington?'

'Yes, of course. I was here. I was cleaning and doing the washing. I'm retired, you see.'

'And how well do you know the lady and her son next door?'

'Sarah? I don't really speak to her that much, but we say hello when we pass. I don't really know her son.'

'Would you happen to know if they were both at home this morning?'

'Well, there were lights on and there was music playing. They have it quite loud, you know. I remember hearing voices at one stage when I was out in the garden... and, yes, I remember I saw Sarah out by the recycling bins. I usually hear the car if she goes out, but I think it's been on the drive all day.'

'Do you know if her son has a car?'

'I doubt it. I think he uses Sarah's. I'm sure he couldn't afford a car. I don't think he's done a day's work since he's lived there.'

'Okay,' said PC Davis, 'so you heard voices, but did you actually see the son at home this morning?'

'Well, as I say, I heard voices. I'm pretty sure they were both there.'

PC Davis finished writing in his notebook. 'Well, thank you, Mrs Warrington; you've been more than helpful.'

'Won't you come in for a cup of tea? It's been a long time since I've had a handsome young man in the house.'

'As much as I'd love to, Mrs Warrington...'

'Never mind. Maybe next time, eh?' Mrs Warrington smiled at him and closed the door.

Sergeant Mason had drawn a blank. The neighbour to the left had been out all morning. When they questioned the owners of the houses opposite, no one had seen anything or really knew much about Sarah Morton and her son, Dylan.

'I think that's all we're going to get, Sarge,' said PC Davis. 'What do you think?'

'I think, on the face of it, there's nothing to suggest that these two have any involvement in the boy's disappearance. However, given the hostility between Sarah Morton and the Blundells and the fact that her son Dylan is a nasty piece of work, I just want to be sure.'

'What do you have in mind?'

'Hell, I know we don't have the resources, but I'm going to suggest we put a car outside this place. Just for the rest of today and tomorrow. There's a kid out there somewhere. If either of them goes anywhere, I want to know about it. If they don't, then the likelihood is they're not involved.'

The constabulary nominated four volunteers. Partnered up, two officers sat in a car parked a short way down the street from Sarah Morton's small semi-detached house in Godshill and rotated with two others across four shifts. For the remainder of that day and all the next, they watched and waited.

In vain.

33

Ransom

Sunday, 20th January 2019

Matthew closed the front door and followed Heather back into the lounge. She had gone over to the window and was looking out as David walked down the path with Noah towards his car.

'It was sweet of him to offer to take Noah out for a few hours,' she said, peering through the net curtains. 'It takes the pressure off us for a while.'

Matthew wandered over to the sofa and sat down. 'The poor kid keeps asking when James will be back,' he said. 'I hate lying to him.'

'Well, David agrees it's the right thing to do.'

Matthew flopped back into the cushions and stared up at the ceiling. 'I know. But it doesn't make it any easier.'

Heather turned and walked into the middle of the room. 'Lying to Noah is one thing,' she said, 'but you can't put off calling Tony and Barbara any longer. I know you don't want to worry them, but this is dragging on and we're going to have to tell them what's happened. Especially as we've told Noah, James has gone to stay with them.'

Matthew and Heather had lied to Noah from the start when he returned home from school on Friday afternoon and asked where James was. On Saturday, the day after James's kidnapping, they had met with Noah's social worker, Louise, and David, and discussed whether they should tell Noah the truth. David said no. Louise agreed with him. 'I think for Noah's well-being and for professional reasons, it's the right thing to do at this stage,' she had said.

Heather turned almost immediately and walked back over to the window. She watched as David secured Noah into a car seat in the back of his red Ford Focus. David had two young children of his own. 'I've been thinking,' she said.

Matthew waited. Heather still appeared to be thinking. 'Okay, spit it out,' he said finally.

Heather turned and walked back towards him. 'I know we suggested to the police that Sarah must be behind all this. But do you really think she's the one who's taken James?'

'I know she's involved.' Matthew patted the space next to him on the sofa. 'Come and sit down. You're making me nervous with all that pacing around.'

Heather ignored him and turned back towards the window. 'Thinking rationally, though, surely Sarah wouldn't be that stupid? With all that's happened, it's obvious she'd be the number one suspect. Would she take that risk? It's got to be someone else.'

'She's stupid, alright. Look at the risks she took to stitch us up.' Matthew got to his feet and walked over to the window to join her. 'She's unhinged, that woman. She's hit self-destruct and now she's going hell-bent for leather for revenge.'

'It feels wrong to me.'

'Well, if it's someone else,' said Matthew, pulling the net curtain aside and looking out, 'what the hell's their motive?'

'Money.'

'Well, now she's lost her forty-grand-a-year job at the council, Sarah's almost certainly got financial issues. There you go, then: revenge *and* money!' David's red Ford Focus pulled away and Matthew let the net curtain fall back into place.

The phone rang.

Heather looked nervously at Matthew. 'You get it...'

Matthew hurried into the hall.

'Hello?'

'Mr Blundell, it's Sergeant Mason. How are you holding up?'

'Desperate for some good news,' said Matthew. 'Do you have any?'

'Well, as you know, we visited Sarah Morton on Friday,' said Sergeant Mason. 'I'm afraid there's no reason to believe she's involved.'

'What did she say?'

'That she was at home that morning with her son.'

'Her son?' For a moment, Matthew was speechless. 'What?'

'Her son, Dylan Dumas,' said Sergeant Mason. 'He's been living there since he was released from Parkhurst last year.'

'You're joking...' Matthew was struggling to comprehend. 'He's on the Isle of Wight? What was he in prison for?'

Sergeant Mason hesitated. 'Well, I'm not telling you anything that isn't a matter of public record,' he said. 'He was convicted for holding a woman against her will and raping her. It was back in 2010 in London. But, so far as James's abduction is concerned, it appears he was at home with his mother. We searched the house and found nothing to implicate either of them. A neighbour we spoke to seemed almost certain they'd both been at home on Friday morning.' He paused. 'I agree, given the serious nature of her past actions, it's tempting to like Sarah Morton, or her son, for James's kidnapping. That's why I put the two of them under surveillance for over twenty-four hours. Neither of them left the house.'

'Isn't that suspicious in itself?'

Sergeant Mason cleared his throat. 'It's possible they clocked us and sat tight, but if they're involved, surely one of them would have left to see to James. But all of this is hypothetical. On the evidence so far, it's unlikely they're involved.'

'Are you still watching them?' Matthew knew the answer.

'We don't have the resources, I'm afraid, Mr Blundell. I had to fight to get what I did.'

'This is bullshit, Sergeant Mason! A child's been kidnapped. You should be throwing everything at it.'

'I'm sorry, Mr Blundell. We're doing all we can.'

Matthew breathed deeply. 'So, where do we go from here, then?'

Sergeant Mason sounded a little more upbeat. 'We've set up an incident room and put every available resource on the case. We're following up every lead. We have to hope whoever's involved makes contact. If you hear or receive anything, let us know immediately. If we get anything concrete, we'll be in touch.'

'Okay, will do.' Matthew put down the phone and swore.

Heather had been standing in the lounge doorway, listening. 'You said "her son".' Her voice was shaky. 'Do you mean Dylan? Is he here on the Isle of Wight?'

Matthew turned to face her. 'Yes. He's been in Parkhurst for rape and now he's living with Sarah.'

Heather gripped the door frame. She was pale. 'I don't believe it...' She steadied herself. 'I guess that explains what Sarah's doing here.'

'The woman he raped. He abducted her; held her against her will.'

'You think he...?'

'Why not? He's a sociopath. What's not to say he's doing Sarah's bidding?'

Heather sank and sat on her haunches. 'What did Sergeant Mason say? I heard you say they're watching them.'

'*Were* watching them. They called it off – not enough resources.' Matthew scoffed. 'You heard what I thought of that!'

Heather folded her arms across her body and rocked gently on her heels. 'So, they don't think she's involved?'

'No.' Matthew stepped towards her. 'Apparently, she and Dylan were home all Friday morning.' He offered Heather his hand. 'They spoke to her, searched her house and neither of them moved a muscle while they were under surveillance.'

Heather looked up at him. 'Couldn't one of them have slipped out the back?'

Matthew shrugged. 'Anything's possible, but if Sarah's car never left the drive, how would they get to where they're holding James? They found the stolen car burnt out in a field near Wroxall.'

'They could've stolen another car...'

Matthew stood patiently, still holding out his hand. 'As I said, anything's possible. We're just speculating. The police are looking elsewhere, and we just have to sit tight and wait.'

‘I feel so helpless...’ Heather reached out and took Matthew’s hand, and he helped her to her feet. ‘We should be doing something,’ she said. ‘We should be out there trying to find James.’

‘I know. It’s like we’re just two lost souls swimming in a fishbowl, idling around here.’

Heather groaned. ‘I’m exhausted. I don’t know what to do.’ She walked back into the lounge and looked down at a pile of toys in the corner. Squatting, she picked up a cuddly pig that belonged to James. She held it to her face and breathed in deeply. ‘Oh, James. I wish you were here, playing with your “-ig”.’

Matthew walked up behind her and placed his hands on her shoulders. ‘Look, you didn’t get any sleep again last night. If we’re just sitting around here waiting, you might as well go up to bed for a few hours,’ he said. ‘Even if you just close your eyes and get some rest, it’s better than nothing. If anything happens, I’ll come and get you.’

Matthew sat in the lounge and put on the TV. It was the usual Sunday morning dross, and he dozed fitfully. Sometime later, the pop, pop, cracking sound of a moped’s exhaust woke him as it sped off from outside the house. On instinct, he got up and went to the front door. He opened it. Hanging from the porch door letterbox was an envelope. The front was blank. He opened it and pulled out a single piece of thick card.

IF YOU WANT JAMES BACK PAY £25,000 IN CASH OR YOU WILL NEVER SEE HIM AGAIN. HAVE MONEY READY BY MIDNIGHT ON TUESDAY 22ND. IF YOU INVOLVE THE POLICE YOU WON’T EVER SEE HIM AGAIN. I’LL BE IN TOUCH WITH INSTRUCTIONS.

Matthew ran up the stairs.

‘Heather! We’ve had a ransom note!’

He ran into the bedroom as Heather sat up in bed. He handed her the card to read.

'Where did this come from?'

'It was in the letterbox in the porch. I think whoever delivered it just left on a moped.'

Heather's hand trembled as she read the note. 'Twenty-five grand! Where the hell are we going to get that sort of money from?'

'It could have been worse,' said Matthew. He sat next to her on the bed. 'Given someone's risked everything to kidnap a kid, that amount seems quite low to me. Perhaps they know our financial circumstances? Perhaps they know banks will hand over that kind of cash without too much bother and they don't want James on their hands any longer than they have to.'

'Well, we don't have that kind of money,' said Heather, 'so they obviously don't know our circumstances. You'd better phone Sergeant Mason.'

'No, hold on a minute,' said Matthew. 'The police don't believe in paying ransoms. They'll try to negotiate some other way. We don't want to put James in danger. It says not to involve the police, so we need to think carefully before we rush in.'

'But if we pay it, we'll have to get a loan of some sort, or increase the mortgage,' said Heather. 'There's no other way.' She handed the note back to Matthew and extricated herself from the duvet.

Matthew stood up as Heather got out of bed. 'We won't get a loan for that amount in time,' he said. 'That's if they even give us one. And the bank will ask all sorts of questions... I need to think.'

Tony's confused face appeared on the screen.

'Do you know you called me on WhatsApp video?'

'Yes, Dad, I do. It was a conscious decision, not a random act of madness.'

'No need to be facetious, Son.'

Matthew grimaced. 'I videoed because I want to speak with you and Mum at the same time.'

'Why, what's up?' Tony's forehead creased into a frown. 'You look and sound agitated.'

'Can you get Mum, please, and I'll tell you.'

'Barbara!' Tony's voice boomed. Matthew saw his mother appear behind Tony. She sat down and huddled beside him, peering into the camera and out at Matthew and Heather, who were viewing on their laptop screen.

'Oh, hello, Heather, love. How are you?'

'Not good, I'm afraid, Barbara.'

'Oh, why's that, love? Has he been mistreating you again?'

Heather made to reply, but Matthew placed a firm hand on her knee and interrupted. 'Mum, Dad. It's a nightmare here, I'm afraid. There's no easy way to say this... James has been kidnapped. Someone snatched him while Heather was in Morrisons on Friday.'

Silence.

Barbara was visibly shaken. The blood drained from her face, and her visage seemed to fade to grey. She gasped and put her hand across her mouth. Tony sat stony-faced, his eyes locked on the screen. For a moment, neither seemed to know what to say.

'I'm so sorry,' said Barbara. Her voice broke and faltered. 'That's shocking news.' She hesitated. 'Is there anything we can do? Would you like us to come over and help you with Noah?'

'Thank you,' said Matthew, 'but for the moment, Noah's still at school.'

'How is he coping?'

'We haven't told him,' said Matthew. 'We don't plan to for the time being, and the social workers agree. I hope you don't mind, but we've told him James is with you...'

'Oh,' said Barbara. 'I suppose so... if you think that's best.'

'I can't believe it,' said Tony. 'Do the police have any idea who might have taken him?'

Matthew briefed them, but kept it short. He pushed on. 'Listen. Mum, Dad, we've had a ransom note. We don't know what to do, and we don't have anyone else to turn to. We just need to talk it through and get someone else's opinion.'

'Well, shouldn't you just go to the police?' said Tony. 'They'll know what to do.'

'That's the obvious thing to do,' said Matthew, 'but, predictably, whoever's responsible has threatened us if we involve them.'

'That's to be expected,' said Tony, 'but surely the police have enough experience to handle these cases?'

'Do they?' said Heather. 'Kidnapping for ransom is quite rare – especially on the Isle of Wight. If they mess things up, we could lose James.'

'Are you saying you're thinking of paying the ransom?' said Tony.

'How much do they want?' said Barbara.

Matthew grimaced. 'Twenty-five thousand.'

'We don't have that kind of money,' said Heather. There were tears in her eyes.

'We do,' said Barbara.

'No, Mum. We couldn't. That's not why we rang.'

'Listen, Matthew,' said Barbara. 'The money's there; it's not doing much. We live comfortably enough on our pensions. James's safe return is paramount, and if you think involving the police could jeopardise that...'

Tony was nodding. 'I have to say, I think not involving the police is a big risk, but James is your son and if you really feel that paying the ransom is the way to go, then I agree with your mum: the money's there and we'll transfer it over to you. I'd never forgive myself if I convinced you to involve the police and something went wrong. But you need to give this some serious thought.'

'Thank you, both,' said Matthew. 'Having that option is a massive weight off our minds.'

'If you pay the ransom, how are they planning to return James to you?' said Tony.

'They haven't said.'

'I mean...' Tony hesitated. 'I have to be blunt here, Matthew. You might not want to hear this, but what if you pay the ransom and the kidnapper doesn't return James?'

'That doesn't bear thinking about,' said Matthew. 'We just have to stay positive and believe that we'll get James home safely. We'll cross any other bridge when we come to it.'

Heather was openly weeping.

'How much time do you have?' said Barbara. 'I mean, to pay the ransom?'

Matthew put his arm around Heather. 'They've given us until midnight on Tuesday to get the cash.' He pulled Heather closer to him. 'Presumably, sometime between now and then, we'll receive instructions where to take it.'

'I guess they'll expect you to involve the police, so it might not be as straightforward as just dropping it off somewhere,' said Tony.

'I've been thinking about what I'd do if we pay the ransom,' said Matthew. 'You can buy those trackers these days. I reckon I could hide it in a bag with the money and track them to where they're holding James and then call the police. Or, if we meet and they do a swap – the money for James – then the police can track the bag and pick them up.'

'This is all sounding a bit James Bond,' said Barbara. 'Are you sure you know what you're doing?'

'The tracker sounds like something the police might do. Won't they be expecting that?' said Tony.

'Hopefully not,' said Matthew.

'What if they transfer the money into a bag of their own and ditch the one with the tracker?'

'Crikey, Dad...'

'I'm just trying to be realistic, Son. You have to think of these things.'

'Okay, so I take the money. They either swap James for the money there and then, in which case, there's a chance the tracker will lead the police to them. But James will be safe, which is what really matters. But if they expect us to hand over the money and take it on trust that they'll tell us where to find James, then at least with a tracker in the bag, there's a chance I can follow them and call the police before they can harm him. And if they ditch the bag, I'll just have to get closer and hope they don't notice me tailing them.'

'It all sounds risky to me. Just as risky as involving the police,' said Tony.

'They've said no police, Dad, and at least we'll have done as they've said. If there are no police at the drop-off, no helicopters, and they are clever enough to suspect a tracker and swap bags, they'll think they've escaped. They'll let their guard down. By the time I've followed them to wherever they go, they won't be expecting the police.'

'And what if you fail to follow them?'

'Then they'll have the money, and we have to trust that they'll return James. Do we have anything to lose?'

'Think about it, Son. If you're sure this is the way you want to go, fine. We'll transfer the money now, so it's there, whatever you decide. If we think of anything else, we'll call you back.'

'Thanks, Dad.'

'And if you change your mind and you want us to come over, let us know,' said Barbara.

'Thank you both,' said Heather. She raised her head from Matthew's shoulder and wiped her eyes.

'You're welcome, my love,' said Barbara. 'And, Matthew, let us know what you decide to do. And for goodness' sake, be careful.'

Monday, 21st January 2019

'Good morning, sir.' The bank clerk employed a well-practised smile that vanished almost immediately. She looked expectantly through the glass.

'Morning,' said Matthew. 'I need to make a large withdrawal from my bank account.'

'No problem, sir. May I ask how much that will be?'

'Yes, twenty-five thousand pounds.'

If the clerk seemed surprised, she didn't show it. 'Normally, for sums over twenty thousand, we require at least three days' notice, sir. May I ask what this amount is for?'

'Certainly. We're having an extension built, and I have to pay for the materials and work done so far, or the builder's going to walk off site. He wants to be paid by tomorrow, or he's going to pack up and move on to his next project.'

'As I said, sir, normally we need three days' notice. It's for your own protection and gives us time to order the cash in whatever denominations you require. I presume you'll be wanting fifty-pound notes?'

'I don't need protection, thank you. I've not fallen foul of fraudsters or scams, and if you look at my account, you'll see the money's been transferred from my parents. I must have the money by tomorrow.'

'Okay, sir. I'll see if there's a manager available. Would you like to take a seat over there?' She indicated a small glassed-off area to Matthew's right. 'I'll get someone to come and speak to you shortly.'

Matthew walked over, stepped into the booth and sat down in a chair at a glass-topped table. He stared at the back of a computer monitor and waited. A minute later, Heather called.

'Have you got the money?'

'For goodness' sake, Heather. I'm still at the bank. I'm waiting for someone to come and speak to me.' He relaxed his tone. 'Apparently, they need more than twenty-four hours' notice for anything over twenty thousand.'

'Oh, Christ. We don't have more than twenty-four hours. We need it tomorrow.'

'That's why I'm waiting to speak with someone. Look, I told you I'd call you when I've finished. Now, stop panicking. Speak to you later.' Matthew hung up and looked around him. The banking hall was quiet, and the two cashiers sat chatting.

Within five minutes, the door to the side of the counter opened, and a middle-aged man came through. He wore a smart blue jacket bearing the bank's logo and neatly pressed grey trousers. He looked like the manager.

'Good morning, sir. I understand you wish to withdraw a large sum of money rather urgently.' He sat at the table on the opposite side to Matthew and logged in to the computer. 'Let's see what we can do. If I can take your account details and some proof of identification.'

Matthew passed over his debit card and passport.

The manager sat tapping away at the keyboard. 'Bear with me...'

After a minute or two, he looked up. 'Okay, Mr Blundell. I can see that your account is in good order, and I understand your parents have transferred the funds to pay off your builder, so you won't be needing a loan from us.'

Matthew smiled politely.

'Right, well, you're in luck,' the manager continued. 'We had a few large pay-ins last week and we've yet to have our collection, so I can let you have the twenty-five. I can probably do most of it in fifties, but some of it will have to be in twenty-pound notes. Will that be okay?'

'Whatever you've got will be fine.' Matthew sat back in his chair. 'Thank you; I appreciate this.'

'Not a problem,' said the manager. 'We've only got a small back-room staff and we're a little busy at the moment, so if you can call in first thing tomorrow morning, we'll have it ready for you. Is that okay?'

'Yes, thank you very much.' Matthew's palms were clammy, and he rubbed them on his trouser legs.

'I'll let the cashiers know,' said the manager. 'Just bring identification, and if there are any problems, just ask for me.'

'Perfect.' Matthew stood to leave. 'Please,' he said, 'don't let me down.' He shook the manager's hand and then hurried out into the fresh air. He felt his tension ease and his shoulders relax. The adrenaline left him feeling slightly weak, and he recalled a similar sensation just after he had passed his driving test. The blessed relief.

He called Heather, who picked up immediately.

'Sorted. I pick up the money first thing tomorrow morning.'

'Oh, thank f...'

Matthew gave a short laugh. 'You were going to swear then, weren't you?'

'Yes, I fucking was,' said Heather. 'Don't be long. I don't like being here on my own.'

Matthew returned home to find Heather busy in the lounge. She had found an old holdall and had picked open a hole in one side of the padded base. A small tracker should fit perfectly. No one would know it was there unless they pulled the bag apart or had some kind of scanning device.

Matthew looked around the lounge. 'Has the tracker arrived?'

'There's a parcel on the kitchen table,' said Heather. 'I imagine that's it.'

Matthew retrieved the parcel and brought it back to the lounge. 'I ordered the smallest I could find, but they're still fairly chunky,' he said, as he ripped through the packaging. 'They're GPS – they track in real-time. I ordered the SIM cards too. It all sounds pretty easy to set up.' He sat down and opened a small black box. He took out a set of instructions and pulled out his phone. 'I'll need to download an app,' he said, beginning to read.

Heather looked over. 'Why have you ordered two?'

Matthew was concentrating. He paused briefly and looked up. 'Huh? Two?... Just in case one doesn't work. And you never know when a spare might come in handy.'

'Your mum called again. She and your dad are still worried. She's now comparing you to Tom Cruise in Mission Impossible. I think they're against it, but they say it's down to us. I don't think they want to be responsible if they influence us and something goes wrong.'

Matthew sighed. He put down the instructions. 'Look, we've thought it through. Yes, of course, there are risks. There are risks if we hand everything over to the police. This whole fucking situation is a stack of dynamite just waiting to blow. But if I'm careful... I'd rather drop the money, walk away and let whoever's behind this see there's no police. We have to assume they're not stupid; they'll have planned for police involvement. They'll be one hundred and ten per cent sure there's no police before they collect, and they'll have a Plan B. Yes, they might well be sensible enough to swap bags if they have the nous to suspect there might be a tracker. If they do, I'll have to hope I can tail them. That's the worst-case scenario.'

'And if you follow them to where they're holding James, you'll call the police then? You won't try any heroics?'

'I promise.'

'I'm serious, Matthew. You could get hurt.'

Matthew bristled. 'I might not be Action Man, Heather, but I can certainly look after myself. My upbringing made me tough. I had to be. I'm not afraid of a scrap.'

'We're not dealing with playground bullies now, Matthew.'

Matthew stood and drew himself to his full height. 'Look at me. Six feet and in my prime. Who's going to mess with this? Besides, this is James we're talking about here. I'll do what has to be done. None of us knows what we're capable of until we put ourselves out there.'

He noticed the horrified look on Heather's face and sat down. 'But it won't come to that,' he said.

A heavy silence lingered and then Heather spoke. 'Sergeant Mason called as well. He asked if we've heard from anyone. I said no. I felt sick lying about something so serious. He can't believe no one's made contact by now. He didn't say outright, but I think they're assuming James is dead.'

'Don't even think about it. We have to believe this is about money. As long as they get their money, they'll want James off their hands, and they'll return him. It's not as though he's ever going to be able to identify them. They've no worries there. Let's focus on the job at hand and try not to think too much about what could go wrong.'

Tuesday, 22nd January 2019

Matthew and Heather had been up early. Matthew had collected the cash from the bank while Heather was dropping Noah off at school. They now had one concern. Second contact. It was Tuesday the 22nd, and the deadline was midnight – surely, they would receive further instructions soon. The first note had been hand-delivered; would someone be crazy enough to ride up brazenly to the front door again and post the second one in broad daylight? It didn't seem likely. But expect the unexpected.

They waited all day. Heather drove to the school and picked up Noah. They ate a meal together, though Heather was not hungry and just picked at the fish fingers on her plate. They watched TV while Noah played, and when it was time for his bed, Heather went up with him and read him a story. When she came back downstairs, Matthew had switched off the television and was sitting in silence, listening to the sound of the clock ticking.

'What's going on?' he said. 'Why haven't we heard anything?'

'I don't know,' said Heather, sitting down next to him on the sofa. 'They said to have the money ready by the end of today. They didn't say when we'd receive further instructions.'

'This waiting is doing my head in.'

Heather switched the television back on and for the next few hours, they stared at it, not really absorbing anything, intermittently speaking, running over the same old ground, over and over. The clock ticked, but they didn't notice it over the noise of the TV, as slowly their minds numbed and their thoughts turned to bed. Eventually, they gave up and went upstairs.

34

Cometh The Hour

Wednesday, 23rd January 2019

The crash woke Matthew and Heather instantly. They sat up. Noah cried out sleepily, 'What's going on?' from his room across the hall.

Matthew looked at Heather. She was clearly shaken. 'You'll have to go down,' she said. 'I'll settle Noah.'

Matthew looked at the time as he swung his feet out from under the duvet and sat momentarily on the edge of the bed: 0:07 AM. They'd barely had time to doze off. He steeled himself, rose and moved silently out onto the landing. There was no sound from downstairs. He took the stairs one by one, taking his time, listening every few seconds. He heard nothing. As he reached the hall, he paused. He heard the muted sound of the clock ticking on the other side of the lounge door, which was closed. He crept over to it. It had multiple frosted glass panels. He could discern no signs of movement on the other side. He placed his ear against the glass. Nothing. He carried on down the hall and stopped in front of the kitchen door. There were knives in the kitchen. He looked around for a weapon of his own. He pulled open the door of the hall cupboard, taking care not to make a sound, and pulled out a golfing umbrella. Better than nothing, he thought. Slowly, he eased the handle of the kitchen door and then shoved it open, standing in the doorway, preparing for an attack.

Nothing.

A waning gibbous moon cast a wan light through the kitchen window over the sink. The window was smashed, and a cold draught caused Matthew to shiver. The moonlight reflected on shards of glass on the kitchen floor. Among the glass was a rock, about the size of his fist. It had paper around it, taped on. Matthew looked up and out through the window. He thought he saw movement in the shadows on the fence in the far left-hand corner of the garden. The unmistakable sound of a moped engine started up, moved away and was gone. Matthew walked into the room, reached down and picked up the rock. Despite his best efforts to avoid the glass, he felt the stabbing pain of tiny shards embedding themselves into the soles of his feet. He winced and trod gingerly back towards the kitchen table and sat in the chair. Heather appeared in the doorway. In her hand, she held the rod for the loft hatch.

'What are you doing down here?' Matthew hissed. 'That wouldn't do much good – it's aluminium.'

Heather looked around the kitchen. 'Did you see anyone?'

'Switch on the light,' said Matthew. 'Whoever it was has gone.'

Heather reached to her left and flicked the light switch. She looked at Matthew sitting at the kitchen table. 'You're bleeding,' she said. 'You've cut your feet.'

'Yes. The kitchen window's all over the kitchen floor.'

'Stay there,' said Heather. 'I'll get your slippers and then get that glass out.'

Heather disappeared into the hall. Matthew sat and peeled the tape from around the rock and opened a piece of folded paper.

YOU BETTER HAVE THE MONEY AND YOU BETTER NOT HAVE INVOLVED THE POLICE. PUT THE MONEY IN A BAG AND DRIVE TO STRAWBERRY LANE. PARK IN FRONT OF THE GATE ON THE RIGHT AND TAKE FOOTPATH TO THE LONGSTONE. GET THERE AT 2AM. LEAVE BAG BY THE STONE.

ONCE I HAVE THE MONEY I'LL GIVE YOU DETAILS WHERE TO FIND JAMES. REMEMBER NO POLICE OR NO JAMES.

Heather reappeared. She saw the note in Matthew's hand. 'What's it say?' Her voice was shaky.

'I haven't got long. They want me to be at the Long Stone by two a.m.' said Matthew.

'That's down by Mottistone. About half an hour away.'

Matthew nodded.

'Here, let me look at your feet first.'

Heather ran some hot water into a bowl, added a splash of TCP and knelt in front of Matthew. She dragged a chair across. 'Put your feet up on here.' She had brought tweezers, which she used to remove the glass, as Matthew sat in silence. Her hands shook slightly as she worked. When she had finished, she bathed and dried the soles of his feet and stuck a few plasters on the worst of the cuts. 'Socks and slippers,' she said, handing them to him. Matthew put them on, and Heather stood up. 'What now?' she said.

'I need to see exactly where I'm going,' said Matthew. 'It says there's a place to pull in on Strawberry Lane, in front of a gate. Then there's a footpath leading to the Long Stone. I'll get the laptop and check it out on Google Earth.'

While Heather swept up the glass, Matthew retrieved the laptop from the office and started it up. He navigated to Google Earth and zoomed down onto the Isle of Wight and the region of Mottistone. He picked out the location of the gate and the footpath, halfway down Strawberry Lane – the first on the right if you headed south from the top end at the junction with Lynch Lane. Distance-wise, there wasn't too much difference driving through Brighstone at the southern end of the lane and heading north, so he decided to follow the instructions to the letter. Next, he homed in on the footpath and the Long Stone. The footpath ran along the hedgerow at the side of a field before disappearing into some trees. When it came out on the other side, it was onto open common land, where the Long Stone stood, a short walk ahead. It was no more than five hundred metres. Matthew packed up the laptop. He knew where he was going. He looked at the clock. It was approaching 1:00 AM. He made his last preparations: dressed in warm clothing and light hiking boots, retrieved the holdall with the money and checked that his two GPS trackers were live and appearing on the app on his phone. And then it was time.

Heather threw her arms around him as he stood by the front door. She clung to him, her head pressed into his chest. 'Now, stay in touch,' she said, her voice breaking, 'and don't do anything rash.' She tried not to let Matthew see she was crying. 'James's life is at stake here,' she said. 'One slip...'

Matthew pulled her in close. 'Don't upset yourself,' he said. 'I know exactly what's at stake. And don't worry; I won't take any unnecessary risks. Now, I best get going.' He kissed her on the top of the head, extricated himself gently from her arms and walked out through the front door, into the crisp, moonlit still of the night.

35

The Long Stone

Strawberry Lane was long and incredibly narrow. As he took the left from Lynch Lane and drove his silver Citroën slowly between overgrown hedgerows on either side, he prayed he wouldn't meet anyone else coming up it at this ungodly hour. It was like running a gauntlet. There was enough moonlight that when gaps in the hedgerows appeared, he saw fields stretching away into the distance with scatterings of trees. An open area appeared on his left, but it was just a track entrance to a field. He drove on.

The lay-by on the right for the footpath was obvious. It appeared almost dead ahead as the lane veered off to the left. He approached slowly and surveyed the area. He drove a short way past a semi-circular space that would accommodate around three cars and then reversed in, leaving the front of the car facing the road, ready to head off in any direction.

Just as he was about to get out of the car, Heather called.

'Where are you now?'

'Jesus. I said I'd call when I got here.'

'Where are you, then?'

'I just got here.'

'Well, there you go...'

'Look, Heather, I need to concentrate. I'll call you after I've made the drop. For Christ's sake...'

Silence.

'Did you hear me, Heather? I said I'll call you. I know it's hard just sitting there waiting, but...' He hung up.

The night sky was clear, and the waning moon was almost two days past full. Matthew had an extra-bright LED torch that Noah and James had bought him for Christmas, but for the time being, he could see without it.

'Okay. Here we go,' he said to himself. He eased out of the driver's seat and stepped onto the stony lay-by. There was a gate leading into a field, off to his left. Directly ahead of him was a wide opening in a hedgerow. A footpath waymarker said, "Public Footpath BS84. The Long Stone, Mottistone..." He leant back into the car and pulled the holdall from the passenger seat. He made one last mental check that he had everything he needed and locked the car. A deep breath and he moved forward through the opening in the hedgerow and into the field.

He stood on the threshold, clutching the holdall in his left hand and the torch in his right. He knew he had to go on, but a small part of him wanted to run like hell and never look back. Looking at the torch in his hand, he thought of Christmas – and James. He looked up at the stars and breathed deeply once more. Then he looked ahead, stepped forward and made his way down the grassy footpath, which ran alongside a hedgerow that barred his way to the left for about a hundred and fifty metres before reaching a stand of trees. A field stretched away to his right. The frozen ground crunched under his boots, and he shivered. When he reached the dense stand of trees and bushes, he stopped and used his torch to scan the way ahead. He saw nothing. Not even the movement of a creature of the night fleeing the intrusion of a stranger. It seemed colder among the trees. Or was it fear? He took a few tentative steps and then stalled to look at his watch. It showed 1:52 AM. He needed to push on. He shook off his hesitation and moved forward again. To his right, the trees were dense, but the path hugged the left edge and almost immediately, he could see a field off to his left just over the hedgeline. A little further forward and the hedge gave way to a small clearing before the path moved back into a final cluster of trees. He followed it in and then held back at the far edge. The open common land lay ahead. He clicked off the torch and put it into his coat pocket. He wouldn't need it now. The pallid, cold light of the moon lit the way ahead over open ground. It gave succour, but no comfort. In the frozen, nacreous light stood the Long Stone, about three hundred metres ahead. It stood four metres tall; supposedly thrown from land to the east by St Catherine in a mythical contest with the devil for control of the island. The devil's smaller stone lay beside it. The scene was supposed to depict the triumph of good over evil. Matthew could do with a similar triumph tonight.

A rush of movement from his right crashed into his reverie, followed by something solid connecting with the back of his head with a sickening, dull thump. His legs buckled, and he fell, face forward, into the dirt and grass, dropping the holdall. Barely retaining consciousness, he teetered on the brink, light and darkness swirling in a vortex that seemed to spin in and around his head. His vision blurred. Sounds were muffled. He felt someone or something pulling at his coat. His body, relaxed and heavy, rolled with the movement. He sensed a scuffling and scraping, then contact ceased, and suddenly he was alone. It felt as if someone had stuffed cotton wool in his ears, and a high-pitched tone persisted, but a few seconds later, the unmistakable sound of a moped starting up to his right broke the muffling barrier. He tried to raise himself, but a sharp pain in his head overwhelmed him, and he failed. He tried again, slower this time, and drew himself up onto his knees. Taking a few seconds to compose himself, he stood uneasily. He reeled but stayed on his feet, fighting the raging pain that was firing like lightning inside his skull. Something trickled down the back of his neck. He reached over his shoulder, and his hand came away covered in blood. His vision swam, and he had only a hazy view of a probing light making its way down the main trail towards the Strawberry Lane car park. The drone of the moped engine faded. His senses were returning. As if in a drunken stupor, he stumbled back into the trees. He knew he had to get back to the car. The tracker. That was all he knew. He made it through the trees and back out into the field, all the while feeling as if he were going to throw up. In the moonlight, he could just about make out the gap in the hedge ahead of him. He lost focus and concentration and stumbled, again falling face-first into the frozen grass. The pain of the frost slowly burning into his skin revived him, focused his senses, and he rose more confidently to his feet. His headache was still raging, his ears ringing, but his vision was a little sharper. He felt the strength returning to his legs, and he broke into a stumbling run. Reaching the car, he patted his coat pockets, forgetting which one his keys were in. It was then he realised his wallet was gone from his inside pocket and he had lost the torch. His keys were in his lower right-hand pocket. He pulled them out and unlocked the car, almost falling into the driver's seat. Pulling the door closed behind him, he sat fumbling with the key. He jiggled it frantically into the ignition and turned it. The engine sparked into life, and he let it run. His mobile phone was still in his trouser pocket, and he managed to bring up the tracker app before putting it into its cradle. He rubbed his eyes and face furiously, ignoring the pain, and then pulled out of the lay-by and headed south towards the Strawberry Lane car park at speed. A red dot pinged on the map on his phone screen. The road it was travelling on was the B3399 heading towards Brighstone. He looked up and then looked back down at the screen again. The dot pinged just short of Brighstone and was moving fast. A pain flashed in his head, and he swerved, jerking his head up only to see the hedge to his left rearing up in front of him. He yanked the wheel right, and his left-hand tyres spun and scuffed as they struggled to grip the sandy, gritty edge of the lane. Swerving back onto a straight course, he powered on. Concentrate. Focus, focus, focus! His head responded with a backlash of pain, but he fought through it and looked again at the screen of his mobile. As he reached the southern end of Strawberry Lane, he slowed, pulling to a temporary halt. The red dot pinged but was stationary. His mobile rang. Heather. He accepted the call and immediately switched the screen back to the tracker app. The red dot had still not moved. Matthew made a left turn and picked up speed along the B3399 towards Brighstone.

'Matthew, are you alright?'

'Yes, I'm fine...' The back of his head throbbed, but he was more alert now. He looked down. The red dot was moving again. But now it had separated into two.

'What's happening?'

'He stole my wallet, Heather!'

'What do you mean? Did you leave the money? Have you got James?'

One red dot blinked but remained stationary. The other was moving away and heading through Brighstone.

'He stole my fucking wallet!' Matthew punched the wheel. Pain lanced through his head, but he was jubilant now. 'Yes! You beauty!'

'Matthew, will you tell me what's happening!'

'He ambushed me. He took the money and ran. He's dumped the bag with the tracker, but he stole my wallet, Heather!'

'Don't lose him, Matthew!'

'I won't lose him! He stole my fucking wallet!'

'Will you stop going on about your fucking wallet!'

'Guess what was in my wallet, Heather.'

Silence.

'The second tracker, Heather. I'd put the second tracker in my wallet. The bastard dumped the bag, but I'm following the tracker in my wallet.'

'Where is he now?'

'He's just gone through Brighstone. He dumped the bag just before he reached all the junctions that head down to Military Road. Clever.'

'I'm staying on the phone. I need to know what's happening.'

'Fine. But when he stops, I'll have to hang up.'

'You keep saying "he", Matthew. Did you get a look at him?'

'No, he jumped me from behind – hit me with a great lump of wood, I think – nearly knocked me senseless, but I managed to get back to the car. I'm a bit more with it now. In fact, talking to you helps...' Matthew looked at his mobile screen. The red dot had stayed on the B3399 and was approaching Limerstone. 'I could just tell, you know... I could just tell. It's a bloke.'

The red dot reached Shorwell and made a right turn. It kept to the B3399, through Sandy Way and Kingston and on towards Chale Green. As Matthew followed, he focused intently on the empty road ahead, aware he couldn't afford any lapse of concentration. Heather's voice calmed him as he steadily closed the gap and then saw the red taillight of the moped in the distance. He hung back, dimming his headlights. He passed the "Welcome" sign to Chale Green and then the road swung left past the top of Chale Lane. Large detached houses appeared on the right-hand side, each on a generous plot of land and backing onto fields that stretched away to the south. He looked at his mobile screen. The red dot still pinged but seemed to have slowed to a stop.

'Where are you?' said Heather.

'Just come into Chale Green. The tracker's not moving. I'm going to get as close as I can in the car and then I'll walk.'

'Matthew. Call the police now.'

'I need to get a little closer, just to make sure. I've got to go, Heather. I'll let you know as soon as I'm outside the place and the police are here.' Matthew hung up and put his phone on silent.

The red dot remained stationary just off the road on the south side. Matthew drove a short way further and then killed the engine and rolled on as far as he felt he could without being noticed. He pulled into a small lay-by on the left-hand side, braked and brought the car to a stop. He took his mobile from its cradle and got out. Chale Green was asleep.

He made his way along the lane until he stood opposite the entrance of a large house screened from the road by a wall and hedging. The bitter chill of the night air had further sharpened his senses. Though he was conscious of the persistent dull ache in his head, it no longer bothered him. He crossed the road. There were no cars on the drive and no lights. Looking down at his phone, Matthew knew he was in the right place. He moved silently, approaching the house, keeping to the right-hand side. The driveway ran up alongside the right-hand side of the house, bordered by a thick laurel hedge. Parked at the far end, deep in the shadows, was a moped. Matthew needed no further convincing. He called 999, gave a brief, urgent outline of his circumstances and his location and was told that the police were on their way. He hung up. Still, he could see no lights, hear no sound. It gave the impression that the house was empty.

He thought of circling around to see if he could discover where James was being held. If he could do that, it would save time when the police arrived. But if he were seen, then it might put James in danger. He moved towards the moped. It was nondescript and black. An idea came to him. As he bent down, pain once again lanced through his skull. He felt the back of his head and the blood, now matted and crusted in his hair. Matthew steadied himself on the frame of the moped and reached into the space between the suspension, the engine and the underside of the seat and felt around until he found a bunch of cables. Grabbing it, he pulled as hard as he could until something gave. Petrol spilled, and he realised he must have ruptured the fuel line. To make doubly sure, Matthew pulled out a miniature toolset attached to his key ring, selected the penknife and punctured the tyres. You won't be driving off on this in a hurry, he thought.

He looked around. Ahead of him was a gate, presumably leading through to a garden at the rear of the house. He listened, hoping to hear police sirens, and then thought that surely the police would arrive silently so as not to give any warning of their approach. He paced around, nervous now. Approaching the gate, he tested the latch. It turned silently, and he nudged it open. He stepped through and moved towards the rear corner of the house. He paused and then peered around it. A small pool of light emerged from a window somewhere in the middle. Satisfied that he had disabled the moped, and that he had the rear of the house covered, he sat back to wait. And then he heard a child scream.

36

Rescue

Matthew didn't stop to think. He ran towards the pool of light. It shone through a set of double doors. Still in stride, Matthew swung out in a shallow arc to give himself a few paces to gain forward momentum. He didn't stop to consider that the doors might be locked or their composition. Fortunately, they were an original feature – paned glass in a wooden frame, and not the latest high-security double-glazing. Adrenaline kicked in. He powered into a quick sprint, lowered his shoulder and hit the doors where they met in the middle. With a splintering crack and a crash of glass, Matthew smashed through. He'd barely had time to register more than a lamp on a side table by a sofa and a figure dressed in a white shirt and jeans on the other side of the door. Now, he crashed into that figure, and it flailed backwards, stumbling and falling. It fell straight back, and there was a sickening crack as it struck its head on a glass coffee table, which splintered. Matthew recovered from the impact and glanced around while the figure lay momentarily stunned. There was a wood-burning stove to his left. He grabbed the wrought iron poker from a companion set to one side and turned back to look at the prone figure on the floor. A man. Medium build, cropped black hair and dark eyes that burned with hate. He had backed up against the sofa, over which a dark blue parka jacket had been slung. His eyes were locked on Matthew.

Matthew steadied himself. 'Let me guess. Dylan Dumas?'

'In the flesh, Matthew Blundell.'

'You look just like your mother.'

'And you look like shit,' said Dylan. He exuded a taut, wiry strength, and his pallid complexion betrayed his time behind bars.

'The police are on their way, Dylan. It's over. Now, where's James?' Matthew sounded more confident than he felt.

Subconsciously, Dylan's eyes flicked left towards a cupboard in the far corner as he manoeuvred his legs and struggled to his knees.

'That's enough. Stay there.' Matthew brandished the poker and glanced around to reassure himself that Dylan was alone. He took in more of his surroundings. The only internal door in the room was in front of him, behind Dylan and the sofa. The ransom money had been on the coffee table and had now spilled over the floor.

Dylan made to move.

'I said, stay there!' Matthew stabbed the poker at him, and the pain in Matthew's head stabbed back.

Dylan raised his hands in a placatory gesture. 'Okay, okay!' He eyed Matthew carefully. 'You know, I'm as much a pawn in this as you are,' he said. His mouth curled into a sly smile. 'She's an evil bitch, my mother. But you don't need me to tell you that.'

'Your mother's going down for what she's done, Dylan; but don't try to kid me; you're as invested in this as she is.'

'Do you read the papers, Matthew? Did you read about that DJ they found half-dead a couple of months back? A witness saw a man in a grey hoodie. Turns out that hoodie has blood on the sleeve. Turns out that bitch I call a mother has it in her possession. All she has to do is hand it over to the police and I'm back inside...'

'You're a sick man, Dumas. That's the only pity you're going to get from me.'

Dylan's face hardened. 'You know, in another life, I could have made something of myself. Passed my GCSEs, found a job, led a normal life. If it weren't for your paedophile of a wife.'

Matthew thought he heard a sound behind him and instinctively glanced back at the French doors.

Dylan seized what he saw as a split-second opportunity and launched like a sprinter at the sound of the starting gun. He sprang forward with outstretched arms. But Matthew was ready for him. In one fluid, brutal motion, he brought the poker down onto Dylan's wrist. It sent Dylan reeling. With a roar of anger, fuelled by pain, he spun and threw himself across the remaining distance between them. Matthew stepped smartly to one side and, as Dylan's momentum took him past, Matthew swung the poker and delivered a backhanded blow to the back of Dylan's skull, which sent Dylan pitching towards the shattered French doors. He landed face-first and rolled in the glass. He came up snarling to face Matthew. The first traces of blood were seeping through his shirt, and he had several cuts on his face, including one on his right cheek, from which protruded a shard of glass.

Matthew's hard stare didn't waver. His head pounded, but he couldn't show any sign of weakness. 'I'd think twice,' he said. 'I'm pretty handy with this.'

Dylan reached up with his good hand and pulled the glass from his cheek. Blood ran freely down his face and dripped onto his chest. He looked past Matthew at the money and then back at Matthew. He cast a half glance back at the French doors and then, again, looked back at Matthew.

'Run if you want to,' said Matthew, 'but the police will be here any minute. You won't get far.'

Dylan winced as he nursed his wrist, which hung uselessly. 'You haven't heard the last of me.' His face set hard, and his dark eyes burned. 'You and your family have a debt to pay. You'll spend the rest of your fucking life looking over your shoulder.' He turned and ran out through the French doors.

He turned right, running towards the gate and the moped. Matthew walked forward to stand in the shattered doorway and looked out, waiting, gingerly feeling the back of his head. A few moments later, Dylan came back through the gate. He stood on the lawn, turning, weighing up his options. Then he headed for the bottom of the garden. In the moonlight, Matthew saw him struggling to climb over a head-height wire mesh fence, hindered by his broken wrist. He clambered over and dropped into the field behind. Matthew watched him just long enough to be sure he wasn't coming back. It was around 3:00 AM; he was on foot, and the police would soon be scouring the area looking for him. He turned and hurried back into the lounge, heading right, towards the cupboard in the far corner of the room.

‘It’s alright, James, Daddy’s here now.’

Matthew grasped the handle and twisted it. He pulled the door towards him to reveal a deep cupboard, with shelves full of books and games. On the floor under the bottom shelf, cowered a child who looked up at Matthew with frightened eyes. Matthew sensed its relief when it saw that he was not Dylan. But whereas two-and-a-half-year-old James had fair hair and distinctive blue eyes, this child had dark brown hair and brown eyes and was somewhere around four years of age.

Matthew reached down and took the child’s hand. ‘It’s okay,’ he said, ‘you’re safe now. What’s your name?’

37

A Matter Of Time

The front of the house was bathed in flashing blue light.

Matthew had briefed a fuming Sergeant Mason and then pleaded with him to step up the search for James. There had been no trace of him in the house, which was now an active crime scene. Officers had been dispatched in the search for Dylan, and Sergeant Mason, having rapidly coordinated the police response, was preparing to drive to Godshill to question Sarah Morton.

'James is still out there,' said Matthew, tailing him out of the house, 'and that madman is still on the loose. If he gets back to James before you find him...'

'He won't go back for James,' said Sergeant Mason. 'He won't take that risk. What we have to worry about is that James is somewhere, possibly with no access to food or water.'

'He didn't give me the details of James's location, so going back for James is exactly what he might do,' said Matthew. 'James is leverage and it's a safe place he can hole up until he decides what to do.'

'If he's got any sense, he'll be trying to get off the island,' said Sergeant Mason, approaching one of the police cars. 'Now, I need to arrange for someone to get this child to the station and reunite him with his parents.' He indicated the boy, who was waiting in the back of the car with a female police officer. 'We'll find Dumas. He can't get far on foot. I suggest you get yourself home, Mr Blundell, and get cleaned up. I'll be in touch.'

'Who is the child?' said Matthew.

'Patrick Hughes,' said Sergeant Mason. 'He was snatched from his home late yesterday afternoon. It hasn't been made public yet.' He turned away and leant into the back of the car to speak with the female officer.

Matthew's phone vibrated. It was Heather.

'What's happening? Have you found him?'

Matthew steeled himself. 'Heather, I'm sorry. James wasn't at the house. The police are back out looking for him.' He swallowed hard. 'Dylan took him. I thought I'd found James, so I let him get away. I'm so sorry. Mason's heading over to Morton's now. I'll fill you in on the rest when I get home. I'm on my way.' He hung up on his distraught wife and hurried back to the car.

Matthew was sitting on the sofa with his arm around Heather. It was 4:44 AM. He had arrived home and led her immediately into the lounge. She was shaking.

'I don't understand why James wasn't at the house.' Heather's words stumbled through her emotion.

'Dylan was using it to hold Patrick Hughes,' said Matthew. 'Another kid – snatched yesterday afternoon. If he was planning to give us James's location, he couldn't very well have them at the same place, could he.'

'Why didn't he tell you where he was holding James? Do you think he was ever planning to let him go?'

'Oh, come on, Heather. How the hell do you expect me to know that? None of this makes any sense. Perhaps he stopped off to stash the money and deal with Patrick before contacting us.'

'And what if Dylan's on his way to where he's holding James? Do you think he'll hurt him?'

'The police don't think he'll go there.'

'But what if he does?'

'For Christ's sake, Heather. He's injured and on foot. I trashed the moped he was using, and the police have drafted everyone in to look for him. Besides, James might be miles from where he was holding Patrick. It might not be possible for him to get there.'

'Do you think Sarah knows where James is?'

'Of course, she does! That bitch knows exactly where he is. She's up to her fucking neck in this. Mason should be hauling her over the coals as we speak.' Matthew punched his fist into his open hand. 'But if he doesn't dispense justice, I will.'

'Yeah, right – that's all we need: you charging around like Charles Bronson and getting arrested.' Heather shook her head. 'I don't understand. If Sarah's involved and this is all about revenge, why did Dylan snatch this other child?'

'Yes, it struck me as odd,' said Matthew. 'Money, I guess. In for a penny, in for a pound.'

Heather took a moment to compose herself. Matthew was silent now, simmering with rage. Heather looked him over. 'You're covered in blood,' she said softly. 'Somehow, I knew you'd end up getting involved. Come into the kitchen and I'll clean you up.'

Matthew sat at the kitchen table while Heather dabbed gently at the back of his head. 'You've got a nasty gash here. You might need stitches.'

'I'm not spending hours up at that hospital over a cut. Haven't we got any Super Glue?'

'Matthew, what happened to you?'

Matthew told her.

When he had finished, Heather looked at him, her eyes rimmed red. 'I'm proud of you, Matthew,' she said. 'We may not have James back yet, but I'm so proud of you.' Heather cupped his face in her hands and kissed him.

The phone rang five minutes later. Matthew glanced at the kitchen clock. 5:40 AM. He rushed into the hall.

'Mr Blundell. It's Sergeant Mason. We've arrested Sarah Morton.'

Matthew thumped his fist on the hall table. 'I told you she was involved! Dylan said as much.'

'Hang on, I'm not necessarily saying she's involved. We're waiting for a lawyer, and then we're interviewing her under caution. She's not been very cooperative so far, but when she was told about her son's actions... well, she was distraught, to say the least. She blames herself, says she was on the verge of kicking him out; that maybe she drove him to it. She broke down. I'm not sure anyone could fake that.'

'Distraught, my arse! The only thing she's distraught about is that we're about to expose her, as well as her son.'

'Expose, *my* arse, Mr Blundell, to borrow your expression. The only thing we're going to expose are the facts. And as things stand, there is nothing, I repeat, nothing to suggest that Sarah Morton had any knowledge of her son's actions. And we've found no trace of the blood-stained hoodie she was supposedly using to blackmail him.'

'She'll have hidden that well,' said Matthew.

'And we'll keep looking, Mr Blundell...'

'So, you tell me, Sergeant Mason,' said Matthew. 'Sarah Morton's son has risked his neck kidnapping two kids, one of whom just happened to be James... Isn't that too much of a coincidence? She's involved! Even if he's gone rogue with the second kid, she knew about James.'

'Maybe, Mr Blundell. Maybe. But Dumas is a nasty piece of work. He could easily have lied about the assault and the blood on the hoodie and done this of his own accord. He'd have known all about his mother's recent run-in with you, so yes, there's an element of revenge. It's cost her dearly – financially and emotionally. She's doing menial work these days – working for a company cleaning Airbnbs. And her loss is his loss. So far as he's concerned, this is the second time Mrs Blundell has messed with his life. He wants to see you suffer, *and* he needs the money. I'd say that's motive enough for him to act alone.'

'You said she's cleaning Airbnbs,' said Matthew. 'That means she knows when homes are empty. How else would Dylan know where it was safe to hide the kids?'

'There could be another explanation,' said Sergeant Mason. 'Just let us interview her and we'll get to the truth. In the meantime, we've got everyone out there looking for Dumas. We get him; we get James.'

Matthew was silent. Then he said, 'You're going to let her get away with this.'

'We're going around in circles, Mr Blundell...'

'He'll kill him.'

Matthew stood in the lounge doorway. 'He won't, Heather...'

'He's on his way there now, and he's going to kill him. It's all about revenge – you said so yourself. It's the ultimate punishment. If he wants to make us suffer, he'll kill him.'

'I should have killed *him* while I had the chance.' Matthew cursed and swiped an imaginary poker. 'What the hell was I thinking?'

'Then we'd never find James.'

'If I ever cross his path again, I swear, I'll send him to the great gig in the sky.'

Heather was pacing the lounge. She stopped, looked up at the ceiling and screamed. 'That bastard said he'd tell us where James is once he had the money!'

'I know – but he didn't,' said Matthew. 'Just calm down. You'll wake Noah.' He put his head in his hands and groaned. 'Maybe, if I hadn't interfered, things would have taken their natural course and he would have got a message to us... Wait...'

'What?'

'Just give me a moment.'

'Matthew?'

'He said that, didn't he – in his note: Once I have the money, I'll give you details where to find James.' Matthew's mind flashed back to the moments after Dylan's assault. 'What if he meant that literally?'

'I don't understand.'

'Just give me a moment...' Matthew rushed to the front door. He opened it and almost fell into the porch.

'Where are you going?'

'Nowhere. Just getting my coat.'

Matthew brought his coat into the lounge. There was blood all over the collar and down the back. 'I felt him, didn't I... rummaging around in my coat. He stole my wallet. But what if...' Matthew was searching his pockets. He looked at Heather. 'No. Nothing.'

'Check again.'

Matthew felt in every pocket and rubbed around the inner linings. Between his finger and thumb, just below his inside pocket, he felt a small square object. 'Christ – my wallet must have worn a hole...' He put his hand into his inside pocket and began manipulating the object up through the lining and through the split seam. It was a small square of folded paper. He opened it.

DOWNSVIEW CARAVAN SITE. TOURING CARAVAN. FIRST PITCH LEFT OF ENTRANCE.

'I'm coming with you,' said Heather. 'I'll get Noah.'

It was 6:21 AM. Matthew pulled on his blood-stained coat and grabbed his keys and phone from the kitchen table. He looked up the caravan site address and put the postcode into his route planner. Heather, meanwhile, was outside securing Noah in his booster seat in the back of the Caravelle. He was already falling back to sleep. James's booster seat remained empty next to him – but expectant.

It was not yet first light. They made their way south through Godshill and turned left onto Whitwell Road. From there, they navigated their way in the dark down a couple of lanes. The caravan site was on the right and was no more than a gated field marked out for around half a dozen caravans. It was winter, and only one caravan, with a tow hitch, occupied the site. A pale golden wash of light appeared to emanate from a rear window.

'What if that's him in there?' Heather peered through the windscreen, fearful. 'It's been over three-and-a-half hours, and we're not that far from Chale Green. What if he's...'

'He'd be mad,' said Matthew. 'He's given us James's location. So far as he knows, this place is crawling with police.'

Matthew pulled up facing the caravan and left the Caravelle's headlights on full beam. Heather jumped out. She raced over and tried the door. It was locked. She turned to look at Matthew, who was running up behind her.

'Where's the key?' She turned back to the door and yanked the handle.

'There's got to be one here somewhere.' Matthew looked around. There was no obvious hiding place.

'You'll have to break in.'

Matthew ran over to a window. Behind it, the blind had been pulled down. He examined the frame. 'You'd need a crowbar to force your way in here,' he said, 'and we don't have one.' He looked up. 'Maybe there's a skylight or something on the roof.'

He glanced around. There was a large green commercial wheelie bin by the entrance to the site. He ran over to it. It was plastic and empty, and he was able to drag it alongside the caravan. He hauled himself up on top of it and looked across the roof. There were two hatches. They were battened down tight. He looked down at Heather.

'We're not getting in through there,' he said. He jumped back down, and they circled the outside of the caravan together. Someone had pulled down the blinds behind all the windows, but there was no sign of movement inside. Apart from the one source of light at the rear, there was no sign of any occupancy. They completed their circuit and returned to stand in front of the door. Matthew studied it as if it were a puzzle waiting to be solved. Then, he cursed, stooped down and ran his hand along the underside of a thin protruding step. 'Very imaginative. I can't believe I missed it the first time!' He removed a key held in place with some duct tape. Heather held out her hand.

'Perhaps I should go first,' said Matthew. He put the key in the lock and turned it. The door swung outward, and he stepped up into the caravan and disappeared inside. Heather followed him in.

A small lamp in the far corner to their right gave them just enough light to see by. Heather peered into the gloom. There was a sofa scattered with cushions against the far wall. Thinking she saw a small body curled up, she covered the distance in a few strides. She scooped up a blanket. It covered two cushions. No James. She turned frantically. Matthew walked up beside her.

'He's not here,' she said.

She pushed past Matthew. The room was open-plan and also contained a kitchenette. At the other end of the caravan was a partition and a closed door. Heather ran to it. She twisted the handle and almost fell through. The room was in semi-darkness. In front of her, she could make out a double bed, with pillows strewn across it. There was another blanket. Again, it covered something from which there was no discernible movement. Heather reached out and pulled it back.

Matthew stepped in behind her, just as Heather was taking James into her arms, sobbing uncontrollably. James awoke and stared sleepily at her.

'Mummy.' A flicker of a smile and his head lolled. It fell against Heather's shoulder, and he was once again asleep.

Heather held him close. She turned to Matthew with tears in her eyes. 'He seems okay. Just a little tired.'

Matthew had turned on the torch on his phone, and he shone it around. There were empty baby bottles of milk and discarded snack and chocolate bar wrappers. The place stank of used nappies that had been carelessly tossed into a metal wastepaper basket. 'It's hardly five-star...' He noticed a pair of trainers by the bed and other articles of clothing. 'I'll call Sergeant Mason,' he said. 'I'm sure he'll want to get his forensics team over here.'

'Come on, little man, let's get you out of here,' said Heather. 'There's someone waiting in the car who's going to be very pleased to see you.'

Matthew emerged from the caravan a few minutes after Heather had taken James outside and placed him in his car seat next to a sleeping Noah. She didn't wake Noah. It would be easier to explain James's return from a supposed visit to Nannie and Grandad at home rather than in a field in the middle of nowhere, just before dawn.

Heather quietly closed the rear door of the Caravelle. She eased into the passenger seat as Matthew jumped in and started the engine.

'Aren't we going to wait for the police?' she said.

'I have nothing more to say to the police,' said Matthew. 'I've called them. They can take it from here. Let's go home.'

Heather put on her seatbelt. 'I'm glad it's over,' she said. She turned and looked back at James, fast asleep in his seat behind Matthew.

'It's not over, Heather.'

'What? Do you mean Dylan? I can't imagine he'll get far. They'll catch him, and that'll be the end of it. Everything will be fine.'

Matthew looked straight ahead, through the windscreen, staring at the caravan. The Caravelle's engine idled. 'Nothing will ever be fine, Heather,' he said. 'Not until Sarah Morton is brought to justice. She needs to answer for what she's done.'

Heather was silent for a moment. Then she spoke. 'Sergeant Mason seems to think she might be innocent. What if she is? She's paid the price for what she did to us. Isn't that enough?'

'Paid the price? Right; if you consider a fair price for blatant fraud is losing your job!'

'The council couldn't find enough evidence to make the charges stick, Matthew. We have to let it go!'

'And what about masterminding the kidnapping of our son? Is she going to get away with that?'

'You don't know that she "masterminded" James's kidnapping,' said Heather.

'I do.'

'No, Matthew. You don't.'

Matthew turned to face Heather. His expression was hard and unyielding. 'Her sociopathic son may have done the deed, but the apple never falls far from the tree.'

'You have to let this go, Matthew. Let the police do their job and let us get on with our lives.'

Matthew turned and again stared out through the windscreen into the muddy light of dawn. 'We'll play happy families, if you like, Heather, but I'm not sure I can let it go. I'm not sure...'

He shifted the Caravelle into gear.

Epilogue

Seven months later...

Thursday, 29th August 2019

Matthew was out early. He was on a big landscaping job on the other side of Merstone, which was running behind, so it was an eight o'clock start. The morning was crisp and clear, not a cloud in the sky. It felt good to be alive. He had Pink Floyd's 'Delicate Sound of Thunder' album playing loudly through the car speakers and was thumping the steering wheel in time to the opening, heavy riff of 'The Dogs of War'. Before he reached Rookley, he took a right turn into Merstone Lane and put his foot down. The silver Citroën C3 responded, and the speedometer pushed past fifty. 'We all have a dark side, to say the least,' he sang. 'And dealing in death is the nature of the beast...' He grinned, a glint of madness in his eye, and drove on. 'One world...' He raised his fist above the steering wheel and smashed it down.

A white "Morton Cleaning Services" van pulled up on a narrow grass verge alongside a hedge, on the opposite side of the road to a residential building in Merstone Lane that had recently been converted into a small, family-run firm of solicitors. It was a Thursday, and the office space needed cleaning before the staff arrived at nine. Not the most glamorous job in the world, but then needs must. The driver's mobile phone rang and was answered.

Matthew slowed as the road ahead veered sharply to the left and then opened up into a long stretch that meandered through a network of fields and hedges. He took the bend and then put his foot down on the accelerator, powering towards Merstone, just over a mile away. As he approached the village, he entered the thirty miles per hour zone doing forty.

In the white "Morton Cleaning Services" van, the driver finished the call and put her mobile phone back into her handbag. She opened the van door and stepped out into the road.

Matthew had slowed to thirty. He was about a hundred metres away when he thought he recognised the woman emerging from the white Ford Transit Connect ahead of him, on his side of the road. A moment later, he knew he did. His eyes locked onto her. It was as if he had lost all other consciousness.

Sarah Morton.

An intense anger flared. A harboured fury. 'You arrogant bitch! You got away with it!'

Sarah Morton was reaching for the handle to slide open the side door of the van. She turned slightly at the sound of an approaching vehicle.

Matthew had dreamt of all the ways he could exact his revenge, and there she was – Sarah Morton – in the road, right in front of him, at his mercy. His eyes remained fixed on her as he closed the distance between them.

Sarah Morton's right hand was on the side door handle. She saw a silver car coming, still a little way off, and paused, waiting for it to pass.

Matthew thumped the steering wheel. It was as if Sarah Morton, by her very presence, was taunting him, goading him. Dark thoughts conjured dark images; conjured dark thoughts... In his head, voices urged him, riled him; rising from a deep, dark well of hate. He shook his head sharply, and his mind fog cleared. He pictured Heather, holding James's hand. She screamed at him. No! The moment of madness passed.

He couldn't murder Sarah Morton in cold blood.

He smiled.

But he could damn well scare the living daylights out of her!

He saw the dawning look of incomprehension on Sarah Morton's face as he accelerated and angled left. It morphed almost immediately into recognition and horror as he drove directly at her, gaining speed. He grinned. That's it, Morton. Shit your pants!

Sarah Morton seemed uncertain. She glanced across the road.

One... two... three seconds; enough to put the fear of God into her. Matthew yanked the wheel hard right to veer away.

But Sarah Morton had already made a split-second decision. A reflex action. She turned awkwardly and made to run.

The car speeding towards them from the other direction was a yellow Vauxhall Corsa. The driver's eyes were down, focused on his satnav, momentarily distracted.

Sarah Morton's sole focus was Matthew's silver Citroën and self-preservation. She was mid-stride, in the road, when she saw him swerve back out towards her. She panicked and stumbled.

Matthew saw her run as he jerked the wheel to straighten up. A glacial rush of fear almost paralysed him. She was in his sights again. He saw her stumble and panicked. Yanking the wheel back hard left, he lost control. He slammed on the brakes, and the tyres squealed. The silver Citroën collided side-on with the back of Sarah Morton's white van and ploughed into the hedge alongside the grass verge.

The driver of the yellow Corsa looked up. The woman he had seen moments earlier on the opposite side of the road, standing by a white van, waiting to cross, was now in the middle of the road. A silver car had swerved to avoid her.

Disbelief. Confusion. Panic.

He stamped on the brake and veered violently to the left.

Too late.

The right side of the yellow Corsa collided with Sarah Morton. She took the full impact on her left side and was flipped like a pinball and spun away. Her body hit the tarmac, rolled and came to rest. It lay crumpled in the road and was still.

In the Citroën, Matthew's airbag had deployed and deflated. The driver's door had melded with the rear of the Transit Connect, and the hedge restricted the passenger door. He was concussed and trapped. To escape the car, he knew he would have to climb over into the rear seats. He felt his nose and winced. It was broken, and his ribs hurt. He wasn't sure he could manage it. He groaned, consumed by his discomfort. Worse, he expected Sarah Morton to appear at any moment, launch a tirade of abuse, then, no doubt, laugh as she saw him laid out like a sacrifice before her. The humiliation...

Thursday, 24th October 2019

'Good morning, Sarah.'

The matron, in short-sleeved navy scrubs with white trim, bustled towards the head of the bed in the Neuro ICU, Southampton General Hospital.

'Let's brush your hair,' she said. 'Your son will be here soon.'

Sarah Morton lay still, eyes open. She stared up at the ceiling, seemingly awake. A tracheostomy tube had been inserted through a stoma in her neck into her windpipe and a gastrostomy tube directly into her stomach. To her left was a mechanical ventilator that hissed gently as it pushed air in and out of her lungs.

Another woman approached her bedside. She was dressed in dark grey scrubs with "Neuro ICU Consultant" embroidered on the left side of her chest. A name badge hanging from an NHS lanyard identified her as Clare Fletcher.

'Good morning, Hayley,' she said to the matron. 'Are we ready?'

'We're almost done, aren't we, Sarah?' Hayley continued to run a brush through Sarah Morton's bleached blonde hair. She finished up and turned to face her colleague. 'This job doesn't get any easier, does it?' she said.

Clare Fletcher eyed the patient. 'No, it doesn't.' There was a moment's silence. 'Her son's on his way up,' she said. 'Cold comfort that'll give her...'

Both women readied themselves, and moments later, a prison officer brought Dylan into the room. Another waited discreetly at the entrance.

'Mr Dumas.' Clare Fletcher acknowledged him with a curt nod.

The prison officer produced a set of keys on a keychain. 'Now, I'll take these cuffs off and we'll dispense with the escort chain,' he said. 'But I warn you... Raise your hands.' He removed the handcuffs. Dylan rubbed his wrists and looked around.

'Mr Dumas. I'm Clare Fletcher. I'm the consultant neurointensivist here. I've been overseeing your mother's care. I believe you've been apprised of the current situation and my recommendations?'

'If I hadn't, I wouldn't be here, would I?' said Dylan. He eyed Clare Fletcher up and down, his eyes lingering on the words embroidered on her chest. 'Let's just get on with this.'

'Well, before we do,' Clare Fletcher looked at him distastefully, 'I want to be absolutely sure you fully understand the seriousness of your mother's condition.'

'Knock yourself out,' said Dylan.

'Okay. Well, we've been monitoring her for eight weeks now, and she's shown no sign of improvement. To all intents and purposes, she's entered what we call a persistent vegetative state.' Clare Fletcher looked into Dylan Dumas's eyes, searching for a glimmer of cognisance or sorrow.

He stared blankly at her. Unfathomable. Unmoved.

'We've run some additional fMRI and EEG tests in an attempt to detect any evidence of brain activity suggesting possible signs of awareness. I'm afraid the tests proved inconclusive.' She continued to study him as she spoke. 'There were indications that some brain activity is occurring, but it's minimal and appears intermittent.' She paused. 'However, these tests cannot determine an individual's level of awareness, even when activity is detected.'

'So?'

'So,' said Clare Fletcher slowly, 'it's possible there is some covert, or hidden, consciousness, but nothing meaningful and certainly nothing that suggests she will make any sort of recovery.'

'Is she suffering?'

Clare Fletcher noticed a flicker of malice.

'Yes, I believe she is, Mr Dumas.' She looked coldly at him. 'The cerebral damage is severe, and the injury to her upper spine has damaged the nerves controlling her breathing, causing irreversible respiratory failure. Those tubes are the only things keeping her alive. Then there are the inherent risks with any life-support function and immobilisation to consider. You know my recommendation.'

Dylan nodded. A faint trace of a smile.

'Would you like to speak to her?' Clare Fletcher stepped aside and gestured towards the bed.

Dylan scoffed. 'Just pull the plug, for fuck's sake!'

The prison officer nudged him forward. 'You damn well show some respect, son. That's your mother lying there.'

Dylan scowled and walked slowly towards the bed. The matron moved away.

A chair had been placed by his mother's bedside. He sat and leant in close, remaining silent for a few moments. Then, lowering his head, he placed his mouth close to her ear. Those around him had positioned themselves at a respectful distance. When he spoke, his words were inaudible to them.

'They're going to let you die, Mum. Put an end to your suffering. But know this: you've been dead to me for years. Why do you think I never let you visit me in prison? Did you really think it was because I was ashamed?' He breathed scorn into her ear. 'No. It was because I couldn't stand the sight of you. After I got out, I tolerated you. Fuck knows that was hard.'

Sarah Morton had spent long hours in the company of regret. A litany of grief lay buried in her subconscious. She could hear words spoken – meaningless words. Yet, in response, fragments of thought surfaced. Triggered. Unbidden. Automatic recall by association, verbal stimulation. Once burdened with sorrow, now they had no meaning, carried no weight.

I loved you…

'I told them you blackmailed me into kidnapping the Blundell kid.'

I did nothing…

'Told them you kept banging on about the Blundells and how they'd ruined our lives.'

I did nothing…

'That you'd threatened to turn me in for that assault if I didn't do something about it.'

… but protect you.

'The dopey fuckers almost bought it.'

I did nothing...

'But here we are. A freak car accident. Problem solved....'

... but love you.

The gentle whoosh of the ventilator was a sound. It meant nothing. Background noise in a meaningless void.

A sound. A hollow laugh in her ear. 'I could probably stop them from killing you if I wanted to. If I screamed bloody murder, I could probably drag this out for years. I could make you suffer... but where's the point in that? I'll sell your cleaning business and the house, and when I get out, I'll be gone. Mummy won't have forgotten her darling little boy in her will.'

Will...

Another hollow laugh.

NSPCC...

'And you owe me big time, "Mummy". While I've been banged up, you've been out there doing alright for yourself, haven't you? Nice house, fancy car. I paid the price for your incompetence, your failure. What's it cost you, eh?'

She had fought tooth and nail for her boy. It had cost her everything.

Marriage...

She and Douglas had been very much in love once.

Friends...

She had moved to the Isle of Wight to be near him, away from everyone and everything she had ever loved.

Chris...

Dylan turned and looked around. Clare Fletcher was in hushed conversation with the other nurse in a corner, and the prison officer was checking his phone.

He turned back and hissed in his mother's ear. 'I guess this is it, then. This is where I get to watch you die. Don't think I feel sorry for you. I don't. I blame you. I blame you for everything. You've got what's coming to you.' He stood.

'Let's get this over with, shall we? I've said all I want to say.'

He walked over to the prison officer as Clare Fletcher and the matron broke off their conversation and returned to Sarah Morton's bedside.

Clare Fletcher reached out and held Sarah Morton's hand. With an automatic reflex, Sarah seemed to grasp it. 'I firmly believe this is in your best interest, Sarah, and my healthcare team and your son agree. This is no kind of life for you. Hayley, will you please?'

Clare Fletcher bowed her head.

The prison officer shuffled uncomfortably. The one at the entrance turned away.

Dylan Dumas looked on and smiled.

Hayley administered a small dose of pain and anxiety relief, reduced the volume on the cardiac monitor and, finally, leaving the tracheostomy tube in place, disconnected the ventilator and switched off the alarm.

'She can't breathe unaided,' said Clare Fletcher, 'so it shouldn't be long.'

There were sounds. Beeps, reducing in frequency, familiar somehow, a precursor to a flat tone and death. A sense of calm, where once such an association would induce a wave of panic. A sense of calm as her brain was starved of oxygen and reacted.

I did nothing...

I did nothing...

But protect you.

Love you.

ALAN was born in Bromley, Kent. He spent twenty years working as a finance analyst for a bank before moving to the picturesque Isle of Wight, where he turned to his passion for writing; honing his craft by undertaking extended writing courses run by 'Writing Magazine'. He is currently a man of leisure.

HARVEY was born in Farnborough, Kent, and now lives in the Lake District. A banking operations manager in a previous life, he has been writing on and off for over thirty years and throughout has been a loyal subscriber to 'Writing Magazine' and its predecessors — once upon a time, enjoying success with the occasional competition entry. He now works for the National Trust.

Alan and Harvey are lifelong friends, having met on a judo mat over forty-five years ago. Both featured regularly on the Kent and Southern Area junior judo teams. 'Lost Lives' has been the glue that has held them together over the last four years, living, as they do, four hundred miles apart. They haven't actually seen each other in the eleven years since they both moved away from Kent...